Home Invasion

Look for these heart-pounding thrillers
by William W. Johnstone,
writing with J. A. Johnstone,
available wherever books are sold.

BLACK FRIDAY

TYRANNY

STAND YOUR GROUND

SUICIDE MISSION

THE BLEEDING EDGE

THE BLOOD OF PATRIOTS

HOME INVASION

JACKKNIFE

REMEMBER THE ALAMO

INVASION USA

INVASION USA: BORDER WAR

VENGEANCE IS MINE

PHOENIX RISING

PHOENIX RISING: FIREBASE FREEDOM

PHOENIX RISING: DAY OF JUDGMENT

HOME INVASION

WILLIAM W. JOHNSTONE

with J. A. Johnstone

PINNACLE BOOKS
Kensington Publishing Corp.
www.kensingtonbooks.com

PINNACLE BOOKS are published by

Kensington Publishing Corp.
119 West 40th Street
New York, NY 10018

PUBLISHER'S NOTE
Following the death of William W. Johnstone, the Johnstone family is working with a carefully selected writer to organize and complete Mr. Johnstone's outlines and many unfinished manuscripts to create additional novels in all of his series like The Last Gunfighter, Mountain Man, and Eagles, among others. This novel was inspired by Mr. Johnstone's superb storytelling.

ISBN-13: 978-0-7860-4534-1
ISBN-10: 0-7860-4534-5

First printing: December 2010

10 9 8 7 6 5 4 3

Printed in the United States of America

Electronic edition:

ISBN-13: 978-0-7860-2585-5 (e-book)
ISBN-10: 0-7860-2585-9 (e-book)

Home, Texas, is a town that lives up to its name—a small, peaceful, off-the-beaten-track West Texas community that seems like a throwback to a kinder, gentler America. Yeah, they have satellite Internet service, but they also have a Dairy Queen where you can go in for breakfast and know everybody there. The school mascot, an antelope, is painted on the water tower at the edge of town, along with the proud declaration 1A STATE CHAMPS 1977. A long time ago, but nobody has forgotten. The words are repainted every year.

Home is a town where on a quiet Sunday morning the main thing you hear are hymns being sung in the local churches. The interstate highway is thirty miles away, so you can't hear the rumble of the eighteen-wheelers. But the mountains, thirty miles the other way, seem to be right in the town's backyard because the air is so clear. Home may not be very big—pop. 1280, reads the sign at the edge of town—but the people who live there like it. Many of them have lived there their entire lives.

They don't realize that Home is about to become Hell.

BOOK ONE

CHAPTER 1

Peter McNamara was sound asleep when his wife, Inez, took hold of his shoulder and shook it. Of course, he was asleep. It was ten-forty-five at night, wasn't it? Pete hadn't been awake past ten-thirty since Johnny Carson retired.

"Pete. Pete!"

He rolled over, let out the sort of moaning sound that a sixty-eight-year-old man makes when he rolls over, and asked, "What is it?"

"Somebody's in the house," Inez whispered.

Pete frowned and lifted himself on an elbow. "What do you mean, somebody's in the house? Nobody's supposed to be here but us."

"You think?"

He swallowed the irritation he felt at her tone of voice. "We don't have burglars around here. Everybody knows everybody else."

"The border's less than an hour from here."

That was true, and Pete knew what went on down there, below the Rio Grande. Over the past decade, Mexico had descended into a state of near-anarchy as the power of the government shrank and the power of the drug cartels grew and grew and grew.

Mexico City and the other large cities were armed camps, patrolled day and night by the army. The problem there was that the army was so corrupt that now it was little more than a branch of the cartels.

Few Americans crossed the border anymore except those bent on some sort of criminal activity. The only places where it was still safe for Americans to visit were the coastal resorts, and those were heavily guarded by special police.

Those special police actually worked for the cartels, although the tourists didn't know that. They didn't want nervousness to interfere with the steady flow of *turista* dollars.

The only reason Pete knew about it was because Inez had a couple of cousins who worked for one of the hotels in Cancún, and she had heard about it from them.

Violence from the gang wars among the cartels was rampant along the border, on both sides of the river. The Texas Rangers, the Border Patrol, and the local police managed to keep reasonable order in the border towns on the Texas side, but there were still a lot of cartel-related incidents. Houston, San Antonio, and Dallas all had their share of problems directly related to the cartel rivalries.

But that sort of trouble hadn't touched Home yet. The biggest problem around here were the fights that sometimes broke out in the honky-tonks out on the state highway on Friday and Saturday nights. Pete read the *Home Herald* from cover to cover every week, and the police report hadn't listed any burglaries in he couldn't remember when.

So even though Inez was worried about somebody breaking into the house, Pete didn't think it had really happened. She'd been dreaming, or she'd heard something else. They didn't have a cat, but they did have a little dog that sometimes knocked things over.

"What did it sound like?" he asked her.

"I heard floorboards creaking. Somebody's walking around out there."

This was an old house, built in 1947. It made noises, like all old houses do. But Pete humored his wife and asked, "Which way were they going?"

"Down the hall, toward the den."

For the first time since waking up, Pete felt a stirring of unease. If burglars *were* going to break into the McNamara house, the den was where they would find the things most worth stealing. Both computers were there, the desktop that Inez used and the laptop that Pete used while sitting in his recliner. Most of his guns were in the den as well, the handguns in a locked gunsafe, the rifles and shotguns in a couple of locked cabinets. Pete had hunted a lot when he was younger, and he still enjoyed having the guns around even though he didn't use them much anymore.

But he still practiced enough to keep his shooting eye, and not *all* the guns were in the den.

He sat up, swung his legs out of bed, and put his bare feet on the floor.

"What are you going to do?" Inez asked.

"Check it out. That's what you want me to do, isn't it?"

"I'd appreciate it. You want me to come along?"

To tell the truth, deep down he did. Inez was a brave woman—hell, she had put up with him for more than forty years, hadn't she?—and she had done enough hard work in her life that she was still tough and strong despite getting older.

But Pete didn't say that. He said, "No, you stay here. I'll be right back. I'm sure it's nothing to worry about."

His eyes were adjusted to the darkness. There was a big moon in the sky outside casting silvery illumination through the curtains, and he had no trouble moving across the room to the closet. He opened the door silently, reached up onto the shelf, and touched the wood-grained plastic box first try. He took it down, set it on the dresser, undid that latches, and lifted the lid.

His fingers curled around the butt of the .45 Colt automatic and took it out of the box. He had carried it in Vietnam and then in West Germany as an MP during his two hitches in the army, and he took it to the range often enough and shot well enough that he thought he might still be able to qualify with it if he had to.

He opened his underwear drawer, slid his hand down beside the stacks of clean underwear, and found the loaded magazine and the box of extra ammunition. He didn't think he would need any more rounds than what were in the magazine, so he didn't bother opening the box. Besides, his pajamas didn't have any pockets. What the hell were they thinking these days, making pajamas without pockets? Just because a man was going to bed, he'd never need to carry anything?

Pete slid the magazine into the automatic until it clicked into place. He pulled back the slide to put a round in the chamber, but he did it quietly. If somebody *was* in the house who wasn't supposed to be, there was no point in giving them any more warning than he had to.

"Be right back," he whispered to Inez.

He went to the door of their bedroom, eased it open, and stepped out into the hall.

Chapter 2

Jorge Corona and Emilio Navarre had grown up together in Piedras Negras, joined a street gang together when they were ten, and committed their first murders when they were twelve. By the time they were recruited to the gang that worked for the Rey del Sol cartel when they were twenty, Jorge had killed seventeen people, Emilio only fifteen. In the three years since then, Emilio had managed to cut Jorge's lead to one. They were best friends, but that didn't mean they couldn't have a little friendly competition between them.

There were two old people in this house, Emilio knew. If he could kill both of them, he would pull ahead.

They had been in Home—and what a stupid name for a town, they both thought; only the Texan *viejos* could come up with something like that—for several days, just checking things out, deciding what they would do. Every morning they sat near the table in the Dairy Queen where the old men gathered.

Listen carefully to the old men talking, without appearing to do so, and before too long you would know everything that was going on in a small town . . . who was getting married, who was having a baby, who was leaving town, who had cancer, who had a prostate the size of a dang grapefruit.

You could also get an idea who had the most guns, because these Texans loved to talk about their guns.

A man named Pete McNamara seemed to be a likely candidate. From the way the other old men talked, this hombre McNamara had quite a collection of firearms. Jorge and Emilio were particularly interested in the pistols and shotguns. Hunting rifles didn't really come in handy in their line of work very often. But a nice heavy handgun was always a good thing to have, and nothing was better than a shotgun for sending straight to hell some fool who dared to cross Rey del Sol.

McNamara's hair was mostly white, with only a little gray left in it. He had a gray mustache that he probably thought gave his lined, weathered face some dignity. There in the Dairy Queen, he wore a flannel shirt, even though it was hot outside. That told Jorge and Emilio that his blood ran thin and he was always cold.

His hand trembled a little, too, when he reached for his coffee cup. A man such as that, so weak, so useless, he might as well already be dead.

The only purpose in life he still served was to be robbed and killed by strong young men.

Jorge and Emilio left the restaurant while the gathering of old men still went on, although it appeared it would be breaking up soon. They waited in the car they had stolen in Eagle Pass and driven up from the border. Emilio pretended to talk on his cell phone so they would have a reason to be just sitting there.

Ten minutes later, McNamara came out, got into a pickup, and drove off. Jorge followed him to an old but well-kept-up frame house on the edge of the town. The house was painted green and had a dark green roof. McNamara parked in the driveway, in front of an attached, one-car garage that had a sedan in it. The wife's car, no doubt. A breezeway connected the garage to the house and had the washer and dryer in it. As Jorge drove slowly past, he and Emilio saw the woman in there, watched as she greeted McNamara. A thick-bodied woman with dark hair, and even the quick glimpse was enough to tell Jorge and Emilio that she was Hispanic.

"Marry a gringo, you deserve whatever happens to you, you dumb bitch," Emilio muttered as Jorge drove on past the house. "Tonight?"

Jorge nodded. "Tonight."

There was no need to wait any longer. They wouldn't find a better target than this. Soon they would be on their way back to Mexico with a carful of guns and whatever else they could loot from the house.

The lights in the house went out a little after ten o'clock. The two amigos waited half an hour, then waited a little longer still, just to be sure. It wouldn't really matter all that much if they woke up the house's inhabitants, because they planned to kill the two old people anyway, but it would be easier to dispose of them if they were asleep. It would be a simple job, no torture, no rape, just murder and robbery. No fuss, no muss, as the anglos said.

They got out of the car and circled around to the back of the house. Back windows were usually easier to break into. And in a place like this, they didn't take elaborate security precautions to begin with.

These people thought they were safe.

A simple hook-and-eye held the screen on the kitchen window. It took Jorge all of ten seconds to cut the screen, reach inside, and unhook it. He lifted the whole screen out of the window frame.

Emilio used a tiny LED flashlight to check for locks on the window. There were none. What was wrong with these people? Did they still believe it was the Twentieth Century?

Emilio slipped the light back in his pocket and started to raise the window. To his surprise, it didn't budge. He got the light out and looked again.

"Painted shut," he whispered to Jorge.

That wasn't good, but it wasn't an insurmountable obstacle. It just meant the window might make a little more noise when they opened it.

They had brought small pry bars. They used their knives to whittle out places in the sill where they could work the bars under the window, then working together, they heaved on both bars and broke the window loose. It made a scraping, squealing sound as it rose.

Jorge and Emilio looked at each other and shrugged. What happened, happened.

They climbed inside.

This wasn't their first burglary. They knew how to find their way around in a strange house. Within minutes, they had located the den. They knew from eavesdropping on the conversation in the

Dairy Queen that this was where McNamara kept his guns. First they would check out the haul they were going to make, then they would deal with the old people.

But as Emilio flashed the little light around the den with its gun cabinents and display cases, its big TV, its stuffed animal heads on the walls, Jorge suddenly gripped his arm and whispered, "Somebody's coming!"

Chapter 3

Pete's chest started to hurt when he saw the reflection of the light darting around inside the den. Somebody was definitely in there. Up until now, he had hoped that Inez was wrong, that nobody had actually broken into the house where they had lived for decades, where they had raised their kids, enjoyed the good things, and endured the bad things that all married couples do.

Somebody was in their *house*, by God. Somebody who wasn't supposed to be here.

Pete's throat was tight with anger, but he had to keep swallowing his fear, too. He'd had a few hairy moments as an MP, but overall his life had been remarkably free from violence and danger.

He stood in the hall considering his age. He could go back to the bedroom, shut the door, and sit there with the gun, waiting if they tried to come in but otherwise letting them take what they want and go. Yeah, he could do that.

But he wasn't going to.

He took a step toward the open door of the den, and damned if he didn't ram his left leg into the little telephone table that stood there, with a cordless phone on it that he owned now, instead of the black rotary dial phone he'd rented from the phone company for all those years. Running into furniture in his own house. How stupid was that?

Pretty stupid, Pete realized, because it warned the guys in the den that he was out here. He heard the swift whisper, couldn't make out the words, but knew there had to be at least two of them.

The element of surprise was lost. Might as well get in there.

He stepped into the doorway and hit the light switch with his left hand as he used his right to thrust the Colt out in front of him.

"Hold it!" he shouted.

The problem was, the sudden burst of light blinded him just as much as it did the intruders. Wincing from the glare, holding his hand up to shade his eyes, Pete tried to take in the scene as quickly as he could so he would know what he was facing.

Two men stood over by his gun cabinets. He could see the shapes of their bodies, even though he couldn't make out many details. He jabbed the gun toward them and said, "Don't move! I've got a gun!"

Well, they could see that, of course. And now he could see the guns in their hands, too, big, ugly things with extended magazines for a lot of firepower.

Pete suddenly knew that he was about to get the shit blown out of him.

Unless he blew the shit out of the burglars first.

And that was the funny thing. All the fear and the other distractions cleared out of his mind. He didn't feel anything except a certain sense of urgency, didn't see anything except what was right in front of him. The annoying little tremor that cropped up in his hands more and more often these days went away. His grip was rock steady as he leveled the .45.

He fired two shots fast, a quick one-two, at the man on the left. He was aiming at the body, the biggest target, and both bullets struck the man in the chest with enough force to knock him back against the cabinet behind him. He threw his arms out to the sides, and as he did, his finger must have jerked the trigger of the gun he held, because it erupted with flame from the muzzle and the most god-awful racket Pete had ever heard. The slugs hammered against the wall of the den in a ragged line from the door to the corner of the room, punching easily through the sheetrock on both sides of the wall.

Pete was half-stunned. Between the double blast from the Colt and the intruder's gun going off, he was deaf. But even though he couldn't hear anything, he could see and knew the second man was still a threat. Pete grabbed his right wrist with his left hand to steady it and pivoted.

Three, maybe four seconds had gone by since he'd stepped into the room and flicked on the lights. It seemed longer than that. The second man had had time to lift his gun and point it at Pete. The only reason he hadn't fired yet was because he was looking at his buddy, who stood there braced against one of the gun cabinets, bloody froth already bubbling from the holes in his chest as he tried to breathe with bullet-torn lungs.

Then his eyes flicked back to Pete, and the two men locked gazes for a heartbeat.

Pete saw a stocky man about five-nine, with dark,

curly hair, a mustache, and a heavy jaw. He wore a short-sleeved shirt, and his arms were covered with tattoos. His dark eyes were wide with surprise.

Pete knew what the man and his companion must have thought. Nobody here but a harmless old couple. Wouldn't be any trouble to break in and steal whatever they wanted. They didn't have to worry about the people who lived here.

Now the first guy knew different, and so did the second one, because he jerked his gun toward Pete as his finger tightened on the trigger.

Pete was just a hair faster. The Colt roared again and the .45 round shattered the burglar's right shoulder, knocked him halfway around, and made him drop his gun. Pete's aim had been just a little off this time, but it got the job done.

Pete didn't stop pulling the trigger, though. The intruder was still on his feet. Pete wanted him on the floor, where he wouldn't be a threat to him or Inez any longer. Three more shots blasted out from the Colt, but only one of them actually hit the man. That one shattered his right kneecap into a million pieces and knocked him down.

The first man had slid down the gun cabinet to a sitting position by now, leaving bloody streaks on the wood. He sat there with his legs sticking out in front of him, leaking more blood on the carpet.

Pete backed out of the den into the hall. Now that the light in the den was on, enough of it spilled out into the hall for him to glimpse something from the corner of his eye. He turned to his left and saw the crumpled figure lying on the floor.

Inez. She must have followed him after all, despite him telling her to stay in the bedroom.

Then Pete thought about the way those bullets from the burglar's gun had punched right through the wall like it wasn't there. . . .

He dropped his own weapon and nearly tripped and fell over his own feet, he was moving so fast as he ran to her side and dropped to his knees and got his arms around her so he could lift her. He saw the way her head rolled loosely on her neck and felt how wet her pajamas were as he pulled her against him, and he screamed her name, even though to his still half-deafened ears the voice didn't sound like his and seemed to come from miles and miles away.

In the dim light, he saw Inez's eyes flutter open for a moment. She looked up at him, but he couldn't tell if she actually saw him or not. Later he liked to think she did. Her lips moved, but he couldn't hear the words, couldn't hear the last thing his wife of more than forty years said to him. It could have been *I love you* or *I told you there was somebody in the house* or *Oh, God, it hurts.*

Pete liked to think it was *I love you.* But he would never know.

CHAPTER 4

Alexandra Bonner tossed the magazine onto the coffee table. She couldn't concentrate tonight. She had read the same paragraph about how to de-stress your life four or five times before she realized what she was doing.

The simple fact was that she wouldn't be able to think about much of anything until Jack got home.

It wasn't really that late. She glanced at the clock. Just eleven. Not that late at all for a seventeen-year-old boy to be out on a summer night, when there was no school the next day. Jack had been out that late lots of times.

But not when he was grounded and wasn't supposed to be out of the house at all. Not when he'd snuck out to do God knows what with those friends of his, Rowdy—what kind of boy went by "Rowdy" in this day and age?—and Steve.

She stood up and raked her fingers through her long, dark blond hair. At work she wore it in a ponytail most of the time, to keep it out of the way, but at home she liked it loose. Eventually she was going to get too old to wear it this long. Mature women had to look dignified, and forty-five was pretty doggone mature.

She wasn't being vain, though, when she told herself she could still pass for thirty-five. Well, thirty-eight, maybe, depending on whether it was a good day or a bad day. Her work kept her in good enough shape that she could still wear her jeans a little tight. Not like when she was eighteen, of course, but when she wasn't wearing her uniform she could still draw some interested looks from men.

She paced over to the front window. Those thoughts weren't doing any better a job of distracting her than the blasted magazine had. She parted the curtains a little and looked out, eyes searching for headlights coming along the farm-to-market road. A car went past, but it didn't turn in at the long driveway, didn't even slow down.

"You're gonna be grounded until you're thirty, kid," she muttered.

Two nights earlier, Jack had been out running around with Rowdy and Steve in Rowdy's pickup when they'd run into a cow that had gotten loose and wandered into the road. Running into a cow wasn't all that uncommon in West Texas, and while it was unfortunate and had done quite a bit of damage to the pickup—not to mention the poor cow—the kicker had been the fact that the sheriff's deputy investigating the accident had smelled alcohol on Rowdy's breath.

That was enough to justify testing all three boys in the car. Rowdy admitted to having one beer, and his blood alcohol level was so low, he'd probably been telling the truth. Jack and Steve told the deputy they hadn't had any, and their tests proved it. Rowdy was underage, of course, but the deputy had decided to let it go, but not before calling all three sets of parents to let them know what was going on. Jack had driven the pickup back to Rowdy's house, just to be on the safe side, and by the time they got there, the parents had gathered to read the riot act to them. All three boys were grounded for two weeks and not allowed to hang around together.

In most places these days, one beer and three teenage boys would have been such a minor matter nobody would have thought twice about it.

But this wasn't most places. This was Home.

The beer incident wasn't the only thing that had caused problems with Jack over the past few months, either. There had been the business with the Internet porn—gee, it would have been handy to have Jack's dad around to handle something like that, if only he hadn't, you know, *left* years ago, she had thought bitterly more than once—plus the falling grades and the fact that he'd barely passed the standardized test, whatever they were calling it now, to get him from eleventh grade to twelfth, plus the general surly attitude that drove her crazy.

Was he a good kid at heart? She thought so. She hoped so. But the defiance and poor judgment he'd been exhibiting lately worried the hell out of her. She tried to tell herself that he was just being a teenage boy, but her instincts told her it might be more than that.

You couldn't really get away from drugs these days, even in a place like Home. She knew that as well or better than anybody, and it just scared her to death.

There was another car coming. Was it slowing down? Yes, it was. The headlights clicked off before it turned into the driveway. He was going to at least try to sneak back in without her noticing, although he was decidedly not very good at it.

The cell phone clipped to her belt rang.

She muttered and shook her head. This was not good timing, not when she was about to catch Jack in the act of sneaking in and rip him a new one.

But they had known at work that she was going home and wouldn't be bothering her if it wasn't something important. She took the phone off its clip and answered it.

"Chief Bonner."

"Sorry to bother you, Alex, but we've got trouble."

Instantly, Alexandra the worried mom was gone, replaced by Alex the chief of police in Home. "What is it, Eloise?"

Eloise Barrigan had worked as the night dispatcher for years. Her husband, Clint, was one of Alex's officers and usually had the night duty, too, so that worked out well for them.

"We got a call about shots being fired on Randall Street, so I sent Clint to check it out. One of the neighbors was out waiting for him to get there, and when he did, the man told him the shots came from Pete and Inez McNamara's house."

"Pete might've had a coyote nosing around and tried to scare it off." Alex knew the McNamaras, just like she knew most of the people in Home. Good folks.

"I wish," Eloise said. "Nobody came to the door when Clint rang the bell, but he could hear crying inside."

"Oh, no."

"Yeah. He went around back, found a window open, went in that way, and found Pete and Inez in the hall. Inez had been shot." Eloise paused to swallow hard. Alex heard it over the phone. "She's dead, Alex."

"Pete would *never* hurt her."

"Oh, no, no! It wasn't that. There's a dead man in Pete's den and another one who's been wounded pretty bad. They were both armed. Looks like Pete surprised a couple of burglars and shot it out with them, and Inez got hit by a stray bullet."

Alex closed her eyes for a moment and pressed her fingertips to her forehead. This was awful. Nothing like this had ever happened in Home since she'd been on the force, not while she was an officer and not while she was chief. It was going to be a terrible mess, but more than anything else, her heart went out to Pete McNamara. To have to defend your home against armed intruders and then to have your wife killed by them . . . It was almost too much to imagine.

The demands of the job took over and shoved the human reaction out. "Has Clint secured the scene?"

"Yeah. I sent Delgado over there right away to give him a hand. You want me to call the sheriff?"

"No, I'll do it while I'm on my way." The city of Home had an agreement with the sheriff's department to handle anything the local police couldn't. With all the complicated demands this crime scene would entail, Alex knew her little four-man force would need help.

"Okay, Alex. Let me know if there's anything I can do."

"Thanks."

Alex closed the phone and went to get her gun and badge from the bedroom, along with the windbreaker that had the word POLICE in big letters on the back. It was too warm tonight for a jacket, but she figured she'd better wear it anyway.

A light shone under the door of Jack's room. As she went by, Alex paused and opened it.

"Hey!" he said from the chair in front of his computer. He was slouched down so far there was no telling how much damage he was doing to his spine, Alex thought. "What happened to respecting each other's privacy?"

"What happened to grounded for two weeks?" she shot back at him. "It's now a month, that's what happened."

He jumped up. "What?"

"I know you snuck out, Jack. I checked your room earlier, and I saw you drive in with your lights out a few minutes ago." She gestured toward the badge she'd clipped to her belt. "Chief of police, remember? I'm observant."

He shook his head and glared at her. "This is totally unfair."

"No, I'll tell you what's unfair," Alex said. "I have to go out now and look at two dead people, including a woman I've known for years and considered a friend. Now *that's* unfair, Jack."

CHAPTER 5

An ambulance and two police cars were already at the McNamara place by the time Alex got there, their flashing lights splashing garishly over the street crowded with onlookers from the neighborhood. Every light in the house seemed to be on.

Alex parked behind the ambulance. On the drive over here, she had been able to force thoughts of her problems with Jack out of her head and concentrate on the horrific crime that had taken place tonight in her town.

Several of the neighbors called out to her as she walked across the yard toward the front porch. They wanted to know what had happened, and you couldn't blame them for that. Evidently there had been a lot of shots fired inside the McNamara house, and then the cops and the ambulance had shown up. You didn't have to be a genius to figure out that something really bad had gone down.

J. P. Delgado stood just inside the open front door with his thumbs hooked in his belt. His lean, handsome face was set in solemn lines as he looked at Alex and shook his head.

"It's bad, Chief, mighty bad."

"Inez is really dead?" Alex asked, keeping her voice pitched low.

Delgado nodded, then inclined his head toward a hallway on the other side of the living room. "She's still in there, down the hall by the den. The M.E. isn't here yet. Dead guy's still in the den, too. Clint's got Mr. McNamara in the kitchen, and the EMTs are working on the wounded perp."

"Is he going to live?"

Delgado shrugged. "He was hit twice, shoulder and leg, but Mr. McNamara got him with an old .45 automatic. Those things can kill you sometimes, even if they just tag you."

Alex knew that. That was why the .45 had been the standard sidearm in the army for many years.

"Eloise said it looked like Mr. McNamara interrupted a burglary in progress. That the way it looked to you?"

She valued Delgado's opinion. Despite his relative youth—he was only thirty-five—he had been a cop for quite a while in Laredo before coming back to Home to care for his aging grandmother. Alex had been happy to hire him and add his experience to her department, although the city couldn't afford to pay him what he'd been making in Laredo.

He said, "I don't think there's any question that's what happened. The two guys are both Hispanic, no I.D.s, probably drove up from the border just to rob somebody. My guess is that they were after Mr. McNamara's guns. There's a constant need for weapons in the cartels."

"You think these two are part of a cartel?"

"There's not much free-lance crime in Mexico anymore except the really low-level stuff. The cartels are like feudal kingdoms in medieval Europe, always at war with each other. There's no effective centralized power in the country anymore."

Delgado came out with stuff like that that would surprise you if you didn't know that he had a history degree from the University of Texas. The academic world didn't really appeal to him, though. He preferred being a cop.

A couple of EMTs maneuvered a gurney out of the hall and into the living room. The man strapped onto it appeared to be unconscious. Some of his clothes had been cut away, and bloodstained bandages were wrapped around his shoulder and leg in their place.

"This one's going to the hospital, Chief," one of the ambulance men said to Alex.

"Is he going to make it?"

"Don't know, but my guess is yes. He lost a lot of blood, but we've got him stabilized right now. Have to wait and see."

Alex nodded and said, "Thanks," as they wheeled out the wounded burglar. She gestured to Delgado. "Go with them. Don't let the son of a bitch out of your sight."

"You got it, Chief." Delgado followed the gurney out of the house.

Alex took a deep breath to steady herself. It didn't help much because there was still a faint reek of gunfire in the air. Waiting wouldn't make it any better, so she stepped over to the hall and looked down it.

She saw the bullet holes in the wall between the den and the hall, her brain automatically noting their location. When the crime scene team from the sheriff's department got here, those holes and all the rest of the physical evidence would be documented with digital photographs and video.

Alex's eyes were drawn to the blanket-shrouded figure lying on the floor of the hall. The EMTs had draped that blanket over Inez McNamara because there was nothing they could do for her other than protect her from the indignity of having people stare at her.

Alex walked over to the body and knelt beside it. She didn't want to, but she forced herself to lift the blanket. Inez's face was gray. The color of life was long gone. From the looks of it, she had been hit twice by bullets coming through the wall, Alex thought, but it could have been more than that. The autopsy would tell for sure.

After carefully replacing the blanket, Alex stood and went to the open door of the den. Since the EMTs had left with the wounded man, nobody was in here except the dead burglar. He sat propped against one of Pete McNamara's gun cabinets, his arms hanging loose at his sides and his head lolled forward over his blood-soaked chest. The high-caliber automatic weapon, some sort of foreign make, lay on the carpet near his right hand.

Alex put the sequence of events together, replaying them in her mind's eye as if she had witnessed them the first time around.

Pete or Inez or both of them hear a noise in the house. Pete gets the .45 and comes to check. Probably he tells Inez to wait in the bedroom while he takes a look around, but Inez being Inez, she follows him anyway. He surprises the burglars in the den, everybody starts shooting, the bullets go through the wall, Pete puts both of the burglars down. . . .

Then turns to find his wife dying on the floor behind him.

Watching where she stepped to make sure she didn't disturb any evidence, Alex moved across the den to the dead man and again hunkered on her heels to study him, as she had with Inez out in the hall.

Definitely just two wounds on this one, both to the chest. Good shooting on Pete's part. If he had just been a little faster, he might have been able to kill the burglar before the man pulled the trigger.

Alex turned her head and looked at the way the line of bullet holes marched across the wall in a ragged but relatively straight line. Pete's bullet had hit the man in the chest and knocked him back into the cabinet, making his arms fly out at the sides just as he pulled the trigger. That theory fit the evidence. There were no other bullet holes, so the wounded man must not have gotten off even a single shot. A similar automatic weapon lay on the carpet next to the bloodstains where the second burglar had fallen.

Forensics would determine the truth of all this, but Alex was confident that she had things right for the most part. She looked into the face of the dead man, which was hard and ugly in death as it had been in life, and wanted to ask him why he and his companion had come here tonight to ruin the lives of two good people.

But there were no answers there and never would be. Evil had invaded the McNamara home, just as evil always invaded paradise sooner or later.

The psychologists and the social engineers wanted people to believe that evil didn't really exist, that it was actually just a series of poor choices forced on individuals by a society that was indifferent at best and hostile at worst.

Alex had been a cop long enough to know what a crock *that* was. Evil existed, all right.

She was looking at it, right here, right now.

And as always, it couldn't explain why it did the terrible things it did. It was just . . . evil.

The nature of the beast.

Alex sighed and came to her feet. It was just about the last thing in the world she wanted to do right now, but she had to go talk to Pete McNamara.

CHAPTER 6

It was four in the morning before Alex got home. Between the lack of sleep and the emotional turmoil of dealing with what had happened, she was exhausted. She took off her gun, badge, and windbreaker and kicked off her shoes, but other than that she was still fully dressed when she fell into her bed and went right to sleep on top of the covers.

She slept like she'd been drugged, but that didn't last. Sometime before dawn, she woke up and realized that she should have checked on Jack when she came in. After the brief argument earlier, she didn't think he would have snuck out again, but although she hated to admit it to herself, she wasn't sure about that.

Jack had changed. Maybe she had, too.

She dragged herself out of bed and went down the hall to his room. No light came under the door, and she didn't hear anything when she leaned closer to it. A lot of times he left the TV or the radio on all night. They had argued about that very thing. Alex didn't see the point of burning the electricity if he was asleep. The fact that Jack's bedroom was dark and quiet actually increased her worry a little.

She turned the knob quietly and eased the door open just enough to stick her head in. Her eyes were adjusted to the darkness well enough for her to be able to make out the shape sprawled on the bed. She heard his deep, regular breathing as well.

That was a relief, she thought as she closed the door as quietly as she'd opened it. She knew now that he was here, and safe, and she could go back to sleep.

If only it had been that easy.

Instead she was restless, dozing off and then waking up with a start, over and over, and when she did sleep long enough to dream, they were nightmares haunted by blood and death. It was almost a relief when the phone rang at eight o'clock, forcing her to get up.

"Hello," she slurred into it.

"I didn't wake you, did I, Alex?"

She recognized Ed Ruiz's voice. Ed owned the local hardware store, which was able to survive because it was such a long drive to the county seat and one of the big box discount stores. He was also the mayor of Home.

"No, I'm fine. What's up, Ed?"

"I heard about what happened to the McNamaras. Terrible, just terrible."

"Yeah." She could hear the sincerity in Ruiz's voice and knew he really felt bad about Pete and Inez. At the same time, he was a politician, and so there was always something a little calculated in everything he said.

Or maybe she just felt that way because he had

dragged his feet about promoting her to chief after Whit Bradford retired and the rest of the city council had had to push him into it.

"There's no doubt about what happened, is there? The two men broke in, and McNamara was just defending himself and his wife?"

"That was Pete's statement," Alex said, recalling the painful ordeal of taking that statement from the sobbing, distraught old man. "That's the way all the evidence looked to me. Pending the report from the sheriff's crime scene team, which I don't expect to change anything, that's how my report will read, too."

"Good." Ruiz sounded relieved. "Let's stick with that."

Alex frowned. Even in her grogginess, she sensed that something else was going on.

"What is it, Ed?" she asked. "Why would anybody even doubt what Pete McNamara said?"

The silence on the other end of the phone told her that the mayor didn't want to answer. When Ruiz finally spoke, his voice was edgy with nervousness. "Mr. Navarre has regained consciousness."

"Who?"

"Emilio Navarre. The man who was wounded by McNamara."

"How do you know his name? He didn't have any I.D. on him. Did Delgado question him? He should've known better than that."

"No, as far as I'm aware, Officer Delgado didn't question the man. Mr. Navarre told his lawyer who he is."

Alex's stomach gave a lurch at the word "lawyer." In her work as a cop, she had run into plenty of attorneys who were decent people, but there was always a core of truth to any cliché, and the sleazy lawyer stereotype was no exception.

"He has a lawyer already?" Alex asked, trying not to clench her teeth in distaste. "Who?"

"I don't recall his name. He's from San Antonio, evidently a partner in a large firm there."

Alex closed her eyes and gave her head a shake. "Wait a minute. How did a lawyer get all the way out here from San Antonio already?"

Home was a drive of several hours from the Alamo City.

"Private jet," Ruiz said. "Mr. Navarre regained consciousness a couple of hours ago and demanded a phone. Since he hasn't been formally arrested, Officer Delgado couldn't stop the hospital personnel from providing one. Navarre dialed a number he evidently knew by heart."

"And less than two hours later he's got a high-powered lawyer with a private jet. Ed, this isn't good."

"I know." Ruiz sounded miserable. "I know. The only bright spot I can think of is that the city can't be held liable in any way. The county contracts with the ambulance service, and they're the only ones who touched him except the doctors and nurses at the hospital."

Alex swallowed her irritation. As mayor, it was Ruiz's job to look out for the city's best interests, even if in doing it he sometimes came across as a little callous.

"He's not going to sue the city or anybody else," Alex said. "He's the one in the wrong here. He's just lawyering up because he knows that he can be convicted of first-degree murder, even though he didn't pull the trigger on Inez McNamara. Accident or not, she was killed in the commission of a felony that he was a party to."

"Are you certain that he didn't fire?"

"Well, no. But the sheriff's people have his gun. I'm sure they'll test it and see if it was fired recently. They may be able to test Navarre's hands for residue, too, although it may be too late for that."

"It would be better if he fired his weapon."

"Better for who?"

"Pete McNamara."

Alex felt sick again. "Oh, no, Ed. You're not saying what I think you're saying."

"Navarre's lawyer has already put out a statement calling for McNamara's arrest on charges of murder and attempted murder."

"That's crazy! *They* broke into *his* house. They shot at him."

"Only the dead man. That's why murder charges probably wouldn't stick. But if Navarre didn't fire his gun . . ."

Wearily, Alex scrubbed a hand over her face. She couldn't believe this was happening. How could a man be attacked by intruders in his own home, see his wife killed practically before his eyes, and then have scum like this Emilio Navarre portray *him* as the bad guy? It was completely insane.

But in a world where elitist politicians just did whatever they wanted to and ignored the will of the people they had been elected to represent, insanity was the new sanity, Alex supposed.

"What do you want me to do, Ed?" She felt like she was a hundred years old as she asked the question.

"Turn on the TV first and take a look at that lawyer's press conference. I'm sure you won't have any trouble finding a station running it. Then get down to the hospital and formally place Navarre under arrest. We're going to try to get out in front on this, but it may be too late."

"Delgado or one of my other officers can make the arrest."

"No, I want you to do it. I think it'll be better if it looks like the chief is in charge."

"I *am* in charge of the department, Ed," she reminded him, not bothering to keep the edge out of her voice.

"I know, I know. But this isn't just a legal matter anymore. It's all public relations now, Alex. It's all perception."

Instead of reality, she thought. That was it in a nutshell. The reason she disliked politics and politicians.

"All right. I'll take care of it."

"Then come by my office. We've got to strategize."

"Sure," she said, although the idea of "strategizing" with Ed Ruiz didn't appeal to her at all. "I'll see you later."

She broke the connection before he could come up with anything else.

She took off the clothes she had slept in and pulled on a robe. No sounds came from Jack's room as she walked past it. There was a little TV in the kitchen, so she turned it on and then turned to get the coffeemaker going.

Ed had been right about one thing: The story was all over the news. It had even made the cable news networks, and after an unctuous, prematurely white-haired anchor made some snarky comments about Texans and guns, the station Alex was watching went to video of a small news conference. A tall, slender man in an expensive suit and sunglasses stood on a sidewalk just outside a building Alex recognized as Home Community Hospital. It was a small, eight-bed facility, and Alex figured Emilio Navarre would be transferred to the county hospital later on, when his condition had stabilized more.

A graphic along the bottom of the screen identified the man in sunglasses as Clayton Cochrum. He was saying, "—terrible injustice inflicted on my client by a trigger-happy, age-impaired vigilante who may well be suffering from dementia. Such a dangerous individual never should have been allowed to possess even one firearm, let alone a veritable arsenal such as the one police discovered inside his house."

"Nobody *discovered* Pete McNamara's guns," Alex muttered. "Everybody in town knew he had 'em."

Clearly playing to the cameras, Clayton Cochrum went on, "This is just one more instance of lax gun laws and even sloppier enforcement leading to a gun-related tragedy in Texas. An innocent woman lies dead, and a blameless bystander is in the hospital behind me, gravely injured because a man who is a danger to himself and the community was allowed to possess a gun. Not just one gun, but many guns!" Cochrum took his sunglasses off so he could peer soulfully into the camera. "Even though as a lifelong resident of the Lone Star State it pains me to admit it . . . this morning I am ashamed to be a citizen of a state that would allow such a tragedy to occur. This morning I am ashamed to be a Texan."

"Yeah, well," Alex said to the TV, "we're not that happy about having to claim a weasel like you, either."

She shut off the TV and went to take a shower while the coffee brewed. She wished she had the time to really soak under the hot water, but unfortunately, she had to get down to the hospital and place Emilio Navarre under arrest.

She had a feeling that after watching Clayton Cochrum, a regular shower just wasn't going to be enough to make her feel clean.

Washington, D.C.

Even after five months in office, there were still times when he looked around the Oval Office and had a hard time believing that he was really here, that he was really the most powerful man in the world.

Of course, he had known all along that it would come to this. Even as a boy, he had known that it was his destiny to be president. He'd always been the smartest one in school, and not just book smarts, either. He was handsome and charming and had a knack for getting people to believe him and to do what he wanted them to do.

All for their own good, of course.

Now he was in a position to remake this country the way it ought to be, to show people who didn't agree with him the error of their ways, to patiently explain to them why he was right and they were wrong and if they would just go along with what he wanted their lives would be so much better.

And if they didn't want to go along for their own good . . . well, the President of the United States wasn't known as the most powerful man in the free world for no reason, now was he?

He would make them go along. Stupid, racist rednecks.

But he had learned from the mistakes of his predecessors. Over the past dozen years, it had become impossible for anyone to be elected to the highest office in the land without the fawning approval of the media, and each victor in turn had tried to push the country farther to the left, convinced that it was his or her mandate to do so.

Unfortunately, there were large segments of the populace who didn't agree with that, mostly from those damned flyover states that nobody who mattered really cared about anyway, and they had made it difficult to get any truly progressive policies implemented. The last two people who had held this office before him hadn't been bold enough. They had clung to some foolish notion that people should be happy with change, even massive change.

This President knew better than that. That was what he had based his entire life on.

He knew best.

And even though he had been biding his time, he knew that when the moment arrived, he would make them all see that he was right.

Maybe today.

He thought that every day when he sat down behind the big desk in the Oval Office.

And today just might be the day, because his Chief of Staff looked very excited when he hurried into the room.

"Have you heard the news, boss?"

"You mean about what the Vice-President said at that dinner last night?" The woman had a positive genius for putting her foot in her mouth.

"No, this," the Chief of Staff said as he picked up a remote from the President's desk and pushed some buttons. A wall panel slid aside to reveal a giant-screen TV, which lit up as the Chief of Staff turned it on.

"Damn it, who left it on that channel?" the President exploded as he saw which of the cable news networks the set was tuned to.

"Sorry, sir," the Chief of Staff said as he hastily switched the channel. "Maybe some of the cleaning crew had it on while they were in here last night, even though they know it's against the rules. I'll find out and deal with it, you can be sure of that."

"Fire whoever was responsible."

"Of course, sir." The Chief of Staff raised the volume. "Just listen to this, if you don't mind."

A man with slicked-back hair and sunglasses was saying, "I am ashamed to be a Texan."

"Well, of course, he is, whoever he is," the President said. "Any sane person would be ashamed to be a Texan. They haven't voted correctly in . . . how many elections in a row is it now?"

"I don't know, sir."

"The whole state's just a bunch of religious fanatic, death-penalty-loving, gun nuts. Praise God, pass the ammunition, and fire up the electric chair."

"They were using lethal injection down there, sir, until we put a stop to it. But if you'd just listen . . ."

"Who was that?"

"A lawyer."

The President smiled. He loved lawyers. He might have been one himself, if things had worked out differently. And they were always good for massive campaign donations.

An anchorman was talking now about some shooting that had left two people dead and another injured. "Gun nuts," the President muttered. "I suppose somebody with a grudge against the government went on a rampage?"

"No, sir. A homeowner shot a couple of men who had broken into his house."

"That's terrible, terrible. People shouldn't be allowed to have handguns. Those men would still be alive today if Texas just had sensible laws. Barbarians."

"One of the men is alive, sir. The man at the news conference is his lawyer."

The President's perfectly trimmed eyebrows went up. "You mean . . . ?"

"Yes, sir. We're looking at a lawsuit, at the very least. The man's attorney is pressuring the local authorities to bring charges against the homeowner who did the shooting."

The President's hand slapped down on the desk as he leaned forward in his chair. "My God! Civil rights violations. Gun laws that are too permissive. Vigilantes on a rampage, and Texans at that! Good Lord, Geoff, this is—"

"Perfect, I know, yes, sir." The Chief of Staff beamed.

The President stood up and turned around to look out the window of the Oval Office.

It was the first day of a new era, and it was a beautiful morning.

Chapter 7

TV satellite trucks from as far away as Dallas/Fort Worth and Houston clogged the street in front of the hospital, and even though Alex turned on the police car's flashing lights and hit the siren for a squalling second, none of the trucks made a move to get out of the way.

As usual, the media's rights trumped everybody else's, at least in the opinion of the media.

Alex gave up, turned onto a side street, and parked there. She could walk back to the hospital quicker than she could get those jackals to move.

She decided to go in the back, rather than running the gauntlet of those perfectly coiffed men and women standing in front of the cameras. She went through the hospital's kitchen, nodding to the workers there.

"It's a regular three-ring circus out there, ain't it, Chief?" one of the women called to her.

Alex smiled and nodded. "It sure is. No shortage of clowns, either."

That brought an appreciative chuckle from the women.

Alex went through the hospital cafeteria, where

several people were eating breakfast, and looked wistfully at the steaming cups of coffee and plates full of food. She'd been in too much of a hurry for breakfast and had settled for a foam cup of coffee from the drive-through window at the Dairy Queen. It wasn't bad, but it still landed like hot lead in her stomach.

After stepping around a corner in the hallway, she approached the nurses' station. She recognized one of the women behind the counter and said, "Morning, Joanie. Where's the famous patient?"

"You mean infamous, Chief." The nurse pointed. "All the way down at the end of the hall in 108. That was Officer Delgado's idea."

And a good one, too, Alex thought. Best to keep the suspect isolated from the hospital's other patients.

"I'm surprised the hall isn't full of reporters," she commented.

"It was. Clint chased 'em out, and he's standin' at the front door to make sure they don't get back in. The hospital is private property, after all, and Dr. Boone asked Clint to keep them out."

Alex nodded. Dr. William Boone owned the Home Community Hospital, so he was within his rights to ask that the reporters be removed. They would probably howl about freedom of the press, but it didn't really matter. Alex knew that if they weren't acting outraged about that, they'd be acting outraged about something else. It was what the media did.

She went down the hall to Room 108 and pushed the door open, saying, "It's me, J. P.," to announce herself to Delgado.

He was sitting in a straight-backed chair at the foot of the bed nearest the door. The other hospital bed in the room was empty and the curtain between the beds was pushed back. It was rare that all the beds in the hospital were occupied.

The patient was hooked up to a couple of IVs and a machine that monitored his vital signs. He glared at Alex, but she could see surprise in his eyes in addition to the hostility. He probably hadn't expected a woman to be the chief of police.

"I wan' my lawyer," he said in accented but passable English.

"I believe you've already seen your lawyer, Mr. Navarre," Alex said as she crossed her arms and looked steadily at the man. "Don't worry, he'll be allowed access to you in accordance with all legal procedures. Right now, though, he's probably off somewhere issuing a statement or preening for the news cameras."

Alex could tell that Delgado was trying not to grin.

"I don't have to tell you nothin'," Navarre said.

"That's true. Right now, you just have to listen." Alex took a small, digital video recorder out of her pocket and handed it to Delgado. "Document this."

"Right, Chief," he said as he got to his feet.

Delgado had the recorder running as Alex faced Navarre and said, "Emilio Navarre, you're under arrest for suspicion of murder and attempted murder. You have the right to remain silent." She went through the rest of the Miranda warning, and when she was finished, she said, "Do you understand these rights, Mr. Navarre?"

He stared back sullenly at her and didn't say anything.

"Do you understand these warnings, Mr. Navarre?" Alex said again, her calm tone indicating that she was willing to stand there and repeat the question for as long as it took to get a response from him.

Navarre must have figured that out, because he said, "Sí, sí, I understand."

"Good. Do you wish to answer any questions?"

"I don't got to tell you nothin'. I talk to my lawyer."

"All right." Alex nodded to Delgado, letting him know that he could shut off the recorder.

"When do I get out of here? You got to give me bail."

"You're injured, Mr. Navarre," Alex said, gesturing toward the bandages that swathed his shoulder and leg. "It'll be up to the doctor to decide when you're well enough to be released from the hospital. When he says that you are, you'll be transported to a holding facility at the county seat where you'll be arraigned."

"You got to give me bail," Navarre insisted stubbornly.

Alex knew that if Navarre made bail, he would be over the border in forty-five minutes and they would never see him again. Navarre was a flight risk if there ever was one. A judge would know that, too, so she hoped bail would be denied.

But crazy things happened sometimes in the legal system. Alex didn't believe that it was actually broken; otherwise, she wouldn't still be part of it, but it sure misfired now and then.

She didn't respond to Navarre, but turned to

Delgado instead. "Are you all right, J. P.? You've been on duty for a long time."

"I'm fine," he said. "Keeping an eye on this . . ." He stopped before saying whatever he'd been about to say, probably something along the lines of "scum," Alex thought. He settled for saying, ". . . prisoner isn't that hard. It isn't like he can jump out of bed and run away."

"Well, I'll get Jerry to relieve you in a little while."

Delgado nodded. "Fine. Don't worry about me, Chief."

"I never do," Alex told him.

She left the hospital the same way she'd gone in, and when she made it back to her car she saw that the street was just as crowded as ever by the news media. Shaking her head, she drove away.

Ed Ruiz's hardware store was only a few minutes from the hospital. When Alex went inside, the handful of customers forgot all about their shopping and clustered around her instead, asking questions. Most of them wanted to know if it was true that Inez McNamara was dead. It seemed too awful to believe, and Alex certainly understood that sentiment. Solemnly, she told them that it was indeed true.

The clerk behind the counter at the rear of the store said, "Ed's not here, Chief. He said you were supposed to stop by, and if you did, to tell you that he's gone over to City Hall."

"What for?" Alex wanted to know.

"He said he had to meet with Dave Rutherford."

Dave Rutherford was the city attorney, as well as having a private practice here in Home, one of only half a dozen lawyers in town. If Ed had dropped everything to go talk with him, that didn't bode well, Alex thought as she thanked the clerk and left.

The coffee she'd had earlier still seemed to be burning a hole in her gut when she reached the small, tan brick building that housed Home's City Hall. The police department and the volunteer fire department were on the same block. She went inside, and before she could even say anything, the city secretary told her, "Go right on back to Ed's office, Alex. He's expectin' you."

With a sinking feeling, Alex opened the door of the mayor's office without knocking and stepped into the room. Ed Ruiz was behind the desk, with Dave Rutherford in one of the chairs in front of it. Both men looked up at her.

Alex didn't waste any time. "What's happened?" she asked.

"Just what we were afraid of," Ed replied, blinking at her through his thick glasses. Despite the flow of cold air from the air-conditioning ducts, his mostly bald head had beads of sweat on it. "That fancy lawyer went over to the county seat and filed suit against Pete McNamara, the manufacturer of the gun Pete used, the city of Home, Hawkes County, the state of Texas, and the federal government. He's made a clean sweep of it, and we're in deep trouble, Alex."

CHAPTER 8

"Calm down, Ed," Alex told the mayor. "He can't possibly win. He and his friend *murdered* Inez McNamara, for God's sake. Navarre's lawyer is just filing all those suits because he thinks it might help him in defending the criminal case against Navarre."

Dave Rutherford shook his head. He was a slender young man who also wore glasses, though his weren't as thick as Ruiz's.

"Not necessarily," he said. "Juries have actually found in favor of the plaintiff in similar cases in the past."

"Cases where a criminal files suit against somebody he tried to victimize?" Alex had heard of such things, but she didn't want to believe they were possible. Surely they were just some sort of urban legend.

"Exactly," Rutherford said. "Not only have the plaintiffs won in such lawsuits, but they've also been awarded significant damages."

"Millions of dollars in damages," Ed Ruiz said with a shudder. "That could bankrupt the town, Alex."

She held up her hands. "Hold on, hold on. We're

getting ahead of ourselves. A judge is liable to toss that lawsuit as soon as it comes up."

"We can't rely on that," Rutherford said. "Just in case the suit ever does come to trial, we need to be very, very careful. Everything that you do in dealing with Navarre has to be strictly by the book and according to normal procedures."

"It has been," Alex said, not bothering to keep the irritation out of her voice. "It will be. That's the way I run my department."

"I know that. I just want to make sure that we don't give Navarre and his lawyer any ammunition to use against us."

Alex nodded. "I understand. And I'll make sure that all my people understand, too."

"Have you placed Navarre under arrest?" Ruiz asked.

"I have."

"He was Mirandized?" Rutherford asked.

"Of course." Alex tapped the little recorder in her pocket. "I have it on tape. Well, so to speak."

Rutherford nodded. "Good."

"He wants a bail hearing."

"That's his right," Rutherford said with a shrug.

"Oh, come on. He's shot up and in the hospital. Where's he going? Besides, you know what'll happen if he gets bailed out. He'll be long gone across the border. *Hasta la vista*, baby."

"Don't say things like that," Ruiz warned. "The news media would make them out to be racist and prejudicial."

"Sorry," Alex muttered. She knew that Ruiz wasn't objecting out of any sense of political correctness or ethnic sensitivity. He was worried strictly about the city's liability in the pending lawsuit.

Rutherford's cell phone vibrated. He took it out of the pocket in his suit coat and answered it. His lean face grew even more grim as he listened. He thanked whoever was on the other end and closed the phone.

"That was my secretary," he said. "Cochrum has convinced a judge over at the county seat to hold a bail hearing in absentia for Navarre at two o'clock this afternoon." He stood up and reached for the briefcase on the floor beside his chair. "I need to get over there and meet with the district attorney so we can prepare for the hearing."

"Navarre hasn't been arraigned yet!" Alex protested.

"Doesn't matter."

Ruiz said, "We have to get that lawsuit quashed, Dave."

"We have to put Navarre in jail where he belongs," Alex said.

Neither of the men even looked at her. It was like they hadn't even heard her.

This case had already gone beyond any concept of right and wrong, she realized.

This was about money now.

Even though everybody in Home was talking about the tragedy that had happened at the McNamara house, it wasn't the only thing going on in town. People had their own lives to lead and their own problems, and they went on about their business. Some of the news crews even left, although they just went back to the rooms they had rented in the two local motels. They wanted to be close at hand if there were any new developments, as it seemed sure that there would be, since Emilio Navarre had been granted a bail hearing.

Alex tried to go on about her business, too. She sent Officer Jerry Houston to relieve Delgado on guard duty at the hospital. Clint Barrigan was working overtime, too, keeping reporters out of the place. Alex called in Lester Simms, one of the part-time reserve officers, to take over for him.

That left her other full-time officer, Betsy Carlyle, to work patrol. Jimmy Clifton was handling dispatch. Jimmy had a mild case of Down Syndrome, but he was an excellent dispatcher and knew as much about what went on in town as anybody, and more than most.

Alex was glad there were no other major problems that morning. She had enough on her mind. Home had always been such a peaceful little town. Did this tragedy mark a shift? Would it be just the first act in an escalating pattern of violence, the sort of thing that had affected so much of the rest of the country?

The citizens of Home had always thought they were safe.

But was anybody ever safe?

In the middle of the day, Alex swung by the pizza place downtown and picked up a large pepperoni. She took it home and carried it into the kitchen, feeling a brief flash of guilt because she didn't cook all that many meals for her and Jack. They ate takeout *way* too much. It wasn't good for either of them.

"Hey, Jack, I'm home," she called as she set the pizza on the kitchen table. "Wake up."

Even though it was nearly one o'clock in the afternoon, she assumed that Jack was still asleep. It was summer, after all, no school, and he was a teenage boy. She sometimes thought he was like a cat, capable of sleeping twenty hours a day. Plus he had come in late the night before, she reminded herself, when he wasn't even supposed to be out at all.

When he didn't respond, she went down the hall to his room and knocked on the door. "Jack. Pizza." That was usually the magic word.

Not this time. For all his passion for privacy, he seldom if ever actually locked his door. She reached down and turned the knob, eased the door open.

He wasn't in his room.

Muttering under her breath, Alex quickly searched the rest of the house. Jack wasn't anywhere to be found. She felt like tearing her hair out in frustration. What was it about the concept of being grounded that he didn't understand?

Or did he just not give a damn what she said anymore?

His car was here, which meant he had either gone somewhere on foot or somebody had come by and picked him up. Alex called the Donovan house, and when Rowdy's mother answered, she said, "Sorry to bother you, Helen, but this is Alex Bonner. Does my son happen to be there with Rowdy?"

"No, we haven't seen Jack all day, Alex," the woman said.

"Rowdy *is* there, isn't he?"

Helen snorted. "I'm looking right at him. In fact,

I don't plan on letting him out of my sight. He's grounded for a month."

Alex heard Rowdy complaining in the background, so she knew Helen was telling the truth. "Thanks anyway," she said. "If you see Jack, I'd appreciate it if you'd tell him I'm looking for him."

"Sure. Say, isn't it just terrible about the McNamaras? I'm glad you've got that monster locked up."

Navarre wasn't exactly locked up, but Alex didn't point that out. She thanked Helen again and hung up, then called the Boone house. Jack's friend Steve was Dr. William Boone's son.

Dr. Boone was a widower, but he had a live-in housekeeper who answered the phone and told Alex that Jack wasn't there and hadn't been there that morning. Alex thanked the woman and hung up. Worry gnawed at her brain, but she wasn't going to let herself panic. Jack had to be around somewhere.

From the corner of her eye, she saw movement through the front window of the house. When she turned to look, she saw one of the police cruisers pulling into the driveway. With the tension inside her growing, she hurried outside to find out what was going on.

The strain she was under got even worse when she saw J. P. Delgado climbing out from behind the wheel of the police car as Jack got out on the passenger side.

"What is it, J. P.?" Alex snapped. "What did you catch him doing?"

Delgado looked surprised. He held up his hands, palms out in the face of his boss's anger. "Wait a minute, Chief," he said. "I didn't catch Jack doing anything."

"Yeah, Mom," Jack said. "Way to jump to a conclusion."

"You be quiet," she told him. "You're grounded."

Delgado said, "I didn't know anything about that. Jack and I had agreed to get together this morning, so I came by after you sent Jerry to the hospital to take over guarding Navarre."

"Get together for what?" Alex asked with a frown.

"We went out to the range and had some target practice."

Alex looked at her son. "You were shooting?"

"Yeah. Anything wrong with that? You shoot your gun all the time."

"I wouldn't say it's all the time," Alex argued. "Anyway, you aren't supposed to leave the house. You're grounded."

"But I was with one of your officers," Jack argued right back. "And I'd think you'd be happy that I want to learn how to handle a gun."

"Well, that's better than not knowing how, I guess, but . . . Blast it, you're grounded!"

Jack looked disgusted and shook his head. "I give up. You just can't be reasonable."

"I can, too! Jack—"

But he stalked past her and went in the house, still shaking his head as he slammed the front door behind him.

"I'm sorry, Alex," Delgado said quietly. "I really didn't know."

She sighed. "That's all right. I know you didn't." She paused. "How long has he been shooting?"

"About a month."

"He never said anything to me about it."

Delgado shrugged. "Kids that age, they like to keep things to themselves."

"Yeah, I guess so. Is he any good?"

A grin broke out on Delgado's face. "Oh, yeah. He's got a good eye, and it doesn't spook him to pull the trigger. He's already a pretty good shot, and he's just going to get better."

"I'm glad to hear that . . . I guess. Now, you'd better go home and get some rest." She thought about the lawsuit Emilio Navarre's attorney had filed. "Things are liable to stay hectic around here for a while."

"You think so?"

"What I think," Alex said, "is that things are going to get worse before they get better."

CHAPTER 9

Dave Rutherford called Alex late that afternoon. "The judge granted bail to Navarre," he told her without any preliminaries.

"Damn it," Alex said with heartfelt anger. "How much?" The best she could hope for was that it would be a large enough amount to keep Navarre in custody.

"Five million dollars."

Alex relaxed a little. "Well, I'd rather there was no bail at all, but I guess—"

"He's out," Rutherford interrupted.

For a second, Alex could only stare. She was sitting in her police car in the parking lot of the First Baptist Church, where she had pulled in to answer her cell phone. When she found her voice again, she said, "He made bail? Five million?"

"He only had to put up ten percent of that. A bonding company put up the rest."

"That's still half a million dollars," Alex protested. "Where does a lowlife like that come up with . . ." Her voice trailed off. She gave a frustrated sigh. "The same place he gets a high-powered lawyer who flies in from San Antonio on a private jet, right?"

"That's right," Rutherford agreed. "Chances are, Navarre works for one of the Mexican cartels."

"The cartel didn't send him up here to burglarize the home of an old couple like the McNamaras."

"No, I imagine he and his friend did that on their own. For kicks, maybe, or just for something to pass the time. But the cartels inspire such fierce loyalty in the men who work for them in two ways: through utter fear, and by standing behind them to the limit when they get in trouble."

Alex's mind worked quickly. "Navarre is still in the hospital here in Home."

"He won't be for long. Cochrum is on his way to get him in a private ambulance."

"We'll see about that," Alex muttered.

"Wait—" Rutherford began, but Alex closed the cell phone and cut him off. The police car was still running. She put it in gear and headed for the hospital. Visions of barricading the hospital doors and not letting Clayton Cochrum in went through her head.

That fantasy didn't last long. She had sworn to uphold the law, not break it. If she was the vigilante type, she never would have become a cop in the first place.

But she could be there to tell Cochrum what she thought of him. There was no law against that.

Alex had no doubt that Emilio Navarre would flee the country and escape justice for his part in Inez McNamara's death. The only remotely good thing about Navarre being granted bail was that it meant the lawsuit Cochrum had filed wouldn't proceed. The judge was sure to throw it out when Navarre didn't show up for the trial.

All the media crews had flocked back to the hospital, Alex saw when she got there. They must have gotten word from the county seat that Navarre had made bail, and they wanted to be here to capture the event when he left the hospital. Alex parked on the side street and went in through the back of the hospital again. As she did so, she wondered if she could persuade Dr. Boone to refuse to release Navarre on medical grounds.

That wouldn't work, she decided. A doctor couldn't actually *force* a patient to stay in the hospital. Navarre would have to sign a release saying that the hospital and its personnel couldn't be sued because of his leaving, but that wouldn't be a problem. The lawyer could probably even sign it for him.

There was just no way to keep him here if he didn't want to stay, Alex thought with a sigh. Like it or not, Navarre was getting out.

Dr. Boone was standing at the nurses' station with several of the nurses. A middle-aged man with the face of a weary basset hound, he said, "There's quite a commotion going on outside, Chief Bonner. Is there anything I should know about?"

"You're going to be losing a patient, Doctor."

"Mr. Navarre?"

"That's right. A judge granted him bail."

Boone nodded. "I'd heard rumors to that effect on the news. There's nothing you can do to stop it?"

"Not a thing. It's legal."

"This man Navarre isn't a U.S. citizen."

Alex shook her head. "Forgive me for being blunt, Doctor, but that doesn't mean a damn thing anymore. With all the changes in the law over the past fifteen years, illegals have just as many rights in this country as anybody else. Maybe more."

"Yes, I know. I never refused to treat anyone who needed help, no matter where they were from, but so much of this other . . . It's not right, Chief, it's just not right."

"Tell me about it," Alex said over her shoulder as she started down the hall toward Room 108. "Just lie low, Doctor. The circus will be over soon." Under her breath, she added, "I hope."

Jerry Houston was young, stocky, and fair, with only a few years of experience as a police officer under his belt. He turned a worried gaze on Alex as she came into the room. Nodding toward the smirking man in the bed, Jerry said, "This guy claims he's gettin' out of here. That's not right, is it, Chief?"

"I'm afraid so, Jerry," Alex said. "Mr. Navarre, I take it you've heard that you were granted bail?"

"My lawyer called," Navarre said with a sneer. "I tol' you you couldn't keep me here."

"Pete McNamara was my Little League coach," Jerry said. "Mrs. McNamara always brought snacks for us. You . . . you can't just let this man go!"

"There's nothing we can do about it."

Jerry put his hand on the butt of his gun and muttered, "There's something *I* can do about it."

Navarre's eyes widened a little in fear. He could see his own death on Jerry's face, just as plainly as Alex could.

"Jerry," she said sharply. "Go out in the hall. Now."

"But, Chief—"

"Do what I told you," Alex snapped. "In fact, go down to the entrance and help Lester. He's liable to need a hand keeping order down there." She paused. "That's an order, Jerry."

He sighed and finally nodded. "All right. But sooner or later, somebody's got to stand up and do what's right, Chief."

"Our only concern is what's legal."

Jerry gave a contemptuous grunt on his way out of the room. Alex felt a flash of anger and thought about calling him back to give him a few choice words about respecting the chief of police, but she let it go.

Right now, she didn't have much respect for the legal system herself, and she was part of it, after all.

Navarre relaxed after Jerry was gone. He grinned at her again and said, "He's a hothead, that one, no?"

"He's just fed up, like the rest of us are when we see—" Alex stopped herself. It wouldn't do any good to argue with Navarre.

He wasn't going to let it go, though. "When you see what?" he demanded. "A dirty Mexican? A spic? You're a racist, lady, like the rest of this Texan trash."

She knew she ought to ignore him, but she couldn't. "You couldn't be more wrong, Navarre," she told him. "I've lived and worked with Hispanics all my life. The mayor, my boss, is named Ruiz, and my best officer is named Delgado. I'd trust him with my life. I don't care what color your skin is. You'd still be a vicious animal if you were black or white or yellow."

"You gonna get what's comin' to you one of these days," Navarre blustered. "All you damn rednecks. Texas will be back where it belongs, as part of Mexico!"

"You tried that a few years ago, remember?" Alex said, referring to the infamous Second Siege of the Alamo. "It didn't work."

Navarre settled back against the pillows propped up behind him and glared at her, but he didn't say anything else.

A short time later, a wave of noise in the hall outside warned Alex of what was coming. As she turned to face the door, it opened and the man she had seen on TV earlier that morning swept into the room. He stopped, took his sunglasses off, and smiled at her.

"Chief Bonner?"

"That's right." Alex didn't return the smile.

"I'm Clayton Cochrum. I represent Mr. Navarre, and I have an order here for his release."

"He's been wounded," Alex said. "He ought to stay here in the hospital."

Cochrum's smile disappeared, to be replaced by a look of grave concern. "I'm well aware that my client has been wounded, Chief. That wanton shooting spree by one of your citizens is the reason I've filed suit on Mr. Navarre's behalf, to try to redress the wrong that's been done him."

Alex opened her mouth to say something, but Cochrum held up a hand.

"As for his medical condition," the lawyer went on, "I have a fully-equipped, state-of-the-art private ambulance waiting outside, along with a crack team of doctors and nurses to provide care for him until we can get him to an adequate private facility. This . . . little country clinic . . . is hardly the sort of place where he needs to be."

"The staff of this little country clinic saved his life," Alex pointed out.

"Which wouldn't have been in danger if you hadn't turned a blind eye to the presence of an armed maniac in your town, Chief."

Alex wasn't sure whom Cochrum was playing to. The news crews were all still outside. Maybe the guy was just in the habit of being a sanctimonious asshole.

"Let's see the paperwork," she snapped.

Cochrum handed over the release documents. They were all in order, no doubt about that. Alex handed the papers back and said, "All right, take him."

Cochrum motioned to the men who had wheeled in a gurney behind him.

Alex stood to the side with her arms crossed as Navarre was unhooked from the IVs and the monitor and transferred to the gurney. A couple of private nurses moved in and reattached him to IVs that they carried. The whole group moved out with the precision of a military unit.

Alex followed them down the hall. They went out through the lobby, into the crowd of reporters and cameramen that had gathered just outside the hospital entrance. Armed rent-a-cops kept the crowd from getting too close. A tumult of shouted questions went up at the sight of Navarre on the gurney.

Cochrum had put his sunglasses back on. He held up his hands for silence and called, "Please, please! We have no statement at this time! Let us through, please!"

It was all for show, which Cochrum proved by turning back to the reporters as soon as Navarre had been loaded into the private ambulance.

"Mr. Navarre will now be transported to a secure private facility where he can receive the proper care. On behalf of my client, I'd like to thank the doctors and staff of Home Community Hospital for their outstanding efforts on his behalf."

One of the reporters managed to say, "Were you worried about your client's safety while he was here?"

"I think that was one of the main factors in deciding to transfer him, yes," Cochrum replied.

"You don't think the local police could protect him?"

"Well, it's a small department, isn't it?" Cochrum asked smoothly. "And to be honest, I'm not certain that my client's safety was at the top of their priority list."

Alex saw some of the cameras swing toward her. She knew the reporters wanted her to react to the lawyer's provocative statement.

She kept her face as stony and expressionless as she could.

When they didn't get what they wanted from her, they turned back to Cochrum. "Do you believe that Navarre is a flight risk?" a woman asked.

"Absolutely not," Cochrum answered without hesitation. "My client *wants* to answer all the absurd charges against him. Even more than that, he wants to be on hand when the lawsuit that I have filed on his behalf comes to trial. You see, ladies and gentlemen, while my client may not be a citizen of this country, he is a great admirer of it and wants to see its system of justice in action. He wants the man who is truly responsible for this tragedy to have to answer for what he has done. To that end, once again I call on the local authorities to arrest Mr. Peter McNamara and charge him with the crimes of which he is guilty . . . *the murder of Jorge Corona and the attempted murder of my client, Emilio Navarre!*"

Once again the cameras turned toward Alex, staring at her with their lenses like the eyes of hungry scavengers. A man called, "What about it, Chief? Are you going to arrest Pete McNamara?"

Alex knew she couldn't get away with a "No comment." She said, "The Home Police Department will take all appropriate action, I assure you."

"Chief Bonner, aren't you friends with Pete McNamara? Is there a conflict of interest here?"

"There's no conflict of interest," Alex said. "My officers and I will follow the law. That's all."

She ignored the other questions they yelled at her and backed toward the glass doors leading into the hospital. Clayton Cochrum stood beside the ambulance, smirking at her.

Less than twenty-four hours ago, Home had been such a nice little town, Alex thought as she retreated into the building. Inez McNamara was still alive, and the streets weren't clogged with vultures masquerading as reporters. She had never even heard of Clayton Cochrum, let alone had to endure his smarmy grin.

Now everything had been turned upside down. A monster was claiming to be the wronged party, the victim of the evil that he himself was responsible for, and he had people lining up to support him. Alex had no doubt that the cable news shows would be full of pundits talking about all those crazy gun nuts down in Texas. If they could get in a few jabs at organized religion, they would do that, too. And all too many of the viewers would sit there, open-mouthed, ready to be spoon-fed that poisonous claptrap.

Maybe someday things would settle down. Maybe someday the world would be right again, and people wouldn't be punished for being hardworking and honest.

But as she stood there watching through the glass doors as the private ambulance drove away with its lights flashing, Alex wasn't sure if that would ever happen. She wasn't sure at all.

BOOK TWO

Chapter 10

Two months later

"Who's this guy supposed to be, anyway?" Brad Parker asked as he sat at the umbrella-shaded table and watched the bikini-clad lovelies strutting their stuff around the pool.

"Hell if I know," Lawrence Ford replied. Like Parker, he wore sunglasses, a Hawaiian shirt, and lightweight trousers. Also like Parker, the long tails of the shirt Ford wore served to conceal the butt of the flat, deadly little automatic that was holstered at the small of his back.

A mandatory accessory for the well-dressed tourist in Corpus Christi, Texas, Ford had called the weapon earlier.

The warm waters of the Gulf of Mexico rolled up on a beautiful white sand beach on the other side of a strip of lush green lawn dotted with palm trees. Despite the nearness of the Gulf, the pool here at the hotel was doing a brisk business. It didn't have any sand or fish in it, and besides, a lot of the beautiful young people gathered around the pool were more interested in being seen and in hooking up with somebody than they were in actually swimming.

"My God, we're a couple of dirty old men," Ford said as two lovely twenty-year-olds in tiny bikinis strolled past their table.

"Speak for yourself, Fargo," Parker said. "I'm still young."

"You just keep on deluding yourself that way." Ford took a sip of his drink. It had a tiny umbrella in it, which he tried to ignore. It was embarrassing for a grown man to drink a drink that had an umbrella in it, he thought. But he and Parker were supposed to look like typical tourists, which meant they were beyond embarrassment.

Both men were in their forties. The tall, burly Ford was from Fargo, North Dakota, hence the nickname, and despite being raised in such a cold climate, since going to work for the Company he had most often found himself on assignment in hot places: Pakistan, Iraq, Saudi Arabia, Central America, now Texas. . . . He had thought more than once that his bosses were engaged in some bizarre conspiracy to make him sweat.

Parker, on the other hand, had been born and raised in Southern California and had the blond good looks to prove it. His face had a rough-hewn quality that kept him from being too pretty, though. A few years earlier, he had been hurt badly during a mission in Afghanistan, and even though he had fully recovered and gone back on active duty, the carefree look he'd had in his eyes as a young man was gone forever.

Nobody who knew the truth of what really went

on in the world could be carefree. And nobody knew that truth better than these shadow warriors.

"So what are we supposed to do here?" Parker pressed.

"Find the guy, grab the guy, hold on to him until somebody picks him up," Ford replied with a shrug of his brawny shoulders. He had a little paunch he struggled with, but like the shorter, more slender Parker he was a very dangerous man in a fight.

"Then he must be somebody important."

"Importance is in the eye of he who pays the bills."

"Don't you ever get tired of putting on that cynical act?"

"Who says it's an act?" Ford smiled lazily. "Don't look now, but there's our pigeon."

Parker didn't react other than to ask, "Where?"

Smiling and nodding, Ford said, "Sixth floor balcony." He counted the balconies from the corner of the building and matched it up with the floor plan he had studied. "Room 627."

"Very good." Parker finished his drink. "What's he doing up there?"

Ford threw his head back and laughed as if his fellow agent had said something funny. That gave him a chance to look directly at the man who had ventured nervously out onto the balcony. The target was small, almost boyish looking with a mop of blond hair.

"Just looking around, as far as I can tell. Watching these nubile young lovelies parade around the pool."

Parker ran a thumbnail along his jawline as he frowned. "So they knew he was in Corpus Christi and even knew what hotel he was staying at, but they couldn't find out his room number?"

"They wanted to leave *something* for us to do," Ford drawled. "You know, so we'll feel like we're earning our wages."

"I feel like it every time the weather turns cold and those busted ribs of mine start aching." Parker shook his head. "Something's not right here, Fargo."

"Something's always not right in this business. If everything was right, they wouldn't need us, now would they?"

"I suppose not." Parker stood up. "There's no point in wasting time. We might as well get started on this babysitting job."

Ford finished his drink and got to his feet as well. "Farewell, ladies," he said to the girls around the pool, quietly enough so that none of them heard him.

The two men strolled into the hotel, went to the bank of elevators, and Parker pushed the button. A family with several kids in tow came up behind them. As the bell rang to signal that the elevator was there, Ford glanced over his shoulder and stepped aside, motioning for the family to go ahead.

"We'll get the next one," he said.

"What did you do that for?" Parker asked when the door had slid closed.

"I didn't like the looks of that little boy. He looked like a farter to me. We didn't want to be trapped in there with him for six floors."

"You're always looking out for our safety, aren't you, Fargo?"

"Of course. It's my job."

As a matter of fact, Ford had saved Parker's life

a couple of times in Pakistan. Neither of them was going to mention that, though. Like Ford said, it was just part of the job.

They took the next elevator and got out at the sixth floor. Signs on the wall told them that Rooms 620 to 640 were to their right. They turned in that direction. The fourth door on the right would be 627.

They had almost reached it when they heard the crash and the cry of pain from inside the room.

CHAPTER 11

Ford's right hand went behind his back and plucked the gun from its concealed holster. At the same time, his left grasped the door handle and tried to twist it.

Locked. The handle didn't budge.

The door had one of those card key locks. Parker had his gun out by now, too, and as he leveled it at the lock, he said, "Step back."

"That won't work," Ford said as another yelp came from inside the room, followed by what sounded like a chair being overturned. "You'll just wind up with a smashed lock and a door that still won't open."

Parker glanced at him. "How do you know that?"

"Those guys on TV proved it. You know, the goofy one and the one with the beret."

"Then what do we do?"

Somebody inside the room screamed, "Help!"

Ford glanced both ways along the corridor. "You take 625, I'll take 629. See if anybody will open up."

They went opposite directions along the hall.

Ford pounded on the door of 629 while Parker did the same on 625. "Police!" Ford yelled. "Emergency!"

The first part was a lie. The second part certainly wasn't.

Nobody answered his knock, but Parker shouted, "Fargo! Down here!"

Moving fast for such a big man, Ford reached the open door of 625 in a couple of leaps. Parker was already in the room, heading for the sliding glass door that opened onto the balcony. Ford followed him, rushing past a fat, middle-aged man who looked terrified to have a couple of armed strangers running through his room.

Parker threw the glass door aside and lunged out onto the balcony. Ford was right behind him.

"You know this is crazy, don't you?" Parker flung over his shoulder.

"Fastest way in there," Ford replied.

As a matter of fact, adrenaline was thundering through his veins and he felt great. For a lot of his career with the Company, he had been a handler, not a field agent. That aspect of the job had its rewards, but it was nothing like being on the ground and feeling like you were actually accomplishing something.

The gap between balconies was about eight feet, plenty wide enough to discourage anybody who might be crazy enough to try to jump from one to another.

Parker barely slowed down, though, as he rested his free hand on the railing, vaulted up, slapped a foot down onto the top of the rail, and pushed off.

With six stories worth of empty air beneath him, he sailed across the gap, clearing the railing on the other balcony by perhaps a foot. He went down to hands and knees when he landed but managed to hang on to the gun.

Ford was right behind him, and as the bigger agent made the leap, reason overwhelmed adrenaline and reminded him of what a big, bloody mess he would make down there by the pool if he failed to reach the other balcony.

It would ruin the rest of the afternoon for the beautiful people around the pool, that was for sure.

Ford didn't completely clear the railing, but he got a foot on it and leaned forward desperately, letting his weight and momentum carry him onto the balcony of 627, where he landed in an awkward heap and rolled across the cement floor, scraping and bruising himself in the process.

He came up on a knee in time to see Parker charging into the room where a struggle was going on. The little blond guy who was their target appeared to be trying to fight off a couple of ugly bruisers who had hired killer written all over them. They must not have been all that good at their job, though, or else the kid would already be dead by now.

Instead, the target had backed into a corner between the bed and the wall and was flailing away at one of the intruders with what was left of a broken chair. He wasn't big enough to have broken it himself, so he must have grabbed it during the fight.

"Get away from him!" Parker yelled as he leveled his gun at the two attackers. The one closest to him wheeled around suddenly and launched a spinning high kick that caught Parker on the wrist and knocked the weapon out of his hand.

Parker didn't let that stop him. He stepped forward swiftly while the guy was still off-balance and grabbed his leg, wrapping his right arm around it. He used his left fist to hammer a blow into the side of the man's head and then heaved on the leg. The man wound up on his butt.

Meanwhile, Ford had made it into the room, too. He pointed his gun at the second would-be assassin as that man grabbed the broken chair leg away from the kid and tried to jab the jagged end of it into his throat. The young man twisted away just in time to avoid the thrust.

Ford wasn't going to give the guy a second chance. He fired across the bed, putting a round through the man's forearm.

The man howled in pain and dropped the chair leg. He whirled toward Ford, leaped onto the bed, and bounced off it like it was a trampoline, using it to send him into the air in a diving tackle. Ford pulled the trigger again but didn't know if the shot hit the man. It certainly didn't slow him down if it did. He crashed into Ford with the impact of a freight train.

Ford went over backwards and the man landed on top of him, driving the air out of his lungs. Gasping for breath, Ford slapped around on the floor for the gun he had just dropped but failed to locate it. He grabbed the phone, though, which had been knocked off the table where it usually sat, and smashed it on the man's head in an explosion of plastic and electronics.

That stunned the man enough for Ford to throw him off. Ford rolled onto his side and dragged air into his lungs. He spotted his gun lying on the carpet and scooped it up just as the man he'd been fighting with pulled a big, ugly revolver from somewhere. Maybe the two men had been trying to eliminate the target quietly at first, with a minimum of fuss, but that ship was *way* out of the harbor by now.

The hell with this, Fargo thought. He emptied the pistol into the man's chest before the guy could pull the trigger.

A bullet hitting a man's body usually wouldn't knock him down unless it was an extremely heavy caliber. That was something else those guys on TV had proven.

But seven bullets, even of a smaller caliber, pounding into a guy's chest in the space of three seconds would certainly make him stagger backwards, and that's what happened now. With blood welling from the bullet holes, the man went back three steps through the open sliding glass door and then three more steps across the balcony. The backs of his thighs hit the railing, and inertia did the rest.

The guy flipped right over it and plummeted toward the ground, screaming as he fell.

Ford had time to mutter, "Look out below," before a loud thud silenced the scream.

He rolled over and reached in his pocket for a fresh magazine as he dumped the empty. On the other side of the room, Parker and the other killer were trading martial arts blows, their arms and legs moving almost too fast for Ford's eyes to follow them.

The blond kid who was the object of all this attention was making a beeline for the door into the corridor, taking off for the tall and uncut.

Ford couldn't really blame him for that, but he couldn't afford to let the target get away, either. He scrambled to his feet and went after the kid, ramming home the fresh magazine as he did so.

A shot blasted in the hall.

By now there was a lot of yelling, cursing, and screaming going on all up and down the corridor, as the hotel guests thought—and rightfully so—that somebody was on a shooting rampage. As Ford stepped out into the hall, he saw the kid stumbling around and clutching a bloody arm. Another shot rang out, chipping wood and plaster from the wall near Ford. He saw the shooter, down in the alcove where the elevators were located, and returned the fire, forcing the man to duck back.

Ford grabbed the target's arm and slung him back into 627. "Stay there!" he bellowed.

Then Ford went to a knee and traded fast shots with the gunman at the elevators.

The kid scampered out of the room behind him and started running the other way along the hall, pushing past people who came out of their rooms to see what was going on. Ford glanced back and saw him fleeing, but there was nothing he could do except bite back a curse. He had his hands full with this firefight.

Inside the room, Parker yelled, "Stop!"

Ford looked back again, saw that his partner had managed to retrieve his gun. The other assassin didn't want any part of it now that the target was gone. He turned and ran toward the balcony. Parker fired a warning shot, but the guy never slowed down.

He bounded across the balcony, leaped onto the railing, and dived off.

Committing suicide because he had failed in his mission? Ford didn't think so. Parker confirmed that when he ran onto the balcony, looked down, and said, "Son of a bitch! Right into the pool!"

It took either a lunatic or somebody who was damned good to dive six stories into a hotel swimming pool and survive. This man must have fallen into one of those categories, although at this point, Ford didn't know if he had actually survived.

The shooting in the hall stopped. Ford heard a door slam open and then closed. There was a stairwell beside the elevators. From the sound of it, the third man was fleeing, too.

Ford was leery of a trap, but he came to his feet and advanced toward the elevator alcove, staying close to the wall and holding his gun ready. He went around the corner in a hurry and tracked the weapon from side to side.

Nobody. The guy was gone, all right. Ford went to the stairwell door, jerked it open, and listened. He could hear hurrying footsteps echoing up from below.

For a second he thought about grabbing one of the elevators and trying to beat the guy to the ground, but he discarded the idea. There was no guarantee the man would go all the way to the first floor. He could leave the stairwell at any of the other floors and blend into the confused crowd that was growing larger all the time as word of the shooting on six spread through the hotel.

"Fargo, you all right?" Parker asked as he trotted down the hall.

"Yeah, you?"

Parker jerked his head in a nod. "The target?"

"In the wind." The words tasted bitter in Ford's mouth.

Parker grimaced and said, "I saw a laptop in there."

"Grab it and let's go."

Parker nodded again, disappeared into 627, and came out with a laptop computer tucked under his arm. "How are we going to get out of here with all this uproar going on?"

"Did that other guy dive into the pool?"

"He did. He climbed out and got away, too." Parker stared at Ford and shook his head. "Fargo, you're not thinking about—"

"Do I look insane to you? There's a walkway from the eighth floor to the top level of the parking garage. Come on."

CHAPTER 12

With the skill of experienced agents, the two men made it out of the hotel, retrieving their SUV from the parking garage, and driving away just before the police arrived in response to the dozens of 911 calls about a shooting and a man falling from a sixth-floor balcony.

Parker was at the wheel. He drove over the towering Nueces Bay bridge and then over Indian Point Bridge into neighboring Portland. He pulled into a nondescript chain motel where he and Ford had rented a room the day before.

Once they were in the room, Ford set the small laptop on the table and opened it. It was already on and in sleep mode. Ford woke it and pointed at the pornographic desktop that appeared.

"What a sleaze."

"Never mind that," Parker said as he leaned over the chair where Ford sat. "How much power is left?"

"Lemme see . . . fifty-four percent."

"Hang on, I think I've got an AC power cord that'll fit it."

Parker fetched the cord from one of his bags and plugged the computer into a wall outlet.

"Now we won't run out of juice," Ford said as he started to work. His big, blunt fingers weren't particularly well-suited for the small keyboard, so he was careful not to push anything he didn't mean to.

He started exploring the files, taking a quick glance through the directory, then opening the e-mail client. The in-box was almost empty.

"Nothing here but spam," Ford muttered. "He must save all his important e-mail on a flash drive and then delete it from the computer."

"It might still be recoverable," Parker said.

"Yeah, but not by me. We ought to send it back to Langley."

"Poke around in there some more first."

"That goes without saying."

Ford went back to exploring the various files. After a few minutes, he muttered, "Looks like this guy didn't use the computer for anything except downloading music and porn and games."

"What's in that folder?" Parker asked. "The one named CDD?"

"Let's see." Ford clicked on it, only to have a dialogue box pop up. "Password protected. You got any idea what his password might be?"

"I don't even know who *he* is," Parker said. He shook his head in disgust. "I'm sure the tech guys can crack it, but I was hoping we could get some clue to what's going on."

"Yeah, me—" Ford began, then stopped short as the lights in the motel room and the screen on the computer suddenly lit up brighter than usual, then abruptly went dark. The overhead lights came back on after a second. The laptop's screen flickered a couple of times, but otherwise remained dark. "Damn!"

"What happened?"

"Power surge." Ford pulled the AC cord loose and flipped the laptop over. His finger pushed the battery release, popping it loose. He held the battery in his hand as seconds dragged by. "Sometimes this works."

The two men waited grimly for about a minute. Then Ford reinserted the battery, hooked up the power cord, and tried to turn the computer on. The lights indicating that it had power going to it came on, but that was all.

"Damn it," Ford said again. "I'd be willing to bet that it's totally fried in there."

"Maybe the data retrieval guys can take it in the clean room and reconstruct what was on the hard drive."

"Maybe, but it'll take a while, and meantime we're still in the dark, with no clue where to start looking for our target."

"Yeah . . ."

Parker wheeled around and ran to the door, throwing it open and hurrying out into the motel parking lot. Ford ran after him. He didn't know what had occurred to his partner, but he trusted Parker's instincts.

Parker looked at the power lines leading into the hotel, then followed them with his eyes down the street to a pole with a transformer on it.

"Look," he said.

An electric company truck was parked beside the pole. The lift on the back of the truck had just descended, and a man in coveralls was climbing out of it.

"Come on," Parker said. He took off at a run toward the truck, reaching to the small of his back for his gun as he did so.

The coverall-clad man saw him coming, reached into one of the garment's baggy pockets, and brought out a gun of his own. Parker darted to the side as the weapon blasted.

He sent a return shot toward the man at the truck, then had to duck behind a parked pickup as the man fired shot after shot while backing toward the truck's cab. He yanked the door open, dived in, and the truck lurched into motion. Another man must have been inside at the wheel, keeping the engine running.

The agents' SUV screeched to a stop beside Parker. "Hop in!" Ford called. He had gone back to get the vehicle rather than following Ford, a hunch telling him that they might have to give chase.

Ford floored the accelerator even before Parker had closed the door on the passenger side. Momentum swung it shut.

"How'd you know?" Ford asked as he took a corner at high speed. The power company truck was a block ahead. It wasn't built for speed. The SUV, with its high-powered and specially-modified engine, was.

"I figured somebody might have seen us leaving the hotel with that laptop. Did you bring it with you, by the way?"

"Yeah, I ducked back in the room and got it. Might still be something salvageable on it."

Parker nodded. "That's what I was thinking.

Anyway, if they saw us with the laptop, they'd have to figure we'd try to find out what's on it. They followed us out of Corpus to the motel."

"They didn't have any way of knowing that we plugged it into the wall."

"No, not for sure, but it's a reasonable assumption."

Ford frowned. "They can put their hands on an electric company truck and cause a power surge to the motel just on the assumption that we might have the computer plugged in?"

"They didn't have anything to lose if they were wrong," Parker pointed out.

"Maybe not, but being able to mount an operation like that on almost zero notice means they've got a lot of pull, whoever they are. That sounds almost like something—"

Ford stopped short as he realized where his thoughts were going.

"Yeah," Parker agreed, his face and voice grim. "It sounds almost like something we could do if we had to."

Ford still had the SUV moving at a high rate of speed, weaving in and out of traffic, blasting through red lights, cutting into their quarry's lead. The power company truck caromed off several parked vehicles as it took a couple of turns too fast. Then it roared onto the freeway frontage road, past a couple of strip shopping centers, and onto the freeway itself.

"He's heading back to Corpus," Ford said as he followed the truck onto Indian Point Bridge, which stretched for more than a mile over the waters of

Nueces Bay. "That's his mistake. He's got nowhere to go while he's on the bridge."

With a screeching of tires and brakes, cars pulled over to get out of the way of the speeding truck and the pursuing SUV. Ford began to pull even with the truck, coming up on the driver's side so the passenger couldn't shoot at them.

The truck swerved toward the SUV, banging into an armored fender. Despite the SUV's built-in protection, the truck had more weight behind it. The collision forced the SUV toward the railing.

Ford fought the wheel and brought the SUV under control again. He dropped back a little and said, "I'm gonna go around them and block the road. Keep the driver busy."

"Will do," Parker said as he lifted his gun.

Ford floored the gas pedal again and sent the SUV surging forward through the gap between the truck and the railing. Parker opened fire from his window, peppering the cab with bullets. He saw the driver hunched low in an attempt to avoid the gunfire.

The SUV roared past the truck, rocketing over the bridge now. Ahead, off to the left, loomed the World War II–era aircraft carrier, USS *Lexington,* now moored permanently at Corpus Christi as a floating museum.

Parker reloaded as Ford opened up a lead on the truck. When he was still a hundred yards or so from the end of the bridge, he slammed on the brakes and spun the wheel, sending the SUV into a sideways skid that brought it to a stop, blocking all three lanes of traffic.

The two agents piled out of the vehicle and crouched behind it, guns leveled across the hood at the truck barreling down on them. They opened fire, concentrating their shots on the truck's front tires, both of which blew with loud explosions. The truck slewed crazily back and forth on the bridge.

"Holy crap!" Ford exclaimed. "He's not stopping!"

There was no time to move the SUV out of the way. All Ford and Parker could do was turn and run as the electric company truck continued toward the SUV, sparks shooting into the air now from the rims of the front wheels as they grated across the concrete.

The crash was spectacular. Both gas tanks exploded, sending a huge fireball into the air and making clouds of oily black smoke roll over the bay. The force was enough to shake the entire bridge and knock Ford and Parker off their feet.

As they picked themselves up, Ford said, "The laptop was still in there."

"I know," Parker said. "Nobody will get anything off of it now."

"So they did what they set out to do. They just had to blow themselves up to do it." Ford turned his head to look at the *Lexington* nearby, with its towering superstructure that had once been the target of Japanese pilots determined to crash their planes into it. "Like kamikazes . . ."

In the underground bunker, a man sat in front of a computer, watching the flow of information from around the world. He leaned forward a little in his chair as a report about all the chaos in Corpus Christi, Texas, came in. He picked up a secure phone that rang in an office upstairs.

A man answered. The watcher told him what had happened, and then the man on the other end of the phone asked, "What about Trussell?"

"No word, sir. I assume he's still out there somewhere."

"Damn it. All they had to do was kill him and recover that laptop, then let those bunglers from the Agency take the blame."

"Yes, sir. But according to eyewitness reports, Parker and Ford didn't have the laptop with them when they fled the scene of the crash on the bridge. It must have been in their vehicle. Our people have impounded the wreckage and are searching it now to confirm that. But I think you can tell the boss that part of it has been taken care of, at least."

"I'll decide what to tell the boss," the man on the other end said coldly.

"Yes, sir, of course." The watcher took the chastisement

in stride. Everything they did here was for the common good.

"Monitor the situation closely and keep me informed of any further developments. Any time, night or day, you understand."

"Yes, sir."

The watcher heard a sigh from the other end. "They may have destroyed the laptop, but Trussell knows everything that was on it. We have to find him, too, and shut him up for good."

"Yes, sir," the watcher said, but the connection was already broken. The other man had been talking to himself there at the end.

Upstairs, he left his office and went up another flight of steps to the second floor, to the residence. He went to a sitting room, where he knew he would find the man he was looking for.

He was there, all right, and he looked up and asked, "What is it, Geoff?"

"A report from Texas, sir. It appears that the laptop computer stolen by Earl Trussell has been destroyed."

"What about Trussell himself?"

"I'm . . . sorry, sir. We had an operation set up to take care of Trussell in a manner that would provide culpability for Langley and deniability for us, but it was unsuccessful."

"Failure is unacceptable." The voice was cold and hard. "I want that little weasel Trussell dead. I've got too much else on my plate right now to have to worry about him."

"Yes, sir, of course, but you really shouldn't, uh, put such sentiments into words."

He laughed. "Are you saying this place might be bugged, Geoff? This *place?"*

"Well, that's not likely, of course, but it never hurts to be careful."

"Don't tell me about careful. I've been careful all my life. That's how I got where I am today."

"Yes, sir."

"Take care of this Trussell problem. The world doesn't need to know about Casa del Diablo."

"No, sir."

"I trust you'll take care of it." The President of the United States looked in a mirror and straightened his tie. "Now, I've got that state dinner to go to."

"Yes, sir."

The President shook his head. "Why does everything seem to happen in Texas? Maybe we should just let the redneck bastards secede if they want to. Good riddance." He smiled brilliantly, knowing that the media would fawn over him as usual. "How do I look?"

Chapter 13

"Well, that's it," Fargo Ford said as he closed the encrypted cell phone. "Mission over."

Brad Parker stopped pacing the motel room floor and frowned at his partner. "They're not even going to let us look for the guy."

Ford shook his head. "Nope. We're done. Stick a fork in us."

"No thanks."

"We don't have any choice in the matter," Ford pointed out. "We've been ordered back to Langley for debriefing. We're supposed to catch a plane out of here tonight for DFW, then switch planes there and proceed straight on to Washington."

"When does the plane from Corpus Christi leave?"

"Eight o'clock."

"That gives us several hours," Parker said.

"Several hours to do what?"

"Go back to that hotel and see if we can pick up the trail of our target."

Ford shook his head, and yet he knew exactly how Parker was feeling. It was incredibly frustrating to go through everything they had, to survive the dangers that had faced them, and yet in the end everything they'd done had to be considered a failure. They didn't have the target or the laptop that must have contained vital intel.

"After all that trouble at the hotel, if we go over there don't you think they might be looking for us?"

"Really? Who got a good look at us?" Parker asked. "The target, and the two guys who were trying to kill him."

"You're forgetting about the security cameras," Ford said. "By now the cops are bound to have studied that footage. They probably have our faces out there. Hell, we may even be on the news, for all I know."

"If that's true, don't you think they'll be watching for us at the airport?"

Ford's frown deepened. "You're right. And yet the orders were to catch that flight this evening."

"Something's not right here, Fargo. These people we're up against . . . they know too much. They get things done too quickly."

"Like we're fighting our own people," Ford mused.

"You said it, not me. But I can't help but wonder."

The two men looked at each other for a long moment, both of them obviously deep in thought. For years they had served their nation, putting their lives in jeopardy again and again with little thought for their own safety, traveling the wild places and the back alleys of the globe in search of America's enemies. Neither man was the sort to make speeches or wave the flag. They were pragmatists who believed they were doing a job worth doing well.

But in recent years, they had seen unwelcome changes creeping over the country. They had watched as the intelligence community became more and more political, and those politics increasingly leaned to the left. They had seen operations fail because the higher-ups had tied the hands of the men in the field. They had seen important information ignored because it conflicted with some bizarre notion of political correctness, sometimes with tragic results. They had seen power concentrated more and more in an elitist minority centered in Washington, with branches in the national news media in New York and in the entertainment capital of Hollywood. To those people, the honest opinions of the vast majority of Americans just didn't count anymore.

As much as Ford hated to admit it, he didn't really know who he was working for anymore . . . or if he could trust them.

"You're talking about going off the reservation," he said now to Parker. "I don't know if I'm ready to do that."

"I'm talking about getting to the bottom of this and finding out the truth. If we're being set up, I want to know about it."

Ever since Parker had been hurt on that mission several years earlier, he had been more reckless, more of a loose cannon. It was like he knew he was living on borrowed time anyway and didn't care about his own safety anymore.

But that didn't mean he was wrong about what was going on here. Something didn't smell right to Ford, too.

"All right," Ford said after a moment. "I suppose it wouldn't hurt to have a look around the hotel and see if we can find out anything. We're gonna have to be careful how we do it, though."

"Whatever you say," Parker replied with a nod.

Ford got to his feet. "I saw a discount store down the road. . . ."

The two men who got out of the pickup in the hotel parking lot an hour later didn't look much like the Hawaiian-shirt-wearing tourists who had been there earlier in the day. Now they wore boots, jeans, shirts with silver snaps instead of buttons, and Stetson hats. The pickup was a plain F-150 with nothing to distinguish it. They had stolen it from the outer reaches of the parking lot at the discount store, the location indicating that it probably belonged to one of the employees there and might not be missed for a while. They had altered the numbers on the license plate with electrical tape, anyway. That wouldn't stand up to close observation . . . but most people didn't pay much attention to anything except their own lives.

The hotel had a small parking lot in front for people who were coming and going, but guests were supposed to park in the attached garage. The first floor of the garage was valet parking. Ford walked in there while Parker stepped into the lobby to talk to the concierge.

In a perfect Texas drawl, Ford asked the Hispanic parking attendant, "I'm lookin' for a friend of mine, little fella about 'yay tall." He held out a hand to indicate a man in the range of five feet, four inches. "Kinda long blond hair, little mustache. Y'all happen to have seen him?"

The attendant shook his head. "No, sir, I don't think so. Have we been parking his car? I wouldn't have seen him if we haven't."

"Well, he usually uses valet parkin' when it's available, so I thought there was a chance."

"Are you sure he's registered here?"

Ford rubbed his jaw and grimaced. "I *thought* this was the place he said, but could be I'm wrong about that."

The attendant pointed to a side door leading into the hotel. "Why don't you go inside and ask at the desk? I'm sure they can help you."

"Thanks. I'll do that." Ford nodded and headed for the door. He paused and looked back. "Say, I heard there was some sort of big trouble here earlier today."

The attendant rolled his eyes and shook his head. "I never saw so many cops and ambulances in all my life. Somebody fell from a sixth-floor balcony and splattered himself all over the concrete next to the pool."

Ford winced. "Man. That's a bad way to go."

"Yeah, well, this guy was dead when he hit, they say. He'd been shot."

"That's terrible. I didn't know things like that happened in a place like this."

"They never have before now." The attendant shook his head again. "I'm thinkin' about quittin'. But I need the job, so I probably won't."

"I hear you, brother," Ford said. "I don't like my job, either, but everybody's got to do somethin', right?"

He grinned, waved, and went on into the hotel, through the side door into a corridor that led past several meeting rooms to the lobby.

Parker was coming down that same corridor toward Ford, evidently looking for him. Parker wasn't moving fast, but Ford saw the glitter of excitement in his eyes.

"You got something?" Ford asked in a low voice as they met.

"The concierge thought she remembered a guy matching the target's description getting into a cab earlier this afternoon, right around the same time all the trouble happened upstairs."

"That must've been him," Ford breathed. "The concierge didn't remember the number of the cab, did she?"

"No," Parker said, and Ford wasn't particularly disappointed. That would have been too much luck to hope for. "But there are only two cab companies in town."

"Then that's our next stop," Ford said.

And now that they had the scent, he wasn't even thinking anymore about how they weren't exactly following orders.

Chapter 14

It took a while and several bribes, but eventually Ford and Parker had the address where a cab driver named Mamoud Hajabanian had dropped off a fare he'd picked up at the hotel at approximately the right time that afternoon. Mamoud didn't remember what the guy had looked like, though. All Americans were the same anyway, according to him.

Mamoud had driven over the bay bridge and delivered the fare to a motel in a strip of low-rent motels, sleazy dive bars, and tourist trap restaurants practically in the shadow of the *Lexington.* The motel had cabins painted pink, each with a plastic flamingo stuck in the ground just outside the door. Swamp coolers chugged in the windows. The place looked like it had been built in 1947 and hadn't been remodeled or updated since, although the coat of pink paint appeared to be relatively fresh.

The office was an eight-by-eight cubicle with a sand-gritty linoleum floor and a counter topped by a sheet of bulletproof glass that had an opening at the bottom where credit cards or cash could be slid through. Ford would have been willing to bet that most of the place's business was done in cash.

On the other side of the glass was an old black man with a stringy neck. He wore a polo shirt and was texting somebody on a cell phone. Without looking up from what he was doing, he said to the agents, "No vacancies. I don't care what the sign outside says. The NO part is burned out."

The old man's voice was muffled by the glass. Ford raised his own voice and said, "We're meeting a friend here."

"No, you're not," the old man said.

"I beg your pardon?"

"This ain't that kind of place. We got a respectable trade. If you're lookin' for dope or hookers, go somewheres else."

"Dope and hookers are the last things we're looking for," Ford said. "Really, we're just looking for our friend." He slid a fifty through the opening in the glass. A few years earlier, it would have been a twenty, but the cost of everything just kept going up.

The old man didn't take the bill, but at least he set the phone aside. "What's this friend of yours look like?"

He didn't ask for a name. Names in a place like this would most likely be phonies anyway.

Ford held out his hand. "About this tall, blond hair, mustache. He's not very old. Not much more than a kid."

The old man's eyes narrowed suspiciously. "What do you want with him? I don't need no trouble here. Last time I had to call the cops, they told me they didn't want to have to keep on comin' out here."

"No trouble at all," Ford assured him. "We're just supposed to meet him, take him around and show him some of the night life. He's from out of town, you know."

"The cousin of a friend of ours," Parker added over Ford's shoulder.

"Uh-huh," the old man said. Clearly, he didn't believe a word they had told him, but he couldn't keep his eyes off that fifty now. His gnarled hand suddenly made it disappear with surprising dexterity. "Cabin Twelve," he said. "But you best not be lyin' to me about that trouble."

"Don't worry," Ford said. "You won't even know we're down there."

As they left the tiny office, Parker said, "What are the odds he was telling us the truth?"

"Pretty good, I think. He was practically drooling over that fifty."

"And the odds that he's already calling the guy in Cabin Twelve to warn him we're coming?"

Ford saw the door of the cabin in question jerk open. "Even better."

They started to run as the young man they had seen at the hotel across the bay that afternoon darted outside. He spotted them, stopped short, and stood there for a second with his head twitching back and forth as he looked for a way to escape.

While he was doing that, a car careened into the motel parking lot with a screech of tires and headed straight for the seemingly immobilized young man.

"Damn it!" Ford said. He knew that he and Parker had unintentionally led the killers right to their quarry.

Parker put on an extra burst of speed while Ford reached under the cowboy shirt and pulled out his gun. He started firing at the driver's window of the speeding car, but the way the glass merely starred a little under the slugs' impact told him it was bulletproof. The car never slowed down.

Parker left his feet in a dive that sent him crashing into the blond man. His momentum carried both of them out of the car's path as it missed them by inches. A second later, with an explosion of glass and pink stucco, the car slammed into the front of the cabin.

Both front doors popped open. The two men in the car had to struggle a little to get out past the air bags that had deployed because of the collision. That slowed them down just enough to give Ford a chance to aim.

He figured they were both wearing bulletproof vests, so he drew a bead on the driver's head and squeezed off two swift shots. The gun in the man's hand went off, firing wildly as Ford's bullets drilled through his brain and flung him back over the vehicle's crumpled hood.

The wrecked car gave the passenger some cover. He was on the same side as Parker and the target. Ford couldn't get a shot from where he was, and as he sprinted toward the back of the car, he didn't know if he could get around there in time to save his partner. The killer wouldn't get away, he vowed, but obviously the men who were after the blond kid were willing to give up their own lives to get rid of him.

Parker wasn't defenseless, though. He rolled, braced himself on his hands, and swept both legs against the side of the would-be assassin's left leg. That knocked the man's feet out from under him.

He sat down hard beside the car. His gun went off as he fell, but it was pointed into the air, not at Parker or the blond man.

Ford pounded around the back of the wrecked car. He fired again, a double tap that turned the second killer's face into an ugly crimson smear.

Parker scrambled to his feet. He had hold of the blond man's arm and dragged him upright, too.

"Let me go, let me go!" the man babbled. "I won't tell, I swear! I swear!"

Ford and Parker ignored his plea. Ford grabbed the blond man's other arm. He was small enough and the two agents were big enough so that when they took off running, his feet lifted from the ground and he dangled between them like a child.

"Oh, my God, oh, my God, oh, my God!" he screamed.

People in the other motel cabins pushed curtains aside and looked out the windows to see what all the commotion was about, but they didn't emerge from the cabins.

The elderly clerk tottered out of the office, though, holding a sawed-off shotgun. "I told you I didn't want no trouble!" he yelled at Ford and Parker as they fled past him with their prisoner. He swung the sawed-off after them but pulled the triggers too soon. The weapon went off with a thunderous roar and pelted some parked cars with its double load of buckshot.

The recoil was powerful enough to throw the feeble old man backward, through the open door into the tiny office.

The agents reached the pickup. Parker jerked

the driver's door open and practically threw the blond man into the cab. He went in next, sliding behind the wheel. Ford's long legs carried him around the F-150 as the prisoner tried to open the passenger door and escape. Ford was right there to stop him, shoving him back against Parker. Ford jumped in and slammed the door. The kid was pinned between them now.

Ford had been driving before. He'd left the keys in the ignition, so all Parker had to do was twist the switch, throw the pickup into gear when the engine started, and tromp the gas. A shower of gravel spurted from under the wheels as the pickup took off. It skidded out of the parking lot onto the street. The freeway was a couple of blocks away. Parker headed for it, knowing they had to put some distance between themselves and this latest scene of violence.

Then they would have to steal another vehicle. This one would be too hot, too fast.

The prisoner was blubbering by now as he huddled between the two big men. "Don't kill me, please don't kill me," he said in a voice choked by terror. "I won't tell anybody what I know. I'll never say anything about Casa del Diablo!"

Ford and Parker exchanged a glance over the prisoner's head as the pickup rocketed along the surface streets, squealing around corners and jumping red lights. The same thought went through their heads. *Casa del Diablo . . . CDD.* It seemed like a safe bet that whatever was in that protected file on the laptop had something to do with a place called in Spanish, "House of the Devil."

"You'll tell somebody, all right, my little friend," Ford said as he laid the barrel of his gun against the prisoner's cheek and made the man quiver and cry even more. It was a shame to scare him that way, but it had to be done. "You're going to tell us everything you know."

CHAPTER 15

In the two months since Jorge Corona and Emilio Navarre had invaded the McNamara home, things had indeed settled down. Nobody in Home had forgotten about the tragedy, but summer was winding down, school was about to start again, and people had to carry on with their lives. The high school football team was already practicing, and so was the marching band. Some families got in last-minute vacations.

For Chief Alex Bonner and the rest of her small police force, the remainder of the summer had been quiet. A few wrecks out on the state highway, some vandalism by bored teenagers, the occasional drunk and disorderly or domestic violence call.

No murders, and no burglars gunned down by homeowners. Alex knew now to appreciate that tranquility.

The interest of the news media had flared up once again in mid-summer, when the district attorney announced that he was dropping the attempted murder charges against Navarre. The man would be prosecuted for trespassing and for possessing a weapon illegally, as well as violating immigration laws, but that was all.

The announcement prompted outrage in Home, and a few people even took to the streets to protest. Alex could have told them it wouldn't do any good. The camera crews would just take pictures of them and the reporters would make it sound like the protestors were more violent and intolerant than the KKK and the Nazis put together, when all the people were doing was expressing their legal right to make their opinions known.

But in this warped version of what America was becoming, tolerance for the opinions of others only cut one way.

At least the district attorney had withstood the continuing pressure from Clayton Cochrum, who still wanted Pete McNamara charged with murder and attempted murder. Cochrum wasn't the only one beating that particular drum. The Mexican government had made a formal protest concerning the death of Jorge Corona and the wounding of Emilio Navarre and demanded that the United States Justice Department launch an investigation into whether or not the civil rights of the two men had been violated. Several prominent Hispanic groups within the U.S. echoed that call, as did numerous international civil rights organizations, and the government of more than one European country, although what business it was of theirs, nobody seemed to know.

The whole thing was crazy . . . and it was exactly what Alex had expected.

But at least the story wasn't front page news every

day anymore. The administration in Washington was busy looking for something else to take over. The big targets—the banks, the auto industry, the insurance business, and most of the hospitals—had already been grabbed by the previous administration. The talk now was that because some school districts had more money than others, that was unconstitutional and local and state control of the public schools should be abolished so that the federal government could establish a nationwide school system with strict control over financing and curriculum . . . "to make everything equal," you know. The politicians and the news media were already lining up to support the idea, because, after all, they said in their most sincere tones, it would be good for the children, and that was what it was all about, wasn't it? Of course, anyone who dared to deviate from that line, be they parent, educator, or local administrator, was swiftly derided and accused of being racist, unpatriotic, homophobic (whatever that had to do with anything), and just plain big ol' meanies.

To people who had even the least lick of common sense, it was the biggest bunch of bullcrap anybody had ever heard. But of course, no one ever listened to them. . . .

But it kept the Navarre story off the front pages and the evening newscasts until the day in August when Dave Rutherford called Alex and said, "Cochrum has convinced the judge to move up the Navarre case."

Alex had been utterly shocked that Navarre hadn't taken off for the tall and uncut as soon as he was free on bond. Navarre was still around, though, probably staying somewhere in San Antonio. He was at every news conference that Clayton Cochrum held, sitting in a wheelchair at first, his arm and leg still heavily bandaged. As the weeks passed and he recuperated some, he was able to limp out at Cochrum's side, looking pathetic like he was in great pain. Maybe he was, but it was no less than he deserved.

Not everybody saw it that way. Navarre was a celebrity. Reporters asked his opinion on everything from politics to who would win the latest reality competition on TV. Women sent him letters proposing marriage, and rumor had it that a famous literary agent was negotiating on Navarre's behalf for a million-dollar book deal.

It went without saying that movie deals were in the works, too. Every Hispanic star in Hollywood wanted to play this poor, noble, victimized man. So did some of the black and Caucasian ones.

Alex hoped all of that would change once Navarre was convicted, so when Rutherford broke the news to her on the phone, she said, "Good. The sooner he's behind bars so all this ridiculous hoopla can die down, the better."

"You don't understand, Chief," Rutherford said grimly. "It's not the criminal case against Navarre that got moved up. It's the civil lawsuit he filed."

Alex's hand tightened on the phone as she leaned forward in the chair behind her desk. "What?" she demanded. "They're going to try the civil suit *before* the criminal case?"

"That's right."

"But . . . but things aren't done that way."

"They are now," Rutherford said. "The judge in the criminal case has been dragging his feet all summer, and everybody knows it. He doesn't *want* to try the case. He knows that no matter what he does, he's going to be in trouble with somebody. If you ask me, he wants the civil court jury to weigh in first, so he'll have some idea of how to proceed with the criminal case."

"That's crazy," Alex responded, well aware of just how often she had made that statement this summer.

"Yes, but I'm just about to head over to the county seat for a meeting with the district attorney, the Justice Department attorney assigned to the case, and Pete McNamara's personal attorney. Trial starts Monday."

Alex knew Joe Gutierrez, the young man who was defending Pete McNamara. Joe's dad, Manny Gutierrez, had practiced law in Home for thirty years and had been McNamara's attorney for much of that time. He had taken his son into the firm with him after Joe graduated from the University of Texas law school a couple of years earlier. Then, six months later, Manny had dropped dead of a heart attack, leaving Joe to handle the practice.

Joe was a good kid, smart and ambitious, but Alex wasn't sure he was any match for a shark like Clayton Cochrum.

"Is there anything I can do to help, Dave?" she asked.

"Not at this point. I'm sure you and your officers will be called to testify during the trial. All you can do then is tell the truth."

"Do you think that'll be enough?"

"I hope so. We have right on our side."

The hollow sound of Rutherford's voice told Alex that he knew how naïve anybody would be to really believe that in this day and age. It used to be thought that whoever had the most money usually prevailed in legal proceedings. That had changed over the past few decades. Now it was whoever had the politicians and the media on their side who won most of the time.

"Innocent until proven guilty" had turned into "innocent until proven politically incorrect." Once the media pundits and the Washington pontificators had rendered that verdict, it was the Salem witch trials all over again.

"Well, if you need anything, you let me know," Alex told the city attorney.

"Will do," Rutherford agreed. "Wish me luck, Chief."

"Good luck," Alex said.

But she had a bad feeling they were all going to need a lot more than luck to come through this unscathed.

CHAPTER 16

Monday, the day the case of Emilio Navarre's civil lawsuit got underway, was also the first day of school. It was Jack Bonner's senior year. One more year until he could shake the dust of this sleepy little town off his feet and start to live his life in some place more exciting and interesting. He had already applied to several universities. He knew his grades were good enough for him to get in, but he didn't know if they would get him a scholarship.

He told himself that it didn't matter. He would work to put himself through college if he had to. He would do whatever it took to get him out of Home.

His friend Steve already had things figured out. Steve was going to Texas A&M as a pre-med, following in his father's footsteps and becoming a doctor. Jack always felt a little confused and aimless around him. Luckily, Rowdy was even more aimless than Jack and didn't have any plans beyond the first football game of the season the next Friday night.

Jack's mom was wearing a dress that morning instead of her usual police chief's uniform. "I probably won't be here when you get home this afternoon," she told him. "I don't know when I'll be called to testify."

"The Navarre case, right?"

"That's right."

Jack had kept up with it over the summer. You couldn't really avoid it unless you never watched TV, listened to the radio, surfed the Internet, or read the newspaper. Jack did all of those things except read the newspaper; print took too long and was boring.

"What happens if he wins?"

"He can't win," Jack's mom said. "He and his friend broke into the McNamara house. They committed a felony. Mr. McNamara acted in self-defense."

She sounded like she was trying to be sincere, but in the back of her voice was a nagging uncertainty.

"Yeah, but what happens if he does win?"

She shook her head. "I don't know. As crazy as the world is these days . . . I just don't know."

It was rare for his mom to admit something like that, Jack thought. She was always in charge, with such a firm grasp of what was right and what was wrong and no hesitation whatsoever about telling somebody what they ought to do. What they *had* to do, in his case. To Jack's way of thinking, she had taken the worst traits of being both a cop and a mom and elevated them to even higher levels. Her attitude had driven him crazy for a while, and he had delighted in pushing back against her, until he realized his life would go along a lot smoother if he just let her believe he was cooperating with her. That way, whenever she wasn't around, he could do what he wanted . . . as long as he was careful about it.

"Well, don't worry about me," he told her. "I've got football practice after school, so I'll be late getting home, too."

She smiled across the kitchen table at him. "Gonna get off the bench more this year?"

He gave her a thumb's up and said, "Way to boost the kid's self-esteem, Mom."

She laughed, and at that moment, he kind of liked her again. They didn't have as much of the ol' give-and-take as they used to when he was younger. He had decided she was too oblivious to get most of his humor and she probably figured he was just a smart-ass kid, but every now and then they still laughed together.

Maybe when he was older, things would be better between them.

She left for the county seat, and he headed for school shortly after that.

Rowdy and Steve were waiting for him in the parking lot. They greeted each other with colorful obscenities, the way teenage boys usually did at the sprawling school. It had been built forty years earlier, but many people in town still called it "the new high school."

"How's your mom think the trial's gonna go today?" Steve asked.

"She won't really say," Jack replied with a shake of his head. "She acts like she's confident Navarre will lose, but I think she's worried that he'll win."

"Things'll really hit the fan around here if he does," Rowdy said. "I mean, how can you break into a guy's house and then sue him for shootin' you?"

Jack shrugged. "People have been doing that for

a long time. And sometimes they win, too. I read about some cases like that on the Internet."

"You should be a lawyer," Rowdy suggested. "You like all that legal stuff."

"Lawyers are weasels. That's what Delgado says." Jack and Delgado were still going to the firing range for target practice at least once every couple of weeks.

"How come everybody just calls him Delgado?" Steve asked.

"I dunno. I've never heard him say what the J. P. stands for."

"Justice of the Peace," Rowdy said. "Anyway, you need to be a lawyer, Jack, so you can defend me when I get arrested."

Jack looked over at his friend. "What're you gonna get arrested for?"

"Well, right off the top of my head, I don't know." Rowdy grinned. "But a screw-up like me's bound to get in trouble sometime, right? Probably wind up in jail more than once." He started to sing. "'Nobody knows . . . the trouble I've seen. . . .'"

"That's enough," the vice-principal said as they went inside the building. He was standing there watching the students stream past him, and he didn't seem any happier about it being the first day of school than they did.

As usual, the first day was busy and confusing, even for seniors. Jack had plenty on his mind.

But that didn't stop his thoughts from straying to the county seat now and then.

He couldn't help but wonder how the trial was going.

Chapter 17

Nine people sat at the defense table: Joe Gutierrez and his client, Pete McNamara; Dave Rutherford, representing the city of Home; Everett Hobson, the district attorney of Hawkes County, and one of his assistants, Janet Garcia; Rosario Encinal, from the Solicitor General's office in Washington, representing the federal government; and three attorneys representing the manufacturer of the gun Pete McNamara had used to shoot Jorge Corona and Emilio Navarre. It made for a crowded table. In fact, the bailiffs had had to bring in a smaller table and put it at the end of the one normally used by the defense, just to have room for everybody.

Despite that, the defense team seemed outnumbered by the three people who sat at the plaintiff's table: Navarre, his lawyer Clayton Cochrum, and one of Cochrum's associates, a stunningly beautiful blond woman.

That was the way it seemed to Alex, anyway, as she sat on one of the benches reserved for spectators. Since she was on the witness list, she would have to leave the courtroom before the trial got underway, but she had slipped in here in hopes of catching Pete McNamara's eye and giving him an encouraging smile. She had known him for years, even before he'd been Jack's Little League coach.

Pete had his head down and didn't seem to be paying much attention to anything around him. His shoulders slumped like he was already defeated. Alex wasn't really surprised to see that. Pete had taken Inez's death hard. The few times she had talked to him over the summer, his eyes had been so haunted that he seemed barely there.

Dave Rutherford seemed to feel her looking at the defense table, though, and turned his head to look back at her. She gave him a brief, strained smile, then stood up and came over to the railing that divided the tables from the spectators' benches.

"You're not supposed to be in here, Alex," he told her in a low voice. "You need to be out in the hall with the other witnesses."

"I know. I just wanted to see Pete. Tell him I said hello, would you?"

"Sure." Rutherford glanced at the crowd that had filled up the benches. "There are lots of people here from Home."

"Of course, there are. We stand by our own."

"I hope they behave themselves. Judge Carson is pretty intolerant of disturbances. If people get loud, it could hurt our chances."

"I'll spread the word."

Rutherford nodded. "Thanks, Alex."

She stood up and gripped his hand for a second, then spoke to several people in the audience she knew, asking them to pass along Rutherford's suggestion that everybody be quiet and polite.

One of Pete McNamara's friends from the VFW nodded solemnly and said, "We'll try, Chief, but it's mighty hard keepin' our feelin's in when we see poor ol' Pete sittin' up there on the wrong side of this trial. It oughta be the other way around."

"I can't argue with that," Alex told the man.

She stepped into the hall outside the courtroom. Chairs for the witnesses lined one wall. A rope line had been set up to keep the press away from them, and a couple of bailiffs stood guard on it to keep the reporters at bay. Alex was grateful for that. The last thing she wanted right now was some news vulture clamoring in her face. Judge Phillip Carson had barred camera crews from inside the courthouse, but there were still plenty of reporters clogging the corridors.

Alex took a seat. She wished she could be inside the courtroom to hear the opening statements and everything else that was going on. Waiting was hard for her, and there was no telling how long it would be before she was called to testify. It might be today, Rutherford had told her, but more than likely it would be tomorrow or the next day. It all depended on how long jury selection took and how Clayton Cochrum presented Navarre's case. It was possible that Cochrum wouldn't put any witnesses on the stand except his own client, but Alex and her officers might be called as hostile witnesses, Rutherford had warned her.

She looked along the line of chairs. J. P. Delgado and Clint Barrigan were here, as were the EMTs who had responded to the call from the McNamara home. Was Cochrum going to try to get their testimony on record before the defense had a chance to do so?

Alex didn't know. All she could do was wait, and

wish the events that had spawned this travesty of justice had never taken place.

Dave Rutherford surprised her during the lunch break by telling her that jury selection was complete and that opening statements would take place as soon as court was back in session.

"Then testimony will get underway, I suppose," Rutherford said with a worried frown. "I can't help but think that Cochrum has some sort of trick waiting for us, though."

"You're probably right," Alex said. "A weasel like him is bound to have something up his sleeve."

Just looking at the smug, self-assured lawyer made her skin crawl. Navarre was just a thug who had never had any morals and never would. Cochrum, on the other hand, somewhere along the way had sold out whatever humanity he had in exchange for money. Although no one had been able to prove it, Alex was sure Cochrum was actually working for the Rey del Sol drug cartel or their enforcement arm, a gang that had originated in American prisons and now had members scattered throughout the border states and beyond. Some were illegals from Mexico, but many were native-born Hispanic Americans who had been lured into joining by easy money or misguided sentiments. Like all law enforcement personnel in this part of the country, Alex received frequent warnings about cartel activities.

About three o'clock that afternoon, Clint Barrigan, as the first officer to respond to the shooting call, was summoned into the courtroom to testify.

That meant Cochrum was going the hostile witness route. That was the only course open to him, really, other than having his client testify and then resting his case.

When Clint came back out into the hall a half hour later, his rugged face was grim. He looked at Alex and gave a little shake of his head, but that was all. They had all been cautioned by Dave Rutherford about discussing the case.

Delgado was next, and then one by one, the EMTs. It looked like Cochrum was saving her for last, Alex thought. But the time was close to five o'clock now, so it appeared her testimony wouldn't take place until the next morning. The case was already a lot farther along by now than she had realistically expected it to be.

Sure enough, a few minutes after the last of the ambulance guys emerged from the courtroom, the doors opened and the spectators and reporters began to stream out. An excited hubbub filled the corridor. When the lawyers appeared, the commotion got even worse. The attorneys for the defense drew a crowd, but Clayton Cochrum drew an even bigger one and obviously reveled in it. Alex didn't see Navarre; she supposed Cochrum's bimbo assistant had probably slipped him out of the courthouse some other way.

Cochrum spewed a lot of high-toned crap about being certain that justice would prevail for his client, and the reporters ate it up. Alex found a harried-looking Dave Rutherford and asked, "What's going on in there?"

Rutherford shook his head. "I don't really know. Cochrum doesn't seem to really care about the testimony. He just uses it as an excuse to work in some speeches about the evils of guns and what racist rednecks we all are. Somebody from our side always objects, of course, and the judge sustains the objections, but that doesn't matter. Cochrum's already hammered that into the heads of the jury. Carson ought to shut him down as soon as he starts up with that claptrap, but he won't."

"Why not?"

Rutherford grimaced. "Carson used to be a federal judge. He retired from that and ran for election as a state judge. But he got his marching orders from Washington for a long time, and you know what that means."

Unfortunately, Alex did. Not much had come out of Washington in the past decade that most folks in this part of the country agreed with.

"Anyway, I think you'll be first up in the morning," Rutherford went on. "Are you ready?"

"Ready as I'll ever be," Alex said.

But she had to wonder what was waiting for her. She had an uneasy feeling that it might be something none of them expected.

CHAPTER 18

Alex tried to put the trial and everything about the Navarre case out of her mind when she got home that evening. It was the first day of Jack's final year in high school, and she wanted to hear all about that instead. She didn't even want to think about what was going on in the county seat.

That was all he wanted to talk about, though. He brushed aside her questions about school and asked her about the trial. Alex told him what she could—Dave Rutherford had cautioned all the witnesses about talking too much about the trial, even with family members—and Jack seemed frustrated that she couldn't tell him even more.

"Really, I don't know anything else," she assured him. "I haven't even been inside the courtroom except for a few minutes this morning before the trial even started."

"There's a lot of talk at school about how mad everybody's gonna be if Mr. McNamara loses," Jack said.

"Everybody needs to just settle down and let the

law run its course. Getting mad isn't going to help anything."

"Yeah, well . . . what if the course the law takes is the wrong one?"

Alex didn't have an answer for that. The part of her that believed in the legal system wanted to think that whatever finding the courts reached had to be the correct and proper one.

The part of her that had watched objectively what had happened over the past ten or twelve years since the liberals had taken over Washington completely knew that wasn't necessarily the case.

She didn't feel any better about things when she arrived at the courthouse the next morning, but at least she didn't have to sit around for very long, stewing and waiting. She had only been sitting in the corridor about five minutes when a bailiff opened the courtroom doors and said, "Ms. Bonner?"

"Chief Bonner," Alex said as she stood up. She didn't want to get pissy about it, but that was her title after all.

The bailiff didn't seem offended. He smiled and said, "Please come in, Chief. You've been called to the stand."

Alex had testified in plenty of court cases before. She knew the drill. She went to the witness stand and was sworn in, then sat down to await the questioning. Cochrum was still sitting at the plaintiff's table, whispering to the blonde.

Judge Carson said, "Mr. Cochrum? Are you ready?" The judge was in late middle-age, a slight, gray-haired man with a heavily lined face.

Cochrum got to his feet. "Yes, sir, Your Honor," he said as he came toward the witness stand. Alex thought the lawyer's suit probably cost as much as she made in a month. He wasn't wearing his sunglasses in the courtroom, of course, but other than that he looked like the same smug, smarmy weasel he did when he was preening for the cameras.

He stopped in front of Alex and said, "Good morning, Chief Bonner. How are you this morning?"

"I've been better," Alex said, not bothering to keep the curt annoyance out of her voice.

"I'm sorry to hear that. Just for the record, you *are* the chief of police in the city of Home, Texas, is that correct?"

"Yes," Alex said.

"And also for the record, you understand that I have called you to testify for the plaintiff as a hostile witness."

"Yes." She was definitely hostile, and she didn't care who knew it.

"Now, I believe that on the night of June eighth of this year, you were at your residence when you received a call from the night dispatcher at the police department?"

"That's right."

"In your own words and to the best of your recollection, please tell us what was said during that call and what you did afterward."

This was simple, straightforward testimony, and Alex went through it as quickly as she could. She expected Cochrum to try to slant things with his questions, but surprisingly, he didn't. He was just as matter of fact as she was.

Somehow, that worried her even more. Cochrum was setting them up for something, she thought, and he wouldn't be doing that unless he was confident that he had a pretty powerful secret weapon on his side.

"Now, this weapon you say was lying on the floor near Mr. Navarre," Cochrum said. "Did you ever see it in his hand?"

"No, I didn't," Alex said. "But a subsequent test showed that his fingerprints were on it."

"Had it been fired?"

"There was no way I could be sure of that, one way or the other."

"But you're an experienced police officer, Chief," Cochrum said. "In your professional opinion, did it *appear* to have been fired recently? Did it *smell* like it had been fired?"

"The whole room still smelled like guns had been fired there," Alex said. "I didn't bother smelling Mr. Navarre's gun in particular because I knew the crime scene technicians from the sheriff's department would test it and make the determination of whether or not it had been fired."

"And did they make those tests?"

"They did."

"What was the determination?"

Alex didn't want to say it, but she didn't have any choice. "The tests showed that Mr. Navarre's weapon had not been fired on the night in question."

Cochrum smiled. "And since that's the only time we're concerned with here, that proves my client could not have shot anyone that night."

"That's not a question, but if it was, I'd have to answer no, that doesn't prove any such thing."

Alex spoke quickly, so she could get it in before Cochrum had a chance to shut her up. She was rewarded by a momentary flash of anger in his eyes. So he was human enough to get mad, anyway.

"What do you mean by that?"

"It proves that your client *didn't* shoot anybody that night. But the fact that his fingerprints were on the weapon prove that he *could* have. He had the potential to—"

"You've answered the question, Chief Bonner."

"You asked me what I meant by it. I was just telling you."

That brought some laughter from the spectators. Judge Carson glared at them, but didn't issue a warning.

"All right, Chief, I have no further questions." Cochrum swung around and went back to the table.

The judge looked at the defense table. Everett Hobson stood up and said, "No questions at this time, Your Honor, but the defense reserves the right to call Chief Bonner as a witness on our behalf."

"Noted," Judge Carson said. "You may step down, Ms. Bonner."

She didn't correct him on the title. She just got out of there.

It hadn't been too bad, Alex mused as she took her seat in the hall again. The little skirmish with Cochrum hadn't amounted to much, and she thought she had held her own against him. She didn't really understand his strategy, but she remained convinced that he was going to pull *something* underhanded before the trial was over.

She had been sitting there for only a few minutes when an uproar suddenly erupted inside the courtroom. It was loud enough for Alex to hear it clearly, including the shocked cries and the banging of the judge's gavel as he hammered for order. A minute later, the doors opened and several reporters burst out. The print reporters were clawing cell phones from their pockets to call their papers. The broadcast reporters were practically sprinting for their camera crews.

Alex's heart sank. Something had happened, and she was sure it was something bad.

She stood up and headed for the door, determined to go in there and find out what was going on. Before she could get there, Rosario Encinal strode out, looking beautiful and regal as she was surrounded by reporters. The federal attorney smiled and said, "Mr. Cochrum and I will be having a press conference shortly, and I'll be glad to answer all your questions then."

Alex stared at Encinal as the woman swept past her. Had she said that she and *Cochrum* were going to be holding a press conference? That made no sense. They were on opposite sides.

Unless they weren't.

As that thought went through Alex's mind, she hurried into the courtroom. Dave Rutherford, Joe Gutierrez, and Everett Hobson were talking animatedly as they stood behind the defense table, and none of them looked happy. Pete McNamara still sat there, looking stunned and more dispirited than ever. The three attorneys for the gun manufacturer were gathering up their papers. They wore disgusted expressions on their faces. When they had finished packing up their briefcases, they stalked out.

The conference between the three remaining lawyers broke up. Gutierrez sat down beside his client and put an arm around the old man's shoulders. Whatever he was saying didn't appear to do any good. Pete McNamara still looked beaten down to nothing.

District Attorney Hobson and his assistant, Janet Garcia, hustled out of the courtroom as well, bent on some errand that seemed hopeless, judging by the expressions on their faces. Dave Rutherford turned, saw Alex, and motioned for her to come over. She went to the railing and rested her hands on it. The benches behind her had cleared of spectators, but there was still an angry commotion going on out in the hallway and the courthouse lobby.

"Dave, what in the world happened?"

Rutherford's mouth quirked in a humorless smile. "Cochrum rested his case."

"Already? He didn't even put Navarre on the stand?"

"He didn't need to." Rutherford drew in a deep breath. "Before he rested, he announced that he'd filed papers to have the United States government dropped from the lawsuit. It seems that Navarre has reached a separate settlement with the feds."

"Wait a minute. A settlement? But that would mean . . ."

Rutherford nodded. "Yes. The federal government is going to acknowledge that Emilio Navarre's civil rights were violated when Pete McNamara shot him. I'm sure that Cochrum and Ms. Encinal will be announcing the terms shortly. I suspect a lot of money will change hands."

The implications of that mushroomed through Alex's mind. Her hands tightened on the railing. "How can the state win a criminal case against

Navarre when the federal government has already said that he's right and Pete was wrong?"

"It can't," Rutherford said as he shook his head. "The jury pool will be irrevocably tainted. Hell, the whole country will be tainted."

"What about this case? Surely what Cochrum has done is grounds for a mistrial."

"Yes, but don't you see, Alex?" Rutherford's face was bleak. "It *doesn't matter.* If the case proceeds, the jury knows that the feds have already sided with Navarre. Maybe they'll rule in favor of Mr. McNamara anyway. But if they do, Cochrum will just appeal, and a higher court will set the judgment aside. Even if it goes all the way to the Supreme Court, in the end Navarre will win. It's over, Alex. No matter how much we try to stretch things out, it's over."

She felt sick to her stomach, and she was dizzy enough that her grip on the railing was all that kept her from collapsing. She had devoted her adult life to enforcing the law—hell, that devotion had cost her her marriage—and now the legal system had just declared that it was all right to break into somebody's home and murder the occupants, and if anybody dared to fight back, *they* were in the wrong, not the criminals who had broken in to start with.

"This is crazy, Dave. Just crazy." She looked at the forlorn figure of Pete McNamara. "Will Pete wind up going to jail?"

"I seriously doubt it, although Everett may have to charge him, just for appearance's sake. But they can work out some sort of plea deal so that Mr. McNamara won't have to spend any time behind bars."

"But he'll be a convicted felon, just for defending his home. This is going to *kill* him, Dave."

Rutherford shrugged. "I hope not, but there's nothing we can do. Cochrum outfoxed us, plain and simple." His face hardened. "I think he's had the deal worked out with that bitch all along. And she's just acting for her bosses in Washington. That's where the real stench comes from. Somebody high up has been planning all along for Navarre to win."

"How high?"

A hollow laugh came from the lawyer. "Who made a call for a lot stricter gun laws a major part of his campaign?"

The same thought had occurred to Alex. "You really think the President would side with a Mexican murderer over a citizen of his own country?"

"If it helps him remake the U.S. into what *he* and his cronies think the country should be, then what do you believe, Alex?"

She knew the answer to that. She hated to think it, but she knew.

"There's something else we have to consider, Dave. This isn't going to go over well with folks in Home. There's liable to be trouble. People are going to be mad, and they may take to the streets to express it."

"The sheriff's department will have to keep order, along with the officers you left back there."

"I need to go—"

Rutherford shook his head. "You can't. The judge called an hour's recess when all hell broke loose, but the trial will resume when that's over. You're still a witness."

"You're going to play out the string, even after what happened?"

"What else can we do?" he asked with a faint

smile. "If we quit now, there's no chance the jury won't find in favor of Navarre."

"I thought you said it didn't matter."

"In the long run, it doesn't. But . . . well . . . some windmills just have to be tilted at, don't they?"

"The Solicitor General is on the phone, sir."

He scooped it up and barked, "Talk to me, Ted. Did it go as planned?" A big smile, the smile that the media loved, spread across his face. "Excellent! Be sure and tell Ms. Encinal how pleased I am with the way she carried out her part. And of course you'll be prepared for further proceedings if necessary? . . . Good."

The smile disappeared as he hung up the phone. A chief executive had to be able to multitask, so there were other things on his mind today.

"Any word on Trussell, Geoff?"

"No, sir. He still appears to have dropped off the face of the earth."

"What about those two rogue CIA agents? They're still missing, too, aren't they?"

"Yes, sir."

"Well, then, Geoff"—the mild, conciliatory tone became a bellow of anger—"did it ever occur to you that they've probably got Trussell and are lying low with him somewhere?"

"Of course the possibility occurred to me, sir." The Chief of Staff's jaw was tight with suppressed anger. "But it's more likely that all three of them are dead. We've had a massive search operation going on now for two months,

and I believe it would have turned up some trace of them if they were still alive."

"You'd better hope they're dead. Things are coming to a head now at Casa del Diablo. They promise me that the first shipment will be ready in less than a month. We can't have word leak out now."

"No, sir." The Chief of Staff hesitated. "Should you issue a statement on the Navarre settlement?"

"Not just yet. We'll wait a little longer. Let those ignorant rednecks stew a while longer. It has to look like the action we'll be taking is justified."

"It will be, sir. Knowing those people in Texas, I think you can count on that."

The arrogant son of a bitch wasn't near as smart as he thought he was, the Chief of Staff told himself as he let himself into his town house near Dupont Circle that evening. He thought that the country loved him so much he could do anything he wanted and get away with it. He never stopped to realize how much work those around him put in to make the country love him and accept his actions, no matter how outrageous and unconstitutional they were.

Thank goodness three of the Supreme Court justices had dropped dead during the previous administration, changing the balance of power on the court so that it went along with whatever the occupant of the White House wanted. The Chief of Staff, long a Washington insider, had wondered on occasion if the previous President might have had something to do with those deaths, even though officially they were from natural causes. He knew that woman, knew the lengths she would go to in order to get what she wanted. After all, it was common knowledge that she'd had at least one man killed, back before she took office.

Ultimately, though, she didn't have the metaphorical balls to finish the job of taking the country in the direction it needed to go. The conventional wisdom was that when her second term neared its end, she would declare some sort of national emergency and suspend the Constitution, thereby postponing the election and keeping herself in office. That hadn't happened, though. She had gone quietly, even meekly, surprising everybody who knew her.

The Chief of Staff supposed the death of the previous President's husband probably had something to do with that. He should have known that he was too old to keep up with that many mistresses. His heart had given out while he was on top of one of them, pumping away. The public didn't know that, but the former President and a limited number of insiders did.

One thing you could say about the guy in the Oval Office now: He had the balls to do whatever was needed. The project at Casa del Diablo was proof enough of that.

"Darling, is that you?"

The woman's voice from the bedroom made a smile break out on the Chief of Staff's face. One mistress was enough . . . if she was the right mistress. Julia Hernandez was brilliant at what she did. She would have drinks waiting for him, and she would be waiting for him as well, naked in his bed. By the time she was through with him, she would have made all the day's stress go away. He was usually so relaxed that he had to take a nap before they went out for dinner.

She was good at her day job, too, one of the assistant social secretaries in the White House. He got to see her every day, but of course, everything between them was prim and proper as long as they were at the most famous building on Pennsylvania Avenue.

Grinning, he went into the bedroom and said, "Yes, it's me. Are you ready for me, darling?"

"Always," she said from the bed.

Yep. Naked. Just like he liked.

He must have been tired. The drugs worked even faster than usual, putting him in that twilight state between waking and sleeping where he was just conscious enough to answer every question she asked him, but too groggy to do anything but tell the truth. He'd babbled on about everything the President was planning, and when he woke up, he wouldn't remember a bit of it except that they had made love.

Nude, Julia padded across the thick carpet of the bedroom and picked up her phone from the dresser. She started entering a text message. To anyone else who read it, the message would look even more like gibberish than the text messages sent by teenagers. When it arrived in Mexico, though, it would be decoded and brought to Enrique Reynosa y Montoya, the head of Rey del Sol.

The idiot now snoring away in the bed had been especially informative this evening. Julia smiled as she pressed the button on the phone that sent the message on its way.

She knew Señor Reynosa would be very interested to hear about what was going on in West Texas, at the place called Casa del Diablo. . . .

BOOK THREE

CHAPTER 19

Just as Alex had predicted, the citizens of Home weren't happy when they heard about what had happened in the courtroom at the county seat. By the time she got back that evening and went to the police department, the sidewalks downtown were full of people, most of them milling around or gathered into tight, angry groups. The feeling of tension in the air was palpable as Alex got out of her car and went into the building.

She had never experienced an actual riot . . . but it felt like that's what was brewing in Home this evening.

Jimmy Clifton looked up from behind the counter where the dispatcher's station was located. "Chief, am I . . . glad to see you," he said. He had a slight slowness of speech. That and a hesitant gait were the only outward signs of his Down Syndrome. "People are sure . . . mad about Pete."

"I don't blame them, Jimmy," Alex said. "He's gotten a really raw deal all the way around. But folks ought to be in their houses, not out stirring up more trouble."

"That's what . . . Jerry and Betsy told 'em. And the . . . sheriff's deputies, too. But it's not against . . . the law for people to be . . . on the street."

"Not yet, anyway," Alex muttered. The way that bunch in Washington tried to suppress dissent, there was no telling what might happen by the time another so-called liberal administration was over. That bunch preached tolerance while practicing some of the worst *in*tolerance Alex had ever seen.

"What do you . . . want me to do, Chief? I can stay here on . . . duty for as long as you need me."

She smiled. "I know you can, Jimmy, and I appreciate that. But you take off when Eloise comes in to relieve you the way she always does. You'd better go home and look after your folks."

Jimmy lived a few blocks away with his elderly parents. Alex didn't want him on the street this evening, not with the trouble that might be building up. She knew that when she told him to take care of his parents, he would listen to her.

"Jack called a little . . . while ago," Jimmy added. "He wanted to know if . . . you were here yet."

"I'll call him back," Alex promised as she started into her office. She had a spare uniform here at the station. She wanted to get out of the dress she had worn to court so she could move around better if she had to.

She wanted to strap on her gun, too. She hadn't taken it to the county seat with her, knowing that she wouldn't be allowed to bring it into the courtroom with her.

As much as she loved and respected the citizens of her town and would never use a weapon against them except as an absolutely last resort, she knew that some of them would be more likely to listen to her if she was armed.

When she came out of her office wearing the brown slacks and tan short-sleeved shirt, with the 9mm automatic in the holster strapped to her belt, she found J. P. Delgado and Clint Barrigan waiting for her, along with the two reserve officers, Lester Simms and Antonio Ruiz, the mayor's cousin.

"We figured you'd need all hands on deck tonight, Chief," Delgado said.

"Well, the nearest ocean is several hundred miles away," Alex said with a smile, "but I appreciate the sentiment. And I'm really glad to see all of you."

Lester asked, "Is what they're saying true, Chief? The federal government is really siding with that . . . that monster who killed Inez McNamara?"

"They reached a settlement with him, yes, and Navarre dropped them from the lawsuit."

"But that's the same thing as saying they think he was in the right and Pete was in the wrong!"

Alex nodded. "I'm afraid so."

"Have you seen the latest news conference?" Delgado asked tightly.

"The one with Navarre's lawyer and that federal attorney?" Alex shook her head. "Not yet. I'll bet it's all over the TV."

"That woman said Pete violated Navarre's civil rights by shooting him," Delgado said. "She claims the evidence at the trial proved it wasn't self-defense. The government's going to pay Navarre five million dollars, and if the state doesn't press charges against Pete, the federal government is."

The craziness just kept on getting crazier, Alex thought with a sigh.

"As ridiculous as it is, none of that is our concern," she said. "Our job is to keep the peace on the streets of Home . . . and that's what we're going to do."

"You know the people of this town, Chief," Clint said. "They're law-abiding folks. But they're starting to figure that they've been pushed far enough."

Alex nodded. "I know, and I can't say as I blame them. But I'm still not going to stand by and let anybody start any trouble." She paused. "I don't think it'll come to that. They can blow off steam all they want, but there's nobody for them to really direct their anger at. That federal attorney and Navarre and his lawyer are all over in the county seat."

"The news media is here," Delgado pointed out. "That's pretty much the fourth branch of government these days."

Alex knew that was true. The media excused everything the President and the liberal-controlled Congress did, while downplaying every gaffe by the Vice-President and exaggerating beyond all sense of proportion anything a conversative politician said or did that they didn't like. And people on both coasts sat there every day and night and lapped up the distortions and outright lies like cream, while the rest of the country could only shake their heads in dismay and think, *That's just not true.*

"You're right," she told Delgado. "All it'll take is some reporter shoving a microphone and a camera in somebody's face and smirking while they pretend to ask a question and really make a political speech instead. People are liable to blow up if that happens. So let's get out there and make sure it doesn't. If folks see us on the street, they'll be a lot more likely to behave."

Alex hoped that was true.

She had left the station with the other officers before she realized she had forgotten to call Jack and let him know she was back from the county seat.

He would be all right, she told herself. He had long since learned that with his mom being the chief of police, there would be times when he was on his own. He'd probably make himself some supper, then spend the evening doing homework, watching TV, surfing the Internet, or listening to music . . . or all of those options at the same time. Jack's generation had learned to multitask while they were practically still in their cribs.

No, Alex told herself, she didn't have to worry about her son.

CHAPTER 20

"It's gonna be historic," Rowdy said. "We don't want to miss it."

"I don't know," Steve said. "It sounds to me like there could be real trouble."

Rowdy made a disgusted face. "Ah, you're just a wuss. What do you think, Jack? The rest of the team's gonna be there to show support for Mr. McNamara."

Jack understood that. There was a lot of anger on the football team about what had happened. Most of them had played Little League in Home, which meant Pete McNamara had either coached them or coached against them, and either way, they knew him and liked him. He was a big supporter of high school athletics, too, always at the games, no matter what sport it was. Sometimes he even announced the games when the regular PA guy couldn't be there.

"I don't guess it would hurt for us to go," Jack said. "Just to see what happens."

"Now you're talkin'," Rowdy said as he slid off the bench in the Dairy Queen booth. "Maybe we'll be on TV. There are still some news crews around town."

The Dairy Queen was busy this evening, and all the talk was about what had happened in the trial at the county seat that day. It was loud, angry talk, too, Jack noted as he and his friends left. Several people had already grabbed the booth they'd vacated.

People were mad, and that made Jack worry a little about his mom. She knew how to take care of herself, though. She was the chief of police, after all. Sure, she annoyed him sometimes, and he didn't understand why she had to be such a hard-ass, but sometimes being a hard-ass was good. She would keep things under control. He was confident of that.

They didn't bother getting into Rowdy's pickup but started walking downtown instead. Home wasn't so big that you couldn't walk all the way from one end of Main Street to the other if you wanted to. There was a lot of traffic, both on the road and beside it. Cars, trucks, and SUVs clogged the asphalt, while people walked along the shoulders and sidewalks, all of them converging on the center of town.

Jack saw a couple of police cars in the parking lot of the supermarket, but they were both empty. He supposed the cops were out on foot, mingling with the crowd so they could keep order. Rowdy saw some of their teammates from the football team and called out to them. As the two groups moved to join each other, a pickup with half a dozen more teenage boys in the back pulled to the side of the road next to them. The kids piled out.

"This is the biggest thing to hit this town in a long time," one of them said.

Another gestured toward the water tower at the edge of town, which was lit up at night. "Biggest thing since the state championship."

"Yeah, but that was a good thing," Jack said. "This sucks. It's not right, what they're doin' to Mr. McNamara."

That brought a burst of profanity-laced agreement from the other boys. One of them added, "It's all because of those damn wetbacks."

Several of them turned to look at the boy who had spoken, whose name was José Gonzales. He spread his hands and said, "What? My family was here when Stephen F. Austin was. We're *Texans.* I got no use for those criminals and drug smugglers from south of the border."

"Yeah, well, I feel sorry for the honest people who have to live over there," Steve said.

"There's not many of those anymore," Rowdy put in. "We oughta go to war with Mexico, that's what we oughta do. It's gonna take our army to put all those damn cartels outta business."

Jack said, "The politicians will never do that. You can just forget it."

José nodded. "Yeah. They don't got the *cojones* for that."

Rowdy nudged Jack with an elbow and nodded toward a blond woman in a dark blue dress making her way through the crowd toward them. He said, "Look at that babe. She's gotta be one of the reporters. Anybody that hot must be on TV."

"Yeah, and the guy behind her with the camera is probably a clue, too," Jack said dryly.

The woman came to a stop and held out a cordless microphone toward them. "Could I ask you boys some questions?" she asked with a dazzling smile.

Rowdy didn't bother trying to tear his eyes away from her cleavage as he nodded and said, "Sure."

"Do you go to school here in Home?"

"Yeah, we're all members of the varsity football team."

She looked like she was impressed by that. Jack would have been willing to bet that she wasn't, not really, but she knew what she was doing and how to get what she wanted.

"Do you know Pete McNamara?"

"Of course, we know Pete," Rowdy said. He had taken over as the spokesman for the group. "He coached Little League when we were all playing."

"So you consider him a friend, a mentor?"

"Yeah, he's a great guy."

"Are you upset about the things being said about him?"

"Wouldn't you be, if somebody claimed that a friend of yours shot some people without good reason?"

"*Do* you think he had a good reason?"

"Of course, he did! Those Mexicans broke into his house and killed his wife."

Jack saw a momentary gleam in the blonde's eyes. Rowdy had played right into her hands by using a phrase like "those Mexicans" and sounding so contemptuous. He had just sent out the message to whoever watched this footage that the citizens of Home were ignorant racists.

Never mind the fact that Jorge Corona and Emilio Navarre actually were Mexican citizens. Truth didn't matter much anymore.

"But it's been established that Emilio Navarre never fired his weapon," the reporter went on. "How could he have been a threat to Mr. McNamara?"

"He had a gun," Rowdy replied with a frown.

"A lot of people have guns. If they don't use them, they can't hurt anybody."

It was hard to argue with a statement like that, even though the logic behind it was false. And the blonde knew that.

"But they broke into Pete's house," Rowdy protested. "And they shot Mrs. McNamara."

"She was injured only *after* Mr. McNamara fatally wounded Jorge Corona. So isn't it possible to say that Mr. McNamara was responsible not only for the death of Mr. Corona, but also for what happened to his wife?"

Jack had had as much as he could swallow. More, even. He stepped forward and said, "Listen, lady, Mrs. McNamara wasn't *injured.* She was *killed.* She's dead, you understand that?"

The blonde's face turned cold. "Of course, I understand that, young man. I'm well aware of the tragedy that happened here."

"Then you ought to understand what a tragedy it is that Pete McNamara's being blamed for something that's not his fault at all. At least, you would if you weren't a moron."

The cameraman lowered his camera and said, "Don't worry, Stacy, that didn't go out on a live feed. We can edit it." He glared at Jack. "And you, kid, you'd better watch your mouth."

"Why don't you make him?" Rowdy demanded, stepping forward. "Or even better, why don't you tell me what to do, mister?"

The man sneered as he lifted his camera again. "You can't touch me, punk. I'm protected by freedom of the press. Ever heard of it, you dumb hick?"

"Freedom of the press *this*, you Yankee mother—"

"Rowdy, no!" Jack yelled as his friend lunged at the cameraman, swinging a punch.

It was too late. Rowdy was an offensive tackle and plenty of size and strength were behind the blow. It landed on the side of the cameraman's head and knocked him sprawling as the blond reporter screamed. The cameraman managed to hang on to the piece of expensive equipment.

The blonde had screamed, but she had also whipped out a cell phone and was recording video on it even as Rowdy started after the fallen cameraman, obviously intent on stomping him. Jack grabbed his friend's arm and tried to hold him back.

"Rowdy, you're just doing what they want," Jack said urgently, trying to get through the anger Rowdy was feeling. "Let it go."

"Too late," Steve said. "Here come some more guys, and they don't look happy."

Jack turned his head and saw several men jumping out of the back of a nearby truck that belonged to one of the cable news networks. The fleeting thought that they were awfully big and burly for audio and video technicians had time to cross his mind, and then José and the other guys whooped in excitement and lunged forward to meet the rush. Shouts filled the air as fists began to fly, and like ripples emanating outward from a rock tossed in a pond, the trouble started to spread through the crowd.

Yeah, it was all hitting the fan, Jack thought, and he was right in the middle of it.

His mom was gonna be royally pissed.

CHAPTER 21

Alex was circulating through the crowd in front of the hardware store, trying to calm them down, when she heard the commotion break out down the street. She had to lift herself on her toes and crane her neck to see what was going on. All she could tell was that there was some sort of fight in the supermarket parking lot.

She bit back a curse. This was exactly the sort of thing she had been worried was going to happen.

As she started pushing through the crowd, hurrying toward the disturbance, she keyed the mike on her shoulder and said, "Supermarket, now!" sending out a call to all the other officers to meet her there unless they were already involved in some other incident.

She wasn't the only one whose attention the fight had attracted. Quite a few people began streaming in that direction, and some of them even yelled, "Fight, fight!" just like they were on a junior high school playground.

When Alex got closer, her heart plummeted for a second as she recognized Rowdy Donovan in the middle of the brawl. If Rowdy was involved, there was a good chance Jack was, too.

A second later, her fear for her son was mitigated somewhat by her anger at him. He *knew* better than to get mixed up in something like this, she thought.

So much for believing he would go home after football practice and do his homework.

A part of Alex wished she could pull the 9mm from the holster on her hip and blast a few shots into the air. That would settle things down in a hurry. Those Old West lawmen in books and movies had some advantages the modern police didn't. Right now Alex wouldn't have minded having a .45-caliber Peacemaker and a double-barreled shotgun.

Instead she settled for raising her voice and shouting, "Hey! Break it up! Everybody stop fighting!" as she plowed into the melée.

She had a strong voice and experience at crowd control, but she had trouble making herself heard over the racket. A couple of guys were rolling around on the cement at her feet, wrestling. Disgusted, she reached down, grabbed the shirt collar of one of them, and hauled him to his feet.

"Mom!" Jack yelped as Alex found herself looking into her son's face.

Before Alex could say anything, a siren snarled loudly somewhere nearby. After a couple of bursts of near-deafening sound, it shut down, only to be replaced by J. P. Delgado's voice amplified through a bullhorn.

"Break it up! Break it up! Or you'll all be placed under arrest!"

Delgado had managed to get into one of the police cars parked in the lot, and between the bullhorn and the siren, he stunned the crowd into submission, at least for the moment. Alex gave Jack a little shake and said through clenched teeth, "Stay here. Do not throw another punch. You understand me?"

He jerked his head in an angry nod. His arm was bleeding from a scraped place and a bruise was already starting to come up on his jaw, but he didn't appear to be badly hurt.

Alex shoved her way through the crowd to the police car. Delgado stood beside the open driver's door, the bullhorn in his hand. She took it from him and lifted it to her mouth.

"Everyone disperse right now," she ordered. "Off the streets! Go home! I'm declaring a curfew in effect!"

From the crowd, somebody yelled, "You can't do that!"

Alex glared in his direction, swung the bullhorn toward him, and barked through it, "You wanna try me?"

Evidently nobody did.

The mob began thinning on the edges as people who hadn't been directly involved in the fight decided it might be best to do as she said and go home. Alex lowered the bullhorn and asked Delgado, "Do you have any idea what started this?"

Before he could answer, a woman's strident voice said, "I can tell you what started it. Those young racists you have growing up here attacked my cameraman!"

Alex turned to see an attractive blonde in her twenties standing there. Her clothes were a little rumpled and her previously perfect hair was in slight disarray. She had a microphone in her hand, and a man with a video camera was pointing it at her.

"That cameraman?" Alex asked.

The guy gave her a hostile glance. He had dried blood on his face from a split lip.

"That's right, Chief," the reporter said. "You *are* Chief Alex Bonner, aren't you?"

"That's right."

"Do you have any comment about the riot that broke out here in Home this evening?"

"It wasn't a riot—" Alex began.

"With all due respect, Chief, you weren't right in the middle of it. Those rampaging citizens were out of control, and I was afraid for my life."

With all due respect, Alex thought bleakly. That was what leeches like this reporter said to people they didn't respect at all.

The blonde went on, "That young man assaulted my associate, and I want him arrested." She turned to point dramatically at Rowdy, who was standing now with Jack and Steve.

Alex narrowed her eyes at him. "Rowdy, what did you do?"

Before he could answer, the reporter said, "Excuse me? Rowdy? Did you say his name is *Rowdy?*" Her condescending smirk spoke volumes.

"Hey, there's nothing wrong with that name, lady," Rowdy protested. "If it was good enough for Clint Eastwood, it's good enough for me."

The blonde never stopped smirking as she said, "What about it, Chief? Are you going to arrest this young man and his friends?"

It was clear she meant Jack and Steve.

Alex faced the three boys. Steve had a hangdog expression on his face, but Jack and Rowdy still looked defiant.

"Did you start this?" Alex demanded of them.

"No, *they* did," Jack replied. "She said that Mr. McNamara was to blame for everything that happened, including his wife getting killed."

"We couldn't let that go," Rowdy said. "We just couldn't, Mrs. Bonner."

"I'm not Mrs. Bonner right now," Alex snapped. "I'm Chief Bonner, and I'm putting all three of you in custody."

Jack's eyes widened. "Mom!"

Through gritted teeth, Alex said, "I told you, I'm not Mom right now. I'm the chief of police." She turned to Delgado and added, "Put them in the backseat of your car."

He nodded and said, "Come on, fellas."

Jack still looked aghast at this turn of events. "You can't be serious," he argued. "They're the ones who ought to be arrested. They came in here where they aren't wanted and stirred up all this trouble!"

The blonde sneered and said, "There's such a thing as freedom of the press, young man. You may not have heard of it, considering the sort of education you probably get in a place like this where all they teach you is football and hate."

"Don't push your luck, lady," Alex snapped. She pointed to Delgado's police car and said, "Go!"

They went, ushered over to the car by Delgado,

who opened the back door and watched as they slid into the uncomfortable confines of the backseat.

Alex nodded to the reporter. "Now, are you satisfied?"

"That you did your duty as the police chief? I suppose. But I heard one of those boys call you Mom. Are you satisfied, Chief Bonner, with the job you've done of raising him?"

For a second, Alex thought about the days of the Old West again, when troublemakers could be tarred, feathered, and ridden out of town on a rail.

It sure was an appealing idea right now.

She took a deep breath and said, "I don't comment on personal matters. I can promise you, though, that there'll be a full investigation of what took place here tonight, and anyone who's at fault . . . *anyone* . . . will face the full penalties allowed by law. Now get off the street."

"You can't—"

"I declared a curfew, remember? That goes for all civilians, including the press."

The reporter glared at her. "I'm going to file a formal protest with the mayor and the city council."

"Go ahead." Alex hoped that Ed Ruiz and the other members of the council would support her on this, but even if they didn't, it would be after the fact. The important thing was to get the streets cleared now, so there wouldn't be any more trouble tonight.

"And my viewers are certainly going to hear about this injustice."

"I'm sure they will. I don't have any further comment."

Alex turned away and surveyed the street and

the parking lot. A few pockets of people still stood around looking surly, but they began to break up as Alex stared at them. The reporters were still there, too, of course, chattering away. Alex told her other officers to shoo them back to their motel rooms, then climbed into the passenger side of the front seat of Delgado's patrol car.

"Mom, this is just wrong!" Jack protested through the wire mesh that separated the front seat from the back. "We shouldn't be under arrest."

"Shut up," Alex told him, still more in cop mode than mom mode. "You're not under arrest, any of you. I placed you in custody, that's all. Delgado will take you all home."

"You mean you did it just to placate that reporter?"

"I mean I was doing what I thought was necessary to defuse an explosive situation. But you should be damn glad you're not under arrest for assault."

Rowdy leaned over to Jack and said, "Hey, dude, your mom said 'damn.'"

Despite everything that had happened, Alex found it hard not to laugh just then. You could always count on Rowdy to be . . . well, Rowdy, she thought.

"This may not be over," she warned them. "It'll depend on what the reporter and cameraman do. They may press for criminal charges to be filed against you, and they can always file a civil lawsuit, too. So be prepared for more trouble as a result of this." She paused. "You really should have gone home after football practice, all of you."

"But it's not fair, what they're doing to poor Mr. McNamara," Jack said.

"I guess maybe that reporter was right," Alex said. "I haven't done a very good job of raising you."

Jack frowned. "What do you mean by that?"

"If I'd done my job, you'd know by now that life isn't fair."

Chapter 22

By the next morning, what the media called "a riot tinged with racist overtones" was national news. Alex felt a surge of despair as she clicked between the various cable network talking heads while drinking her coffee, but the despair was quickly replaced by simmering anger.

How dare they distort everything that's happened? she thought. The fact that Corona and Navarre were Mexican didn't have anything to do with the outrage that filled the town . . . other than the additional fact that most of the crime within a hundred miles of the border originated in one way or another south of the Rio Grande.

Didn't facts mean anything anymore?

Then she thought about the way things had played out politically in the United States over the past dozen years and realized that no, they didn't. Facts didn't mean a blasted thing anymore if they were inconvenient for the power-mongers on the left. They would just yell their lies even louder, and the media would parrot them.

It reminded her of the big stink over so-called ethnic profiling a number of years earlier, after the terrorist attacks on the U.S. The liberal mind-set that no one should ever, ever be the least bit offended by anything (unless they were white and middle-class, of course) had led to eighty-year-old grandmothers being detained and searched in airports while young Arab men in the country on expired visas swept blithely through security checkpoints.

The threat from the Middle East was still a problem, and one day it would come back to bite the country on the ass, big-time, Alex thought. But for now, the terrorist warlords in their caves had scaled back their activities. They *liked* the guy in the White House. They didn't want anything happening on his watch that might damage his administration. That was Alex's theory, anyway, and she knew a lot of people in law enforcement who shared it.

The bigger threat these days was much closer at hand, as the cartels in Mexico had grown so powerful that they were the de facto government south of the border. The Mexican politicians were just figureheads, mouthpieces for the various cartels, and the army generals took their orders from those same cartels.

Like feudal barons, the drug kingpins made war on each other, and those epic clashes often spilled across the border into the U.S. Alex could see a day coming when there might be an actual war down here, unless the United States was willing to meekly give up Texas, New Mexico, Arizona, and a big chunk of California. Of course, if that same spineless bunch was still in power in Washington, that might be exactly what happened.

She forced those bleak thoughts out of her head

as she finished her coffee. "Jack, you'd better be awake," she called down the hall. "I'm leaving, and you've got school."

"Yeah, yeah, I'm awake," came the sleepy answer. "Don't worry, I'll be there."

"Straight there, straight home after football practice, remember?" She would ground him until he was thirty if she had to, and he could damned well like it. It was better than being arrested.

"Yeah, I got it."

Alex rinsed her coffee cup, put it in the drainer, and left the house. Home appeared to be quiet this morning, she saw as she drove through town, and she was grateful for that.

Everybody was probably inside, watching TV as the reporters made them out to be a town full of monsters.

She was wearing a dress again, because she had to go back over to the county seat and be on hand if she was called by the defense to testify. Clayton Cochrum had rested his case. Now it would be up to Joe Gutierrez, Dave Rutherford, and the other defense attorneys. Alex didn't expect the trial to last much longer. Everything was pretty cut and dried.

Or at least it would have been if not for that backstabbing federal bitch, Rosario Encinal, Alex reminded herself. After what had gone down yesterday, there was no telling what might happen today.

Ed Ruiz was waiting for her when she came into the station. "I need to talk to you about that curfew you declared last night, Alex," he said, launching right into the business that had brought him here without any small talk, as usual.

"Sure, just a minute," she said. It was early enough that Eloise was still on duty at the dispatcher's station. Alex asked her, "Any trouble overnight?"

Eloise shook her head. "No, after you quieted everything down, it stayed quiet, Chief." She added, "You look nice today."

Alex smiled briefly. "Thanks." She looked at Ruiz and nodded toward her office. "Come on, Ed."

Once they were in the office, Ruiz said, "I just wanted you to know that we've already had an emergency meeting this morning, and the council voted to authorize the curfew. And we, uh, put yesterday's date on the paperwork."

Alex raised her eyebrows. "That's putting your ass on the line to cover mine, Ed," she told him bluntly.

"Maybe, but you're our police chief and you're trying to do what's best for the town, so the council thinks you deserve our support."

She noticed that he didn't say the council had voted unanimously to take the action they had. She wasn't sure which way Ed had voted. But he was willing to along with what the council decided and deliver the news to her, and she had to give him credit for that.

"Thank you," she said, and meant it. "I appreciate that more than you and the other council members know. I just hope this mess is over soon."

"It's not going to end well," Ruiz warned. "Not for Pete McNamara, anyway."

Alex sighed, nodded, and said, "I'm afraid you're right."

* * *

When she came into the courtroom forty-five minutes later, the first thing she noticed was that Joe Gutierrez and Dave Rutherford were sitting alone at the defense table with Pete McNamara. The crowd from the previous two days was gone.

Alex went to the railing, leaned over it, and called, "Dave."

Rutherford turned around to look at her. His expression was grim as he stood up and stepped over to the railing.

"What happened to all the lawyers from the gun manufacturer?" she asked.

Rutherford shook his head. "They've cut and run."

Alex stared at him in disbelief. "They're not even going to defend against the suit?"

"Word is that they're having a settlement conference with one of Cochrum's associates later today. They'll fight for a non-liability clause, but other than that they're going to roll over and give Navarre whatever he wants."

"My God," Alex murmured. "So you and Joe are the only ones still fighting?"

"That's right . . . and I advised Ed that it might be best to explore the possibility of the city settling, too."

"No! You can't. Everybody else has already deserted Pete."

A rueful smile appeared on Rutherford's face. "Don't worry. Ed showed more backbone than I thought he would, although I'd deny under oath that I ever said that. He said fight it out to the end, so that's what I'm going to do."

"Well . . . good. Somebody needs to keep fighting."

"Even though it's a lost cause?"

"Do you really believe that?"

"After that press conference Cochrum and Ms. Encinal held yesterday, we don't have a chance in hell," Rutherford said, lowering his voice so that only Alex could hear.

Her heart sank at hearing it put into words like that. She said, "I hope you're wrong," and put her hand on Rutherford's arm for a second to give it an encouraging squeeze. Then she went back out into the hall to wait and see what happened.

The morning was mostly a rehash of what had gone before, with Alex and the other officers being called to the stand to testify as to what they had seen and done on the night in question. Cochrum asked each of them two questions in cross-examination:

"Did you see the gun allegedly belonging to my client in his hand at any time?"

And, "Did tests indicate that the gun allegedly belonging to my client had been fired on the night in question?"

The answer to both questions was no, of course.

By the time the trial resumed after lunch, the only thing that was left was for the defense to call Pete McNamara to the stand to testify in his own behalf.

Rutherford told Alex later, "Cochrum's cross-examination was awful. He never badgered Pete or anything like that that might have made him sympathetic to the jury. No, Cochrum was as polite and respectful as he could be. And he *still* made Pete seem like a doddering old fool who didn't really know what happened that night and never should have had a gun in the house in the first place. It was terrible, Alex. You could see that the jury was actually sorry for Pete . . . but they blamed him for what happened, anyway."

"But what about the fact that Corona and Navarre broke into the McNamara house?"

Rutherford sighed. "Cochrum took care of that in his closing. He put all the blame on Corona. He claimed Navarre had no idea Corona planned to burglarize the house. He said the only reason Navarre went inside was to try to talk Corona out of it. Then Pete busted in and started shooting with no warning, and for no good reason. Navarre claims that they both called out for Pete not to shoot and tried to surrender."

"But Navarre never took the stand and testified to any of that!"

"Of course not. That would have opened him up to cross-examination."

"Cochrum can't get that sort of thing in during a closing statement, can he?"

"Joe and I both objected. Judge Carson overruled us."

Alex looked around the courthouse hallway where they were sitting, waiting for the jury to return with a verdict, but she wasn't really seeing her surroundings. She was too stunned by everything Rutherford had just told her.

"The fix is in," she muttered.

"You'd better not say that in there," Rutherford

warned. "The judge will hold you in contempt of court."

"But it is, isn't it?"

Rutherford shrugged. "I honestly don't think so. I believe that Judge Carson is just so dedicated to his liberal ideals that he's willing to cut someone like Navarre any break that he possibly can. His instructions to the jury practically told them they had to find in Navarre's favor."

"Well, it's just crazy."

"How many times have you said or thought that since this whole thing started?"

"Too many," Alex admitted.

"The only silver lining—and it's a small one—is that they never really made any sort of case against the city. You and your people handled everything strictly by the book and made sure that Navarre's rights were protected every step of the way."

"You don't know how hard it was to do that, either," Alex said.

"I can imagine. But maybe we're going to dodge the bullet on this one, at least liability-wise." Rutherford winced. "That was a poor choice of words, wasn't it?"

Alex looked down the hall to the chairs where Pete McNamara and Joe Gutierrez sat side by side. Joe was trying to talk to his client, but Pete's head was down and he didn't appear to be paying attention. He looked like he was in shock, the same way he had looked ever since that tragic night.

"Nobody's dodged the bullet," she whispered. "Least of all Pete."

Rutherford shrugged and was about to say

something else when the courtroom door opened and a bailiff stuck his head out.

"Jury's back," he called.

That started an immediate hubbub and a rush toward the courtroom.

"Isn't that awfully fast?" Alex asked Rutherford as they stood up.

The city attorney nodded. "Very fast. A little less than an hour."

"Is that a good sign or a bad one?"

"When you got whipped like our side did, all signs are bad."

Alex hoped that wasn't true, but she suspected Rutherford was right.

She was allowed to be in the courtroom while court was in session now, since the case was in the hands of the jury. Along with the other witnesses, a gaggle of reporters, and as many spectators could squeeze in, they crowded the courtroom while the jury was brought back in. The twelve men and women looked solemn and not the least bit happy, as if they had just performed an unpleasant task that left a bad taste in their mouths.

One of the bailiffs called on everyone to rise. Judge Carson came in and took his seat on the bench. When everyone had settled down again and an air of tense expectancy gripped the courtroom, Carson called on the jury foreman to rise.

"Has the jury reached a verdict in the matter before the court, the case of Navarre versus McNamara and the City of Home?"

Alex noted that the gun manufacturer had indeed been dropped from the lawsuit. They must have paid off handsomely for that, she thought.

The jury foreman nodded and said, "Yes, Your Honor, we have."

Carson looked at Pete McNamara. "The defendant will please rise."

Slowly, painfully, the old man climbed to his feet. Gutierrez and Rutherford flanked him.

"What is your verdict?"

The jury foreman took a deep breath. "We find in favor of the plaintiff, Emilio Navarre."

Even though that was expected, hearing it caused a loud reaction from the crowd in the courtroom. Angrily, Carson gaveled for silence. When he finally got it, he turned again to the jury foreman.

"Do you find liability on the part of both defendants?"

"We do, Your Honor."

"And in the matter of damages?"

"We recommend that the plaintiff be awarded actual damages of one million dollars and punitive damages of five million dollars."

The courtroom erupted again. Alex felt sick to her stomach. She had seen Pete McNamara flinch with every word spoken. With every flinch, he seemed to shrink.

Beside him, Dave Rutherford looked stunned. Rutherford had at least held out some hope that his client, the city, would escape from the self-righteous liberal wrath. Now that hope had been dashed.

It took a while for the courtroom to quiet down again. When it had, Judge Carson told the jury members, "Your recommendation in the matter of damages will be taken into account. The court thanks you for your service, and you are dismissed." He picked up his gavel. "These proceedings will resume at nine o'clock tomorrow morning and take up the matter of damages and the final disposition of the case. Until then, court is adjourned."

Before the gavel could fall, though, Pete McNamara lifted his head and asked, "Don't I get to say anything?"

A smirking Clayton Cochrum, who had been shaking Navarre's hand and slapping him on the back, shot to his feet. "Your Honor, the defendant had his chance to testify earlier. Allowing him to speak now would be highly irregular."

"Don't tell me how to run my court, counselor," Carson snapped. "But Mr. Cochrum is correct, Mr. McNamara. Testimony is over. You'll have a chance to speak your piece again during the next phase of the trial, during which damages will be awarded to the plaintiff."

"So nothin' can change the fact that I've been found guilty? That's over and done with?"

"I'm afraid so."

McNamara shook off Joe Gutierrez's warning hand on his arm. "Well, I don't have much money, so it don't really matter what I say, does it? I lost my wife, and you can't do anything worse than that to me. None of you can." He pointed at Navarre, who sneered at him. "That son of a bitch and his buddy already done it. They killed my wife, the damn thieves."

"Counselor, you'd better get your client under control," Carson barked at Gutierrez. "If you don't, he's going to be found in contempt of court."

"Oh, I got plenty of contempt," McNamara lashed out, and a cheer came from many of the spectators. Alex felt like cheering herself as this old man, who had been beaten down so unfairly, found the strength somewhere deep inside to stand up against the evil that had come down on him, futile though the fight might be. "I got contempt for you, Judge, and for that rattlesnake of a lawyer, and for that ugly monster who calls hisself human." He waved an arm toward the eagerly watching reporters. "I got contempt for them coyotes who call themselves the press. They done made me out to be the bad guy here." McNamara's voice broke. "Me, the man who's lost everything that mattered to him, includin' his good name—"

He broke off with a strangled sound and took a stumbling step forward. "Pete!" Gutierrez said as McNamara slumped over the defense table. "Pete!"

McNamara slid off the table and fell to the floor in a limp heap as shouts and screams filled the courtroom. Alex saw Judge Carson hammering frantically on the bench with his gavel, but she couldn't hear anything over the tumult of the shocked spectators and the roaring that filled her own head.

CHAPTER 23

"The doctors are sure it was a stroke?" Alex asked as she stood in the hospital corridor with Joe Gutierrez and Dave Rutherford.

Joe nodded. "Yeah. They think there's a good chance Pete won't ever regain consciousness. And even if he does . . ." The lawyer shrugged as his voice trailed off.

"There's so much damage to his brain that he'll never recover," Rutherford finished what his colleague couldn't bring himself to say.

For a long moment, Alex didn't say anything. Then, "I know it's terrible to feel this way, but maybe it's for the best. My dad always said that going fast was like winning the senior citizens' lottery. And after everything Pete's gone through, he probably wouldn't have wanted to live."

"Maybe not, but he shouldn't have been hounded to death by scum like Cochrum," Joe said angrily.

"He's not dead yet," Rutherford pointed out, "and this is going to throw the whole legal situation into limbo."

"I'm filing an appeal. Judge Carson gave us

plenty of grounds in his instructions to the jury. He was clearly prejudicial."

"And the way the courts have been packed by the liberals in the past dozen years, do you really think that's going to do any good?"

Alex held up her hands. "You two can wrangle out the legal issues later," she said. "For now, what do we need to do for Pete?"

Joe shrugged again. "There's nothing we *can* do for him. It's all up to the doctors now . . . and to El *Señor Dios,* as my grandmother would say."

Alex nodded. "All right, then. I'm heading back to Home. The news of the verdict and Pete's stroke is bound to have gotten there by now, and it's liable to make the trouble last night look like nothing."

"Maybe I'd better go, too," Rutherford said, "in case the mayor needs my legal advice on anything."

"Both of you go," Joe said. "I'll stay here and look out for Pete's best interests, whatever they may be."

They said their farewell, and Alex and Rutherford headed for the elevator used by hospital personnel that they had come up in earlier. Local police from the county seat were posted in the corridors to keep the media and everybody else away from the ICU.

There was a mob on the lawn in front of the hospital, too. Everybody in town knew Pete McNamara had collapsed at the conclusion of the trial, and most of them knew he had been brought here. *Damn gawkers,* Alex thought as she circled the sprawling building in her car and headed out of town on the state highway.

It was just human nature, though, to stop and

stare at a tragedy . . . and there was no other word to describe this situation.

She turned on the radio as she drove, and the first thing she heard was Clayton Cochrum's oily voice saying, ". . . regret that Mr. McNamara was stricken. Mr. Navarre also wants it known that he bears no personal ill will toward Mr. McNamara and wishes him a complete and speedy recovery."

"Oh, barf," Alex muttered.

The press conference was probably live, not on tape. Reporters shouted questions at Cochrum, their voices blending together. After a moment, Cochrum must have singled out one of them, because a woman's voice rose and asked, "What effect does this have on the verdict reached by the jury today?"

"None whatsoever," Cochrum replied without hesitation. "That verdict stands. Of course, under the circumstances, my client and I will not press for any hurried disposition of the damages phase of the trial until Mr. McNamara has recovered."

"What if he doesn't recover?" another reporter asked. "He's in critical condition, according to our sources at the hospital."

"Then in due time, we'll deal with his estate."

"What about the other settlements, the ones with the federal government and the gun company?"

"Those negotiations are proceeding, and announcements will be made shortly concerning them."

"Do you feel that your client has been vindicated?"

Cochrum laughed. "Well, of course, I do. The jury sent a clear message today, don't you think?"

"What about the criminal charges still pending against him?"

"I filed a motion a short time ago to have them dismissed. It'll be up to District Attorney Hobson to decide whether to go forward with them."

Alex had a pretty good idea what Everett Hobson would decide, too. It might not be impossible to try Emilio Navarre now . . . but it was mighty close to it.

For the first time in her life, thoughts of vigilante justice flickered through Alex's brain. She was a cop, she had dedicated her life to law and order. . . .

But right about now, she knew how soul satisfying it would be to put a bullet through Navarre's head and splatter his evil brains all over the wall.

She shoved the thought away. "Don't you do that, Alex," she whispered to herself. "Don't you ever."

When people were pushed far enough, though . . . when pure evil flaunted itself right in their faces and dared them to do something about it . . . well, she could understand why some folks reacted the way they did. She might not condone it, but she could understand it.

It was suppertime when she got back to Home, normally a quiet time of day. Not today, though. The streets were jammed with cars, and even more people were on the sidewalks and in the parking lots than there had been the night before. And every face wore an angry expression, too.

She had sent Clint and Delgado back here before she ever started to the hospital in the county seat, so they were already on duty, thank goodness.

So were all the other members of her department, and some deputies from the sheriff's office were on hand, too. Alex was in her personal car, but it had a radio in it. She picked up the mike, keyed it, and said, "Jimmy, are you there?"

"Right here, Chief," the dispatcher answered immediately. "Where are . . . you?"

"Just driving into town. Trying to, anyway." Traffic had slowed to a standstill. Alex thought about getting the portable flashing light from the glove compartment and putting it on top of the car, but she realized that wouldn't do any good. The vehicles ahead of her didn't have anywhere to go to get out of her way.

Instead she turned onto a side street and figured she would wind her way through the back roads if she had to. She went on, "Tell me what's happening. Any trouble so far?"

"Not so . . . far," Jimmy replied. "Just lots of folks . . . millin' around. They're really . . . mad about Pete, Chief."

"I know, Jimmy," she said. "I am, too. Is everybody out on patrol?"

"Yeah. I can . . . go out, too, if you . . . need me to. I can get Eloise . . . to come in early."

"No, you stay right where you are. I need you there at the station. Got it?"

"You bet."

Alex relaxed, but only slightly. "I'll be there in a little while. Hold down the fort until then, okay?"

"Okay, Chief."

Alex put the mike back on its clip and took her cell phone from her purse. She didn't have to look at it to speed-dial her house.

Jack answered after one ring, and Alex felt relief go through her. "You're there," she said.

"Of course, I'm here," he replied. "Where did you think I would be, after I got in so much trouble last night?"

"You came straight home after practice?"

"We didn't have practice. Coach canceled it. He'd heard about Mr. McNamara, like everybody else in town."

"Did the other boys go home, too?"

"I don't know. Rowdy and Steve are here with me, though. We've been playing video games."

"Good. Keep them there, if you can. You boys don't need to be out on the street tonight. Can you rustle up something for the three of you to eat? I don't have any idea when I'll be able to get home."

"Look, Mom, don't worry about us, okay?" Jack said. "We'll be fine. Just go do your job."

"All right." She had reached the back parking lot of the police station. As she pulled into it, she added, "You know, you're a good kid when you want to be."

Jack snorted. "Yeah, yeah." He paused. "Just be careful, all right? People were upset last night, but now they're *really* mad."

"You don't have to tell me. I'll see you later. Don't wait up."

But he probably would, Alex thought as she went into the station.

That's the kind of kid he was.

Chapter 24

Alex went in through the back door and up to the front of the building, where Jimmy gave her a huge grin.

"Now I know that everything . . . will be all right. The chief is . . . back."

Alex returned the smile. "I hope I live up to that faith you have in me, Jimmy. I'm going to get my uniform on."

She came out of her office a few minutes later, feeling glad to have the gun on her hip again.

"How's Mr. McNamara?" Jimmy asked.

Alex shook her head sadly. "Not too good. He's really sick, Jimmy. He may not get well."

"I'm gonna . . . pray for him."

"That's a good idea." She pushed open the front door and paused. "Say one for the rest of us while you're at it, why don't you?"

She had a feeling they could use all the help they could get this evening.

She wasn't going to take a car out, not with the streets hopelessly jammed like they were. Instead she set out on foot, using her portable radio to check in with the other officers as she made her way downtown.

One by one they reported in and gave her their locations. Delgado was at the supermarket where the brawl had broken out the night before. Clint was on the corner where a farm-to-market road crossed the state highway at the very center of town. There were two convenience stores, the bank, and an insurance office at that intersection, along with a mob of angry people, Clint informed her. Jerry, Lester, Betsy, and Antonio were scattered around town, at the lumberyard, the hospital, the Dairy Queen, and Sally's Steak House, respectively. The sheriff's deputies were using the same frequency, and they called in as well, letting Alex know that they were at the hardware store, the auto supply store, the propane company, and the telephone company offices.

Between them, they had the town pretty well covered, Alex thought. No matter where trouble broke out—if trouble broke out—an officer wouldn't be too far away.

She hoped she was wrong, but she had a feeling there was no *if* about it.

As she made her way along the street, a lot of people stopped her to ask her if she'd heard anything more about Pete McNamara. When she told them she hadn't, they expressed their anger about the whole situation.

"I hear you," Alex said each time. "I feel the same way. But it won't help Pete or anybody else to cause trouble."

"We didn't start it, Chief," more than one person protested, using similar words to lambaste the politicians, the media, and everybody else who had completely lost touch with the regular people of the country.

Something Alex didn't see were the news trucks with the dishes on their roofs for their satellite uplinks. The media seemed to be avoiding Home this evening. Maybe for once they were acting half as smart as they claimed to be. When night fell, she began to hope that maybe people would start to return to their homes now that they had blown off some steam. Maybe she and the officers could actually skate by tonight without any real trouble.

In the back of her mind, though, she knew that was too much to hope for, and sure enough, around seven o'clock hordes of people began to stream toward the western edge of town as if they had all heard some sort of announcement.

Alex grabbed a man's arm as he went past her and stopped him. "Where's everybody going?" she asked.

"I heard that there's gonna be a prayer rally at the high school football field for Pete," the man replied. "Haven't you heard about it, Chief?"

"Not until now," Alex said. She let the man go.

This might be a good thing, she told herself. Get everybody in the stadium instead of milling around the streets. Praying was bound to calm them down a little.

She looked toward the high school and saw the big lights on their tall standards around the football field flicker on as somebody threw a switch.

How much trouble could a prayer rally cause, anyway?

But still, she knew she needed to be there. She

joined the crowds headed in that direction, feeling a little like a lemming, and used the radio to tell her officers to converge on the football field.

Despite all the terrible things going on in this part of the country, and all around the world as well, it was a beautiful evening. The sun was going down and lighting up the sky with a glorious display of red, gold, and orange against a backdrop of deep blue, and the air was pleasantly warm with just a hint of welcome coolness. Alex found it somehow reassuring that while people could do their best to mess things up for themselves and everyone else, somehow the world kept turning and there was plenty of beauty if you knew where to look for it.

She had attended scores of high school football games over the years, sometimes on duty and sometimes not, and that's what this felt like, she thought as she watched people streaming into the stadium adjacent to the high school campus. There were still some loud, angry voices to be heard, but for the most part people seemed to be calming down, as Alex had hoped would happen. A certain solemnity took hold when people gathered to pray. It made them realize that there were things bigger than this world.

Alex climbed to the top of the bleachers, just below the press box, and looked out over the crowd, searching for any signs of trouble. Thankfully, she didn't see any. Down at the bottom of the stands, just in front of the first row of seats, a couple of men were setting up a portable public address system. Alex recognized them as the pastors from the local Baptist and Methodist churches. Evidently they were going to use the portable PA, rather than the stadium's sound system. That was probably so they could walk up and down while they were praying. Alex hadn't seen too many preachers who were good at standing still, she thought with a faint smile. The spirit moved them.

Standing up high like this, Alex could see for a long way over the flat West Texas landscape. Her gaze followed the state highway toward the county seat. A frown creased her forehead as she saw a lot of headlights coming toward Home. That didn't have to mean anything, but worry stirred inside her anyway.

She saw her officers standing here and there in the bleachers. The sheriff's deputies had stayed over in the business district, just in case anything happened there. They were all ready for trouble, but with a crowd this size, and emotions running as high as they were . . .

Alex didn't like to think about the sort of things that might happen in circumstances like that.

Her nerves stretched even tighter when she saw a dozen vehicles turn off the highway into the stadium parking lot. The lot wasn't full, since most of the people had walked here, so the newcomers were able to get in. The sun had set, but enough dusky light remained in the sky for Alex to pick out the shapes of satellite dishes on top of some of the trucks.

The media had arrived.

They had just been biding their time, she realized, waiting for the situation in Home to get tense enough that something might happen. They were like buzzards, she thought, scavengers feeding off human misery. She didn't want them in her town.

She couldn't stop them from flocking to tragedy, though. Nobody could. And if they were here only to report, it wouldn't be so bad. That wouldn't be the case. They would try to mold and shape the thinking of their viewers according to their own warped perspective on the world, where everything America did was bad, every problem could be solved by raising taxes, and regular people were morons who were so stupid that they needed the federal government to take care of them from the cradle to the grave. That was the media's version of Utopia, and nothing could shake them from that belief, which they held with a religious fervor that put that of regular Christians to shame. Big government was the left's religion.

"The reporters are here," Alex said into her mike as she started down from the top of the bleachers. "Keep your eyes open. I'm going to talk to them."

She wanted to persuade the news crews to leave people alone while they were praying. It probably wouldn't do any good, but she felt like she had to try.

Alex reached the bottom of the bleachers, turned and went down a ramp into the area underneath the stands. As she did that, the Baptist minister began leading the crowd in a prayer for Pete McNamara.

The first of the reporters to get set up was coming toward the ramp, carrying a microphone and trailed by her cameraman and a light man. It was the arrogant blonde who had clashed with Jack, Rowdy, and Steve the night before, Alex realized.

She held up a hand to stop the advancing trio. "That's far enough," she said.

"You can't stop us, Chief," the blonde said. "This is public property and a public gathering."

"Actually, it's not," Alex shot back. "This stadium belongs to the school district."

"Which is financed by taxes, which makes it public property."

"*You* don't pay school taxes here," Alex pointed out. "Anyway, people are praying up there, and it's just common courtesy not to bother them."

The blonde shook her head stubbornly. "We have a right to cover this event . . . especially since it sounds like whoever is speaking is inciting these people to riot."

Alex turned her head to listen to the words coming from the portable PA system. The minister was saying, "—smite down the evildoers, Lord, and show them the error of their unholy ways."

"He's not inciting anything," she told the reporter. "He's praying, that's all."

"It's a call for violence against immigrants," the blonde insisted. "Anyone can see that. That so-called man of God is telling his redneck followers to ignore the verdict fairly delivered by our legal system and seek vengeance on Emilio Navarre."

Alex could only stare at her in disbelief. "You're crazy," she finally said. "How do you get that out of a prayer?"

The reporter's chin jutted out contemptuously. "I know what I hear with my own ears, Chief. Are you sure you want to go on record as supporting a plea for vigilante injustice?"

Alex felt like tearing her hair out in frustration. How could you talk sense to these people? To them, day was night, up was down, and the sky was the color they said it was. They screamed about other people's intolerance and bigotry and had no clue about their own.

Several other news crews had come up behind the blonde. They wanted to crowd up the ramp, and Alex's presence was the only thing keeping them from doing so. She felt a little overwhelmed, but she stood strong. If they were going to disrupt this prayer rally, they would have to trample over her to do so.

And she wasn't going to let that happen. She put her hand on the butt of her pistol and said, "All of you clear out now, or I'm going to arrest every one of you for trespassing and disturbing the peace."

The blonde smirked. "The courts will never let you get away with an unconstitutional action like that."

"Maybe not, but you'll spend some time in our holding cells anyway. And with this big a crowd, it won't be a very pleasant experience for you." Alex couldn't resist adding, "You might even get your hair mussed."

The standoff stretched out for a moment. Alex had no idea how it was going to end, but she had a hunch that it wouldn't be good.

It was even worse than she expected, as the sudden roar of a shotgun filled the night.

CHAPTER 25

At the sound of the shot, the blonde screamed and jumped. Clearly she had never done any reporting from a war zone.

Alex reacted instantly, too, but not in panic. She drew her weapon, shouted, "Everybody on the ground!" and started looking for the shooter.

The coiffed and manicured on-air talent all scurried for cover. The cameramen and technicians conducted themselves in a more professional manner, crouching in hopes of avoiding any flying bullets, but continuing to tape what was going on around them.

Alex rushed past them. The shotgun boomed again, and she could tell that the sound came from the small parking lot in front of the stadium, next to the ticket booth, the athletic director's office, and the field house. That was where the line of satellite trucks had come to a halt.

Alex saw that the dishes on top of the first two trucks had been blasted by buckshot and heavily damaged. The man holding the shotgun pumped another shell into the chamber and took aim at the dish on top of the third truck. Alex didn't recognize him from the back. All she could tell was that he wore blue jeans, a flannel shirt with the sleeves rolled up, and a gimme cap.

Before he could pull the shotgun's trigger for the third time, she shouted, "Hold it! Drop that gun! Get on the ground!"

She had her own pistol leveled at him. If he swung around and pointed the shotgun at her, she would shoot him. No doubt about it.

Instead, he looked back over his shoulder at her and grinned. "Oh, hey, Chief! These suckers can't broadcast their bullshit without any antennas, can they?"

She recognized Billy Squires. He had gotten in the occasional drunken brawl in the past, but had never caused any real trouble until now. He sounded like he'd been drinking this evening.

"Billy, put that gun down," Alex ordered. "You can't go around shooting up TV trucks. You know better than that."

From somewhere behind her, she heard the blonde's voice. "I should have known whoever it was shooting would be a friend of yours, Chief. You're always quick to excuse violence when it's being done by your cronies, aren't you?"

Alex ignored the taunt. She just wanted Billy to put the gun down so she could take him into custody and put an end to this debacle that was probably being broadcast live all over the country.

Billy looked sort of hurt, like a little kid who'd been reprimanded when he didn't think he was doing anything wrong. "Aw, Chief," he said, "you shouldn't take up for these people. They come in here and they spread all those lies about us, and they don't give a damn about poor Pete." Billy wasn't grinning now. He sniffled a little. "Pete was a good guy. He coached my Little League team ten years ago. What happened to him was *wrong*."

Alex couldn't argue with that. "I know," she said, "but shooting those satellite dishes isn't going to change anything. You know that, Billy."

By now people who had been praying along with the pastor had flocked down from the stands to see what was going on. Alex could sense hundreds, maybe even thousands of eyes on her. Millions if you counted the ones watching on TV.

Billy sighed and lowered the shotgun. He started to turn toward Alex.

"All right, Chief," he said. "If that's the way you want—"

The blonde screamed. "That redneck madman's going to kill us all!" she cried.

People on the outskirts of the crowd couldn't see what was going on. The reporter's panicked screech sent them stampeding for cover. As panic always did, it spread rapidly, and within a heartbeat, the area under the stands was a seething mass of frightened people.

Alex ran toward Billy, grabbed the shotgun out of his hands, and kicked his legs out from under him. "Stay down!" she told him as he fell to the ground.

Alex turned toward the chaos and shouted, "Stop it! Settle down! Nobody's in danger!"

Most of the people didn't hear her. The ones who did ignored her.

Alex saw the blond reporter giving her a sly, triumphant smile. The blonde hadn't panicked at all.

The whole thing had been an act, calculated to set off something that they could propagandize as yet another redneck riot.

She had been successful, too. Things were out of control, and Alex didn't have enough people on hand to settle them down. All she could do was let it play out and hope that nobody was hurt too badly in the stampede.

From the ground at her feet, Billy Squires said sheepishly, "I screwed up, didn't I?"

"Yeah, Billy, you did," Alex said without looking down at him. "Big-time."

It was a little surprising how quickly the crowd dispersed. Since people had walked to the stadium, they were able to walk away, so there wasn't the usual Friday night post-game traffic jam as folks tried to get their cars out of the parking lot.

Despite the best efforts of Alex and her officers, there were several shouting matches between townspeople and news crews. Fists were clenched, but no punches were thrown, at least not as far as Alex knew. She thought they had gotten off lucky.

That wasn't the way it sounded by the time she got back to the police station with Billy Squires in handcuffs. As Alex came in, Eloise pointed to the TV set mounted on the wall. A cable news talking head was saying, "—another outbreak of violence in Home, Texas, tonight, scene of massive anti-immigrant protests in recent days and also the place where a man was shot to death earlier this summer for being in the wrong place at the wrong time."

A bold graphic at the bottom of the screen read TEXAS SHOOTING SPREE—ATTACK ON PRESS.

The news anchor continued, "At another anti-immigrant rally held tonight in Home, one of the gun-toting citizens opened fire on news crews from this network and others, attempting to murder them with a shotgun. Here's footage of some of the damage done to news trucks by stray gunfire as the assailant tried to mow down reporters and cameramen."

"Wait a minute," Billy said. "I didn't shoot at nobody. I just shot up them antennas."

"Billy Squires, did you do that?" Eloise asked. "Shame on you!"

Alex motioned for both of them to be quiet. On TV, the camera panned across the two ruined satellite dishes, then the footage immediately cut to close-ups of gun racks in several pickups, showing rifles and shotguns hanging on them.

The implication was obvious. Home was full of gun-toting lunatics who would open fire at anything that moved.

The cameraman hadn't been content with that slanted image, however. Next the round face of the local Baptist pastor leaped onto the screen as he prayed for God to smite the evildoers. His face was flushed and covered with beads of sweat. To viewers on both coasts, the message would be clear: Home, Texas, wasn't just full of gun-nuts. It was full of religious fanatics, too.

A bitter taste filled Alex's mouth. Liberal spin,

half-truths, and outright lies . . . those were the media's stock in trade these days.

Betsy Carlyle came into the station. Alex took hold of Billy's arm and gave him a gentle push toward her. "Betsy, would you put Mr. Squires in one of the holding cells?"

"Sure, Alex." Betsy nodded toward the TV. "The story's all over the radio, too. They're sure makin' us look bad."

"Nothing new about that."

"Yeah, but it's not right." Betsy took hold of Billy's arm. "Come on, you."

"Didn't we go to high school together?" Billy asked the petite, redheaded officer.

"You really are drunk, aren't you? We dated for two months in tenth grade, you damn fool."

Billy's face lit up in a grin. "Oh, yeah! I remember you now. Lil' Betsy. We went out to Fletcher's stock tank one night and—"

She shoved him down the hall and into the holding cell before he could continue reminiscing.

"What happens now, boss?" Eloise asked Alex as she leaned on the counter.

Alex sighed wearily. "I'm hoping it's all over. The news media will smirk at us for a few days, then move on to whatever the next big story is."

"What about Pete?"

Alex shook her head. "He probably won't make it."

"And that man Navarre?"

"Out of our hands now," Alex said. "He won his court case, and he'll collect his millions from the federal government and the gun manufacturer. He won't get much from Pete's estate, though. There won't be much there."

"What about the criminal charges against him?"

Alex grimaced. "I'm betting that Everett Hobson will practically break his neck getting into court tomorrow morning and asking that the charges against Navarre be dropped. The slimy lawyer of his made an end run right around justice."

"That's a real shame," Eloise said as she shook her head. "It's just not right."

"No, it's not," Alex agreed. "I just hope this fuss tonight was the last of it. I'd like to see the town get back to normal. We've had enough trouble."

Now, she thought, if everybody else would just go along with that . . .

"It's extraordinary, isn't it, Carl, for the President to comment directly on a civil settlement reached by the government?"

"That's right, Roberta, but the rumor going around Washington today is that the President will have a major announcement to make regarding the Navarre settlement. So far there's no hint of what that announcement might be, but sources close to White House Chief of Staff Geoffrey St. John indicate that it's something very important to the President. He—"

"Excuse me, Carl, but we go now live to the Oval Office."

"My fellow Americans, good afternoon. The past few days I've been very troubled, and no doubt you have, too, by the continuing reports of violence that threatens to spiral out of control in the Texas town of Home. Racial unrest and disrespect for law and order and our justice system, aggravated by a court decision in favor of a Mexican national gunned down for no discernible reason by an elderly citizen of Home who had amassed an arsenal of weapons in his house, has spawned several riots and

near-riots in the community, culminating last night in an attack by shotgun-wielding vigilantes on gallant members of the media attempting to uphold the constitutional rights of a free press. These unconscionable actions, to which local and state authorities have turned a blind eye, leave me with no choice but to step in.

"In addition, the federal government, in its recent settlement with Mr. Emilio Navarre, one of the victims of the unwarranted attack earlier this summer that left him severely wounded and killed his best friend, has agreed to take action which will insure that no one else will meet such a tragic fate, at least in Home, Texas.

"Therefore, as of noon today, I am placing Home, Texas, and an area for ten miles around the geographical center of the town, under federal martial law, to be enforced by the newly-created Federal Protective Service, which was commissioned by Congress to serve as a national police force in times of emergency.

"If, like I have, you've watched the news reports recently, you know that the situation in Home constitutes an emergency, and a grave one, at that.

"Pursuant to the Executive Order I signed less than an hour ago placing Home under martial law, all citizens of Home and the surrounding area will be required to surrender, temporarily, any firearms in their possession, until order is restored. This Executive Order applies to all citizens and all types of firearms. None are exempted except the members of Home's police force, who will be allowed to keep their weapons, at least for the time being.

"There will be those argue that disarming an entire town like this is unconstitutional, but I would point out that as President, the Constitution gives me broad and sweeping powers to deal with emergency situations, and I believe that the easy availability of guns has fueled

the discontent in Home until something must be done. The temporary suspension of rights granted by the Constitution is within the scope of my power, according to both the Attorney General and the Solicitor General of the United States.

"Therefore, I call on the citizens of Home and the surrounding area to peacefully surrender your firearms. Representatives of the Federal Protective Service are now on hand in Home and will be glad to take charge of your weapons for you. Refusal to surrender your arms will be considered a breach of martial law and will be dealt with accordingly, to the full extent allowable under the terms of this Executive Order.

"My fellow Americans, I promise you that I do not take these actions lightly or without careful, reasoned consideration. I know they are extreme, and I know they will not sit well with many of you. But this is the only way, and it's for the good of the country. The violence must be stopped, and stopped now.

"Now, I call directly on the citizens of Home. Surrender your firearms. Cooperate with the Federal Protective Service. They're there to help you and keep you safe. If you fail to cooperate and comply with the Executive Order, you will be arrested, you will be prosecuted, and you will face the consequences of defying the federal government. Choose wisely, citizens of Home.

"Your fate is in your own hands."

"What do you think, Geoff?"

"The instant poll numbers are good, Mr. President. It's certainly a bold move, and it seems to be playing well with the electorate, although there are a few holdouts who are clinging to the view that it's unconstitutional."

"Those people do love to cling to their God and their guns, don't they? Well, they're just going to have to learn to accept that those days are over. This is just the beginning, Geoff, just the beginning. We're going to get the guns out of the hands of every right-wing fanatic out there, mark my words."

"I agree with you, of course, sir . . ."

"But? I sense a but, Geoff."

"Some of those people aren't going to cooperate, sir."

"Well . . . that's why we have Casa del Diablo, isn't it?"

Chapter 26

It was eleven o'clock in the morning—noon, Washington time—and Alex was in her office at the police station wondering if she was ever going to get any work done. The phone rang every couple of minutes, as reporters from all over the country called wanting some comments on the "anti-immigrant riots and out-of-control violence" that had erupted in Home.

None of them wanted to hear it when she told them there hadn't been any riots or any out-of-control violence. They just kept asking questions as if the scenario they had laid out was completely correct. The truth didn't interest them.

So she had started saying she couldn't comment on matters that were still under investigation, although the last few times she'd been more curt and just said, "No comment." She was considering telling Jimmy to tell callers she wasn't here. She didn't want to do that unless she absolutely had to, though. She had always prided herself on being available to the people she served.

So she already felt pretty tense and impatient

when Jimmy called through the open doorway of her office, "Delgado's on the . . . radio, Chief. Sounds like we've got more . . . trouble."

Alex sighed as she got up and went out to the dispatch station. She took the microphone from Jimmy and keyed it. "What's up, J. P.?"

"The cavalry's here," Delgado's voice came back over the speaker. "Or rather, the Federal Protective Service."

"It looks like a damn invasion, Chief." Delgado sounded angry and worried at the same time. "They've got armored cars and personnel carriers. We're about to have a full-fledged panic on our hands again as people hear about this."

"Where are you?"

"At the high school. They're setting up a command post on the parking lot."

"Son of a—" Alex swallowed the rest of the exclamation. "I'm on my way."

Jack was at the school, she thought as a cold chill went down her back. And so were several hundred other kids.

Alex tossed the microphone back to Jimmy and said, "Call in everybody who's off duty. Lester works patrol. Everybody else meet at the high school, ASAP."

"Got it, Chief." Jimmy began barking the call over the radio. When trouble broke out, he was able to lose some of the halting pattern to his speech.

Alex ran out to her car and headed for the school with lights flashing and siren blaring. As she approached the campus, she saw that Delgado was right. A dozen black SUVs were parked in the lot, along with four deuce-and-a-half trucks of the sort used to carry troops and a couple of armored cars with— Good Lord, Alex thought as her eyes widened in shock. Were those *machine guns* mounted on the vehicles?

Yes, she realized. Those were machine guns.

Like most people in law enforcement, as well as civilians who actually paid attention to what was going on in Washington—a dwindling number, unfortunately—Alex had heard plenty about the so-called Federal Protective Service while its formation was being debated in Congress.

The President, who was a strong backer of the idea, along with the senators who had sponsored the bill commissioning the organization, made it sound so benign and helpful. The Federal Protective Service would be a sort of national police force, available to help local authorities in times of disaster or strife. It would be better for everyone to have such extra assistance on hand, the President had mentioned several times in speeches. And there would be checks and balances on the system, because supposedly the Federal Protective Service could be called in only if local authorities requested its help.

A few politicians and commentators on the right had noticed that the actual language of the bill did, in fact, *not* make it a requirement that local authorities request aid from the FPS before it could be mobilized. Instead, the organization was to be considered part of the executive branch, which meant the President could send them in wherever and whenever he deemed it necessary. It was a perfect example of a technique perfected by the liberal politicians who had ruled Washington for the past decade or more: convince the public of one thing with a lot of lofty-sounding speeches, aided and abetted by the media, of course, when the truth was actually the direct opposite of what they claimed.

Unfortunately, one of the conservative politicians who had tried to expose this fraud had made the mistake of comparing the FPS to the Gestapo of Nazi Germany, and the media had gone ballistic, screeching nonstop about how anyone opposed to the FPS's formation was just fear mongering and, anyway, how dare anybody compare the President and Congress to a bunch of Nazis? That just wasn't called for and was an example of how people who were opposed to their policies were just evil and stupid and unpatriotic. And on and on, *ad nauseum*, as usual, cheerleading for the radical politicians they adored.

So it was no surprise that the FPS bill had passed Congress in a strict party-line vote a couple of weeks earlier, the same way every bill in this administration and the previous one had passed, and the President had signed it into law immediately, hailing it as a new step forward for the country.

Everyone involved with the FPS claimed that no one had been recruited, trained, and equipped for it yet. That process was just now supposed to be getting underway.

And yet, as Alex pulled into the high school parking lot and saw all the vehicles with hundreds of armed, black-uniformed, helmeted figures moving around them, she knew that was yet another lie from the left. A military force like this one couldn't be pulled together in a couple of weeks. It was clear to her that for all practical purposes, the FPS had existed for at least a year before the bill authorizing its creation became law.

Chances were, nobody could prove that, and even if they did, the media would ignore it, the politicians would deny it, and the gullible sheep who had put those people in office would believe whatever they were told.

Alex knew that, but the knowledge didn't make her any less angry right now. She had heavily armed personnel setting up shop in her town, and she didn't like it.

Not one damned bit.

She brought her police car to a screeching halt, got out, and started toward a huge black RV bristling with antennas. All that communications equipment told her that this was the FPS command post. It had the organization's logo emblazoned on its side: an eagle surrounded by a band of stars and also encircled by the words FEDERAL PROTECTIVE SERVICE.

A couple of men carrying assault rifles moved to block her path. "Excuse me, ma'am," one of them said. "Please state your name and your business here."

Alex bit back an angry retort. She knew how to deal with the military, and despite the idea that the FPS was supposed to be a "police" force, she recognized these men for what they were, elite shock troops.

"I'm Alex Bonner, chief of police here in Home. I'd like to speak to your commanding officer."

One of the men nodded. They wore black goggles that were attached to their helmets, so she couldn't see their eyes.

"Yes, ma'am. Colonel Grady wants to speak to you, too, and gave orders that you were to be escorted to him as soon as you arrived."

"So he knew I was coming, did he?"

"I guess he figured you'd want to know what was going on, ma'am."

"He was right about that," Alex muttered.

The two men parted, then flanked her as she walked toward the RV. Someone inside must have seen her coming—they probably had video cameras monitoring everything—because a door in the side of the vehicle opened and another black-uniformed man lowered some folding steps to the asphalt of the parking lot.

"Right this way, Chief," he said.

Alex climbed the steps into what could have passed for a control room at NASA. There were video screens and computer monitors and gauges and blinking lights everywhere. She experienced a moment of mild disorientation because it appeared that the inside of the RV was larger than its outside, which was physically impossible, of course. But that was the way it looked to her stunned eyes. Male and female technicians in black uniforms were packed into the command post.

The man who had let Alex in told her, "The colonel is right over here, ma'am." He led her to a video screen where another black-uniformed figure stood watching what was on the display. This man stood erect, with his hands clasped behind his back. He didn't wear a helmet like the others but was bareheaded instead, revealing a thatch of iron-gray hair that matched his tanned, rugged face. The soldier with Alex said, "Colonel, here's Chief Bonner."

The colonel turned to her, nodded, and extended his hand. "Chief," he said. "I'm glad to meet you. I'm Colonel Charles Grady."

Alex shook his hand. "With all due respect, Colonel, what are you and your soldiers doing here in my town?"

Grady smiled faintly. "These men and women aren't soldiers, Chief. They're officers. Police officers, just like the men and women who work for you."

Alex wanted to say *Not hardly,* but she controlled the impulse. Instead she said, "But you're a colonel. That's a military title."

Grady shrugged. "I'm a retired colonel, actually. Now I work for the Federal Protective Service. My superiors have been kind enough to allow me to keep the rank."

"Which still doesn't answer the question of what you're doing here."

"Following orders," Grady said. "I would have notified you in advance of our arrival, but those orders specified that I not do so. From one commanding officer to another, ma'am, I apologize for that."

"The President sent you here, didn't he?"

"The FPS is part of the executive branch, yes, ma'am."

Getting a straight answer from this man seemed

well-nigh impossible. Alex kept trying, though, asking through clenched teeth, "Why?"

Grady glanced at a watch strapped to his wrist and then gestured at the video screen in front of him. "I believe if you'll just watch this for a few minutes, Chief, you'll have all the answers you need."

Impatiently, Alex glanced at the screen and saw that it was showing a cable news feed. A man and a woman were talking, then a moment later, they shut up and the broadcast switched to a location Alex recognized.

The Oval Office in the White House.

The President sat behind his desk, looking as handsome and photogenic and sincere as ever. He spoke in a calm, assured, rational voice.

And yet as Alex stood there watching and listening, the world seemed to start spinning crazily around her. She couldn't believe what she was hearing. Even after all the outrageous things this president and the previous one had done and gotten away with, this new trampling of the Constitution was shocking.

When the President's speech was finished and the news anchors came back to talk about how wonderful he was and how everything he had said was right, Alex turned to Colonel Grady and said, "So you're here to take away all the guns that belong to the citizens of Home."

"And the surrounding area, yes, ma'am," Grady replied. "Those are our orders."

"You can't do that."

"Actually, Chief, we can. The area is now under martial law. Technically, you no longer have any authority here." Grady smiled. "However, for the sake of the public good and to make the entire process run smoother, I'm asking you and your force to cooperate. The citizens are much more likely to comply peacefully with the order if they see that their own police force thinks it better for them to turn in their guns."

"I won't do it," Alex said flatly. "It's not legal."

"If the President says that it's legal, then it's legal, as far as I'm concerned." Grady frowned. "As he said, you and your officers will be allowed to keep your weapons, Chief. I want you to continue enforcing the law in Home, just as you have been. *But* . . . that decision can be suspended if I see fit to do so. I have the authority to demand that you and your officers surrender your weapons as well. I'd prefer that you not force me to do so, Chief."

It was all Alex could do to control the fury that welled up inside her. She knew she was outnumbered and outgunned. She couldn't stop Grady from doing whatever he wanted to do.

But she didn't have to help him, and so she shook her head. "I won't try to stop you," she said, "but I'll be damned if I'm going to help you."

"Then just stay out of our way," Grady snapped. "I won't be needing you anymore."

"You mean—"

"I mean you're free to leave, Chief. Have a good day."

Yeah, Alex thought bitterly. Like that was going to happen.

She had a feeling that the good days in Home were over.

Chapter 27

When she left the command post RV, Delgado was waiting for her, guarded by a couple of the black-clad soldiers.

"Is it true?" Delgado asked tensely. "They're here to take everybody's guns?"

"How do you know about it?"

"Jimmy called me. Enough people in town saw that news broadcast that the word is spreading fast. Jimmy says the station is being flooded with calls from people wanting to know if its true."

Alex sighed and nodded. "It's true. *These* people"—she glared scathingly at the so-called "officers"—"have been sent here to disarm all the civilians."

"But not us."

"Not yet. But I'm sure if we give them any trouble, that'll be the next step. The commanding officer made that clear." Alex started toward her car and jerked her head for Delgado to follow.

The other members of the force were waiting for them. Alex called them together and explained the situation.

"What are we gonna do?" Jerry Houston asked when she was finished.

"I don't know." Alex hated to appear indecisive, but the sheer enormity of the situation had all but overwhelmed her. "There are too many of them. I told the colonel we wouldn't help them, but we won't try to interfere with them, either."

"The hell with that," Clint said with a snort. "I quit."

Alex shook her head. "Clint, don't. Please. I'm going to need all the good people I can get to maintain order."

"No, you won't," he argued. "This bunch of goose-steppers will maintain order, at gunpoint, I expect. You just wait and see."

Alex didn't have to wait. She was sure Clint was right.

Unbelievably in this, the Twenty-first Century, the day of the jackboot and the iron fist had dawned in America. The forces of the left, so arrogant and self-righteous in their belief that their way was the only way for the country, had bided their time, waiting for the right moment to step in and force their agenda on everyone, and the anger over the tragic injustice that had happened to Pete McNamara had served as their excuse.

This was just the first step down a long, nightmarish road that would ultimately find the formerly free United States transformed into a socialist dictatorship.

That was a harsh judgment, Alex knew, but she didn't doubt the truth of it for an instant. That was exactly what the man in the Oval Office intended.

As if to confirm her fears, several of the sinister-looking SUVs pulled out of the parking lot and headed downtown. Alex couldn't see through the blacked-out windows in the vehicles, but she was sure they were full of FPS "officers" setting out on their mission to disarm the town.

At that moment, static crackled from the radio on her shoulder, and then Jimmy said, "Chief, I got a call that Wendell Post is . . . barricadin' himself inside his store. He says he's gonna fight if anbody . . . tries to take away his guns."

"Damn it," Alex muttered. Still, Jimmy's news came as no surprise. A lot of people would probably react the same way as the hardware store owner. Wendell Post was just the first one to do so.

She leaned her head toward the radio and keyed the mike. "On my way, Jimmy," she told the dispatcher. "If any more calls like that come in, send an officer to each location." She broke the connection and turned toward them. "Do *not* let those goons shoot any of the townspeople. Clint, are you with us or not?"

Clint sighed. "All right, all right. I'll stay on . . . for now. I don't want them shootin' up the town any more than you do, and that's what it's liable to come to."

Alex got into her car and headed downtown. Post Hardware was at the intersection of the state highway and the farm road, in the very center of town. When she glanced at the rearview mirror, she saw more of the SUVs leaving the high school as the FPS began spreading out on its unholy mission.

It didn't take long to drive from the outskirts of town where the school was located to the downtown area. Alex saw several of the black SUVs parked at intervals along the blocks of businesses. The soldiers had gotten out and were striding along the sidewalks, the highly visible presence of their weapons causing a lot of alarm and commotion among the citizens. They hadn't gotten to the hardware store yet, she saw, and she was grateful for that. She might still have a chance to talk some sense into Wendell Post.

As she parked in a fire zone and got out of the car, she heard the bullhorn-magnified tones of one of the troopers saying, "Attention, citizens of Home! Attention, citizens of Home! As per the Executive Order of the President of the United States, Home and the surrounding area are now under federal control! You are required by law to cooperate and comply with this order! All firearms must be surrendered! Repeat, all firearms must be surrendered! Take your guns to the Federal Protective Service command post located at the Home High School and turn them in! FPS personnel are on duty there to collect your firearms and issue receipts for them! This is a temporary measure, but all firearms must be surrendered!"

Where was the news media now? Alex wondered fleetingly as she moved toward the door of the hardware store. Where were all those gallant reporters devoted to the pursuit of truth now? Why weren't they showing the world pictures of how soldiers under the direct command of the President had invaded and occupied an American town? Where was the outrage at such a heavy-handed and unconstitutional action?

She knew the answer, of course. The FPS had probably thrown a cordon around the entire area placed under martial law. The media wouldn't be allowed in while the disarming of Home was going on. And even if they had been, they would have downplayed and excused the whole thing, so it didn't really matter.

Alex grabbed the handle on one of the glass front doors of the hardware store and pulled it open.

A shot blasted, shattering the glass and spraying shards of it over the sidewalk. Alex crouched, instinct making her draw her pistol as broken glass crunched under her feet.

"Wendell!" she shouted. "Wendell, it's Chief Bonner! Don't shoot!"

From where she was, she could see that the hardware store appeared to be empty of customers. That was good, anyway. This wouldn't turn into a bloodbath.

Not unless the blood was hers, she thought.

From the corner of her eye, she spotted movement and turned her head to see several of the FPS troopers rushing toward the hardware store. She motioned with her free hand for them to stop. They slowed down but kept coming.

"Wendell, can you hear me?"

There hadn't been any more shots. Now Post called from the back of the store somewhere, "Chief? Is that really you?"

"It's really me, Wendell." Alex took a deep breath. "I'm coming in."

"Are there any of them government thugs with you?"

"No, just me." She motioned again to the FPS men, more sharply this time. They stopped at the end of the block, and one of them gave her a curt nod. She took this as permission to go in and talk with the barricaded store owner.

"Well . . . all right, I guess," Post called. "Come on in. Just you, though."

"Just me," Alex said, loud enough for the men at the end of the block to hear her. She motioned for them to stay where they were as she pulled back the undamaged door and stepped into the store.

"Back here behind the counter," Post said.

Alex holstered her weapon. She didn't believe Wendell Post would shoot her. They had known each other for years.

The rawboned sixty-year-old straightened from his crouch behind the old, scarred wooden counter where he had filled orders for his customers for decades. He had a deer rifle in his hands.

"I'm sorry, Chief," he said. "I thought you was one of them government Nazis."

"No, just me, same as I've always been. Why don't you put that rifle down, Wendell?"

He looked at the weapon as if he had forgotten he was holding it. "Oh. Yeah, sure." He laid it on the counter between them, the barrel pointing to the side. "It's not true, is it? They can't take our guns away just on that damn politician's say-so, can they?"

"They've got the men and the firepower on their side," Alex pointed out. "It may not be right, but if we try to put up a fight . . . well, I'm afraid some innocent people might be killed, and I don't want that."

"Neither do I. I always swore I'd never let 'em take my guns away, though. My daddy fought in the Big One when he was just a boy, and he always said that if they ever come to take away our guns, that'd be the end of the country he fought for."

"They're saying that it's just temporary."

Post shook his head. "Do you really believe that, Chief?"

Alex had asked herself the same question, and she had to answer honestly. "No, I don't. I think once they get their hands on everybody's guns, we'll never see them again."

"That's right," Post said. "Then they'll go to some other little town and pull the same stunt there, and some place after that, and another and another until the only ones who got guns are the army . . . and them thugs who come up across the border, like the ones who killed poor Inez McNamara."

There wasn't a thing he had said that Alex could dispute. She believed he was right. And yet there were cold, hard facts to face.

"They didn't come up with this idea overnight. They're ready for anything we might do, Wendell. We're going to have to cooperate with them and hope that somehow the courts will step in and put things right."

Post snorted in disbelief. "That ain't never gonna happen, Alex, and you know it."

Alex sighed. "We have to hope." She put a hand on the rifle that rested on the counter. "Can I take this and turn it over to them? If I don't, they'll come in here and arrest you. If you shoot at them, they'll kill you."

She didn't doubt that for a second.

Post sighed and pushed the rifle toward her. "Take it. There's gonna come a time, though, when you and me and ever'body else in this town is gonna have to ask themselves what's worth fightin' for . . . and dyin' over, if need be."

Alex knew he was right about that, too.

Holding the rifle well away from her body, she stepped out onto the sidewalk. "Clear!" she called to the FPS troopers at the end of the block. More men had joined them. "I've got his gun. You can have it."

They rushed down the sidewalk toward her. One of them snatched the rifle out of her hands, and several more charged into the store, broken glass crunching under their boots.

"Wait a minute!" Alex cried. "What are you doing? I got the gun!"

She heard angry shouting inside that was cut off abruptly. She moved to go in, but black-clad men blocked her. A moment later, the men who had gone inside reappeared, dragging a groggy Wendell Post between them. The storekeeper's head was bleeding from a place where he had obviously been hit with a gun butt or something else.

"This man is under arrest for failing to comply with the executive order," one of the FPS men said.

"But I got his gun," Alex protested.

"Doesn't matter, ma'am. He's in our custody now."

"You can't—"

Alex stopped short. Of course, they could do it. They could do whatever they wanted. They were in charge now, them and their liberal masters back in Washington. They had waltzed right in and taken over as if it was their right to do so—and that was exactly what they believed.

And she had let them do it. God help her, Alex thought as sickness roiled her stomach, she had let them do it.

BOOK FOUR

Chapter 28

"How long are we going to stay here?"

"Relax, Earl. Nobody's trying to kill you, are they?"

"Well . . . no." A bitter tone entered Earl Trussell's voice. "Not for the past couple of days, anyway."

"Then you're ahead of the game," Ford said. "I'm grateful that nobody's tried to kill me for more than forty-eight hours."

"You would be, you Neanderthal."

"Sticks and stones may break my bones, but they won't do nearly as much damage as automatic weapons."

"Will you two shut up?" Parker asked from the window of the camper, where he moved aside the curtain every so often to check on what was going on outside. "It's bad enough that we're stuck here in Pissant, Texas, without the two of you yammering at each other all the time."

"He started it, the big gorilla," Earl complained.

"And you can finish it," Parker pointed out. "Just tell us what we need to know."

Earl was pale to start with, but his pallor deepened as he shook his head. "I can't. They'll kill me."

"Maybe we'll kill you if you don't," Ford said.

"No, you won't. You're the good guys, remember?"

"This day and age, it's gettin' harder and harder to tell the good guys from the bad guys," Ford drawled.

He was stretched out on one of the camper's bunks with his hands behind his head and his legs crossed at the ankles. The casual pose belied the fact that he was ready for trouble. They had been lucky since escaping from Corpus Christi with Earl Trussell as their prisoner, but Ford knew good luck never lasted. Bad luck always came along to replace it.

They had bought this used camper for cash in a little town south of Corpus, hooked it onto a pickup they had stolen that also had stolen license plates on it, then headed west into the largely empty southern tip of Texas.

The camper wasn't all they bought. Parker and Ford picked up a couple of throwaway cell phones to replace the government-issued phones they had, well, thrown away. Off the bridge into Nueces Bay, in fact. Those phones would have been too easy to trace, and after everything that had happened, the two agents were no longer a hundred percent certain who they could trust.

It was a debate they'd had several times while driving all night across the flat Texas landscape. Ford was ambivalent about calling in and reporting that they had the target in custody. Parker was dead set against it.

"We were set up, Fargo," he had declared as they

argued. "The only reason we were there at that hotel in Corpus was so those guys could kill the little guy here and pin the blame on us. And there's only one way they could have known we'd be there."

"Our bosses told them," Ford had said.

"Exactly. Or somebody who works for our bosses, anyway. If we let them know where we are, there'll be another hit squad on us in a matter of hours."

Ford hadn't been able to dispute that logic, but he was still uneasy about their best course of action. "As long as we're in the wind, they're going to think we've gone rogue," he had warned.

"Better that than being dead."

Again, indisputable logic.

"I vote for staying alive," the prisoner had piped up from between them on the pickup seat.

"You don't get a vote," Ford growled. "At least, not until you spill who you are and why so many people want you dead."

"We want to know what was on that laptop of yours, too," Parker had told him.

So far, though, they hadn't gotten him to reveal anything except his name: Earl Trussell.

Early the next morning, they had stopped at this RV park in a small crossroads town and laid low ever since. Parker had walked across the highway several times to get food for them at the Tasty Kreme drive-in, which appeared not to have changed a bit since being built sometime in the 1950s.

Now Ford continued, "Speaking of lines blurring, we could always torture the little weasel, Brad."

Earl sneered at him. "Do your worst, big shot."

"Wouldn't the worst torture be torture that *didn't*

make you talk? The best torture would be the stuff that makes you talk."

"You can't make me talk."

"That's just little-guy bravado. Next thing you know, you'll be threating to murdalize me."

"Yeah, well, if I could—"

"Pipe down," Parker said, tensing at the window. "An SUV just pulled up and stopped at the office."

Ford swung his legs off the bunk. "So?"

"So it's black and the windows are heavily tinted."

"Doesn't have to mean a thing," Ford said, but he reached for his gun anyway. He felt better with it in his hand.

"Guy's getting out and going in to talk to the park manager."

"You recognize him?"

"Never saw him before."

Both agents knew that didn't mean a thing. The Company had plenty of assets working for it that they had never seen, and freelancers could always be hired for a sensitive job, too.

But at least the man in the RV park office wasn't a known killer.

That didn't mean he wasn't dangerous.

The problem with a camper trailer like this was that you couldn't just park it. There were things you had to do in order to set it up properly. Which meant that you couldn't just hop in the pickup and drive off at a moment's notice, either. You had to take time to unhook.

"Nobody else has stopped here since we came in yesterday morning," Parker said. "If the guy's looking for us, he's gonna have to check us out."

The camper had only one door, and it was facing

the office. They couldn't get out, climb in the pickup, and drive away without being seen by anybody who was looking in this direction.

"Anybody still in the SUV?" Ford asked.

"I think so. Hard to tell through that dark glass, but I believe there's another guy in the front seat."

"Yeah, they travel in pairs, at least."

From the stool where he was sitting next to the tiny kitchen counter, Earl asked, "Guys, are . . . are we gonna be all right?"

"I don't know," Ford said. "If you're going to tell anybody why you ran away from Casa del Diablo, now's the time, Earl. You may not get another chance."

It was almost a blind shot, but the sudden flare of surprise in Earl's eyes told Ford that he had scored. Earl had run away from a place called Casa del Diablo. That was more than they had known for sure a moment earlier.

"The first guy's coming out of the office," Parker reported. "He's shaking hands with the manager. Now he's getting back in the SUV. . . . It looks like they're leaving."

"Really?" Ford asked, unwilling to believe just yet that their luck had held.

"Yeah, they're pulling out onto the highway—" Parker's breath hissed between his teeth. "No, wait a minute. They're backing up. The tailgate's starting to come up—"

Ford lunged off the bed, grabbed Earl's arm, and yanked him off the stool. Earl yelped in pain as Ford said, "Go! Go!"

Parker slapped the door open and the three men leaped out of the camper. Ford just had time to think that if he was wrong, they had not only revealed their presence unnecessarily, but they were going to look mighty silly, too.

But alarm bells were clamoring in his head, and as the SUV's tailgate lifted even more, he saw that he was right. A man crouched in the back of the SUV, pointing a grenade launcher at them.

The RPG shot out from the weapon, trailing smoke and fire as it rocketed toward the camper.

Ford and Parker launched themselves into dives that carried them away from the camper, and since Ford still had his hand clamped on Earl's arm, he dragged the little guy with him. They hit the ground next to the pickup just as the grenade struck the camper and exploded. The earth jumped violently beneath them. The blast blew a huge hole in the camper and knocked it over on its side.

Parker came up on one knee, gun in hand, and opened fire on the SUV. It was probably armored and had bulletproof glass in the windows, but with the rear gate open, that gave him an opening. He poured several shots into the back of the SUV while Ford and Earl scrambled to their feet.

Neither agent asked the other if he was hurt. As long as they could move and fight, they would keep going. Ford jerked the pickup's passenger door open and shoved Earl in. Then, joining Parker in firing at the SUV, he ran around the front of the truck and slid in behind the wheel.

The seat was littered with broken glass. The blast that had wrecked the camper had blown out the pickup's rear window. The engine was all right, though, and turned over as soon as Ford hit the key.

Parker put a foot on the rear bumper and vaulted

into the pickup bed. "Go!" he yelled to Ford, who floored the gas. The pickup leaped ahead.

Another RPG sizzled toward them, but Ford had gotten the vehicle moving just in time. The rocket-propelled grenade burned past, only a few inches from the pickup's tailgate, and slammed into some mesquite trees at the edge of the RV park, turning them into kindling.

A barbed-wire fence loomed in front of the windshield. Ford never slowed down. He aimed the pickup between two fence posts and hit the wire at full speed. It parted with several loud *twangs*! The truck bounced across an open field, smashed through another fence, and slewed onto a dirt road.

"At least one of the bastards is still alive!" Parker called through the broken rear window. "The SUV just pulled out of the park and is coming after us."

"If I let it get close enough, can you shoot out a tire?"

"Hell, no! It's bound to have run-flats on it, anyway."

In the pickup cab, Ford turned his head to look at Earl as the vehicle raced along the dirt road, raising a cloud of dust behind it.

"There's only one thing to do," Ford told Parker. "We've got to give them Earl."

"What!" Earl said in a high-pitched squeak of terror.

"Good idea," Parker agreed. "They'll still have to come after us, of course, but since Earl's the one they've really been after all along, they'll have to stop and kill him first. That'll give us a little breathing room."

"Wait, wait!" Earl babbled. "You can't—"

"He's already told us he's never gonna talk," Ford said. "I'll be damned if I'm gonna die for something without even knowing what it is."

"And you saw the way they broke out the heavy artillery right away, back there at the park," Parker said from the pickup bed. "They didn't even know for sure it was us in that camper. They want Earl dead so bad they were willing to take a chance on slaughtering innocent people, just because it was possible he was there."

"All right, I'll talk, I'll talk!" Earl screeched. "Don't throw me out! Please! What is it you want to know?"

"What's Casa del Diablo?"

"A research lab in the mountains out in West Texas. I worked there."

"Research into what?" Ford asked.

Earl took a deep breath. "Biological weapons."

"Bio-weapons have been banned."

"Tell that to the guys running the place, and the guys who give them their orders."

"What did you do there?"

"I'm a chemist. You might not believe it to look at me, since I'm so handsome and all, but I'm actually pretty smart."

"Not smart enough," Ford muttered. "What did you do, think you could blow the whistle on them and they'd just let you get away with it?"

Muddy sweat coated Earl's face. He wiped some of it away and said, "You don't get it, Ford. The stuff they're making there . . . it's bad. Really, really bad."

"And the government's funding it?" Parker asked. He had been listening through the broken window.

"Somebody is. I don't know who. I just figured . . . well, it had to be somebody pretty high up."

Ford glanced back at Parker, and as the eyes of the two men met, Ford knew they were sharing the same thought:

There were several people in Washington who *might* be able to marshal the sort of forces that were arrayed against them.

But there was only one man in Washington who *definitely* could.

"Yeah, I think we're gonna be about as rogue as rogue can get," Ford muttered.

That is, he amended to himself, if they survived the next few minutes with pursuit closing in behind them.

Chapter 29

Ford hoped that the dirt road they were on would lead to a highway, or at least another paved road. The pickup they were in almost certainly didn't have the power of the SUV following them. The SUV's engine probably had been souped up so it would be capable of more speed.

So maybe it was a good thing after all that they were on a dirt road, Ford decided after a moment's thought. That way the SUV's extra power was less of an advantage for the pursuers.

The problem was that the road was getting narrower and rougher, and if that trend continued, it was liable to peter out completely, leaving them with nowhere to run.

Ford glanced at the side mirrors. The pickup's tires were kicking up so much dust he couldn't really see anything else behind them, but he knew the would-be killers were still back there. Based on the intel Earl Trussell had just spilled, they couldn't afford to let him live, or anyone else who had been in close contact with him and might have found out about Casa del Diablo.

Might as well put the time they had left to good

use, Ford thought. He said, "All right, Earl, tell me more. What are they making at this House of the Devil?"

Earl hesitated, then shrugged his narrow shoulders. "I don't guess it really matters anymore, does it? We're all gonna die anyway."

"Just in case we don't, the more people you tell, the better. The more people who know the secret, the less reason those guys back there have for wanting you dead."

Earl frowned. "You know, I never really thought about it that way."

"You planned on blowing the whistle when you stole that laptop and ran away from there, right?"

"I didn't *steal* the laptop," Earl objected. "It was mine. Well, the government owned it, I suppose, but it's the one I used all the time. And yeah, I figured I ought to tell somebody what was going on there before a lot of people died."

"Why didn't you?"

Earl shook his head and sighed. "I . . . I got scared. I thought maybe I was making a big mistake. So I decided to take a few days and think it over while I made up my mind."

"And to do that you rented a room at a fancy resort hotel in Corpus Christi?"

"Hey, did you see the babes at that place? I figured I might as well partake of a little eye candy while I was pondering the fate of the world."

Ford couldn't help but laugh. "You're a skuzzy little weasel, aren't you?"

"Maybe, but that doesn't mean I want to see the government murdering its own citizens."

Ford glanced sharply at him as the pickup

bounced over a stretch of road that resembled an old-fashioned washboard. "What the hell are you talking about?"

"Those bio-weapons . . . they're not being developed for the military. I don't think the army even knows about them."

Ford muttered a curse. This was starting to sound even worse than he'd thought.

"Start at the beginning," he said.

"Okay. There are several projects in development at Casa del Diablo, but the one that's closest to being finished, the one I was working on, is a new nerve gas. It's incredibly lethal. A tiny amount will stop a person's heart in less than two seconds."

"Nasty stuff, but it doesn't sound like anything all that new."

"There are two things different about it," Earl explained. "The first is that it's tailored to the human genome. Dogs, cats, livestock . . . they can breathe the stuff all day without it doing a thing to them. Even chimps have enough genetic differences from humans that it doesn't affect them. The second thing is that the gas's window of viability is extremely narrow. It lasts less than five minutes. After that it becomes inert and harmless."

"So you could spray a town with the stuff from the air and then waltz in five minutes later to find all the people dead but everything else intact, including the pets."

Earl nodded. "That's right. Like you said, nasty stuff."

"It seems to me, though, that its only applications would be military in nature. You'd only use it in a war, right? And we couldn't even do that now, with all the laws against bio-weapons."

"You could use it against anybody you wanted to get rid of. The thing that made me decide I had to get out of there was . . ." Earl stopped and blew out a breath, as if he had to work himself up to telling what he knew. "Was when I found some documents I wasn't supposed to find. A report from the chief of the project to the Department of Homeland Security and the director of the Federal Protective Service."

Ford's hands tightened on the pickup's steering wheel. He had been overseas a lot during the past ten or twelve years, but that didn't mean he was completely ignorant of what was going on in the country. Like many in the intelligence community, though, he had believed that what he did was separate, for the most part, from politics. It didn't matter who was in the White House. The country would always have enemies who wanted to take it down. It was the job of Ford and Parker and all the other warriors who operated in the shadows to see that that didn't happen.

But he had heard the rumors about how under the previous administration, the Department of Homeland Security had turned most of its attention away from outward threats and begun to concentrate on what it considered homegrown terrorism.

In theory that wasn't necessarily a bad thing. There were violent nutjobs of all nationalities and beliefs. Always had been and always would be, more than likely.

But the previous President's paranoia about right-wing conspiracies against her had infected

Homeland Security until anybody who expressed the least bit of disagreement with her policies, from an editorial writer for a small-town paper to a radio talk-show host to the executives of the one cable news network that didn't toe the liberal line, had an official file in Washington labeling them as potential terrorists.

It wasn't just Homeland Security that was affected, either. People who disagreed publicly with the President suddenly found their tax returns being audited at a much higher rate than those of the general public. New wiretapping and surveillance laws that were much more intrusive and frightening than previous ones were rammed through Congress by the very liberals who had decried such tactics only a few years earlier, a blatant example of the double standard that ruled Washington.

The new Federal Protective Service was part of the Department of Homeland Security, Ford knew. But it had just been formed, and as far as Ford was aware, a director for it hadn't even been named yet.

When he said as much to Earl Trussell while he wrestled the pickup around a bend in the road, Earl asked, "Have you heard of a guy named General Stone?"

"Weldon Stone?"

"That's him."

Ford grimaced. "Yeah, I know who he is."

General Weldon Stone was a career military man who had been eased into retirement a couple of years earlier after a series of public clashes with the Joint Chiefs of Staff. Stone had been in command of U.S. forces in the Middle East, and his growing reluctance to pursue Islamic terrorists because of what he termed "their legitimate grievances against Israel and the United States" had finally led to his removal. That had brought on an anti-Semitic tirade to the news media that was bad enough to force the previous administration to sever its ties with him.

"Stone's the director of the FPS," Earl said. "As least according to the file I saw, he is."

So the new administration, which was cold if not openly hostile to Israel, had brought back General Stone and placed him in charge of the new national police force. That was not good, Ford thought. Stone was a maniac, the sort of inflexible fanatic who thought that anybody who disagreed with his political views was not only stupid but evil and ought to be wiped off the face of the earth. And since his political views had slanted more and more to the left over the years, he was now very much at home in Washington.

"This is the guy they're going to give that new nerve gas?" Ford asked. Despite the heat of the day and the sweat that made his shirt stick to him, he felt an icy chill inside.

"Yeah," Earl said. "You can see now why I was worried."

"There's no way they can get away with using it against our own people. The country wouldn't stand for it."

"Are you kidding? The country will stand for anything if the guy in the White House says it's the right thing to do."

Unfortunately, that was probably true. A large

part of the population thought the President could do no wrong, and with the media constantly reinforcing that idea, that percentage grew larger and larger all the time.

"Anyway," Earl went on, "they'll probably try to keep it quiet. Say somebody's giving the administration a lot of trouble. They pipe the stuff into his house, kill him and his family, and then blame it on a carbon monoxide leak or something. Even if they wanted to use it for something bigger, like taking out a whole town, they could say the water supply got contaminated by some corporation. You know how those people like to blame corporations for everything bad that happens."

Ford nodded slowly. "Yeah, yeah, I see where you're going. No wonder finding out about it shook you up."

"I may be a weasel, but I'm still an American," Earl said with a note of pride in his voice.

Suddenly, Ford yelled, "Hang on, Brad!" He jammed on the brakes and hauled hard on the steering wheel, sending the rear end of the pickup slewing around. The truck went into a sideways skid and came to a stop about two feet from the edge of a sheer drop-off where the dirt road ended. The road had been going up a slight rise, so Ford hadn't been able to see the drop-off until it was almost too late.

He twisted around in the seat to look through the broken window into the pickup bed. Parker was still back there, clinging to the side of the pickup with a slightly wide-eyed look on his face.

"What the hell!" he said.

"We've run out of room to run," Ford said. "Last stop, everybody out!"

CHAPTER 30

The dust cloud swirled over the pickup and began to thin as Ford and Earl climbed quickly out of the cab and Parker jumped down from the bed. Out here in the middle of nowhere, it was quiet enough so that the growl of the SUV's engine as it powered toward them was shockingly loud.

Ford saw the black vehicle. It was about three hundred yards behind them and coming fast. The drop-off wasn't too deep, only about a dozen feet to a narrow creek that twisted across the countryside. He saw what was left of some thick posts that indicated a bridge had crossed the creek at some time in the past. It must have been swept away by a flash flood, he thought, and was never rebuilt. What remained had been left to rot.

"Get down there," he told Earl as he and Parker crouched behind the pickup bed and leveled their pistols at the onrushing SUV.

"What?" Earl yelped. "There's no trail."

"Then jump! It won't kill you. Take off up the creek."

"What about you two?"

Parker said, "We'll slow those bastards down. Go, Earl!"

Earl swallowed hard, sat down on the edge of the bank, and slid off. Ford heard him thud to the ground at the bottom of the drop-off but didn't turn around to look at him.

"You land all right, Earl?" he called.

"Yeah. Yeah, I guess I'm okay."

"Then get the hell out of here!"

The two agents opened fire. They knew their shots were hitting the heavily armored SUV, but it was like throwing pebbles at a runaway locomotive. The SUV didn't slow down.

"Get ready to jump," Ford warned.

"Yeah," Parker said. It would be like on the Indian Point bridge back in Corpus.

Only it wasn't, because the driver of the SUV suddenly braked, too, and brought his vehicle sliding to a halt with the passenger side toward the pickup. Someone inside kicked the door open and the chatter of an automatic weapon ripped through the air.

Ford and Parker ducked as the slugs pounded into the pickup. Ford knew it was a lot harder to make a vehicle's gas tank blow up than the movies made it appear, but when the sharp reek of spilled gasoline filled his nose, he knew the tank had been holed and it was only a matter of time until a spark set it off.

"Jump!" he said.

He and Parker whirled around and leaped off the edge of the bank. Behind them, a ball of flame erupted and engulfed the pickup. That was yet another vehicle he and Parker had gotten blown up, Ford thought as he landed in the shallow creek and went to his hands and knees, feeling the heat of the blast on the back of his neck. They were racking up quite a score in automotive destruction.

The sound of splashing made him glance to his left. Earl was running away down the creek with desperate speed. Ford and Parker went after him. They heard the men from the SUV shouting above them.

"Sounds like . . . just two of them," Ford said between panting breaths. "Stop and . . . make a stand?"

"They've got us . . . outgunned," Parker said. "Better try to give them the slip."

What Parker said was true. All they had were the two pistols. The guys after them had automatic weapons and a grenade launcher, for God's sake! Ford promised himself that if they made it out of this mess alive, he would never go on a mission again armed with anything less than a bazooka.

But, knowing what he knew now about Casa del Diablo and its connection to the guy in the White House, he figured he would never be going on a mission for the Company again anyway. Those days were over and done with. He would have a target on his back for the rest of his life. . . .

Unless they could somehow get the truth out and convince enough people to believe it.

They could worry about that later, Ford told himself. Right now his only concern was their immediate survival.

Parker said, "Fargo! Where the hell did Earl go?"

Ford looked along the creek, but didn't see the little scientist. Earl had been moving fast, but not fast enough to get completely out of sight.

Then an arm emerged from a clump of brush and dead limbs against one side of the bank and waved frantically to them.

"Guys! Guys! Over here!"

Ford and Parker ran to the brush and pushed it aside. Behind it was a depression that erosion had hollowed out of the bank. It was too shallow to be called a cave, but Ford thought it was big enough so that all three of them could crowd in there.

They did. Ford and Parker pulled the dead brush back in place in front of them. Their bodies shielded Earl, who was pressed against the hollow's rear wall.

"Careful," Earl said in a strained voice. "I've still gotta breathe back here."

"Pipe down," Ford whispered. "Not a sound, understand?"

They stood there in complete silence. Using the iron discipline they had learned from years in a dangerous profession, the two agents slowed their breathing until it was inaudible.

A few moments later, they heard footsteps crunching through the sand not far away. The searchers were still above them on the bank. The footsteps grew even louder, until they were right above the hollow.

Then, while the three men hidden there held their breath, the searchers moved on.

Not for long, though. The footsteps stopped,

and a man's voice said, "You're sure they came this direction?"

"I heard the splashing as they ran along the creek this way," another man replied.

"Then where the hell did they go?"

"I don't know. Let's climb down there and see if we can find any tracks."

They wouldn't find what they were looking for, Ford thought, because they had already gone farther than their quarry. But when the killers realized that, they would probably double back.

He and Parker looked at each other. This would probably be their only chance to get the drop on the would-be assassins, and they knew it.

The sounds they heard told them that the men were climbing down the bank about twenty feet to the left. When they heard feet splashing in the creek, they looked at each other again and nodded.

With a splintering of dead limbs, they burst out of the brush and leveled their guns at the two men.

Unfortunately, the men didn't have their backs to Ford and Parker, but at least they were half-turned away. The split-second delay in being forced to turn and raise their automatic weapons gave the two agents time to fire. Shots blasted from the pistols.

They had expected the pursuers to be wearing flak jackets, so Ford and Parker both went for head shots. They drilled their targets, sending slugs coring through the brains of the two men. The killers flopped bonelessly into the creek, polluting the water with the blood and brain matter that seeped from the holes in their skulls.

More footsteps pounded on the bank above them. There had been three enemies left, not just two. Ford cursed as he and Parker swung around and lifted their guns. The third flak-jacketed killer had already slid to a halt and his finger was tightening on the trigger of the assault rifle he had pointed at them.

Earl burst from the brush and flung a broken tree limb at the man just as he fired. It was a good throw, right at the man's face so that he flinched involuntarily and the bullets from his gun whipped through the air above Ford and Parker. The two of them fired at the same time. Their bullets, traveling at an upward angle, tore through the assassin's throat, severed his spine, and pulped his brain. He jerked spasmodically, dropped his rifle, and pitched off the bank to land facedown in the creek with a huge splash.

"God, I hope there's not any more of them!" Ford said fervently.

"Get back in the hole, Earl," Parker snapped.

"Hey, in case you guys didn't notice, I think I just saved your lives," Earl said.

"Yeah, thanks," Ford said. "Get back in the hole until we check things out."

Parker backed off to the far side of the creek and scanned the bank as far as he could see. Ford made sure the three men were dead and gathered up their weapons.

"Anything?" he called to Parker.

"Nothing that I can see or hear. I think that was the last of them."

"All right. Earl, come here and help me with this gear."

Earl pushed his way through the brush and walked toward Ford. He made a point of not looking directly at the bloody corpses. His face was a little green now.

"You, uh, killed them," he said.

"Yep. Seemed like the thing to do at the time," Ford drawled.

"Doesn't it, I don't know, bother you? Now that it's all over, I mean, and you're not caught up in the heat of battle."

"We weren't caught up in the heat of battle. That'll get you killed. The man who keeps his nerves cool is the one who usually survives." Ford handed him web belts full of ammunition that he had stripped off the dead men. "You can carry these."

Earl grunted under the weight of the belts. "Aren't you going to give me one of their guns?"

"Have you ever shot a gun?"

"Well . . . no. Only in video games."

"Then I think it's safe to assume that you don't know how to use one of these babies that fires more than a thousand rounds in a minute."

"Uh, no, I guess not." Earl hefted the belts. "What are we gonna do now?"

"Take their SUV and get the hell out of here," Parker said as he rejoined them. "We have to find some place to hole up and figure out our next move."

"Before they find us again and try to kill us again, you mean."

"I'd say that's pretty inevitable," Ford told him.

They found a place where they could climb out of the creek bed and started toward the black SUV, which was about a hundred and fifty yards away. Black smoke still rose from the burned wreckage of the pickup they had been using.

"You think they left the keys in it?" Earl asked.

"Doesn't matter," Parker said. "We can get it running."

"Once we've made sure it's not booby-trapped," Ford added.

"They'd do that? Booby-trap their own vehicle to make sure no one else used it?"

"Oh, yeah. That'd be the smart move, wouldn't it? Those boys weren't quite as lucky as we were, but they were smart enough."

"FPS wouldn't hire dummies," Parker put in.

"You think that's who they worked for?"

Parker nodded. "I'd bet on it. In fact, I'd bet the whole thing is nothing but a cover for a black ops shop."

"Is there *anybody* left in the government you can trust?"

As they came up to the SUV, Ford said, "That, my little friend, is the jackpot question."

But before they could attempt to answer it, a man stepped out from behind the black vehicle, pointed a rifle at them, and said, "Y'all just hold it right there where you are, fellas, or by God, I'll have to shoot you."

CHAPTER 31

Ford knew instantly that the man wasn't one of the government assassins who'd been sent after Earl Trussell and the two rogue CIA agents traveling with him. This man wore boots, jeans, a faded work shirt, and a cowboy hat with a tightly curled brim. His hawklike face was permanently tanned by long exposure to the sun until his skin looked like old saddle leather.

Even though the man looked like something from the Nineteenth Century, the rifle he pointed at them certainly didn't. It was modern and high-powered, and he handled the weapon like he knew how to use it.

"Well," he said after a tense minute, "y'all don't look like a bunch o' damn drug smugglers. You're sure loaded down with guns, though, like they usually are."

"You've had trouble with smugglers before?" Ford asked.

"Everybody in this part of the country has. They fly that poison over the border, then pick it up in trucks and spread it out all over the place. Shootin's too good for scum like that."

"I agree with you," Parker said. "And we're definitely not drug smugglers."

"We're not even Mexicans," Earl said.

The leathery stranger snorted. "Hell, there's some anglos work for them cartels. I saw the smoke and heard a bunch o' shootin', so I figured a couple of rival gangs were tryin' to kill each other. Then I come out here and find a couple o' fellas who look like cops and a pasty-faced little gent who looks about as dangerous as a twelve-year-old girl."

"Hey!" Earl protested.

"Shut up," Ford told him. "We *are* cops, sort of. We work for the government."

Or at least we used to, he added to himself.

"Border Patrol?" the man asked, squinting suspiciously at them over the barrel of the rifle, which he still hadn't lowered. "DEA?"

"Not exactly," Parker said. "We work for a, uh, government agency, though."

"Got I.D.?"

Ford smiled humorlessly. "They don't issue it to guys like us."

"Oh. You're spooks, are you?"

"Something like that."

The man snorted. "Yeah, and I'm John Wayne come back to life."

"Actually, you look more like Lee Van Cleef."

"You know who Lee Van Cleef was?"

"Doesn't everybody?"

Earl said, "Look, they work for the CIA, all right? They've been trying to protect me because some other guys from the government want to kill me, because I know about this new nerve gas that's being developed at a place called Casa del Diablo and it looks like the President might try to use it against American citizens who disagree with what he's doing, and I decided to blow the whistle on the whole thing and somebody sent that new Federal Protective Service after me and they tried to kill me and frame these guys for it and—"

"Damn it, boy, take a breath!" the stranger exclaimed. "You expect me to follow that crazy line o' bull?"

"It only *sounds* crazy," Ford said. "I'm afraid there's a lot of truth to it. Now, we don't want to hurt you, mister—"

"Hurt me? I'm the one who's got the gun pointin' at you, remember?"

"Yeah, but by the time you shoot one of us, the other one will kill you," Ford said calmly, "and there's no need for that. Just let us get in this SUV and drive away, and you can forget you ever saw us."

"What about that blowed-up pickup? I'd be willin' to bet that there's some bodies around here somewhere, too."

"Wait a couple of hours and then call the sheriff's office like you just discovered that something happened," Parker suggested. "By then we'll be long gone, and there won't be any need to mention that we were here."

"I got a better idea." The man finally lowered the rifle. "Come on back to my ranch house with me, and y'all can clean up, get somethin' to eat, and try to spin some yarn that actually makes sense."

"So you've decided to trust us?" Ford asked.

The man shrugged. "Hell, if you're so all-fired

deadly as you claim to be, you could'a killed me already if you really wanted to. Right?"

"Well . . . yeah," Ford admitted.

"And as pale as that little fella is, if he don't get out of the sun pretty soon, he's gonna be blistered." The man turned away. "I left my horse back yonder a ways. Shoot me or come on, whatever."

The rancher's name was Rye Callahan. Ryan, actually, but as he explained to Ford, Parker, and Earl, he wasn't that fond of the name, and since he was fond of rye whiskey, it seemed like a good idea to shorten it. Since he was an old bachelor, he was in the habit of doing what he wanted.

Rye whiskey was the drink he poured for them as they sat in the comfortably furnished living room of the large, sprawling ranch house where several generations of his family had lived. Callahan tossed back the fiery liquor, licked his lips appreciately, and then said, "All right, start at the beginnin' and tell me this story again."

Earl opened his mouth to talk, but Ford stopped him with an upraised hand. "I'll tell Mr. Callahan what's been going on, and then he can decide what to do about it."

"What do you mean, decide?" Earl asked. "Since when is the decision up to him?"

"He's opened up the hospitality of his home to us," Parker said. "We owe him some consideration."

"And he's a fellow American," Ford added. "We don't shoot our fellow Americans."

"What about those guys from the FPS?"

"We don't shoot our fellow Americans unless they're trying to shoot us," Parker said.

"And unless they're probably conspiring to murder a bunch of other Americans because of some power-hungry politician," Ford said.

Callahan pointed out, "That ain't startin' from the beginnin'."

Ford lifted his glass of whiskey and nodded to the rancher. "You're right, sir. As far as we've been able to put the story together, it's like this. . . ."

Callahan listened without interrupting as Ford explained what had been going on during the past week. Parker and Earl spoke up a time or two to clarify a point.

As Ford wrapped up the summary, he said, "I understand if you think we're lunatics. But I swear, that's the way it all happened, and as far as we've been able to figure out, there's only one man who could be responsible for it, as hard as it may be for you to believe that."

Callahan let out a dismissive snort. "You really think that because a bunch of damn fools were crazy enough to vote the man into office, I wouldn't believe he's capable of doin' what you say?" The rancher shook his head. "I've heard the man talk on TV. He thinks he's smarter'n everybody else and that him and his buddies ought to be in charge of everything 'cause they're smarter'n us. The people who work and pay the taxes and keep the whole damn country goin'! Hell, is there anybody in that whole damn crowd who's ever held down a real job? They're all professional politicians."

"So you *do* believe us?" Parker asked.

"You sound surprised, boy."

"Well . . . most people wouldn't."

"You mean most people who let Hollywood and New York and Washington tell 'em how to think wouldn't believe you. With all the things that've been goin' on in Texas lately, I wouldn't put anything past that skunk in the White House."

Ford asked, "What do you mean, the things that have been going on in Texas?"

Callahan leaned forward in his overstuffed armchair and frowned. "You haven't heard about Home?"

"Home?" Ford repeated. "Whose home?"

Callahan shook his head. "That's the name of a town. It's a ways north and west of here. Hell, it's been all over the news the past few days."

"We've been a little busy," Ford said. "Trying to stay alive and all, you know."

Callahan snorted again. He picked up a remote control from a table beside his chair, pointed it at a wall full of bookshelves, and pushed a button. Two sections of the shelves slid back to reveal a giant-screen TV. Ford, Parker, and Earl stared at the rancher.

"What?" Callahan said. "I reckon you didn't see the satellite dish out back. Remind me to show you my computer system later."

Another push of a button turned the TV on.

It was tuned to one of the cable news networks. "Only one of the bunch I can stand to watch," Callahan said, "and even they've gotten a mite too cushy there in Washington and New York. They've started pullin' their punches lately. I reckon they're runnin' scared like ever'body else who don't say and think exactly what that bunch wants 'em to."

The anchor was talking about a bill making its way through Congress that would expand the federal government's control over education nationwide. When that story was finished, he said, "Now, in other news . . . Tensions continue to run high in the small Texas town of Home today after the President issued an executive order yesterday placing the community and the surrounding area under the control of the Federal Protective Service. After several so-called anti-immigrant riots in Home in recent days, the President declared martial law and sent in the FPS to disarm the citizens."

"He's trying to take away a whole town's guns?" Ford asked in disbelief.

Callahan motioned for quiet. "Just listen."

"Yesterday when the FPS arrived in Home to set up a command post, one of the citizens went on a shooting spree, the second such incident in less than twenty-four hours. He was taken into custody without any casualties, but there have been other incidents of defiance directed at the officers of the Federal Protective Service."

Parker shook his head. "They're operating openly now. Amazing."

The newsman continued, "Last night, a number of people gathered with their guns in the First Baptist Church of Home and refused to come out and surrender the weapons."

Nighttime footage of a church appeared on the screen. The building was surrounded by armored cars and black SUVs, behind which black-uniformed men crouched and pointed assault rifles at the church.

"This potentially disastrous situation was defused by the actions of local chief of police, Alexandra Bonner, who managed to talk the insurgents out of the sanctuary."

"Insurgents?" Ford repeated angrily. "They're calling Americans *insurgents*?"

"And this is the unbiased channel," Callahan said with a dry, humorless chuckle.

Chief Bonner appeared on screen, a harried-looking but attractive woman who appeared to be in her thirties. "Kinda hot for a police chief," Ford commented.

"None of this would have happened if the federal government hadn't bulldozed in here where they're not needed or wanted," Chief Bonner told the microphones extended toward her. "The city leaders and I firmly believe that the actions being taken by the Federal Protective Service are unconstitutional."

"Ooh, there's gonna be red flags all over her tax return next year," Earl said.

"We believe that the courts will eventually side with us on this issue," Bonner went on, "but in the meantime, because the people of Home are all good, law-abiding American citizens, we're going to cooperate with the FPS in hopes that this will soon be settled."

"If they give up their guns, they'll never see 'em again," Ford said. "Surely they know that."

"Yeah, but how can a bunch of regular folks from a small town argue with the sort of firepower the

FPS has?" Parker asked. "They can't, not without getting slaughtered. They have to cooperate."

Callahan pointed the remote at the screen and muted the sound. "You know what started this whole business?" he asked. Without waiting for an answer, he went on, "A few months ago, a couple of low-level thugs who work for one o' them Mexican drug cartels came across the border and broke into the house of an old couple in Home. The fella who lived there had quite a few guns, and I reckon the thugs were after them. But the old-timer surprised 'em and fought back. He killed one of the varmints and wounded the other, but his wife was killed in the shootin'."

"That's terrible," Ford muttered. "How does a tragedy like that lead to this?"

"Because the thug who survived turned around and sued the old fella, along with the city and ever'body else he could think of to sue, includin' the federal government. And he won."

The other three men stared at him. "That's crazier than the story we just told you," Parker said.

"Yep, but it's true, too. The Feds settled with him, and as part of the agreement, they said they'd disarm the whole town. And now they're doin' it. Sooner or later, they're gonna get all the guns, and then folks won't have any way to defend themselves anymore."

"Except to rely on the government," Parker said.

Callahan shook his head. "They won't have any way to defend themselves *against* the government. You boys probably aren't old enough to really remember what it was like back in the old Soviet

Union, but I do, and I'm here to tell you that's just what we're headed for here." A sigh came from the rancher as he looked at the TV and shook his head. "We're not that far from this country bein' turned into a dictatorship, fellas, and what's goin' on in Home right now . . . that's just the first step down that road."

Chapter 32

Alex couldn't remember the last time she'd slept. It had been forty-eight hours, at least. The longest two days of her life. She had been kept busy the whole time by continuing confrontations between the citizens of Home and the Federal Protective Service.

Wendell Post barricading himself inside his store had been just the beginning. Other people had forted up in their businesses and homes, culminating in the standoff at the Baptist Church. That had held the potential to be the worst of all, since there were quite a few armed people inside the sanctuary. If the citizens had put up a fight, the FPS would have won in the end, no doubt about that, but people would have been hurt and probably killed on both sides. That might have set off an outright war in Home, and *that* would have wound up being a bloodbath.

Luckily, in each case the civilians had looked at the odds and the firepower facing them and done the sensible thing. They were ordinary people, not misguided, suicidal zealots like that bunch in Waco a couple of decades earlier. In the end, they had come out and surrendered their guns, and Colonel Grady had surprised Alex by not arresting them.

Maybe he just didn't have the facilities available to arrest an entire town.

But even though killing had been avoided so far, Alex had had to be on hand every time something happened, had to be there to talk sense to the citizens who wanted to defy the government. In truth, she wanted to be just as defiant as they were and tell Colonel Grady, the FPS, and the President to go climb a stick because what they were doing was illegal, and she said as much to the steadily circling buzzards of the news media.

She was sworn to protect the people who lived here, though, and right now, keeping them alive meant getting them to swallow the bitter pill of government oppression.

She had been either at the police station or out on call ever since the FPS had rolled into town, except for a few brief moments when she had stretched out on the cot in the station's back room. She hadn't slept, though. Things hadn't stayed quiet enough, long enough, for that.

That meant she hadn't seen Jack for forty-eight hours, either, and the thought that she was a terrible mother gnawed insistently at the back of her brain. She knew that wasn't true—he was a senior in high school, after all, a smart, responsible kid despite the occasional lapse in judgment or outbreak of rebelliousness—and she trusted him to take care of himself. But that didn't stop her from wanting to be there for him.

As she drove around the streets now, she saw the black SUVs of the Federal Protective Service everywhere. Heavily armed men and women in black uniforms moved along the sidewalks. The citizens who encountered them looked the other way and tried to stay out of their path, at least for the most part. A few bolder ones gave the troopers hostile stares.

Home looked like an occupied town in a defeated enemy country, Alex thought.

And that was pretty much what it amounted to. The ruling elite in Washington regarded everyone outside the Beltway as an enemy, except for a few privileged enclaves of sycophants here and there, in New York, Boston, Hollywood. . . . For years they had been waging a not-so-secret war against the beliefs and values of average, everyday Americans, and now it appeared they had won.

Static crackled from the radio. Jimmy said, "Chief, you there?"

Alex picked up the mike. "I'm here."

"Report of shots fired at . . . Pearson's Feed Store."

Oh, no, Alex thought. She had been waiting for this to happen, even though she hoped it wouldn't.

"I'm on my way," she told Jimmy. She hung up the mike, hit the lights and siren, and tromped down on the gas.

As fast as she got to the feed store, the FPS was faster. Alex saw a couple of the sinister-looking SUVs careen around a corner ahead of her. She knew they were on their way to the feed store, which was on a side street not far from the high school.

Black smoke suddenly plumed into the sky. Even though she hadn't heard an explosion over the howling siren and the roar of the car's engine, she knew that was what had just taken place. Something had blown up, and she was afraid it was the feed store.

She hoped there hadn't been any civilians inside it.

The car slewed around the corner. She spotted the old building with tin siding up ahead and realized the feed store hadn't been destroyed after all. The smoke came from a burning pickup parked in front of the store. A man she recognized as Phil Pearson ran around the pickup, spraying it with a fire extinguisher in an attempt to keep the flames from spreading.

Several of the FPS men stood back with guns cradled in their arms, watching the pickup burn. They weren't lifting a finger to help Pearson. Another trooper had somebody on the ground, pinning him down with a knee in the small of the back. Two more troopers covered the prisoner with their weapons.

Alex brought the police car to a halt and leaped out. She ran toward the troopers, calling, "Hey! Hey, what's going on here?"

A couple of the men who'd been watching the truck burn swung around sharply and lifted their guns. As they pointed the weapons at Alex, one of them yelled, "Stop right there!"

Alex skidded to a halt and held up her hands, palms out. "Take it easy," she said. "I'm Chief Bonner."

"We know who you are," the man snapped. "You're a civilian, just like the rest of these people."

Alex forced herself not to bristle at being called

a civilian. Losing her temper with these goons wasn't going to help matters.

"What's going on here?" she asked. "Who's that you have on the ground?"

"Terrorist, ma'am," replied the trooper who had just finished slipping plastic restraints around the prisoner's wrists.

Alex was close enough now to recognize the thinning white hair and overalls. "Terrorist, hell!" she burst out. "That's Elmer Davis!"

"He not only refused to surrender his weapon, he attempted to use it against us," the trooper replied as he got to his feet. "That makes him a terrorist."

Alex sighed. She had known Elmer for years, ever since she was a little girl, in fact. She knew he carried an old Winchester pellet gun in a gun rack in his pickup and used it to shoot at rattlesnakes when he saw them on the side of the road. The pellet gun was at least as old as Elmer was, probably older, but he kept it in good repair.

"I know this man," she told the troopers. "That Winchester of his is practically an antique. It may be an antique. And it's not even a real—"

"Doesn't matter," one of the black-uniformed men replied with a shake of his head. "A firearm is a firearm. They're all forbidden."

"Did he try to shoot you? I have a hard time believing that."

Phil Pearson just about had the fire out now. The fire extinguisher sputtered as it ran out of chemicals. He tossed it aside and turned to face Alex and the troopers.

"No, he didn't try to shoot at them," he said angrily. "I'll tell you what happened, Chief. Elmer and I were just standing there on the loading dock talking when the first one of those SUVs came up. A couple of fellas got out and started yellin' about how Elmer had to turn over that old rifle he had in his pickup."

"That'll do, citizen," one of the troopers said. "We're in charge here."

"No, by God, it *won't* do," Pearson said. "Elmer came down the steps from the dock and tried to tell 'em about how he never used the rifle for anything except shootin' at snakes. He said he'd show 'em it was just a pellet gun, and then they opened fire on him!"

"Is that true?" Alex demanded.

"The suspect never said the weapon was a pellet gun," the spokesman for the troopers said. "He just said that he'd show us, and we took that to be a threat and fired a warning burst. A moment later reinforcements arrived, and one of them took out the truck with a grenade to make sure that the suspect wouldn't use the weapon against us while we took him into custody."

Alex stared at the men for a long moment before saying, "Let me get this straight. You fired automatic weapons at a seventy-five-year-old man, knocked him to the ground, cuffed him, and blew up his truck . . . *because he had a pellet gun in it?*"

"This is none of your affair, ma'am," the trooper snapped. He turned to the others and ordered curtly, "Take the suspect back to the command post for interrogation."

"What?" Alex said. "After all this, you're going to take him in? Really?"

"Colonel Grady will want him questioned about possible affiliation with other terrorists."

Alex didn't know whether to laugh or cry. As the men lifted a scared and befuddled-looking Elmer Davis to his feet, the decision was made for her as a tear rolled down her cheek. Was this what the country she loved had come to? Was it really?

"I'm sorry, Elmer," she said. "I'll talk to the colonel."

The trooper who'd been doing the talking said, "If the suspect is cleared of any criminal charges, he can file a claim with the government to be reimbursed for his truck."

"And how long will *that* take?" Alex asked. "You think he'll live long enough to see the government admit that it was wrong? Do you honestly think any of us will?"

"I don't know, ma'am. Issues like that are above my pay grade."

They dragged Elmer over to one of the SUVs and put him in the backseat. He gave Alex a despairing look as they slammed the door and cut him off from her view.

Phil Pearson came up beside her and said, "I know you said we have to cooperate with those black-suited thugs, Chief, but can they really get away with this? I mean, for God's sake, calling Elmer Davis a terrorist and roughing him up like that! Elmer never hurt a soul in his life."

"I know, Phil," Alex said with a sigh. "I just keep hoping that somehow, somebody will come to their senses and see how wrong this whole thing is."

* * *

"Violence broke out again today in the infamous town of Home, Texas, which the Federal Protective Service has placed under martial law. The FPS is attempting to curb the recent outbreak of bigotry, rioting, and attempted murder which has plagued Home. Earlier today, one of the community's citizens attacked officers of the Protective Service with an illegal firearm. This wanton lawlessness resulted in the destruction of a vehicle. The gallant officers were able to subdue the suspect and place him in custody without suffering any casualties. The suspect, Elmer Davis, has been charged with attempted murder and terroristic acts, and faces a sentence of life in prison if convicted.

"In other news, what is now being called the National Education and Re-education Act moved another step toward passage today, and the President promised to sign this important legislation as soon as it lands on his desk. In impromptu remarks at a White House gathering, the President said that this bill is vital to his administration's continuing efforts to make sure that students know exactly what they need to know in order to reach the proper decisions on the vital issues that face us all today, young and old. . . ."

CHAPTER 33

By the time the Federal Protective Service had been in Home for a week, the town's guns were gone. They had been turned in voluntarily, albeit grudgingly, or confiscated wherever and whenever the FPS found them. Alex suspected that some of the citizens had managed to hide a few guns, but probably not many. She had heard that other people had left town, slipping through the FPS cordon and taking their guns with them. She suspected that Colonel Grady didn't really care about that. He just wanted to be able to say that Home had been disarmed, as the settlement agreement with Emilio Navarre called for . . . and as the President had ordered.

She faced Grady now across his desk in the mobile command post. The colonel had ordered everyone else to clear out. It was just the two of them.

"You'll be glad to hear, Chief, that we have fulfilled our mission in your town."

"Does that mean you'll be leaving?" Alex asked, not really thinking for a minute that it did.

"As a matter of fact . . . yes," Grady said.

Alex's eyes widened in surprise. "Really? I mean, you're really leaving town?"

Grady nodded. "My officers and I will be packing up and pulling out later this afternoon."

Alex sat back in the folding chair. "I don't believe it. This is some sort of trick."

"I work for the federal government, Chief," Grady said with a flash of anger in his eyes. "We don't play tricks on people."

She managed not to laugh at that statement. Keeping her face and voice solemn, she said, "With all due respect, Colonel, I won't be sad to see you go."

"It won't make me sad to leave, either." For the first time, Alex sensed a slight chink in the man's armor. "I haven't enjoyed cracking down on my fellow citizens like this. But I signed on to faithfully carry out the orders of the President, and I have done so. There are no longer any illegal firearms to be found in Home, or in the surrounding area."

Technically, that was true, Alex supposed. Any firearms still here *hadn't* been found.

Not that there were very many of them. She didn't know for sure, of course, but she guessed there probably weren't much more than a dozen guns left in town, including the ones she and her full-time officers had been allowed to retain. The reserve officers had had to turn their guns in like everybody else. There might be a few more in the area outside the city limits within that ten-mile cordon, but not many. The FPS had been remarkably thorough with their searches, sweeping through the area like locusts.

"What happens now?" Alex asked.

Grady smiled thinly. "We'll be setting up permanent checkpoints on the main roads leading in and out of town. Anyone attempting to bring in a gun or guns will be subject to immediate arrest."

"What's happened to the people you've already arrested?"

"That's none of your concern. They're being held in a secure location."

"What about their rights?"

"Under martial law, they have none."

"But Home isn't staying under martial law, right? Isn't that what you meant when you said the FPS was leaving?"

"That's true. But those suspects were arrested under martial law, so they will remain under our jurisdiction."

One more twisting and perverting of the Constitution, Alex thought. After everything they had done so far, what did one more outrage really amount to?

"Did you call me in here just to tell me this, Colonel?"

"I thought you'd want to know."

"Oh, I do, don't get me wrong. I just wish it had never come to this."

Grady leaned back in his chair and steepled his fingers. "You know, Chief Bonner, you're a very intelligent woman. To protect your people, you've kept this situation from escalating until someone got hurt. If you're ever interested in moving up in law enforcement, say on a federal level . . ."

Alex stared at him in amazement. "You're offering me a job? Working for this . . . this modern-day Gestapo?"

Grady's features hardened. "It was just a thought,"

he said. "Obviously, not a good one. Forget I said anything."

"I'll try, you can count on that."

The colonel stood up. "All right, I believe we're done here. Best of luck to you, Chief." He gave her a curt nod but didn't offer to shake hands. That was fine with Alex.

She left the giant mobile command post and found Delgado leaning against the fender of his police car that was parked next to hers.

"I heard that the colonel sent for you," he said. "What's going on?"

Alex told him. Delgado looked surprised, too.

"I figured we'd be stuck with them from now on," he said when Alex finished explaining the situation.

"So did I. But I suppose they have other things to do. Other constitutional rights to violate somewhere else."

"It wouldn't surprise me a bit."

Alex debated briefly with herself whether to tell him the rest of it, but it was so outrageous she had to share it. "You know, J. P., he offered me a job."

Delgado's eyebrows went up. "The colonel?"

"Yeah. He said that I'd done a good job of controlling the situation so that my people didn't get hurt."

"Like the Vichy government in France during World War II."

Alex grimaced. "You had to be a history major. I feel a little dirty, though, like I have been collaborating with the Nazis."

"It's a funny thing," Delgado mused. "The liberals have always accused anyone who didn't agree with them of being fascists. They'd even play the

Nazi card from time to time. And yet, less than fifteen years after they took over everything in Washington, they're the ones who come marching in dressed like storm troopers and occupy an American town. They wiretap ten times more than conservative administrations ever did, they run up the national debt to astronomical levels that will leave the country crippled for decades, if not centuries, they take over more and more of the industries . . . and still they turn around and act noble and claim they're just doing it for the good of the country. I'm not sure there's ever been a society where those in charge preached one thing and did just the opposite to the extent that these people do." He stopped, shook his head, and chuckled. "I didn't mean to start lecturing like a college professor."

"Don't worry, you weren't," Alex told him.

"No?"

She shook her head. "No college professor would ever say anything like that about the left. They adore the President and his bunch as much as the media do."

"You're probably right about that." Delgado straightened from his casual pose. "Some people would say that our job's going to be easier now."

"How could they think that?"

He shrugged. "There are no guns. Everybody knows that if there are no guns, there won't be any crime, ever again."

Alex knew he was being sarcastic, but she shook her head anyway.

"Something tells me our job just got a whole hell of a lot harder, J. P."

* * *

The splashing of the water in the fountain was like the merry notes of a guitar playing. Enrique Reynosa y Montoya leaned back in his comfortable chair, closed his eyes, and smiled. He heard the girls splashing and laughing in the pool at the other end of the courtyard, and that pleased him as well. Soon he would join them. He loved visualizing them in their sleek young nudity, all smooth skin and dark hair and flashing eyes, the sort of erotic image that many men conjured up in their minds. The difference was that when he opened his eyes, the beautiful girls were really there, at his beck and call, ready to whatever he wished in order to please him.

But first there was business to be dealt with.

Herman had been waiting patiently. What else was he going to do? As the head of Rey del Sol, Señor Reynosa had the power of life and death over thousands of people, including Herman Guzman.

But there was no point in making Herman wait any longer. Enrique sat up, smiled across the table at his second-in-command, and said, "You have a report from across the border?"

"Yes, Señor Reynosa. The American Federal Protective Service has withdrawn its forces from the town."

"Permanently?"

"It appears so."

Reynosa reached for the glass of lemonade that was coated with moisture from the heat and humidity. He drank only non-alcoholic beverages, and he never used the drugs that his cartel smuggled so successfully over the border. He believed in keeping his body healthy, so that he could fully enjoy other pleasures.

Such as the young girls who swam naked in his pool like seals.

After taking a sip of the cold lemonade, Enrique said, "So, the town of Home has no guns."

Herman shrugged. "The police are still armed, but there are less than half a dozen of them. And some of the people no doubt hid their weapons, but there cannot be many."

"Not enough to matter," Enrique said with a dismissive wave of his hand. "There is nothing to stop us from putting our plan into operation."

"The American soldiers have set up checkpoints on the highways, to make sure no one brings guns back into Home."

"We have our agents in this so-called Federal Protective Force, have we not?"

Herman smiled. "We do, Señor Reynosa. We have agents in places the foolish Americans would never dream of."

Enrique nodded, thinking of the beautiful Julia Hernandez. She had been brought here to his villa when she was, what, fifteen? He couldn't remember for sure. She had been quivering and innocent, but he had taught her well, and she had learned quickly. Her intelligence was just as important as her physical skills. She moved now in the highest circles in Washington, and no one there ever dreamed that she was not who she appeared to be. No one had any idea who her true master was.

Enrique forced his thoughts back to the matter at hand. "When General Garaldo's forces take over those checkpoints, our agents with the FPS will be able to tell him what to do to keep their superiors from finding out what's going on until it's too late."

"Certainly. We should need no more than twelve hours at most. Our timing will be precise, as always."

"Very well. Contact General Garaldo and issue the orders. Sunday morning, we strike."

"Sunday morning," Herman repeated, his voice soft and silky with anticipation. Operation Casa del Diablo would be the boldest stroke Rey del Sol had ever attempted. If they were successful, the cartel wars would be over. There would be only one left, standing victorious over all the others.

With his business concluded, Enrique Reynosa y Montoya drank the rest of his lemonade, stood up, and walked past the gurgling fountain toward the pool, stripping off his robe and tossing it aside as he went.

"Señoritas!" he cried as he reached the edge of the pool. "Bid welcome to the King of the Sun!"

Then he made a clean dive into the cool water and came up surrounded by lovely, young, nude, and willing female flesh.

It was good to be him.

Chapter 34

With the resources that the enemy had at their command, Fargo Ford knew it was only a matter of time before he and Parker and Earl Trussell would have to run again.

It felt so good to rest and catch their breath at Rye Callahan's ranch, though, that they allowed a couple of days to slip past.

On Saturday morning, though, Ford called a summit meeting of him, Parker, and Callahan. The three men nursed cups of coffee on the ranch house patio while Earl stayed inside to put away a huge plate of pancakes, scrambled eggs, and bacon. For a little fella, he sure could eat.

"We need to get out of here," Ford said.

"Not on my account," Callahan replied. "You're welcome to stay as long as you want."

Parker shook his head and said, "We know that, Rye. But by now the men who are looking for us are bound to have found those bodies and that burned-out pickup. They'll know that we're probably still somewhere in the area, and they'll start checking out the ranches around here."

Ford gestured toward the slate-tiled roof that

overhung the patio. He and his companions had been careful not to venture out into the open while they were here, and the SUV they had brought with them was stashed out of sight in one of Callahan's barns. They had gone over the vehicle, making an intensive search of it to be sure there were no tracking devices hidden in it.

"They've probably got an eye-in-the-sky satellite up there right now, taking surveillance photos of the whole area. I know you've been going on about your business, but they'll still wonder if we're here."

"Maybe you could slip out durin' the night," Callahan suggested. "I've got a couple of pickups. You can use one of them."

Parker shook his head again. "Those satellites have infrared capability, too. It'll look bright as day out here."

"Then what are you gonna do?"

"You have any friends you could invite over for a fandango?" Ford asked, drawling out the last word.

"So you can mingle with them and slip out that way?"

"That's the idea."

Callahan rubbed his angular jaw. "Yeah, that might work. It'd have to be folks I trust, but there's a few of those around here. Not as many as there used to be. A lot of the old guard's died out."

"You don't have to tell them anything about us," Parker said. "Maybe just that we're cousins visiting from somewhere. Would the guests know you well enough to know that wasn't true?"

"Not really. I've never been a real talkative sort, I guess you could say."

Ford grinned. "All right. Can you get them here tonight?"

"That's short notice . . . but most people will turn out for a barbecue."

"All right. We've got ourselves a plan."

They went inside and found that Earl wasn't just eating breakfast. He had turned up a map of Texas from somewhere and was poring over it.

"What are you looking at, Earl?" Parker asked.

The young man frowned as he studied the map. "I got to thinking about that town called Home."

They had kept up with the story on the news channels the past couple of days. After a few scattered incidents of violence, the Federal Protective Service had succeeded in disarming the town. According to a statement issued by the commander of the FPS forces, Colonel Charles Grady, all firearms in Home and the surrounding area had been either turned in or confiscated, and so the FPS had withdrawn the previous afternoon.

Neither Ford nor Parker believed that everyone in the town had turned in their guns. A few people probably had some stashed that the FPS storm troopers hadn't found. By and large, though, the town probably was disarmed.

Except for the tiny police force. That good-looking female chief had been interviewed several times, and she had declared that she and her officers would keep the town safe until everything was settled and the people had their guns returned to them.

The CIA agents knew *that* was never going to happen. Not with the way the President was smirking and preening for the cameras, obviously filled with arrogant pride that he had succeeded in taking away the guns of a whole town.

"What about Home?" Parker asked Earl.

"Look." Earl put a finger on the map. "This is where Home is."

Curious, Ford peered over the little scientist's shoulder. "Yeah. So what?"

Earl moved his finger over a short distance, into a range of small but rugged mountains. "And *this* is where Casa del Diablo is."

Parker frowned. "How far away is that? Fifty, sixty miles?"

"Yeah," Earl said. "And the highway that's closest to the lab is the same state road that runs right through Home."

Ford and Parker glanced at each other, and each of them knew that alarm bells were going off in the other's head.

"What exactly are you getting at, Earl?" Ford asked.

"I don't know. I just got this uneasy feeling all of a sudden. . . . The project was getting pretty close to finished when I decided to jump ship. Enough time has gone by since then that they could have finished up the prototype batch of the nerve gas."

"How much of the stuff are we talking about?" Parker asked.

Earl took a deep breath. "I don't know for sure. I was high enough in the pecking order to be privy to some of the details of the project, but not all of them. My guess? Maybe a hundred canisters."

"How big would those canisters be?"

Earl held up his hands to indicate dimensions. "About the size of an oxygen tank like the ones you see old guys using sometimes."

Parker's voice was sharp. "How would they be transported?"

"Very carefully," Earl said. "Lots of protective packing, to make absolutely certain that they wouldn't be jostled around and spring a leak."

"What about temperature?" Ford wanted to know.

"Best to keep the stuff cool. It's less volatile that way."

Ford frowned in thought as he tugged at his earlobe a couple of times and then ran his thumbnail down the line of his jaw. "So we're talking about refrigerated trucks, big enough to carry, say, fifty canisters each."

"Yeah," Parker agreed, "they wouldn't put the whole shipment in one truck. They'd split up in at least two, maybe three or four."

"And they'd have to take it somewhere, because it doesn't do them any good just sitting in a lab," Ford mused.

"That's what I was thinking," Earl said. "Homeland Security and the FPS put a ton of money into this project. The bosses are going to want to have the stuff where they can get at it easily in case they need to use it."

A shudder went through Ford. "I hate to think about Weldon Stone having the capability to wipe out a whole town so easily."

"Son of a . . ." Parker said in a low, stunned voice. His finger stabbed down on the map at the dot marking the location of Home. "You think there's going to be a test, Fargo? Is that really why the FPS disarmed the whole town?"

Ford thought about it for a moment and shook

his head. "No, if the stuff is really as fast and lethal as Earl says it is—"

"It is," Earl said. "Don't doubt it for a second."

"Then it wouldn't matter whether the people in Home still had their guns or not," Ford went on. "All the FPS would have to do is fly over the town, release the gas, and then waltz in a little while later to collect the bodies. The citizens wouldn't ever know what hit them."

Callahan spoke up. "Wait just a damn minute. I been listenin' to what you boys are sayin', and while I'm as upset about what's goin' on as anybody, you're talkin' about the U.S. government murderin' a whole townful of its own citizens in cold blood. You really think they'd do that?"

"I'd like to believe they wouldn't," Ford said, "but I'm convinced it's the FPS that's been trying to kill the three of us for the past week. I don't know what I believe anymore."

"You're right, though, Fargo," Parker said. "It's not going to be a test. That doesn't make sense when you factor in the business of disarming the town. I think it's just a coincidence. The President and his cronies saw their chance to make a move when the lawsuit came up, and they grabbed it."

"Yeah, but there's something going on here," Ford insisted. "My gut tells me there is, and I've learned to trust it."

"Mine, too." Parker's finger tapped the map again. "I think when we leave here tonight, we'd better head for Home."

CHAPTER 35

Callahan called six of the local ranching families and invited them for a barbecue at his place that night. Five of them accepted. The other family already had plans.

But that was enough. Counting the kids, there would be more than twenty people at Callahan's house that evening. With the two agents and Earl dressed in boots, jeans, Western shirts, and Stetsons, they would blend right in and be able to leave without being noticed when the barbecue was over.

That was the plan, anyway. They would just have to wait and see how it played out.

Ford and Parker had mapped out the route they would take in Callahan's old pickup. They checked the guns and ammunition they had taken from the dead FPS agents. Callahan used his tractor to haul a trailer loaded with bags of feed and fertilizer up to the patio. They unloaded enough of the bags to form a hollow, then concealed the weapons in it and covered them with some of the unloaded bags. Callahan drove the tractor back into the barn and hid the guns under a tarp in the back of the pickup. The truck was full of gas and ready to go.

All that was left was waiting, and while they were doing that, they tried to figure out the connection between the disarming of Home and the town's proximity to Casa del Diablo. As Parker had said, the whole thing might be a coincidence, but the agents were going to try to prepare for any eventuality.

That was the way they had stayed alive in such a dangerous profession.

That afternoon, Callahan asked them, "What're you boys plannin' to do once you get there?"

"We'll get the lay of the land, figure out what's going on there, if anything."

Callahan snorted. "No, I mean about this whole nerve gas shit. You can't let those people in Washington get away with plottin' against our own citizens."

"We have to get proof, and we have to get the word out," Parker said. "If the public knows about the gas, the government won't dare use it. They wouldn't be able to cover it up. There would be such an uproar, the President would probably have to resign."

Callahan shook his head. "I don't know about that. I ain't sure you'll ever get that fella out of office, now that he's there. If he can get enough of the military on his side, he'll just up and declare himself President for life, like those little tinpot dictators down in the Caribbean."

"The country won't stand for it," Parker insisted.

"And while General Stone and the FPS may have signed on to do his dirty work," Ford said, "there are enough members in the regular branches of the service who have enough sense to know they're not supposed to be fighting their own countrymen. Remember that mess at the Alamo a few years back?"

Callahan nodded and said, "Hard to forget about it. You're talkin' about a military takeover, though. That ain't the way we do things in this country."

"I know. And so do enough members of the President's own party, or at least I hope so. I hope enough of them still have enough decency to stand up to him once they find out what he's been doing. They're the ones who'll have to throw him out of office, if he won't go voluntarily."

"You fellas are more optimistic than I am," Callahan said with a sigh. "His own bunch won't ever turn on him. And you'll have a damn hard time gettin' the word out, anyway, what with all the TV folks kissin' up to him all the time."

"There are still some honest people on the radio," Ford said.

"And don't forget the bloggers," Parker added. "They've shown that they can spread news the mainstream media doesn't want heard. All it'll take are a few brave men and women at first who are willing to tell the truth. It'll mushroom from there."

"I hope you're right," Callahan said, but he didn't sound convinced.

The guests began to arrive while the sun was still up. Callahan already had meat smoking in a barbecue pit, and delicious aromas filled the air. Ford, Parker, and Earl were dressed in their cowboy clothes. Callahan introduced them as his cousins from Houston, as they had planned. None of the guests seemed to doubt the story.

As they stood near the barbecue pit, Earl complained under his breath, "I look like an idiot in this getup. You two can pass for cowboys, but me . . ." He shook his head.

"You're right, Earl," Ford said. "You look like a little kid in a Hallowe'en costume. Or you would if kids still dressed like cowboys for Hallowe'en." Ford grinned. "You just need a cap pistol."

"Oh, thanks," Earl said dryly. "That makes me feel a *lot* better."

Parker took a pull on the beer he held. Callahan had filled a big washtub with ice and shoved a few dozen bottles of beer down into it.

"We'll leave when everybody else does, right?" he asked.

"Yep," Ford said. "I doubt if anybody's watching close enough to notice there's one more pickup leaving than drove up earlier."

Earl said, "Uh . . . guys? What's that thing?"

The agents turned to him. He nodded toward a range of hills about half a mile north of the ranch house.

Ford's eyes narrowed as he spotted the aircraft flying slowly over the hills. It had an odd, streamlined look about it, and Ford recognized it instantly.

"Drone," he said as the craft swung toward the ranch. "Damn it! Somebody's decided to take a closer look."

"You mean it's a remote-controlled plane?"

"Yeah, with high-powered cameras mounted in the nose," Parker said. "We'd better get in the house, otherwise it can look right into our faces from that altitude."

Moving unhurriedly so as not to attract attention, the three men turned and walked across the patio into the house. Outside, Callahan's guests noticed the drone plane as well and started pointing and talking about it.

"You think the guys flying that thing saw us?" Earl asked nervously once they were inside.

"I hope not," Ford said. "Maybe we made it inside before it got close enough."

He had a bad feeling, though. The cameras on a surveillance drone like that were powerful enough to zoom in from a long distance and pick up quite a few details. Even before the drone finished its pass, it could have captured digital images of everybody at the gathering, and right now somebody could be running those images through government computers at mind-boggling speeds, searching for matches.

The drone circled back over the hills. Ford thought for a second that it was leaving, but then it swung around again so that its nose pointed toward the ranch house. He grabbed a pair of binoculars Callahan kept on the mantel over the fireplace and lifted them to his eyes, peering through them and locating the drone in time to see the hatch in its belly slide open so something could poke out.

"Damn!" he exclaimed as he threw the binoculars aside. "It's armed with a missile."

"Oh, no, oh, no, oh, no!" Earl babbled. "Not again!"

Ford slammed the sliding glass doors aside and ran out onto the patio. "Everybody out!" he bellowed. "Get out of here! We're under attack!"

It made him sick to think the lives of all these innocent people were in danger because of the plan he and Parker had come up with. They had known the government—or at least, certain people inside the government—wanted them dead at all costs. And yet they had brought these civilians into the line of fire because there was no other way.

They hadn't counted on a surveillance drone discovering their presence on Callahan's ranch before they could make their getaway. Now it was too late for second-guessing. All they could do was try to scatter the people caught on the bull's-eye.

Parker and Callahan joined in on the yelling, too, shouting at the guests to move. Ford saw a sudden plume of smoke in the air near the drone and knew the missile was on its way.

"Incoming!" he roared. "Incoming!"

Screaming and yelling incoherently, the guests ran toward the barn as Parker waved them in that direction. They had only seconds, but at least they put some distance between themselves and the house before the missile came whistling in and slammed into the building. The massive explosion shook the earth, sent debris flying high into the air, and created a cloud of dust and smoke.

Ford and Earl were the closest ones to the blast. The impact knocked them off their feet. With his ears ringing, Ford grabbed Earl's arm and hauled him upright.

"Are you okay?" he shouted.

"What?" Earl was deafened.

"Okay?"

Earl must have read his lips, because the little scientist nodded his head.

The drone flew overhead and swung around for another pass. Ford knew some of the drones carried only one missile, but some were armed with two.

Just their luck, this craft was a two-fer.

As the drone lined up for a second missile run, Parker stepped out of the barn holding the RPG launcher that had been in the SUV belonging to the Federal Protective Service. He lifted the weapon to his shoulder, lined up the shot, and fired. The grenade streaked through the dusk toward the drone.

The second missile launched, but it had barely cleared the drone's nose when the RPG struck it. Both of them detonated, and the huge, mid-air explosion was close enough to the drone to send it spinning crazily out of control across the sky. A couple of seconds later, the drone slammed into the side of a hill and blew up in a brilliant burst of flame.

Realizing that they had gained a few moments' respite, Ford shouted to the stunned party-goers, "Move! Get in your trucks and get out of here!"

Everyone had arrived in either a pickup or an SUV. They were parked in the open area between the barn and the ranch house. The house was on fire now from the explosion. That was good, Ford thought. The blaze would confuse the footage from any heat-sensitive cameras pointing down at them from orbit. With a big, intense source of heat like that, it would be harder for the camera to pick out individual figures.

As scared people began piling into their vehicles, Ford and Earl ran over to join Parker and Callahan in the open double doors of the barn.

"Come on!" Ford said. "We've gotta get outta here now, while everybody else is scattering. Maybe they won't be able to pick us out on the satellite footage."

"Those sons of bitches!" Callahan said bitterly as he looked at the wreckage of his home. "They blew up my house!"

"Yeah, and they'll figure out that you know who we are and what we're after," Parker said. "You've got to come with us, Rye. It won't be safe for you to stay here."

Callahan glared at him. "This place has been in my family for generations. I won't abandon it."

"You're not abandoning it forever," Ford said. "You're just giving yourself a chance to stay alive so you can reclaim it later."

"Well . . ."

"Come on, Mr. Callahan," Earl urged. "We don't have any time to waste."

That was true enough. With the skidding of tires on gravel, the guests were getting the hell out of there while the getting was good.

"All right," Callahan said abruptly. "I don't like it, but I reckon you fellas are right."

The four of them crowded into the pickup. They wouldn't have made it if Earl hadn't sat on Ford's lap.

"I don't like it any better than you do, you big ape," Earl said.

"Remind you of sitting on Santa's lap, does it?" Ford shot back.

"Shut up, both of you," Parker grated from behind the wheel. He stomped the gas and sent the truck racing out of the barn. They fell in behind the others who were fleeing from the devastation.

Sitting in the middle, Callahan twisted his neck to look back at the burning ranch house. "By God, I got a score to settle with them FPS varmints now, too, and I intend to settle it!"

"You'll probably get your chance," Ford said. "But for now, you're coming with us while we check out things in Home."

Knowing that it was possible they were being watched and that a small army of cold-blooded killers might be moving to intercept them at that very moment, the four fugitives headed west across the Texas plains, into the dwindling light of a dying day.

BOOK FIVE

CHAPTER 36

Except for a few fluffy white clouds over the mountains to the west, Sunday morning dawned clear and beautiful. It was a late summer day with a hint of coolness in the air that presaged the autumn and winter to come.

The Federal Protective Service troopers manning the checkpoint on the state highway approximately five miles east of Home had painted the words STOP HERE in big letters across the westbound lane of the highway. A couple of orange traffic cones were set up behind the words. One of the black RVs was parked beside the road to serve as the command post for the checkpoint, and also as a place for the men who weren't on duty at the moment to sleep, eat, and chill out.

As the sun rose, two men in full gear were standing beside the road, watching for traffic. There hadn't been much. Not many people other than the media were going in and out of Home these days, and the troopers didn't have to worry much about the media, although they checked all the vehicles. The reporters were on their side.

Hector Reyes stifled a yawn. It was contagious.

Adam Sutherland, on the other side of the highway, yawned, too. Hector grinned across at him.

"I don't know why we're out here," Adam said. "Nothing's gonna happen today. Everybody knows they can't get away with bringing guns into town."

"You can never be sure of that," Hector said. "Sometimes things happen to surprise you."

Adam shook his head. "Not on this mission. Nobody even wants to come to this backwater town anymore. It wouldn't surprise me if the whole place just dries up and blows away in a few years."

"Me, neither," Hector agreed.

Adam suddenly stiffened and peered off into the distance to the east. "*Something's* coming," he said. "Can't tell what it is yet."

Hector stepped out into the road and shaded his eyes with his hand. The sun hadn't been up very long and was still low to the horizon.

"Looks like a truck," he commented a moment later.

"More than one, I'd say," Adam responded as he joined Hector in the middle of the highway. "Looks like a couple." He shrugged. "Not too surprising, I guess. The people in Home may not have their guns anymore, but they still have to eat. I'll bet those are grocery trucks."

"Maybe." Hector shrugged. "We'll find out in a minute."

It was true. The trucks advanced at a steady speed, the growl of their engines audible now in the early morning air.

Adam started to frown. "Are . . . are they not slowing down? Surely they're not going to try to bust through here!"

But then he relaxed as the whine of brakes joined the engine sound. The two trucks slowed gradually. Adam and Hector moved to opposite sides of the road again and covered the vehicles with their assault rifles. The sound of the brakes grew louder until the pair of trucks finally came to a stop. The front wheels of the first one sat on top of the words painted on the highway.

Adam walked toward the driver's door while the man behind the wheel rolled down his window. "You'll have to step out, sir," Adam called up. "These trucks and their contents will have to be inspected before you can continue, by order of the Federal Protective Service."

Hector came around the front of the truck and stepped up beside him. Adam didn't do more than glance at him. Most of his attention was centered on the man behind the wheel of the truck.

So he never saw the silenced pistol in Hector's hand. He just felt the muzzle of it press against his ear for a second before Hector pulled the trigger and sent a .32 round bouncing around inside Adam's skull. The beautiful morning turned red and black and then went away forever for Adam Sutherland.

Hector caught the body and lowered it to the ground. He nodded to the driver, who pressed a button on the truck's dashboard that lit up a light in the enclosed back.

Hector walked around the truck again and went to the RV. He opened the door and called, "Hey, guys, come out here for a minute and give us a hand."

The other four members of the detachment

emerged from the vehicle a moment later, a couple of them yawning sleepily. Hector waited until all four of them were out, then shot the last one in the head, just as he had Adam.

Before the other three realized what the coughing sound behind them really was, several men armed with automatic weapons stepped out from behind the first truck parked on the highway and covered them. The FPS troopers reacted instantly and started to swing their own weapons up, but Hector said, "No! Stand down!"

The men were well-trained, so they hesitated. Only for a second, but in that second, every hope of fighting back was lost. Hector said, "Put your guns on the ground."

"Reyes, you son of a bitch," one of the men said as they reluctantly complied. "What's going on here?"

"Destiny," Hector said.

A few minutes later, all the troopers except Hector were dead, each shot once in the head after Hector made them remove their helmets. The men from the trucks stripped their uniforms off them, and five of the men from the cartel began to put them on. Hector handed around lists of the day's call signs and radio broadcast protocols.

"There are three more checkpoints," he said. "One on the state highway on the other side of town, and on the farm-to-market road north and south of town. Colonel Grady talked about how there would be checkpoints on the smaller roads, too, but that was just a bluff. General Stone decided it wasn't necessary to go to that much trouble."

"Why not?" one of the killers asked.

Hector waved a hand toward the town, which was out of sight in the distance except for the barely visible water tower. "Because those people have given up. Hell, they let the government come in and take their guns. Most of them swore they'd never do a thing like that, but when it was their own skins on the line, they caved. They're beat, man. Beat down all the way. They got no fight left in 'em anymore."

"I hope you're right," the other man said as he settled one of the FPS helmets on his head. "But in the end, it won't really matter, will it?"

Hector smiled. "Not one bit, man."

The ringing of the phone on the table beside the bed woke Alex. She groaned and rolled over, reaching blindly for it. She couldn't find the phone and had to open her eyes and, when she did, the first thing she saw was the clock. It was only a few minutes after seven. She had planned on sleeping in this morning in hopes of making up for some of the sleep she had lost over the past few days, and she had gotten a start on it, but now that plan was ruined.

Because nobody was going to be calling at seven o'clock on a Sunday morning with good news.

She finally got a hand on the phone and lifted it from its base. She thumbed the Talk button and said, "Yeah?"

"This is Ed Ruiz, Alex. Sorry to call you so early, but I thought you'd want to know."

Alex sat up and pushed tangled hair out of her eyes with her free hand. "Know what, Ed?" Why couldn't the mayor just spit it out, whatever he wanted to tell her.

Ruiz did. "Pete McNamara died early this morning, about an hour ago."

Alex drew in a deep breath and blew it out. "Damn," she said softly.

"Yeah," Ruiz agreed. "I guess we all knew it was coming. Nobody expected him to last this long, especially the doctors. But it's still hard."

It was. Pete had never really regained consciousness after the stroke that had felled him in the courtroom, although he had shown signs of awareness on occasion. He didn't have a DNR order on file, and he and Inez hadn't had any kids to make the decision for him. So after his condition had been stabilized enough for him to be moved, he'd been brought back to the small nursing home near the hospital and placed under Dr. Boone's care. They'd put a feeding tube in his stomach and waited for nature to take its course, one way or another.

Now, several months later, it had finally gotten around to finishing the job of killing Pete McNamara, Alex thought, the job that Jorge Corona and Emilio Navarre had begun the night they broke into his house.

"All right, Ed. Thanks for telling me."

"I kept hoping and praying that maybe the doctors were wrong, that maybe one of these days Pete would wake up and be himself again." A hollow laugh came from Ruiz. "But if Pete had been aware enough to know what was going on in his hometown, he wouldn't have wanted to live. He would have been so sickened by all of us that he would have rather been dead."

"We don't know that," Alex said. "And we did what we had to do to keep a bunch of our people from getting thrown into some secret prison or worse. Nobody knows where they took Wendell Post and Elmer Davis. Dave Rutherford doesn't think we'll ever know . . . or see them again."

"Maybe not. Maybe we don't want to know. There's nothing we can do about it, is there?"

Alex didn't answer that. There was no answer she could make, not one that she wanted to admit to, anyway.

She said goodbye to Ruiz and hung up the phone. Knowing that she wouldn't be able to get back to sleep, she got up and pulled on some jeans and a T-shirt. Jack would still be asleep—the phone wouldn't have awakened him, since he could sleep through anything short of an earthquake—so she thought she might as well have a look around town before coming back here to fix some breakfast.

She clipped her holster to her belt, pulled her hair into a ponytail, and put on a cap. As she went out to her patrol car, she slipped on a pair of sunglasses. She drove downtown and parked in front of the bank.

Nothing was much quieter than a little town this early on Sunday morning. In a little while, people would start moving around more, pulling into the parking lots of the Baptist Church, the Methodist Church, the Catholic Church. One of the convenience stores at the crossroads was closed; the other was open but didn't have any customers. A gasoline truck was parked at the side of the road, its driver filling the convenience store's tanks. Alex leaned against the fender of her car and looked up and down, both ways along the highway and the farm road. Peace and quiet.

The *whup-whup-whup* eggbeater sound of a helicopter suddenly intruded on the tranquility. She looked up, searching the pale blue sky for the aircraft. When she spotted it off to the east, she realized it was coming toward Home.

It was low, too, and getting lower. Alex straightened from her casual pose, her muscles stiffening with tension. It looked like the blasted chopper was going to land somewhere in or near the town. She hurriedly got into the car as the helicopter dipped out of her sight.

The high school, she thought. It looked like the helicopter was landing on the high school parking lot.

And whatever it was carrying couldn't be anything good, she thought as she gunned the patrol car in that direction.

Chapter 37

She was right. She recognized the tall, slender, expensively-dressed figure standing next to the helicopter with his longish dark hair blowing in the propwash. As she entered the school parking lot with a squeal of tires, the man turned his head to peer at the patrol car through a pair of sunglasses even darker than the ones Alex wore.

What the hell was that slimy weasel Clayton Cochrum doing landing in Home in a helicopter?

A moment later, Alex told herself she should have known the answer to that question. All became clear as an attractive blond woman climbed down from the chopper and joined Cochrum, followed by a cameraman.

Cochrum was here for a photo op, and he had brought his own tame news crew with him.

That bastard, Alex thought. He's heard about Pete McNamara dying, and he wants to get some publicity out of it.

Cochrum motioned for the reporter and the cameraman to follow him and strode toward the police car as Alex got out. He wore his usual arrogant smirk as he raised his voice to be heard over the still-turning blades of the helicopter and called, "Chief Bonner! Good morning!"

"There's nothing good about it," Alex snapped.

"I suppose you must have heard about Pete McNamara's death?"

Alex jerked her head in a curt nod. "I have."

The blond reporter, who managed to look perky and attractive even this early on a Sunday morning, said into her microphone, "And how do you feel about Mr. McNamara passing away, Chief Bonner?" She thrust the mike toward Alex.

Reining in her temper, Alex said, "How do you think I feel? I'm mourning a friend. Pete McNamara was a good man."

"According to the courts, he was an unstable, gun-wielding vigilante."

Alex took a step toward the reporter. She couldn't stop herself.

Smoothly, Cochrum got between them. "This isn't really a legal matter anymore," he said. "The courts have ruled, and the case will be disposed of properly in due time. Right now, I don't think we should intrude on the good people of Home."

"Then what are you doing here?" Alex asked tightly.

"When I heard about Mr. McNamara's passing, I knew I had to fly right over here from San Antonio and convey my client's sympathy to Mr. McNamara's friends and neighbors. Mr. Navarre bears no personal ill will toward anyone involved in the tragedy that crippled him and killed his good friend."

Alex wanted to ram those words back down Cochrum's throat, but she knew if she did, the video would be viral worldwide in less than an hour.

Cochrum went on, "If there's anything I can do to help, perhaps with the funeral arrangements . . ."

"You'd like that, wouldn't you?" Alex said. "Put on a big show for the cameras."

Cochrum shook his head. "I don't know what you're talking about, Chief. If you doubt my sincerity, then that's your problem, not mine."

"Why don't you get back in that chopper and go back to San Antonio?" Alex suggested. "We don't want you here."

Cochrum shrugged and shook his head. "This is still a free country, Chief."

"Did the school district give you permission for that thing to land here?" Alex nodded toward the helicopter.

"Well, no, there wasn't time to obtain permission, and this is really the best place in town to land—"

"Then you're trespassing," Alex cut in. "Either get out, or I'll arrest you."

Cochrum's face hardened as he stared at her through the dark sunglasses. "You can't do that."

"Try me," Alex said.

She didn't know how the standoff would end. In a way, Cochrum would probably relish being arrested. That would get him even more publicity.

The rumble of a truck engine intruded on her thoughts and made her turn her head to look along the highway. A couple of unmarked trucks rolled past, evidently on their way through town. Truck traffic through Home wasn't an uncommon sight, but the early morning hour and the fact that these vehicles were unmarked struck Alex as odd. She heard their brakes engage and watched curiously as the two trucks slowed to a stop in the middle of the crossroads.

"What in the world?" she muttered as she started toward her car. Her instincts as a law enforcement officer had kicked in, and for the moment she had forgotten about Clayton Cochrum, the reporter, and the cameraman.

"What is it?" Cochrum called from behind her. "Is there some sort of trouble, Chief?"

She ignored him and got in the car. She had left the engine running, so all she had to do was put it in gear and head for the center of town.

She wasn't the only one who had noticed the trucks' arrival, she saw as she approached. Jerry Houston was already on hand, pulling up next to the lead truck in his patrol car. He got out and approached the cab, lifting a hand in greeting to the driver. The cab door opened.

At first Alex's brain couldn't comprehend what her eyes were seeing. Jerry flew backwards like he was a puppet attached to strings jerked by a puppeteer. He landed across the hood of his car, lying there for a second while bright crimson blood spouted from the bullet holes stitched across his chest. Then he slid off the car into a crumpled heap on the pavement next to the right front wheel.

Alex's instincts took over. Her gut knew she had just seen one of her officers gunned down, even if her brain couldn't quite grasp it yet. She stomped the brakes and spun the wheel, sending the police car into a skidding, screeching halt that left it sitting crossways in the street.

She threw the door open and rolled out as the hammering sound of automatic weapons fire blasted apart the early morning tranquility. Slugs pounded into the other side of the car. It was all that saved her from being killed like Jerry.

Her gun was in her hand. She didn't even remember pulling it from its holster. As the yammering guns fell silent for a moment, she risked a look over the hood and saw dozens of armed men pouring out of the trucks.

Home was being invaded . . . again.

These men weren't from the federal government, though. They were civilians, or at least they were dressed like civilians. They moved with military precision, though, as they began spreading out along the streets.

Alex couldn't reach the radio in the car, but she had a portable clipped to her belt. She grabbed it and keyed the mike.

"Eloise! Jimmy! Whoever's there! Officer down, officer down! I need help now in the center of town! Now!"

But was she just calling her people in to their deaths? she wondered. The strangers had way more firepower than her little department could muster.

When she released the microphone button, all she heard from the speaker was static. She tried calling the station again but got no response.

Alex dropped the radio and grabbed her cell phone. She flipped it open.

No signal.

That was crazy. All of Home had good cell phone reception.

The explanation hit her brain like a bombshell. The invaders had somehow knocked out all communications in the vicinity. They had to have some sort of machine emitting a powerful electromagnetic pulse that blocked digital signals. All the computers in town had probably gone haywire, too.

This bunch was ready for trouble, no doubt about that.

Alex heard shouting in Spanish. Somebody was giving orders. She risked another look. A man in fatigues and campaign cap had gotten out of one of the trucks. He was the only one in uniform and was obviously in command.

Alex heard a rush of footsteps nearby. She wheeled around and saw that a squad of the invaders had flanked her. She went to the pavement and fired three rounds. The shots missed, but the men ducked back.

She was going to die here. She was sure of it. She would never see Jack again, never get a chance to tell him goodbye. Never get a chance to tell him how much she loved him. She prayed to God that he knew that anyway. Her hand tightened on the gun butt and she swallowed hard as she waited for the killers to charge her again.

"Hold your fire!" a man called in English. "Hold your fire, *por favor.*"

A couple of tense seconds went by. Then the man said, "Señorita, can you hear me? I know you are either Chief Bonner or Officer Carlyle. Please throw out your weapon and surrender."

Alex hesitated. The idea of surrendering didn't sit well with her, especially after everything that had happened in the past week.

On the other hand, taking on a small army alone was just another way of committing suicide.

Before making up her mind, she wanted to know something.

"Who the hell are you?" she asked. She had a feeling she was talking to the man in fatigues.

That hunch was confirmed when he replied from the other side of the car, "General Jose Luis Garaldo. This town is now under my command."

"What gives you that idea?"

A chuckle came from him. "The fact that my men have all the guns, *señorita*."

And who was to blame for that, Alex asked herself bitterly?

One man . . . and his current address was 1600 Pennsylvania Avenue.

"What is it you want, General?" Alex asked, still stalling for time. She wasn't sure why she was doing that when she faced odds like these.

"Do not concern yourself with that," Garaldo snapped. "But I give you my word, those who cooperate will not be harmed."

"That's a damned lie," Alex snapped. "I saw your men shoot down my officer."

"Ah, you are the chief of police," Garaldo said. Alex chided herself for giving away even that much information. "You and your officers are the only ones in this town who are still armed," Garaldo went on. "You must understand that we will take no chances with you. Nothing must be allowed to interfere with our mission."

"And what's that?"

"Enough," Garaldo replied in a harsh, impatient tone. "Throw out your weapon and surrender, Chief Bonner, or you will be ki—"

The leader of the invaders didn't get to finish his threat. Tires squealed around a corner, and suddenly the street was filled with gun thunder once again.

Chapter 38

Alex ducked lower as bullets whipped through the air, whined off the pavement, and thudded into buildings and parked cars. She saw one of her own department's police cars barreling toward her. J. P. Delgado had his left hand out the window, firing his service revolver, while his right hand suddenly spun the wheel. The patrol car slid to a stop only a few feet from Alex.

"Come on!" Delgado yelled through the open passenger side window.

Alex didn't have to be invited twice. She didn't take the time to open the door, either.

She just surged to her feet and dived headfirst through the open window.

She wound up with her face in Delgado's lap, but under the circumstances neither of them had the time nor inclination to think about how awkward that was. Bullets continued to slam into the car as Delgado hauled the wheel around and tromped on the gas. The rear window starred under the impact of the slugs, then suddenly shattered, spraying glass through the interior of the car.

Alex pulled her legs in and levered herself up

into a sitting position. Keeping her head low, she twisted in the seat and fired back through the broken window. A fierce surge of satisfaction went through her as she saw one of the men shooting at them double over and collapse.

"Got one of the bastards!" she said as her gun clicked on empty.

"Yep, but there's still a bunch more of them," Delgado said. He cranked the wheel again and sent the car careening around a corner into one of the side streets. For the time being, bullets quit smacking into it.

Alex had a spare magazine clipped to her belt. She shoved it into the automatic and asked, "How'd you happen to show up just in the nick of time? Did my radio call get out before they shut all the comms down?"

Delgado shook his head. "No, I didn't hear a call. But I did hear the shots. I had a bad feeling about things and held off on the lights and siren until I got close enough to see what was going on." He laughed humorlessly. "Which I still don't know. Who are those men, Alex? Is the town really under attack?"

"That's what it looks like. The guy I was talking to calls himself a general. Jose Luis Garaldo, he said his name was."

"I know the name," Delgado said. "He's a general in the Mexican army, but he's even more open than his fellow officers about the fact that he really works for the Rey del Sol cartel."

"Navarre's bunch."

"Navarre was the lowest of the low. Garaldo is

almost at the top, not much below Enrique Reynosa, the boss of the whole thing."

Now that he reminded her of it, Alex recalled reading reports for the Border Patrol and the Drug Enforcement Agency about the Rey del Sol cartel, including mentions of its leader. Garaldo's name was vaguely familiar, too.

"The town's being taken over by a drug cartel?"

"Sounds like it," Delgado said. "Were all the men you saw Hispanic?"

"Well . . . yeah. And they were yelling orders in Spanish."

"God, I hate being related to those people," Delgado said fervently. "People hear my name and see my brown skin, and they think I'm like those . . . those . . . people is too good a word for them. They're animals."

"Nobody who knows you feels that way, J. P.," Alex said.

They had reached the edge of town. No one seemed to be pursuing them . . . yet. Alex knew it was just a matter of time before Garaldo sent his men after them, though.

"Now what?" Delgado asked as he slowed the car.

"We need to get to the police department. That's where all our other weapons are. Maybe the rest of the officers will head for there, too, and we can fort up inside the building. Word of what's going on here is bound to get out, and maybe we'll get some help from outside."

"That's going to be our only chance," Delgado agreed. "The problem is that Garaldo will be smart enough to know that he needs to take out the police station as soon as he can."

* * *

The shift change was at eight o'clock, so Eloise Barrigan was getting ready for Jimmy to show up, and then Clint would swing by the station and pick her up so they could go home. Their schedule made it hard for them to attend church on Sunday morning, but they always showed up for the Sunday evening service.

It had been a peaceful night and was turning into a mighty quiet morning. Too quiet, Eloise suddenly thought, like in those old Western movies when the hero starts to worry that the Indians are sneaking up on him. She picked up the microphone on her desk and said, "Clint, you hearin' me?"

There was no answer.

"Hey, Jerry? J. P.? Anybody out there?"

Alex had tried to talk Eloise into being more formal on the air, but it was hard when she had known all these people for years and considered them to be her friends.

Still getting no response, she picked up the phone and hit the speed-dial button that would connect her to her husband's cell phone. It took her a second to realize that the phone wasn't dialing. In fact, there was no dial tone on it at all. The landline was dead.

Well, that was odd, Eloise thought. She opened the drawer where she kept her purse and reached inside to take out her own cell phone.

No service. Stubbornly, Eloise tried to call Clint anyway, but what the display told her was true. The cell phone was as dead as the landline.

"Well, if that doesn't beat all," she said as the

front door of the station opened. Eloise looked up, figuring it was Clint coming in. Maybe he'd have some explanation for why the radio and all the phones were out.

Instead, the cell phone slipped out of Eloise's fingers and fell to the floor as she stared in shock at the men with guns who were coming into the station.

Jimmy Clifton didn't have a driver's license, but he had the best bike in the whole town and could get anywhere he wanted to in Home without any trouble. This morning he had gotten up and made breakfast for himself because his mom and dad were still asleep. While he was eating his cereal, he thought he heard some odd sounds from somewhere else in town, like somebody hammering nails real fast, but he wasn't sure. Whatever it was, it didn't have anything to do with him.

Now he was on his way to work, and as always, that thought never failed to make him experience a surge of pride. He knew perfectly well that he was different from most folks and couldn't do a lot of the things they could do, but he could do some things they couldn't, too. He had won awards for his excellence as a dispatcher. He might get mixed up about some things, but he never got a call wrong.

He recognized trouble when he saw it, too. When he came around the corner on his bike and started pedaling toward the station two blocks away, he spotted armed men entering the building.

That was wrong, really wrong. The men weren't soldiers, like the ones who had come into town a few days ago and taken everybody's guns. These men looked more like criminals. And those sounds he had heard earlier . . . could they have been gunfire?

Jimmy brought the bike to a skidding halt and frowned as he thought about what he had seen. His heart pounded with fear for his friend Eloise.

He didn't hear any shots from inside the station, though, so maybe she was all right.

Somebody else was going to have to figure this out and tell him what to do. Clint would know, or J.P., or the chief.

That was it. He would go to the chief's house and tell her what he had just seen.

And then the chief would fix everything. Jimmy was sure of it.

Clint Barrigan was driving past the high school when he saw the helicopter on the parking lot. It distracted him from what he had already seen, several blocks on down the highway in the center of town: some trucks stopped in the middle of the road, and a police car parked sideways across both lanes of Main Street. That had to be trouble. Clint was already worried because he hadn't been able to raise Eloise on the radio.

Now he hit the brakes as a man in a suit ran out from behind the helicopter, waving his arms as if he were trying to get Clint to stop. Clint did so, and as he did, he recognized that sleazy lawyer Cochrum. What was that weasel doing here in Home? Clint wondered. And did it have something to do with what was going on in the center of town? Lots of people were milling around down there, he noted. Maybe the Feds had come back to raise more hell.

Clint lowered the passenger-side window. Cochrum rested his hands on the sill and stuck his head into the car.

"Thank God you're here, officer!" the lawyer said. "There was a lot of shooting down the street a few minutes ago, after Chief Bonner went down there."

Alex! Clint hadn't heard an officer-needs-assistance call, but then, he wouldn't have with the radio out.

"Back away from the car, sir!"

Cochrum ignored the order. "Are we in any danger? Should we evacuate?" He waved a hand toward the helicopter.

"I don't care. Get the hell out of town if you want. Just get your head out of my car!"

Clint wasn't going to wait any longer. He stomped the gas just as Cochrum leaped back away from the patrol car. The side of the window barely cleared the lawyer's head.

Clint had a shotgun clipped under the seat. He reached down and pulled it free as he drove one-handed toward the crossroads at the center of town. He was almost there before somebody opened fire on him. One of the shots blew a front tire on the police car, and suddenly Clint found the world revolving crazily in front of his eyes as the car skidded and then rolled. It went over twice and was upside-down when it slammed into the empty car sitting in the middle of the street.

Badly shaken up but not really hurt, Clint fumbled for the release on his seat belt as he hung there. It came loose and dropped him in an ungainly sprawl on the ceiling of the car. He heard flames crackling somewhere and knew he had to get out before one or both of the gas tanks blew up. Still clutching the shotgun, he crawled through broken glass onto the pavement. He staggered to his feet and started running, instinct making him want to get as far as he could from the burning cars.

Then men with guns loomed up in front of him. Clint raised the shotgun and yelled, "Drop those guns! Get on the ground!"

They laughed at him.

And then they shot him.

But as the high-powered slugs ripped into him, dozens of them shredding his organs, he managed to pull the trigger and send a load of buckshot into one of his killers. The blast blew the man backwards.

That was the last thing Clint saw with his eyes.

But in his mind and in his heart, for an instant he saw his wife, whom he had loved ever since they were both seniors in high school, and then he was gone.

Whoever they were, they were killing cops, Clayton Cochrum thought as he ran toward the helicopter. That reporter, Wilma What's-her-name, and her cameraman, Bud, both looked terrified by all the shooting they had heard. Obviously not veterans of war zone journalism, Cochrum thought.

He revolved his hand over his head in a signal to the pilot. They were getting the hell out of Dodge, and the sooner the better.

Problem was, the son-of-a-bitch pilot didn't wait. He must have been scared, too. The rotors began to turn faster, and suddenly the chopper was in the air, and the three former passengers were still on the ground. Propwash pounded down around them. Wilma was screaming something, but Cochrum couldn't hear her over the roar of the helicopter.

The chopper lifted higher and higher, and its nose swung toward the east. Suddenly, from the corner of his eye Cochrum saw something streak through the air, trailing smoke. It headed straight toward the helicopter. . . .

Which exploded in a huge ball of fire as the surface-to-air missile struck it.

Cochrum stared openmouthed and uncomprehending at the destruction as bits of flaming wreckage began to rain down. He could have been on there, he thought. Mere moments earlier he had been cursing the pilot for leaving him behind.

The realization that he had narrowly escaped death sunk in on him, and so did the need to do something. He grabbed the arms of his two companions and shoved them toward the school.

"Run!" he urged them. "We gotta get out of here!"

"What is it?" the blonde cried. "What's going on? Who are those people?"

"I don't know," Cochrum said, "but I got a bad feeling that they're gonna be coming after us next."

CHAPTER 39

Jack Bonner's mother liked to say that he could sleep through an earthquake, but that wasn't strictly true. Yeah, he was a sound sleeper, but some things would wake him up, especially if they went on long enough.

He didn't know how long somebody had been pounding on the front door of his house, but the racket finally dragged him out of bed.

A glance at the clock told him it was a little after eight o'clock. On a Sunday morning, yet. His mom should be here. Why wasn't she answering the door?

With a vague stirring of unease inside him, Jack stumbled through the house wearing only his boxers. "Mom?" he called. "Mom, are you here?"

No answer. Well, she *was* a cop, after all, Jack told himself. She probably had to leave to take care of some sort of trouble.

He jerked the front door open and said, "Yeah, what—"

The words choked in his throat as he saw Jimmy Clifton standing there, with his bike lying on its side in the front yard. Jack had known Jimmy for what seemed like his whole life, and he liked the dispatcher.

Now Jimmy looked scared, really scared, and suddenly Jack was scared, too.

"What is it, Jimmy? Did something happen to my mom?"

"The chief's not . . . here?" Jimmy asked.

"No, I don't think so. I just got up, and I called to her, but she didn't answer."

Jimmy put his hands to his head. "I gotta find . . . the chief. Somethin' bad is . . . happenin'."

Jack wasn't the least bit sleepy anymore. "What is it, Jimmy? What did you see?"

"Men with guns . . . goin' into the police station."

Jack's first thought was that the Federal Protective Service had come back to town for some reason. "Like the ones who were here before?"

Jimmy shook his head. "No, they weren't . . . soldiers. They looked more like bad guys. And then . . . and then . . ."

"And then what? You can tell me, Jimmy."

"There was a bunch of . . . shootin'."

Alarm surged through Jack. "From the police station?"

"Nuh-uh. From downtown somewhere. And then I saw . . . a whirlybird . . . blow up."

"A whirlybird? You mean a helicopter?"

"Yeah."

"It blew up while it was in the air?" Jack had a hard time believing that, but Jimmy looked and sounded absolutely sincere.

"Yeah. I think somebody musta . . . shot it down."

Now that was just crazy, Jack thought. All this

crap couldn't really be happening. Not in Home. Not on a Sunday morning.

Tears rolled down Jimmy's cheeks. "I'm really scared, Jack," he said. "I don't know what to do. I'm s'posed to be . . . at work, but I'm scared to . . . go in the police station. I want the chief . . . to tell me what to do."

"She's not here, but I'll tell you what." Jack made up his mind. "Let me put some clothes on, and you and me'll go down to the station together. How about that?"

"O-Okay. I guess. I hope Eloise is all right."

So did Jack, but he was more worried about his mom. If some sort of gun battle had broken out downtown, the chances were that she would be right in the middle of it.

He pulled on blue jeans and a T-shirt, shoved his feet in some running shoes. "We'll take my car," he told Jimmy.

They were just about to pull out of the driveway when Rowdy's pickup screeched to a halt in front of the house. Rowdy beckoned to them from behind the wheel.

"Come on!" he called through the open window. "There's all kinds o' shit going down! It's war, dudes, war!"

Rowdy's pickup was bigger and had more power than Jack's car. They'd be better off going with him, Jack decided. "Come on, Jimmy," he said. They piled into the cab, with Jack in the middle and Jimmy next to the passenger window.

"War with who?" Jack asked.

"I dunno," Rowdy replied. "But there's been a bunch of shootin', and somebody told me there was a helicopter got shot down by a missile, out by the high school!"

Jack glanced at Jimmy. The story about the helicopter, outlandish as it was, was gaining credence.

"Maybe we should have guns," he said tentatively.

Rowdy jammed on the brakes. "That's a good idea. Are there any left at your house?"

"My mom's got a couple extra pistols she didn't turn in. And there's a deer rifle my dad didn't take with him when he split."

Rowdy turned the pickup back toward the Bonner house. "Let's get 'em, then. We may need some firepower."

"Now that I think about it, I'm not sure this is a good idea. I mean, how can we fight 'em? We're just two kids and, well, Jimmy."

Rowdy glanced over at him and grinned. "If we're bein' invaded, somebody's got to fight the sons o' bitches, dude. And it looks like we're elected."

Fargo Ford yawned and ground a knuckle against the corner of his right eye. He had dozed a little while Parker was driving, earlier in the night, but not enough to do much good.

They were all running on empty, with the exception of Earl Trussell. The little scientist had snored for hours while the others took turns driving across Texas. Earl was awake now and fiddling with the radio buttons while Ford drove and Parker dozed in the other corner of the cab. Rye Callahan was in the back of the pickup with the guns, his Stetson tipped down over his eyes.

Mostly static came from the radio speakers, with

an occasional burst of music or incomprehensible speech. Earl muttered, "Boy, you get out here in West Texas and the reception sucks."

"That's because of all these wide-open spaces," Ford said.

"Well, I'm a city boy. I need music. And concrete. And there's too much *sky*. I need buildings."

"I thought you worked at that Casa del Diablo place. It's in the middle of nowhere, isn't it?"

"Yeah, and that's one thing I didn't like about it. That and the fact that they're making bio-weapons to use on American citizens."

"Yeah, that's a bummer, all right," Ford drawled.

They were on a state highway now, having traveled on a crazy network of farm roads and county roads, some of them unpaved, for most of the night. That had taken them away from Callahan's ranch, though, and as far as Ford could tell, they weren't being followed. Once again, they had slipped away from the men who wanted them dead.

It was early Sunday morning, and the sun was up behind them, painting the flat, mesquite-dotted, unprepossessing landscape with splashes of orange and gold that made it look prettier than it really was. Mountains bulked on the horizon in the distance. Ford knew those were the mountains where Casa del Diablo was located.

He drove past a sign that read HOME 10. "Almost there," he said.

"And what are we gonna do when we get there?" Earl asked. "We need a plan, don't we?"

"We have a look around first to see if we can figure out if anything's going on. If you make a plan before you have the proper intel, you're liable to get locked into a mind-set that won't work."

"In other words, we improvise."

"Exactly."

"With our lives and the lives of God knows how many other people on the line."

"It won't be the first time," Ford said.

"And it's worked all the other times," Parker said without opening his eyes. "If you don't count the times we got shot and nearly killed."

"Oh, now I feel much better," Earl said.

"Even when we got hurt, we stopped the bad guys," Ford pointed out.

The radio was nothing but static now. Earl turned it off, then squinted through the windshield.

"What's that up ahead?" he asked.

Ford had already moved his foot from the gas to the brake, although he didn't actually press down on the pedal yet. On the other side of the cab, Parker sat up and opened his eyes.

"Trouble?"

"Don't know yet," Ford said. "Appears to be a roadblock of some sort."

"Wasn't the FPS supposed to set up checkpoints to keep guns out of Home?"

Ford nodded. "Yeah. Maybe that's all it is."

Earl pointed over his shoulder with a thumb. "John Wayne back there is sitting on a whole pile of guns."

"He doesn't look like John Wayne," Ford said. "He looks like Lee Van Cleef. Can't you get that right?"

"Whatever, dude. Hadn't we better turn around?

We don't want them to find all that hardware, do we?"

Parker said, "Hang on a minute. There's a police car and a couple of local officers up there, too. Maybe they're not looking for guns. Let's check it out, Fargo."

"All right. Tell Mr. Callahan to make sure the tarp's down good over those weapons. Maybe we can claim that it's pipe for a windmill or something."

"There you go, improvising again," Earl said.

Ford slowed the pickup. There was a black RV parked off the side of the road that probably belonged to the FPS, but a Home police car was on the shoulder with its lights flashing. Two officers walked toward the pickup as Ford brought it to a stop.

"Trouble up ahead, fellas?" Ford asked through the open window. "A bad wreck, maybe?"

"No, it's worse than that, sir," one of the officers said. Both of them were Hispanic, but that wasn't unusual out here in West Texas. "Some sort of epidemic. We're trying to keep it contained until the CDC gets here."

Ford's heart slugged harder in his chest at the mention of the word "epidemic." Had the bastards already field-tested their nerve gas by wiping out an entire town?

These two cops didn't seem upset enough to be the sole survivors from Home, though. They looked somewhat tense, but at the same time, they were just doing their jobs.

"We're just passing through on our way to El Paso," Ford said. "If we roll up all the windows and drive straight through town without stopping, don't you think it would be all right?"

The cop who had spoken before shook his head. "No, sir, I'm afraid our orders are clear. Nobody gets in or out of Home until further notice." He pointed east. "But if you go back that way for a few miles, you'll come to a county road that'll take you up to the Interstate. That'll get you to El Paso faster, anyway."

"Yeah, I suppose you're right. Thanks." Ford put the truck in reverse. "Sorry to hear about folks being sick."

"We'll deal with it, don't worry."

"Well, so long." Ford backed the truck around and headed back east.

"You believe him?" Parker asked.

"Hell, no," Ford replied without hesitation. "Too many coincidences have piled up. Casa del Diablo being so close by, the citizens of Home being disarmed, now the town's closed off. . . . *Something* is happening back there, and my hunch is that it's happening today."

"Now what?" Earl asked. "We can't get into town to look around, the way you wanted."

"Oh, we're going to town," Ford said. "We just have to find another way in, that's all."

Chapter 40

Alex and Delgado abandoned the police car behind the old abandoned cotton gin on the edge of town. The car would just draw attention, and they didn't want that.

They took the two riot guns with them, though.

That wasn't going to be enough firepower, Alex thought grimly as they made their way on foot, sticking to the outskirts of the community. They had heard all the gunfire from downtown, and it killed Alex not to be there protecting the people she had sworn to serve. Until they knew exactly what was going on, though, it was better for them to stay free to take whatever action they could.

Then they saw the helicopter get blown out of the air on the other side of town. "That was a SAM that took out that chopper," Delgado muttered. "Where do those drug cartels get their hands on weapons like that?" He made a curt gesture. "Never mind. Everything's available on the black market, and with the tons of money they make, they could afford to buy a nuke."

"Don't even think about it," Alex said, knowing that one day it might come to that.

"It still baffles me why they're trying to take over the town."

"I don't know, but we're going to stop them."

Delgado flashed her a grin. "I share the sentiment, Chief, but not the confidence. We're about as outnumbered and outgunned as anybody could be."

"We need reinforcements," Alex said, thinking about the people she most suspected of hiding guns from the FPS. "I think we're going to have to split up, J. P."

He didn't like the idea, but she named half a dozen families in town and told him to go to their houses and see if they had any weapons.

"If this is war, then we have to start putting together a resistance," Alex said. "Get all the guns you can, and people willing to use them, and head for the high school. If it hasn't been taken over, we'll use it as a staging area."

Delgado nodded. "That makes sense, I guess. What are you going to do?"

"Scout out the station. I'd still like to get in there . . . if they haven't taken it over already."

"I don't suppose it would do any good to tell you to be careful."

"I think we're well past that point," Alex said.

"Better take it slow and easy," Jack cautioned as Rowdy turned the pickup onto Main Street.

"Slow just means you're givin' the bad guys more time to aim at you," Rowdy said. Before Jack could warn him again, he tromped the gas pedal.

The pickup surged forward, heading toward the municipal complex and the police station. Too late, the three occupants saw the heavily-armed men posted along the street to keep everybody inside and traffic at a standstill.

"Look out!" Jack yelled. "They've got guns!"

"So do we!" Rowdy let out a whoop and stuck his left arm out the window so he could blaze away with the pistol in that hand.

He wasn't a very good shot with either hand, and his bullets went wild, ricocheting off the pavement. That was plenty to make the invaders return the fire, though.

When they got back in the pickup at Jack's house, Jack had put Jimmy in the middle, even though the dispatcher was bigger. Jack wanted to be at the window so he could shoot if he needed to.

He needed to now. He put his left hand on Jimmy's shoulder and pushed. "Get down, Jimmy! Get as low as you can!"

At the same time he stuck the other pistol out the window and started squeezing off shots. All that time he had spent on the firing range with Delgado paid off now. He saw one of the invaders spin off his feet, and another dropped his gun, clutched his shoulder, and staggered backwards as the pickup raced past.

"We're runnin' the gauntlet, boys!" Rowdy yelled. The pickup's engine roared. Rowdy had the truck moving at eighty miles an hour down the deserted street.

The sheer audacity of it probably saved their lives. By the time some of the gunmen realized what was going on, the pickup had already zoomed past them, through the hail of lead criss-crossing the street. Jack heard some of the bullets thud into the truck, but the hits didn't slow them down.

The police station came into view. Rowdy said, "Holy crap!" and Jack thought that was putting it mildly. A couple of big trucks were parked in front of the place, and there had to be at least fifty or sixty of the invaders waiting for them, including several manning something that looked like—

"Oh, my God!" Jack said. "That's a machine gun! Left, Rowdy, left!"

Rowdy's reaction time was the only thing that saved them. He spun the wheel and sent the pickup plunging into the narrow driveway between the saddle shop and the drugstore just as the machine gun opened up. Slugs chewed great gouges out of the pavement mere inches behind the pickup as it slewed out of the street. The driveway was only wide enough for one vehicle. Rowdy floored the gas pedal.

An SUV started to pull across the far end of the driveway. Rowdy never slowed down. The right front fender of the pickup slammed into the left front fender of the SUV. The impact threw all three young men in the pickup to the side, but Rowdy managed to hang on to the wheel and powered on past the SUV they had hit. The mirror on that side was gone, scraped away by the collision, along with a lot of paint.

"Son of a *bitch!*" Rowdy said. "That was close!"

Jack lifted his left hand and looked at it for a second, watching it shake. "Yeah."

They were on a side street now, but they weren't out of trouble. Armed men were still running after them, firing automatic weapons. Rowdy cut to the right.

"I'll come up to the back of the police station," he said.

"There's no point in it," Jack told him. "You saw how many of them there were back there. They've already taken it over."

Jimmy was still bent over so his head was below the level of the dashboard. He looked up past his shoulder at Jack and asked, "What about Eloise?"

"I don't know, Jimmy. I hope she's all right, but I just don't know."

"Those men are bad!"

"Yeah. Yeah, they sure are."

Jack was trying to figure out who the invaders were. He had gotten a pretty good look at quite a few of them, and every one he'd seen was Hispanic. Was the U.S. at war with Mexico? Was this just the first step in an actual invasion of the entire country?

Jack didn't believe he was a bigot, no matter what those eastern politicians and reporters said about Texans. Like most kids in this part of the state, he had grown up bilingual and was just about as fluent in Spanish as he was in English. He'd had Hispanic friends for as far back as he could remember. He just flat didn't care what color somebody's skin was, only how they acted.

But it was just a fact that the situation in Mexico was bad now. The drug cartels ran everything, and for everybody else, poverty was rampant. Jack knew enough history to know that circumstances like that were breeding grounds for resentment and jealousy, and corrupt leaders could play on that to get people to do whatever they wanted. That was the classic way a lot of America's own politicians gained power in the first place and then hung on to it once they had it.

So, yeah, an actual invasion from Mexico was a possibility, Jack thought. Home, Texas, might be ground zero in a new war.

Or it might just be something as simple as some of those drug smugglers flexing their muscle. Everybody knew they were better armed than the Mexican army. They would have what it took to shoot down a helicopter and take over a town.

"Stay on the back roads and head for the high school," Jack told Rowdy.

"The school? Why?"

"It's Sunday. Nobody will be there. Maybe those guys know that and won't pay much attention to it. We can get in and hide out there while we figure out what to do."

"Hide out?" Rowdy frowned. "I don't much like the sound of that. I want to fight these guys!"

"We tried that, and it's pure luck we didn't get ourselves shot to pieces. We've got to lie low for a little while, maybe find a way to get some reinforcements."

"Well . . . all right. But I want another shot at those guys before this is over."

"I'm sure you'll get it," Jack said.

Alex sank down on the roof and put her back against the low wall that ran around it. Even this early in the day, the black asphalt that coated the roof was hot under her butt. She wouldn't stay here long, but she had to get her nerves back under control.

She was on top of Wendell Post's hardware store, closed down since Wendell had been taken into federal custody a few days earlier. She had been sneaking along behind the building when she spotted a ladder lying on the ground along the base of the rear wall. That was when it had occurred to her the roof might be a good vantage point for her to have a look around. She had propped the ladder against the wall and climbed up, swinging quickly over the lip and staying low so no one down below would be able to spot her as she crawled to the front of the building.

She had just gotten into position when a pickup she recognized as belonging to Rowdy Donovan roared down Main Street. At least two people were inside the truck, trading shots with the invaders, and Alex had no doubt the second person was Jack.

The crazy kids! . . . Crazy, valiant kids . . .

She had done what she could to help them, all the while gripped by utter terror that she was about to watch her son die right in front of her. Using her pistol, she had picked off several of the gunmen who were shooting at the pickup. She didn't care if the killers spotted her, not as long as it helped Jack and Rowdy get away.

But that was the funny thing. With all the shooting going on, none of them seemed to notice the sharp cracks of the pistol from the top of the hardware store. Alex pushed her luck, killing half a dozen of the invaders before the truck disappeared down an alley. She stopped shooting then and listened, wincing when she heard the tortured crash of metal against metal.

The engine of Rowdy's truck continued its distinctive roar, though. Alex knew the sound of it quite well. The pickup might have collided with another vehicle, but it was still going. The sound of it, along with the shots, gradually died away.

Alex started to breathe again. Maybe Jack was all right after all. Maybe he had survived that foolhardy stunt.

When she saw him again, she was going to have a long talk with him about taking such stupid chances. . . .

After her heartbeat settled down, she turned and knelt at the low wall around the roof, surveying what she could see of the town. Nobody was moving around now. Home appeared to still be asleep in the morning sun, as if no one's alarm clock had gone off today.

That so-called general, Garaldo, had sent his thugs out all over town to frighten the citizens and seize control. For now, he appeared to have succeeded. Quiet gripped the community.

But it was an uneasy quiet, with a brooding sense of something about to happen.

Nearly a hundred years earlier, Alex recalled from her history lessons, Pancho Villa and his followers had crossed the border and raided a town over in New Mexico, bent on plunder and destruction. She had thought the same thing might be going on here, but as time passed, it seemed less and less like these invaders intended to loot Home. They were here for some other reason, she sensed, although Alex had no idea what it might be.

She couldn't get to the police station. She had seen how many of the gunmen were gathered there now. That was out. The only course of action remaining open to her was to head for the high school and hope that Delgado had been able to find some citizens willing to fight.

They should have fought harder against letting the FPS take their guns away from them, she thought bitterly as she crawled across the hot asphalt toward the ladder. Then they wouldn't have been defenseless when those damned cartel thugs came in here.

A quick check of the alley told her it was still deserted. She went down the ladder as fast as she could.

Her feet had barely touched the ground when the rear door of the hardware store was kicked open and men with heavy rifles and automatic pistols rushed out into the alley to surround her. She started to reach for her pistol but froze as she realized that if she pulled the gun, she would be riddled with bullets in a matter of seconds.

General Garaldo sauntered out of the store and smirked at her. "Chief Bonner," he said. "How pleasant to see you again. One of my men thought he saw someone up on the roof, but I did not anticipate that it would be you."

One of the invaders plucked Alex's gun from its holster.

"Come," Garaldo went on. "We will go back to the police station, and you will be my guest for the momentous events transpiring here today."

And since Alex wanted to know just what those events were going to be—not to mention the fact that she was surrounded and had no choice—she went.

CHAPTER 41

Jack, Rowdy, and Jimmy approached the high school from the back, past the baseball diamond, the soccer pitch, the tennis courts, and the outdoor basketball and volleyball courts the P.E. classes used. They didn't see anybody moving anywhere as they approached the back of the gym.

The latch on one of the windows into the boys' locker room had been broken ever since the past school year. A lot of the guys knew about it, but they kept it quiet so they could sneak in and play basketball whenever they wanted to.

That was going to come in handy today, although Jack never would have dreamed before now that sneaking into a gym could play a part in a war.

"I can't go in . . . there," Jimmy said when Jack and Rowdy had levered the window open.

"Sure you can," Rowdy said. "Jack can go in first, and then he'll help you while I give you a boost out here."

"No, I mean . . . I can't break into the school."

"We're not breaking in, Jimmy," Jack said. "The

window was unlocked. You saw how we got it open without any trouble."

"It's still . . . trespassing. We don't have permission to . . . be here."

Jack saw the exasperation on Rowdy's face, so before his friend could say something hurtful, he went on quickly, "This is an emergency, Jimmy. You know all about emergencies. You've handled enough of 'em over the years."

"Well . . . yeah, I . . . guess so."

"Sometimes you have to bend the rules a little in an emergency, right?"

Jimmy shrugged. "The chief says . . . we go by the book."

"I know. Believe me, I know. But I also know she'd want us to get somewhere safe and out of sight, so those bad guys can't get us."

"Yeah, that's . . . true." Jimmy sighed and nodded. "All right, but it's . . . high. I don't know if I can climb in."

Rowdy slapped him on the shoulder. "Sure you can, buddy. Like I said, we'll help you."

It took a few minutes, but all three of them managed to get inside. Jack felt better right away because of the familiar surroundings, and because they weren't out in the open where they could be spotted easily anymore.

"We'll go to the library," he said. "That'll give us a good view of the front of the school. We'll be able to see if anybody's coming."

Rowdy had brought the deer rifle from the pickup. "Yeah, maybe we can pick 'em off."

"We don't shoot unless we have to," Jack said. "That'll just draw attention to us."

"Don't you want to kill as many of those bastards as we can, Jack?"

"Yeah. Yeah, I do." And Jack was surprised to realize he was telling the truth. He had never considered himself a really violent person, but those guys had come into his town and shot it up and killed God knew how many people already. Yeah, given the chance, he could pull the trigger on any of them.

Hell, yeah.

With all the lights off, the hallways of the school were dim and shadowy and kind of spooky. Jack had never seen them this empty. Their footsteps echoed hollowly as they made their way through the wings of the sprawling building to the area where the administrative offices and the library were located. The library had several big windows that looked out over the front of the school.

The library doors might be locked, Jack thought, but they would force their way in if they had to.

When they reached the double doors that were half-glass, Jack grasped the handle of one and pulled. It opened easily. That was a relief. With everything that had gone wrong so far today, it was only fair that something go right for a change.

He went in and half-turned to motion for Rowdy and Jimmy to follow him. The door swung shut behind them as they came in.

Someone lunged out of the shadows between some sets of shelves, tackled Jack, and drove him to the floor, knocking the air out of his lungs and stunning him.

* * *

Eloise was still alive. That was something to be thankful for, anyway, Alex thought as she was prodded through the police station at gunpoint. Eloise had been tied into her chair at the dispatch station. Her face was pale and tear-streaked, and when she saw Alex, she exclaimed, "Oh, my God! Alex, they got you, too?"

"Yeah, I'm afraid so."

"What about Clint? Have you see him? Do you know if he's all right?"

Alex could only shake her head and say, "I don't know. I haven't seen him."

Sounding amused, Garaldo asked, "Who is this Clint?"

"One of my officers," Alex grated.

Garaldo shrugged. "Then he is probably dead. We have killed all of them we have found, except for you, of course. Four men and a woman."

Eloise began to sob, and Alex felt her stomach clench in horror at the casual way Garaldo talked about murdering her officers.

But Garaldo had said four men and a woman. The woman was poor Betsy, of course, but there were five male officers in Home, counting the two reserves. Alex was sure that Lester and Antonio would have tried to reach the station when the trouble broke out, only to run into Garaldo's killers.

That left one man unaccounted for. There was really no way of knowing who it might be, but Alex hoped it was J. P. Delgado. Then she felt an immediate twinge of guilt, because if Garaldo was telling the truth, and if Delgado was alive, that meant Clint Barrigan was dead and Eloise was a widow.

But it was possible none of them would survive

this bloody Sunday, she reminded herself. Highly likely, in fact.

Garaldo had her taken on into her office. Hands pushed her down into a chair in front of the desk, while Garaldo himself went behind the desk and sat down in the comfortable old leather chair. He drew his pistol, a heavy Colt .45 automatic that looked like U.S. Army issue, and laid it on the desk in front of him. Then he made a shooing motion with his hand. The men who had brought Alex in withdrew, closing the door behind them.

She was alone with the general now. She gauged the distance between them and tried to figure the odds of her being able to grab that gun before Garaldo could pick it up and kill her.

Of course, even if she was successful, the men in the other room would just rush in and shoot her to pieces.

"You probably are wondering why I don't simply kill you as we have killed the rest of your police force," he said as he pushed his campaign cap to the back of his head. He was a stocky, ugly man with the very dark skin, hair, and eyes that said he had a lot of Indian ancestors in his background. "I've given orders that as many of the city leaders are to be left alive as possible. The citizens will remain calmer if they know the mayor and the police chief are cooperating with us."

"I'm not cooperating with you," Alex pointed out. "I'm your prisoner."

Garaldo inclined his head. "True, but in a little while you'll be coming with me. We will drive around town, and using the speaker on my vehicle, you will tell the people to stay in their homes and not cause any trouble. When we have what we want, we will leave and no one else will have to be hurt."

"What *do* you want?" Alex asked. "Why have you and your men invaded my town?"

"Your town," he repeated with a grin. "I like that. I would feel the same way if I were in your position, Chief."

"You didn't answer my question."

"And why should I? I am in charge here, not you." Garaldo shrugged. "But what can it hurt? We have time . . . time to kill, as the old saying goes. The shipment will not be here for several hours yet."

"Shipment?" Alex frowned. "What sort of shipment? Drugs? One of the other cartels is bringing through a big load that you're going to hijack?"

Garaldo put his head back and laughed. "This goes far beyond drugs, Chief Bonner. What we are after today is nothing more or less than destiny." He clenched a fist and thrust it out in front of him. "Destiny! For Rey del Sol, and for me, and for all of Mexico! Destiny, in canisters not much bigger than a tank of oxygen. . . ."

And as Alex listened in horror, General Jose Luis Garaldo continued to talk.

"Hang on to him! Get his gun! Don't let him up!"

"Then help me, for God's sake!"

Jack fought back wildly as the men yelled and grappled with him. Then a woman screamed, "Look out for the others!"

Jack heard a grunt, and the weight that was on top of him went away. Chairs toppled over with a clatter and a crash. A face loomed over Jack, and he struck instantly, driving his fist into it. The man rolled away, groaning in pain.

Jack scrambled to his feet. He saw Rowdy wrestling with another man next to one of the library tables. A pretty woman with disheveled blond hair grabbed one of the overturned chairs and lifted it like she was going to hit Rowdy with it.

"Jimmy, grab her!" Jack said. "Don't let her hurt Rowdy."

Jimmy did as he was told, looping one arm around the woman's waist from behind and grabbing the chair with his other hand. She screamed again as he lifted her off the floor.

With clenched fists, ready to continue the fight, Jack swung toward the first man who had tackled him. That man had made it to his knees. He held up his hands, palms out, and yelped, "Hey, no more! Take it easy, compadre! I think there's been a mistake made here."

A surge of surprise went through Jack as he realized the man looked familiar. A second later, he placed the face from various newcasts. This was Clayton Cochrum, that scumbag lawyer who had represented Emilio Navarre.

And the blonde was a TV reporter. Jack remembered seeing her, too. He didn't know who the other guy was, but obviously not one of the army of thugs that had invaded Home this morning.

"Rowdy," Jack said. "Rowdy, take it easy. I think we're all on the same side."

Cochrum struggled to his feet. "There you go, kid. You're thinking straight now." He took hold of his chin and wiggled his jaw back and forth, wincing as he did so. "Damn, you pack a hell of a punch for a youngster."

"You're the one who jumped me, mister," Jack said coldly.

"We thought you were some of those . . . those killers. The ones who blew our helicopter out of the sky."

"I saw . . . that," Jimmy said.

The reporter twisted and slapped at him. "Put me down, you big oaf! What the hell's wrong with you? Are you retarded or something?"

"I have . . . Down Syndrome." Carefully, Jimmy put the woman back on her feet. "I'm sorry."

Jack said, "You don't have anything to apologize for, Jimmy. She would've hit Rowdy with that chair if you hadn't stopped her."

"So who's this guy I'm sittin' on?" Rowdy asked from the floor. "Do I let him up?"

"He's Wilma's cameraman," Cochrum explained.

"Yeah, let him up, Rowdy," Jack said. "What are you people doing in here?"

"Trying to stay alive. What about you?"

Jack shrugged. "Same thing, I guess."

Rowdy stood up. The cameraman climbed to his feet and glared at him.

Cochrum said, "After those guys shot down the helicopter, we figured they might come looking for us, so we ran around the school and broke a window. That let us into the kitchen. From there we came up here so we could keep an eye out through the windows. Nobody's come poking around, though, until you kids."

"They probably figured you were all on the helicopter," Jack said. "And we're not all kids. Jimmy there is a grown man. In fact, he's one of the dispatchers for the police department."

"Really?" Cochrum looked at Jimmy. "What are the cops doing to stop those crazy killers?"

"I don't . . . know. We can't find the . . . chief. She's Jack's mom."

Cochrum turned his attention back to Jack. "You're Chief Bonner's son?"

"That's right. We tried to get to the police station, but there were too many of them for us to get through. We retreated here."

"You've got guns," the reporter said. "Nobody in Home is supposed to have guns."

Jack frowned. "Well, lady, you'd better hope that we're not the only ones, because if we are, there's a good chance none of us will live to see the sun go down today."

He might have said more, but at that moment, voices sounded somewhere outside the library, echoing in the school's deserted hallways. Jack held up a hand and whispered, "Somebody's coming!"

CHAPTER 42

Since it seemed likely that whoever was responsible for the roadblocks would have all the routes into Home closed off, Ford, Parker, Earl, and Callahan abandoned the pickup and approached the town on foot. Ford, Parker, and Callahan were armed with pistols and rifles. Reluctantly, Ford had even given Earl a pistol, warning him, "If you shoot me, I'll never forgive you."

"I'll try not to, but you're an awfully big target," Earl had said.

Callahan had done enough hunting in his life to know how to move across the landscape undetected. So had Ford and Parker, but they had been hunting men, not wild game.

"Just do what we do," Parker told Earl.

"I'll try."

Ford recalled seeing a creek that ran close to Home on the map they had studied the day before. They had circled to the north, found where the road they were on crossed the creek, and pulled off to park the pickup under the bridge where it wouldn't be noticed. Then they set off, following the creek as it meandered south toward the town, several miles away. The banks of the streambed were high enough, and enough brush grew along them, that it was unlikely anybody would spot them as they moved along.

The creek ran to within five hundred yards of the edge of the town, then curved west before looping south again and crossing the state highway a mile or so west of the city limits. The four men stopped when they were north of Home and lay at the top of the sloping bank where they could look through the brush at the community. Callahan had brought binoculars from the pickup. He trained them on the town and studied it for a few minutes.

The rancher grunted and passed the binoculars to Ford. "Take a look for yourself," he said. "I don't see anybody movin' around except some fellas carryin' automatic weapons."

"The FPS?" Parker asked.

"No," Ford said as he peered through the glasses and spotted some of the men Callahan had mentioned. "Civilians. Hispanic males, all appearing to be in their twenties and thirties."

Parker frowned. "And they're armed?"

"Oh, yeah."

"That sounds like drug cartel goons. But we're north of the border."

"That doesn't matter much anymore. The Rio Grande is less than fifty miles away. From what I've heard, the cartels have a lot of influence over here, and they're getting more powerful all the time." Ford passed the binoculars to Parker. "Whoever those civilians are, it looks like they've taken over the town."

Parker studied the situation for a moment and then said, "Yeah. It looks like a military occupation, the way they've got guards posted and patrols moving around the streets. What the hell's going on?"

Earl said, "This is just off the top of my head, you understand, but, uh, what if they're transporting the first shipment of that nerve gas out of Casa del Diablo today? Wouldn't that be something those cartel types would like to get their hands on? They're always at war with each other, right?"

The other three men stared at the young scientist. Earl said defensively, "Hey, it's just a theory. I don't know anything about this kind of stuff."

"It's a good theory," Ford said. "It would explain a lot."

"How would a bunch of Mexican drug smugglers find out about Casa del Diablo?" Parker asked.

Callahan snorted. "Shoot, they got folks workin' for 'em all over Texas. Most of the people who come over here from Mexico are just lookin' for a better job, but some of them already got a good job . . . workin' for the cartels. And some of 'em go along with it because they still got relatives below the border who'll be in danger if they don't cooperate. When somebody crosses the cartel, it's not just them who pays the price. Their whole family usually gets wiped out, too."

Ford nodded and said, "That's right. There's no telling where they have agents these days. They could find out when a shipment is scheduled."

"But we don't *know* they're bringing out the nerve gas today," Earl pointed out. "I just said they might be."

"And that's what we have to find out," Ford said. "Earl, why don't you stay here?"

"By myself?"

"No, Mr. Callahan will stay with you," Parker said.

The rancher objected. "Wait just a cotton-pickin' minute. I got shot at, too. I want to know what it's all about."

"Yeah, but somebody's got to live through this so that the truth will have a chance to get out," Ford said. "That's gonna be up to you and Earl here. Besides, getting in and out of places where everybody wants to kill us is what Brad and I are good at."

Callahan rubbed his jaw and frowned. "Well . . . I don't like it. But I reckon you've got a point. The boy and me will stay here . . . for now."

"Don't I get a say in this?" Earl asked.

"No," the other three men said together.

"All right, all right. Go do your secret agent, commando thing. Just don't forget that we're out here, okay?"

"We'll be back to get you," Parker promised.

"If we're alive," Ford added.

"Have you heard of a place called Casa del Diablo?" General Garaldo asked.

"House of the Devil," Alex automatically translated. "No, that doesn't sound familiar."

"I am not surprised. Few know of it except the people who work there, and their masters at the very highest levels of your government. It's a scientific research facility located in the mountains west of here. They're developing nerve gas and other biological and chemical weapons."

Alex's eyes widened. "Nerve gas?" she repeated. "The U.S. doesn't use things like that on other countries. We never have."

Garaldo laughed and shook his head. "You misunderstand, Chief. The gas is not intended to be used in a war against another country. It will be used *here*, in this country, against the enemies of the man who is now your President."

The horror of what Garaldo had just said, the sheer enormity of it, was almost too much for Alex's brain to comprehend. She shook her head and said, "No. That's not possible. I don't agree with the man's politics, but he wouldn't . . . he'd never get away with such a . . . it's just not possible!"

"Of course, it is," Garaldo said calmly. "If a man believes strongly enough in something, he will do anything to accomplish it. I have never met your President, but I have looked into his eyes in news broadcasts and seen what is there. He is like the Spanish priests of the Inquisition. He believes so strongly that he is correct in his thinking, he will do anything in his power to impose his will on the country. Do you not understand? You foolish Americans have put a man in office who truly loathes his own country and blames it for everything that is wrong in the world. Therefore, he must reshape it into what he believes is right: A country that is weak and defenseless, a country where a relative few do all the work and support the many who will not, a country where success is punished and lack of effort is rewarded. What is *wrong* with you people?

Did you not *see* for yourselves what sort of man he is while he was running for election?"

Garaldo shook his head as if he were honestly baffled. "Elections are for fools. If a man is strong enough, he should seize power for himself! But I will give your President credit for one thing. The sheep you call voters may have put him in office, but now that he's there, he will stop at nothing to stay in power. *That* is the reason for Casa del Diablo's existence. He plans to wipe out his enemies and everyone who disagrees with him. There will be no more elections in the United States, at least not for this President." Garaldo smiled. "That is his intention, anyway. But today will change all that."

Alex struggled to make sense of everything Garaldo had said. "What are you talking about?" she asked now in a voice hollow with strain.

"Today, the first shipment of nerve gas will leave Casa del Diablo and be brought through your town on its way to Washington. My men and I will stop it and take it for ourselves." Garaldo's smile widened into a wolfish grin. "Señor Reynosa y Montoya, the head of Rey del Sol, believes that I will bring the gas to him so he can use it to eliminate his rivals and make himself the most powerful man in all of Mexico."

"But . . . that's not what's going to happen?"

Garaldo made a curt, slashing motion with his hand. "Reynosa is a criminal, a common thug addled by perversion! All he wants is to make himself the boss of all the criminals. He lacks the vision a man needs in order to truly take advantage of this opportunity."

"And you have that vision," Alex guessed.

"Indeed I do, Chief." He closed his hand into a fist again. "The leadership of the other cartels will be wiped out by the gas, but so will Señor Reynosa and his inner circle. Then it will be *I* who seize power! I will be the one to truly unite Mexico for the first time in many years. Then it will be time to turn our attention northward, to the cruel giant who has dominated my country for far too long."

"You're talking about the United States."

"Of course! With the weapons at my command, it will be my turn to impose my will on your country, and I will begin by demanding the return of the land stolen from us so long ago!"

"You mean Texas?" Alex asked.

"Texas, California, New Mexico, Arizona . . ." Garaldo shrugged. "Your President will be glad to return them to their proper owners. Has he not already figuratively given away much of your country to foreign powers? Now he shall give some of it away literally, and the *reconquista* movement will not stop there. Eventually, Mexico under my command will become the world's one, true superpower, as it should have been all along!"

Well, that cinched it, Alex thought. General Jose Luis Garaldo was crazy. Certifiably insane. He would never be able to make his mad plan a reality.

But in attempting it, he might kill hundreds of thousands, maybe even millions of innocent people, in the U.S. and Mexico both. If he got his hands on that new nerve gas—the very existence of which Alex still struggled to grasp—there was no telling how much damage he might do before he was stopped.

And there was just the slimmest of chances that he might succeed, at least in blackmailing the U.S. into ceding the southwestern states back to Mexico.

After all, nobody with any sense would have dreamed that the President could get away with as much as he already had.

Garaldo spread his hands. "So, Chief Bonner, now you know what I intend to do. You can see that your only choice is to cooperate with me."

Alex glanced again at the gun on the desk. Cooperating wasn't her only choice, not at all. She could still make a play for the pistol. If she could get her hands on it, she could kill Garaldo, even though it would surely cost her her own life a moment later when his men rushed in. But without their leader, could the plan go forward?

That was a chance she might have to take.

Garaldo raised a finger. "I can see what you are thinking, Chief. I beg you, consider not only your own life, but those of the citizens of Home."

"What are you talking about?" Alex asked tightly.

"My intention is to leave them alive when my men and I pull out later today. But I would not have to be merciful. In fact, it might be good to have a small field test of the nerve gas. . . ."

Alex went cold all over. "You wouldn't," she said. "That would be cold-blooded murder."

"No. It would be the first act in a long-overdue war." Garaldo shrugged. "Anyway, what makes you think I would hesitate at cold-blooded murder?"

He had a point there. Still, every fiber of Alex's being itched to make a grab for that gun. . . .

And she might have, if the ground hadn't suddenly jumped under them from the force of an explosion that shook the whole town.

It was a minor seismic disturbance, barely enough to make the needles on the gauges wobble. But on this particular day, that was just enough to trigger a red flag and send an e-mail. That e-mail prompted a technician in the basement room that didn't officially exist to tap some keys on his computer terminal and call up current surveillance satellite footage for the area of West Texas where the ground had shaken briefly a few moments earlier. The tech frowned at what he saw as he zoomed in.

That resulted in a phone call to the Chief of Staff, one of the few people who knew this room existed. He was so disturbed by what he heard that he came down to the basement himself to look at the footage.

Then he rushed upstairs.

"Sir?"

"What is it, Geoff? I'm getting ready to go play golf with the Speaker of the House. She won't like it if I'm late."

The Chief of Staff swallowed hard. "It appears that something is happening in Home, sir."

"Home? The place where we took away their guns?"

"The town that's sitting right on the route out of Casa del Diablo. You know what's happening today—"

The President turned sharply and held up his hand to stop the Chief of Staff. "I don't know anything,*" he said.*

"Yes, sir, I realize the plan is maximum deniability, and that's why we've committed so few resources to the operation, for the sake of secrecy and not calling attention to it, but—"

"But nothing. Don't tell me anymore."

The Chief of Staff knew what he was risking, but he had to do it. He had to speak.

"Sir, it appears that a military force of some kind has occupied and taken over Home."

The President was so stunned that he sat down. "A . . . a military force? Our military? The FPS, maybe?"

The Chief of Staff shook his head. "No, sir. I wish that was the case. I don't know who these people are, but if they're able to stop that shipment and take control of the cargo themselves—"

The President held up a hand to stop him again. "This is unacceptable. How could anyone have found out about this, after everything we've done to keep it quiet?"

"I don't know, sir. I truly don't."

But the Chief of Staff had just had a terrible thought. It had to do with Julia Hernandez, and the fact that the Mexican border was less than fifty miles from Home. . . .

Deal with that later, he told himself. One crisis at a time. And this was a real crisis, no doubt about that.

The President took a deep breath. "All right, Geoff. You know what to do."

"Sir . . ."

"Execute the emergency plan," the President said heavily. "When will the trucks reach Home?"

The Chief of Staff checked his watch. "A little less than two hours from now. I'll get in touch with them immediately and have them turn back to Casa del Diablo."

"No."

The Chief of Staff stared at his boss. "No?" he repeated. "Did you say no, sir?"

"That's right."

"But . . . that's the emergency plan, and we have plenty of time to implement it."

The President shook his head. "No, I'm talking about Operation Omega."

The Chief of Staff was shaken to his core. "Sir, we can't—"

The President seemed oddly calm now, as if he had accepted the inevitability of what had to happen. "We knew we'd be taking this step someday, Geoff. It's the reason for Casa del Diablo's very existence. It's happening sooner than we expected, that's all."

"But if we stop the trucks—"

"Whoever those men are who have taken over the town, they know what's coming. They must, otherwise they wouldn't be there, today of all days. If they know, then it's possible some of the citizens of Home have found out by now, too." The President shook his head again. "No, Geoff, I'm afraid this is the only way. I want a team of General Stone's special operatives in the air ASAP. They'll intercept the trucks before they reach Home and take charge of the canisters. They're to bring all but one of them back to FPS headquarters."

"All but one," the Chief of Staff repeated hollowly.

The President smiled. "I think one canister of the gas will be enough to make sure no one in Home ever reveals what they know, don't you?"

CHAPTER 43

Ford and Parker waited until what looked like a hundred or more armed men rushed out of the police station and headed down the street toward the site of the explosion.

Finding that gasoline tanker parked at the edge of town had been a stroke of luck. Neither agent knew for sure what it was doing there, but they could make a guess. There were several places in Home that sold gas. The truck had probably been stopped at one of them when the invaders came in and took over. Nobody would want stray bullets flying around anywhere near a tanker full of gasoline, so they had moved it to the outskirts of town to get it out of the way.

For men with their specialized skills, it wasn't that hard to rig the truck's fuel tank to blow, and when it did, the gas in the big tank went up, too. That made one heck of a nice distraction. The invaders had to figure that they were under attack, so most of them would rush to the scene to repel that attack. They wouldn't find anything except a burning tank trunk.

But by that time, Ford and Parker would be in

the police station. They wanted to get their hands on some communication equipment, on the off chance that the invaders weren't jamming everything. If that were the case, at least they could grab some more weapons and maybe find somebody who could tell them exactly what was going on here.

They ran along the alley toward the police station's back door. The guard who had been standing there before the blast had ducked inside, probably to check for new orders. He reappeared just as Ford and Parker reached the door. Parker's hand shot out and grabbed the front of the man's shirt. The guard was too startled to put up a fight as Parker jerked him forward and head-butted him.

Ford slammed the butt of his pistol into the back of the guard's head a split-second later. The double blow, front and back, was enough to knock the man out cold.

Parker lowered the guard to the ground and took his rifle. They had left the rifles they'd brought from the ranch with Callahan and Earl, since the weapons would have been in the way while the agents crawled into town.

Parker looked at Ford and nodded, then went into the station, moving fast. Ford was right behind him, pistol gripped tightly and ready for use.

They were in a hallway that led past an open door into the station's lobby. Several men armed with rifles were in the lobby, looking out the windows and the open front door. One of them must have spotted the two American agents from the corner of an eye, because he yelled a warning in

Spanish. The men whirled around and raised their rifles.

Parker had already dropped to a knee and brought the rifle he had taken from the guard to his shoulder. He opened fire with it as Ford began shooting over his head. Their bullets raked the lobby and sent the gunmen tumbling off their feet, except for one who dived through a window in a shower of glass to escape the hail of lead.

"Damn it," Ford said. "He'll fetch his friends."

"The shots would do that anyway," Parker said as he lowered the rifle.

They had just started past the open door when shots blasted inside the room.

The explosion made Garaldo snatch up the gun from the desk, and Alex cursed herself for missing her chance. He sprang from his chair and covered her.

"What was that?" he asked as a snarl pulled his lips back from his teeth.

She shook her head. "I don't have any idea."

"If any of your people are foolish enough to think they can fight back, they will all die!" Garaldo practically spat. "They cannot interfere with destiny."

"They don't care about your so-called destiny nearly as much as they do their freedom."

Garaldo laughed. "Then why did they allow their own government to come in and disarm them? Why have they allowed their own government to take more and more of their rights away from them? Your people willingly gave up their own freedom long ago, Chief, in return for cheap handouts."

As sick as it made her to agree with this maniac about anything, Alex knew that what Garaldo had just said contained a kernel of truth. In return for more and more "entitlements" paid for by confiscatory taxes on anybody the government considered rich—meaning anybody who was actually willing to work hard and make a little money—people had handed over power to those who would ensure that the system would remain in place. And now there were too few people working, and they were having to struggle too hard just to keep their heads above water, for that downward spiral to be reversed.

At the moment, though, politics was the farthest thing from Alex's mind. Survival was front and center. With Garaldo's gun pointing at her, she stood up slowly and backed against the wall when he gestured for her to do so. Outside in the hall, one of the guards trotted by.

A minute later, someone in the lobby yelled in alarm, and guns started to go off. Some of them were right outside the door in the hall.

The fight didn't last long. As the shooting and the echoes died away, Alex heard something from the other side of the door. Voices . . . American voices. Two men, from the sound of it, and they were about to step past the opening, even as Garaldo leveled his pistol at the door, obviously intending to ambush them.

Alex wasn't going to let that happen. She launched herself at Garaldo.

She got her hands on his arm and shoved it up just as he started pulling the trigger. Several shots roared out, deafening in the small confines of the modest office, before Garaldo jerked free from her grip and backhanded her with the pistol as he cursed frenziedly in Spanish. The barrel of the pistol smashed against the side of Alex's head and sent her spinning backward, stunned.

Not too stunned, though, to hear one of those wonderful American voices order, "Drop it, you son of a bitch!"

Alex caught herself on the back of the chair in which she'd been sitting earlier. A man in jeans and work shirt, holding a rifle, came into the room and leveled the weapon at Garaldo. Another man, this one with a pistol, remained in the doorway, keeping an eye on the lobby.

Garaldo sneered at the men, but didn't try to shoot again. If he had, the rifleman would have blasted him before he could pull the trigger. Garaldo set the pistol on the desk, and Alex lunged forward and snatched it up.

"Lady, what're you—" the man with the rifle bit out as Alex pointed the pistol at the middle of Garaldo's face.

She thought about how her friends and coworkers had been slaughtered wantonly by killers under the command of this man. She thought about everything Garaldo planned to do if he got his hands on that nerve gas, quite possibly including wiping out the lives of every man, woman, and child in Home. They would all be better off, safer, if she just pulled the trigger and turned that ugly, arrogant face into a crimson ruin.

But even after everything that had happened, she was still sworn to uphold the law, and killing Garaldo in cold blood would be murder.

She lowered the pistol a little and said, "He's in

command of the invasion. Who are you men?" They were dressed like cowboys, but something about them didn't really fit the part.

"We heard about what happened and came here to help," the man with the rifle replied, an answer which, Alex realized, wasn't really an answer at all.

From the doorway, the second man said, "Hey, you're that hot police chief . . . I mean, the police chief of Home. I've, uh, seen you on TV." He stiffened suddenly and barked, "Hold it!"

"Don't shoot, please don't shoot!"

Alex knew that voice. "That's Eloise," she exclaimed. "That's my dispatcher."

The man with the pistol relaxed a little. "All right, lady, come on around the corner. Anybody else up there?"

"Just the . . . the men you killed," Eloise said.

"Keep him covered," Alex told the rifleman with a jerk of her chin toward Garaldo. She stepped past the other man into the hall and put her arms around Eloise, being careful with the general's pistol as she did so. "Are you all right?"

"Yeah, I . . . I guess. Just scared."

Alex gave her a smile. "Welcome to the club." She turned back to the two men. "What are your names?"

"I'm Lawrence Ford," the one with the pistol said. "My friends call me Fargo." He nodded toward the other one. "That's Brad Parker."

"Well, Mr. Ford, Mr. Parker, as you know, I'm Chief Bonner, and I'm mighty glad to meet you. But now we need to get out of here before some of Garaldo's men come back."

"What'll we do with him?" Parker asked.

"Bring him with us," Alex decided abruptly. "He'll make a good hostage."

"Never!" Garaldo said. "You'll have to kill me!"

Parker grunted as his finger started to tighten on the trigger. "That works, too."

"Wait!" Garaldo held his hands out to them. "All right. I'll come with you. But you might as well surrender and throw yourself on my mercy. You can't win, only a handful of you. I have too many men. You'll all die."

"Maybe there's more than a handful of us," Alex said, thinking of how she had told J. P. Delgado to round up some people willing to fight and get them to the high school. "And maybe we'd rather die than let you win."

They jerked Garaldo's arms behind his back, fastened his wrists with plastic restraints, then hustled him out of the office and left the police station through the back door. Ford had gathered up all the rifles from the dead men in the lobby and carried them in his arms, except for the ones he gave to Alex and Eloise.

"Follow me," Alex said as they trotted along the alley. "We need to get to the high school."

"Why there?" Ford asked.

"Because that's where the resistance is gathering," she replied, hoping that was true.

"What resistance?" Parker asked. "I thought everybody in this town gave up their guns."

"Well, I'm hoping not everybody did. And even if they did, we've got a start on re-arming, haven't we?"

"Not a very big one." Parker hesitated. "Do you know what this is about, Chief?"

"Do you?" Alex shot back at him.

"I think we should tell her the truth, Brad," Ford said. "Hell, we're all on the same side."

Parker thought it over for a second and then nodded.

"We're American intelligence agents," Ford told Alex.

"Then this must have something to do with Casa del Diablo and that damn nerve gas they're bringing out of there today."

Ford and Parker both looked shocked. "How does a small-town police chief find out about something like that?"

"He told me," Alex said as she waved a hand toward Garaldo. "What do you think they're after?"

"Who in blazes *are* they, anyway?"

"Thugs who work for the drug cartel Rey del Sol."

Garaldo snapped, "Visionaries who believe in the destiny of Mexico!"

"Don't pay any attention to that line of bull—" Alex began as they darted across the mouth of an alley.

That was when somebody opened fire on them, steel-jacketed slugs whistling around their heads.

CHAPTER 44

In the high school library, Jack motioned quickly to Rowdy and Jimmy. "Get on either side of the doors," he told them in a half-whisper. "We'll jump whoever it is when they come in." He waved a hand at Cochrum, the blond reporter, and the cameraman. "You three hide between the shelves."

"The hell with that," the cameraman said. His name was Bud, Jack recalled. "We'll help you grab them."

"We will?" Cochrum said.

"Yeah, the odds will be better that way. Wilma, you should hide, though."

The blonde didn't argue. She scurried off and crouched nervously between two sets of bookshelves.

Jack and Cochrum joined Jimmy to the right of the doors, while Bud partnered up with Rowdy on the other side. The voices and footsteps were louder now as people came down the hall toward the library.

Jack knew perfectly well that if the newcomers were some of the heavily-armed invaders, he and his companions would probably be dead in a few minutes. But if they could take the men by surprise and get their hands on some of those automatic weapons, there was a slender chance a couple of them might survive.

Anyway, the alternative was to surrender, and Jack was in no mood to do that. Those sons of bitches had taken over his town and killed innocent people. He wasn't going to stand for that.

The library doors swung open and a man strode in. Jack launched himself in a diving tackle at his back.

Unfortunately, the man twisted around with great instincts and reflexes, grabbed Jack, and flipped him with a neat wrestling throw. Jack came crashing down on his back, and an instant later the man's knee dug into his belly, pinning him down to the library floor.

"Jack!" the man exclaimed.

Gasping to reclaim the breath that had been knocked out of his lungs, Jack found himself looking up into the startled face of Officer J. P. Delgado, his friend and the man who had taught him to shoot.

Commotion and angry yells filled the library. Delgado jerked his head around and ordered, "Hold your fire! Take it easy, these are friends."

Jack looked around, saw that Rowdy and Bud had tried to attack some of the people with Delgado, only to find themselves looking down the barrels of several rifles and shotguns.

A dozen men and women had crowded into the library with Delgado. Each of them was armed and wore a grim expression that said they were willing to fight to the death. Jack felt a wave of relief go through him as he recognized most of them.

"Don't shoot, people, don't shoot," Cochrum said. "I think we're all on the same side."

"I don't know about that," Delgado said dryly. "You're the lawyer who represented Navarre, aren't you?"

Cochrum looked nervous. "That, uh, doesn't have anything to do with our current situation."

"The hell it doesn't. If the town hadn't been mostly disarmed, we could have put up a better fight when those cartel thugs came in and took over." Delgado got to his feet and extended a hand to Jack, helping him up as well. "These people may be the only ones in town who were able to hide some guns from the Feds."

"I don't make the law, Officer," Cochrum said. "I just—"

"Shut up," Delgado said. "Are you all right, Jack?"

"Yeah, I think so," the young man replied. "It just, uh, knocked the wind out of me when you flipped me over like that. You gotta teach me how to do that!"

Delgado smiled. "If we live through this, I will. In the meantime, is there anybody else here at the school?"

Jack shook his head. "Just the six of us."

"Well, that gives us almost twenty people," Delgado mused.

Rowdy asked, "Can we put our hands down now?"

"Oh, yeah. Sure." Delgado motioned for his

"troops" to lower their weapons. He turned to Jack again. "Your mom's not here?"

"I haven't seen her all day," Jack said, trying not to let too much worry creep into his voice. He was trying to stay confident that she was all right. He asked hopefully, "Have you seen her?"

"Yeah, she was okay a little while ago. She was going to try to make it to the station."

"No!" Jack couldn't hold in the exclamation. "That place is full of those guys!"

Delgado nodded grimly. "That's what I was afraid of. She sent me sneaking around town to gather a resistance force and bring it here. She said she'd meet me here."

"She's not here yet . . . but I'm sure she will be." Jack tried to feel as confident as he hoped he sounded.

"Yeah, I'm sure she will be, too," Delgado said, but Jack had a feeling that the older man was sort of whistling in the dark, too.

Cochrum said, "Listen, is this all the people you could get? There's gotta be at least a couple hundred of those Hispanic guys, and I'll bet they're all cold-blooded killers."

"Unlike that client of yours, eh?"

Cochrum's face flushed in what appeared to be a mixture of anger and embarrassment. "This doesn't have anything to do with Emilio Navarre," he snapped.

"I wouldn't say that. Those are his amigos out there."

"You don't know that. Nothing has been proven.

Anyway, my point is that you can't fight an army with less than two dozen people! It'll be suicide!"

"Didn't you ever hear of going out fighting, Cochrum?"

The lawyer sneered. "That's just another way of describing losing. I'd rather win."

"So would I. You got any ideas?"

"Well . . . we could call for help."

Delgado shook his head. "Won't work. Somehow they've blocked all communication with the outside world. Radios, cell phones, computers, none of 'em work. My guess is that they've got some sort of machine broadcasting an extremely powerful electromagnetic pulse. No, Cochrum, win or lose, I think we're on our own." He paused. "But this may not be all of us. I couldn't cover the whole town, so several men I talked to volunteered to try to round up some more fighters. If they're successful, they'll be rendezvousing here, also."

"There still won't be enough to make it an even fight."

Rowdy said, "Hey, sometimes you've got to buck the odds, dude. We're Texans. That's what we do."

"He's . . . right," Jimmy said. "We can . . . do it."

Wilma had emerged from hiding by now. She stared at the group gathered in the library and demanded in astonishment, "Seriously, are you people actually going to listen to this . . . this retard? You can't fight an army. You'll just get yourselves killed! We'll be better off just waiting. They don't seem to know we're here, and if we stay hidden, maybe they'll just leave without bothering us."

"The lady has a point," Cochrum said. "They can't hope to hold on to the town for very long. They've got to be here for some specific reason, and once they get what they're after, they'll go." He shrugged. "We should just lie low. I say we put it to a vote. That's the American way, isn't it?"

One of the townsmen said, "You don't know a damned thing about the American way, mister. You've proven that."

"And you shouldn't call Jimmy bad names, either," one of the women said as she glared at the reporter. "He's a fine young man."

"He's not playing with a full deck," the blonde shot back. "None of you moronic hayseeds are, evidently."

Bud stepped forward and said, "That's enough, Wilma."

She looked at him in surprise, then her face darkened with anger. "Don't you talk to me like that. You're just a cameraman. I'm on-air talent!"

Bud shook his head and looked disgusted. "I've always backed you up on most stuff, but you're wrong here. This is like nothing we've ever seen before. Whatever those invaders are up to, it's got to be something really bad, and somebody has to stop them. Looks like that's up to us." He gave Delgado a nod. "I'm with you, pal, if you'll have me. But . . . I don't have a gun or anything. I don't know what I can do."

"We'll have to find something else to fight with, for those who don't have guns, I guess," Delgado said.

Jack suggested, "How about baseball bats? There's

a closetful of 'em by the gym. The P.E. classes use them."

Delgado nodded. "That's not a bad idea. Get close enough to one of the guys, brain him with a bat, and take his gun."

"Get shot, that's what you mean," Cochrum muttered. "That's what's gonna happen."

"You can stay here, counselor." Delgado nodded at Wilma. "So can the lady. We can't force you to join us."

Wilma sniffed. "Of course, you can't. We still have freedom of the press in this country, you know."

That brought scornful laughter from several of the people gathered in the library. Wilma flushed a deeper shade of red, but didn't say anything else.

"What about that vote?" Cochrum prodded.

"We don't need a vote," Delgado said. "These folks wouldn't be here unless they were willing to fight. And they know they don't have to come with us unless they want to."

Jack asked, "Where are we going?"

"Nowhere, right away. We're going to wait here for a while and give others a chance to join us. It's not easy to move around town without being spotted, but we've all proven it can be done. They've spread themselves a little too thin. Even with guards out and patrols moving around, they can't watch everywhere at once."

"What about after that?"

Delgado grinned ruefully. "I'll tell you, kid, I haven't figured that out yet. There has to be *something* we can do that would help."

Bud said, "I have a suggestion, if you want to hear it."

"Sure, why not?" Delgado replied with a shrug.

"What you said about an EMP got me to thinking . . . one pulse strong enough would knock out most, if not all, of the communications devices in town, but they couldn't count on the fact that they'd all be out for hours. There might be somebody with the know-how and equipment to fix whatever damage they did."

Delgado nodded. "That makes sense. So you think they're broadcasting a continuous jamming signal."

"That's exactly what I think. In order to cover the whole town, it would have to be centrally located."

"We saw unmarked trucks parked at the police station," Jack put in.

"Did any of them have unusual antennas on them?"

"I don't know." Jack shook his head. "They were sort of, uh, shooting at us at the time, so I didn't look real close."

Delgado said, "That's the most logical place for the jamming equipment to be. We knock it out, we can call for help."

"Which probably won't get here in time to save any of you," Cochrum pointed out. "You'll still die."

"Maybe, but those invaders won't get away with whatever it is they're trying to do. That may be the best outcome we can hope for."

Delgado looked around the room and received grim nods in return from everybody except Cochrum and Wilma. "You're all crazy," the lawyer told them.

"If that means we don't think anything like you . . . I'll take that as a compliment, counselor," Delgado said. "Now we just have to wait and see who else shows up to join forces with us."

If anybody did.

Chapter 45

Alex jerked back as slugs flew around her, but she had the presence of mind to grab Garaldo's collar and haul him with her behind a corner of the nearest building. Eloise pressed herself to the wall behind them.

Ford and Parker had been a few steps ahead, so they had lunged on across the alley and taken cover on that side. "We'll cover you!" Ford called. "Make a run for it!"

Alex was ready to do so, but Garaldo suddenly twisted and rammed his head into her face. She cried out in pain as the blow drove her head back against the wall. Garaldo took off running back the way they had come.

"Stop him!" Alex choked out. Garaldo knew the resistance was gathering at the high school, and if he reached his men with that information, it would result in a bloodbath.

Eloise brought the rifle she held to her shoulder and squeezed the trigger. The weapon was set to automatic fire, so a burst of shots ripped out from it. She probably wasn't expecting the recoil, because all the bullets went high except one.

That one clipped the upper part of Garaldo's right arm and knocked him spinning off his feet.

Alex had recovered from the blow by now. She dashed after Garaldo while Ford and Parker continued trading shots with the invaders at the other end of the alley. The general was cursing and trying to struggle to his feet when Alex reached him and put the muzzle of her rifle against the back of his head.

"Don't make me regret the decision to keep you alive," she said coldly.

Panting a little from the pain of his wounded arm, Garaldo said, "You cannot blame a man . . . for fighting for his destiny, Chief."

"Your only destiny is prison."

"We shall see."

"Get up," she ordered curtly.

"I am wounded."

"And you're lucky you're not dead. If Eloise was used to handling an automatic rifle like that, you would be. Get up."

Awkwardly, Garaldo got to his feet. Blood dripped from his arm. Alex took hold of his collar again and swung him around. She prodded him back to the alley mouth.

"Did I do all right, Alex?" Eloise asked.

Alex gave the dispatcher a quick smile. "You saved the day, that's for sure."

"Enough talk," Parker said. "Those guys look like they're getting ready to charge us. When we open up again, you go."

"Hear that, Garaldo? You come with us, or I kill you right now."

He nodded. "Yes. I understand."

With Ford aiming high and Parker aiming low, the two agents thrust their rifles around the corner of the building and opened fire. Alex sent Garaldo across first, then Eloise, then dashed out into the open herself. She felt as much as heard a bullet passing within inches of her head, but then she was behind the sheltering corner of the other building.

"Lead the way," Ford told her, and the five of them set off at a run again.

The pair of trucks set out from Casa del Diablo a little before eleven o'clock that morning, winding through the mountains on the narrow blacktop road until they reached the larger road that led through the foothills to the flatland. Each truck had a squad of armed men riding in the back with the cargo, but there were no jeeps leading the way, no armored SUVs following, no visible security at all. Secrecy was the greatest security of all, and there was nothing special about these trucks to attract anyone's attention. That was the way it had been planned all along.

The guards didn't know what they were guarding. A lot of the scientists who had worked on the various parts of the project didn't know exactly what they were working on. Fewer than a dozen people at the facility knew the whole story, and even fewer people in Washington were aware of the truth. That was the only way this could work.

Construction of Casa del Diablo had started under the administration of the previous president, but at that point the possibilities for it had been only theories. Contingency plans at most. In the end, the President had decided not to go forward with any of it. Despite all her lust for power and her self-righteous zeal, she had finally drawn the line at murdering Americans whose only crime was disagreeing with her politics.

The man in the Oval Office now had no such compunction, and as soon as he had been briefed on the Casa del Diablo project, he had given the go-ahead for it. In fact, he had instructed the project leaders to work as quickly as possible. His instincts had told him that he might need the fruits of their labors sooner rather than later. So far, the American people had been amazingly tolerant about letting him do whatever he wanted, but he knew that couldn't last.

Now, in these old, nondescript trucks, the means to crush any opposition was almost within his grasp. The cargo would be driven all the way to Washington and delivered to a military installation there. Not regular military, though. The Federal Protective Service would take charge of it until it was needed.

That day had arrived much sooner than even the President had expected, but the drivers behind the wheels of the trucks didn't know that. Neither did the guards. And so the trucks rolled on, under the arching vault of the blue Texas sky.

Alex knew about the unlocked window in the gym. She had heard Jack, Rowdy, and Steve talking about it, although they had no idea that she knew. She led Ford, Parker, Garaldo, and Eloise right to it.

Parker went in first to reconnoiter, and when he gave the all-clear, Alex told Garaldo, "Up you go."

"I cannot. Not with my hands fastened behind my back and a wounded arm."

"He's got a point," Ford said. "I'll cut you loose, Garaldo, but if you try anything else, you'll be a dead hostage instead of a live one."

Alex started to bristle. Garaldo was *her* prisoner, and she ought to be the one to decide what to do.

But Ford was right and she knew it. Garaldo had to be cut loose. Ford did so with a clasp knife he took from one of the pockets in his jeans.

While they covered him, the general climbed through the window. Eloise followed, then Alex, and finally Ford. Once they were all inside, they listened intently but didn't hear any sounds of movement from elsewhere in the school.

"If some of your people are here, where would they be?" Parker asked Alex in a half-whisper.

She thought about it for a moment before saying, "I don't know, unless they're in the library. It has some big windows and gives a good view of the front parking lot. If they're in there, they could see anybody coming."

"Sounds reasonable," Ford drawled. "Can you take us there?"

"Sure. Come on."

As they made their way through the halls, Alex felt someone watching her, and when she glanced back, Ford looked away quickly. She looked forward again and smiled faintly. Earlier, he had let slip some comment about her being hot. He was kind of a big, good-looking guy himself. Not classically handsome, by any means, but he had a rugged appeal to him.

And this was *so* not the time to be thinking about such things, she reminded herself. Not with the lives of everybody in town still in danger, not to mention the terrible threat that nerve gas would be if it fell into Garaldo's hands.

They reached the hall that led past the library doors. Alex whispered, "I'll go first."

"Maybe I should—" Ford began.

"This is *my* town, Agent Ford," Alex cut him off. "If some of my people are in there, they need to see me first."

Ford made a go-ahead gesture. "That's a good point, Chief. Just be careful."

"A little late for that, don't you think?" she asked with a curt laugh.

She cat-footed toward the doors with the rifle clutched tightly in her hands. Each door had a window set into it. When she got close enough, she leaned over to peer through the glass. Plenty of light came through the big front windows, but the library had some dark corners, too, because of all the shelves.

Alex didn't see anybody moving around. She pushed one of the doors open a few inches and listened intently without hearing anything. It appeared that no one was here after all. A pang of disappointment went through her. She pushed the door back even more and stepped into the big room.

A hand came out of nowhere, grabbed the rifle barrel, and thrust it toward the ceiling. Alex didn't fire because she didn't know who had grabbed the gun. Then strong arms went around her from behind and lifted her off the floor. She let go of the rifle with her right hand and drove that elbow back into the stomach of her captor. The man grunted in pain and let go.

Alex jerked the rifle loose and spun around,

ready to slam the stock into the face of whoever had grabbed her. She stopped short when she realized it wasn't a man at all, but rather a teenage boy.

"Rowdy!" she exclaimed.

"Oh, shit!" he said. "I mean, I'm sorry, ma'am. I didn't mean to grab your boobs, honest I didn't."

Other figures surrounded her. "Alex," she heard J. P. Delgado say, and then an even more familiar voice said, "Mom!"

Alex handed the rifle to Rowdy and then turned to embrace her son.

It was a tight, desperate hug on the part of both of them. "Jack," she whispered. "Are you all right?"

"I'm fine," he told her. "What about you?"

Alex managed to nod. "Yeah. Yeah, I'm okay." As much as she enjoyed being reunited with him and knowing that he was all right, there were other considerations. She turned her head and called, "Come on in."

Eloise entered the library first. She hugged Jack and Delgado while Ford and Parker prodded Garaldo into the room at gunpoint. Eloise stepped back from Delgado and gripped his arms.

"Clint?" she asked.

"I don't know," he said gently. "I haven't seen him."

Alex knew what Delgado being here really meant, though. Garaldo had boasted that all of her officers were dead, but he'd miscounted. One had survived . . . and now it was obvious Delgado was that one.

Which meant Clint hadn't made it, along with Jerry, Betsy, Lester, and Antonio. Grief was a powerful force inside Alex at that moment, along with a justified outrage.

More people were emerging from the shadows between the sets of shelves. Alex saw Clayton Cochrum, the blond reporter, and the cameraman. So they hadn't been on the helicopter, after all, when it was blown out of the sky. When everyone had come out, she did a quick headcount.

"Twenty-eight," she announced. "That's not a very big bunch to take on an army."

"It's more than we started with," Delgado said. "People have been showing up by ones and twos over the past half-hour. If we wait, maybe more will get here."

"I'm not sure we can afford to wait." Alex looked at Garaldo. "When's that shipment of nerve gas supposed to come through here?"

"Nerve gas?" Rowdy repeated in a surprised yelp. "What the heck's goin' on here, Chief?"

Alex glanced at the two renegade CIA agents. "Is it all right to tell them?"

"The more people who know about it, the better as far as I'm concerned," Parker said.

Ford nodded in agreement. "Getting the story out to the public is the only chance we have of surviving this with our careers even reasonably intact. At that, I doubt we'll ever be trusted out in the field again."

"All right." Quickly, Alex told everyone in the library about Casa del Diablo and the shipment of deadly nerve gas that was leaving there today.

"That's crazy," the reporter said angrily. "That's nothing but a pack of right-wing lies. The President would never do such a thing. He's an honorable man."

"You've blinded yourself to the truth," Alex

snapped. "He's used all the power at his command to try to keep the truth from getting out."

"I don't believe it, either," Cochrum said. "I voted for the guy. I donated money to his campaign. He . . . he'd never . . . well, hell."

The blonde turned on him like a she-badger. "Don't tell me you believe those awful lies! The President would never do anything bad. He's a liberal!"

Cochrum grimaced. "Sorry, babe. I've seen what happens to some guys when they get power in their hands. I don't want to believe it, but I can't rule it out."

"Oh!" The blonde fumed. "You're all just a bunch of . . . of *conservatives!*"

"Liberal or conservative doesn't have much to do with it at this level, lady," Ford said. "We're talking good and evil here. This guy"—he jerked a thumb at Garaldo—"this guy's evil. So's the guy who decided it was okay to use nerve gas on his own people if they disagreed with him. Doesn't matter what party you're from, doesn't matter what your motivation is. It's still mass murder you're talking about, and we've got to stop it."

That was the longest speech Alex had heard from Ford so far. It was inspiring, but it didn't answer the most important question.

"How are we going to stop it?" she asked.

Delgado motioned the cameraman forward. "We've been talking about that," he said, "and we've come up with an idea. . . ."

Chapter 46

The helicopters seemed to come out of nowhere, swooping down from the sky to land on the highway both in front of and behind the trucks carrying the shipment from Casa del Diablo. The spot chosen for the intercept was a good one. A deep gully ran along the right side of the highway for several hundred yards, so the trucks couldn't swerve and take off across country in that direction in an attempt to escape. The left was open, but even as the eyes of the drivers swung in that direction, another gunship landed, blocking that path, too.

The drivers had no choice except to bring their vehicles to a halt. They had been warned about avoiding accidents during the trip to D.C. Crashing into a helicopter would certainly qualify.

"Code Red, Code Red!" the driver of the first truck said into the intercom connecting him with the guards in the back of the vehicle. They were outgunned, no doubt about it, but they would fight to defend the cargo. Satellite surveillance was supposed to be following them on their journey, and this interception would prompt a rescue team to be scrambled and sent out. Maybe they could hold out long enough for help to get here.

Surprisingly, only one man jumped down from the chopper that had landed in front of the trucks. He strode toward them, a stiff-backed, middle-aged man with a wind-burned face, graying sandy hair that was cut close to his head, and a small mustache. He wore close-fitting black combat gear, and the only weapon he appeared to be carrying was a holstered pistol strapped to his hip. He looked familiar to the driver.

As the man approached, he motioned for the driver to lower his window. The driver did so, wondering if he was going to be killed.

"At ease, son," the man barked. "I'm General Wendell Stone, director of the Federal Protective Force. Change of plans."

The driver recognized General Stone from news reports about the man's ouster from the army and his subsequent appointment as head of the newly-formed FPS. That made the driver relax a little, but not much. Nobody had told him about a change of plans. Fortunately, there was a protocol for handling things like this.

The driver put his right hand on the gun beside him. "Sir? Are you sure about that?"

Stone smiled thinly. "Authorization Zulu Niner Bird Dog. That good enough for you, son?"

The driver blew out his breath in a sigh of relief. That authorization code came from the top. The very top. He nodded and said, "Yes, sir, what can we do for you?"

"My men and I are here to take charge of that cargo you're carrying."

"I thought it was supposed to be low-profile all the way to Washington."

"Like I said, change of plans. You'll cooperate, of course?"

The driver wondered for a second if there was a veiled threat in that question. Deciding that there wasn't, he nodded and said, "Sure. We were supposed to turn the stuff over to you, anyway. We're just doing it a few days sooner, that's all."

Stone grinned. "You're right, that's all." He turned and motioned to the choppers. Men clad in similar black outfits disembarked and started to gather around the trucks.

The drivers and the guards climbed out to watch as nine of the ten cases containing the mysterious cargo were unloaded from the trucks and placed aboard two of the helicopters, four cases in one and five in the other. The tenth and final case was carried to the command chopper.

General Stone nodded in satisfaction when it had been loaded aboard. "Thank you for your cooperation, son," he said to the lead driver.

"Just following—"

That was as far as the driver got, because at that point Stone drew his gun and shot him in the head, killing him instantly. The driver was dead when he hit the pavement, so he didn't hear the yells and the gunfire as the rest of his companions were wiped out.

Less than ten minutes later, the bodies had been tossed in the now-empty trucks. Some of Stone's men got into the cabs to drive the vehicles out into the empty West Texas landscape and dispose of them in a ravine that had been located on satellite photos. A few expertly placed charges would collapse the wall of the ravine on the trucks, burying them and their grisly contents forever.

And no one would ever know what had happened on this lonely stretch of West Texas highway.

From several blocks away, Bud focused the lenses of the binoculars on the trucks parked in front of the police station. He grunted as if he had seen what he was looking for and said in low tones, "Check out the one on the left. See that little dish antenna on top?"

He passed the binoculars to Ford, who studied the trucks for a moment and said, "Yeah, I see it. You think that's where the EMP is coming from?"

"I don't know if it's a regular series of EMPs or a continuous jamming signal of some sort, but yeah, that's why nobody's phones or computers will work. I'd bet on it, anyway."

"You are."

"Are what?"

"Betting on it," Fargo said as he lowered the glasses. "Betting a lot of lives, in fact."

Bud swallowed hard. "All right."

"What's the best way to disable a gizmo like that, anyway?"

"Well . . . the sure-fire method would be to blow up the truck."

"Short of that?"

"It's bound to have an on-off switch," Bud said. "Worst comes to worst, I could kill the power to it."

"And everybody's phones would start working again?"

"Probably not all of them. Some of them are probably damaged and would need to be repaired. But as many cell phones as there are bound to be around here, some of them should work, yeah."

The two men were crouched inside a big Dumpster at the side of the grocery store. A few minutes earlier, the two men had taken cover in the Dumpster to avoid being seen by one of the Rey del Sol patrols, and they had stayed there since it had proven to be a viable, if somewhat smelly, observation post for their needs.

Since they had found out what they needed to know, they climbed out and trotted around the back of the grocery store, carrying their rifles. The rest of the group had split up, since nearly thirty people couldn't move around a town the size of Home without being spotted. General Garaldo had been tied up securely and left at the high school with Cochrum and the blond reporter, who had refused to join the fight. Jimmy and Eloise had stayed there as well to keep an eye on them.

Parker and Alex were waiting in a beauty shop called the Hairateria, which sat a block off Main, facing a side street. Alex and Delgado had deployed everybody else in specific places around town, contingent on the small groups being able to reach those locations without running into any of the patrols. Since they had no way of communicating with each other, they had established a signal that would mean everyone should converge on the police station and be ready to fight. That signal was three evenly spaced shots, followed five seconds later by two more. The invaders would be able to hear those shots, too, and might figure out that they were intended as a signal, but there was nothing that could be done about that.

Parker had broken the lock on the beauty shop's back door, but the damage wasn't noticeable. Ford and Bud slipped inside the darkened interior. Parker and Alex lowered the rifles they had trained on the door when it swung open.

"Bud's pinpointed the truck we're after," Ford said. "It's parked in front of the police station, just like we thought it would be. But if we can fight our way to it, Bud says he can disable whatever's jamming communications."

Bud nodded. "Yeah, shouldn't be too big a problem. Other than staying alive, that is."

"Yeah, that's all," Parker said dryly. He turned to Alex. "We're going to need a distraction, like the one we came up with when we sprang you from Garaldo and his men."

"Why are you looking at me?" she asked. "That sounds more like a job for you two spooks."

Ford shook his head. "No, we'll be leading the attack on the trucks. You know this town better than the rest of us. Surely there's something here that'll get their attention. I don't think we'll be lucky enough to find another tanker truck to blow up."

Alex frowned in thought. After a moment, she said, "There's a warehouse full of hay on the edge of town. If somebody set fire to it, it would make quite a blaze. It might even blow up. Hay will do that sometimes, when it's been sitting around for a while and it gets too hot."

"Sounds like it's worth a try," Ford said with a nod. "If nothing else, all the smoke will get them looking away. How long will it take you?"

Alex shrugged. "Fifteen minutes, maybe, to get there and start the fire."

"All right," Parker said. "We'll use that time to get as close to the trucks as we can. When you get the fire going, give the signal for the others to attack the police station. The three of us will wait for the fighting to start, then make a run for the trucks." He looked at Bud. "Are you up for this?"

The cameraman swallowed hard, but nodded without hesitation. "Yeah. I don't know how good a fighter I'll be, but get me in that truck alive and I can handle the tech stuff."

"We're good to go, then," Ford said. "In fifteen minutes."

Alex looked at him. "Fifteen minutes," she agreed.

And she knew it might be the longest fifteen minutes of her life.

Jimmy wished there was something he could do to help his friend Eloise. She was pacing back and forth, and he knew she was really worried about Clint. So was he. He hadn't seen any of the officers except Delgado, and he wished he knew whether they were all right.

General Garaldo was sitting in a chair at one of

the library's study tables. Not only were his hands tied behind his back, but he was tied into the chair as well. His shoulders slumped in defeat.

Eloise suddenly stopped pacing and pointed her rifle at the general. "I ought to kill you right here and now," she said.

Garaldo lifted his head. He still had enough defiance in him to sneer at her. "You won't do it," he said. "You're too weak, just like the rest of your countrymen. You let your own government do anything it wants to now, and you do nothing but whine and complain! In my country, the government does what those with real power tell it to. Men like me."

"You're not telling . . . anybody what to do," Jimmy said. "You're tied up."

"That's right," Eloise said. "And if I want to, there's not a thing stoppin' me from blowin' you away, mister."

"Nothing except your own weakness," Garaldo mocked.

Eloise glared at him for a moment, then turned away with an exasperated sigh. Jimmy was glad she hadn't shot the general. The chief hadn't said anything about shooting anybody.

Eloise went over to look out the window. Jimmy moved to stand beside her. "It'll be all right," he told her. "You just gotta . . . have faith."

"I'm trying, Jimmy," she said as tears ran down her cheeks. "I'm tryin', but it's really hard."

Behind them, Garaldo caught the blonde's eye and motioned her over with his head. Wilma hesitated, but after a moment she walked up to him.

"What do you want?" she asked.

Garaldo nodded toward Jimmy and Eloise at the front windows. Keeping his voice low, he said, "The woman is insane, and the man is mentally deficient in other ways. They're going to kill me, *señorita.*"

"I don't think they will. If they wanted to, they would have done it before now."

"You know this ridiculous tale about nerve gas and your American President isn't true, don't you?"

"Of course, it's not. The President would never do anything like that." Wilma frowned. "But you're a bad man, General. You're probably here after drugs or something like that, aren't you?"

Even tied up, Garaldo managed to give an eloquent shrug. "I see no point in denying the obvious. It is true that I work for the Rey del Sol cartel. Our enemies are bringing a shipment of cocaine through here today, and we plan to hijack it. But that's all, señorita. This talk of nerve gas is loco!"

Wilma crossed her arms and nodded. "I knew it. I knew the President couldn't do anything bad. He's so nice. I've met him several times, you know."

"If you could help me get free," Garaldo said, "I could stop all this killing right now. And you . . . you could get an exclusive for your network out of it, my dear."

Excitement leaped into Wilma's eyes, but only for a second. Then she said, "How stupid do you think I am? Never mind, you must think I'm pretty stupid. I'm not going to trust a Mexican drug lord."

Cochrum ambled up behind her and grinned. "I was waiting to see whether you'd fall for his pitch, sweetheart."

"Don't call me sweetheart," she snapped. "That's

sexual harassment. You're a lawyer. You ought to know that."

He held up his hands. "Sorry, sorry. Didn't mean anything by it. I was just saying that you did good not to believe this guy. He's not on our side."

"I never claimed to be," Garaldo said. "But I can speak your language, and I don't mean English. I mean . . . one million dollars if you turn me loose."

"You want me to betray my country for a million dollars?" Cochrum demanded.

"I'm sorry. I meant five million."

"You might as well shut up—" Wilma began.

Cochrum stopped her with a curt gesture. "Don't pay any attention to her," he told Garaldo. "Keep talking, General . . ."

CHAPTER 47

Alex wasn't sure what worried her the most: the dangerous mission she was on, the possibility that the deadliest nerve gas on the planet might fall into the hands of a madman . . . or the fact that in a few minutes her son, her only child, would be in the middle of a fight to the death. There was no way she could have talked Jack and Rowdy out of taking part in the battle with Garaldo's men. At least they had gone with J. P. Delgado, and Alex knew he would do his best to look out for them.

In the meantime, she had a job to do, and she couldn't afford to waste any time. She had already had to hide a couple of times to avoid the cartel patrols, and that had delayed her. But now she was at the rear door of the warehouse where Phil Pearson stored the hay he sold at his feed store. He kept a truckload at the store, but the rest of his stock was here.

"Sorry, Phil," Alex muttered under her breath as she used the barrel of her rifle to wrench the lock off the door. The hasp came free with a screech of nails.

She stepped into the shadowy, cavernous warehouse. The piled-up bales of hay loomed on both sides of a narrow aisle like twin mountains. A forklift was parked in the aisle. The air was thick with the smell of hay and floating dust motes. That dust would help the fire burn with a fierceness that was akin to an explosion.

Alex had a cigarette lighter in the pocket of her jeans. She didn't smoke, but like a lot of law enforcement personnel, she carried a lighter with her because it often came in handy. That was certainly the case now. She trotted to the far end of the aisle and flicked the flame into life. Dashing back and forth between the two piles of hay, she set the stuff on fire in several different places as she hurried toward the back door. Behind her, the flames began to crackle as the blaze caught hold.

Alex was running by the time she reached the door and burst outside, and it was a good thing because the hay went up with a gigantic *whoosh*! behind her. A wind sprang up in her face as oxygen rushed into the warehouse to fuel the conflagration, but that wasn't enough to keep the heat from battering her back. Alex kept moving until she was a good hundred yards from the building.

She stopped and turned to look at the thick cloud of gray smoke billowing up from the fire. It would be visible all over town . . . hell, from all over the area, she thought. And some of Garaldo's men would have to come check it out. They were probably pretty jumpy by now with their commanding officer missing.

Grim-faced, Alex set her rifle on single fire, pointed it toward the sky, and pulled the trigger three times, then waited and fired twice more.

No turning back now, she thought. The signal had been given.

Let the battle for Home begin.

"I can't stand it no more," Rye Callahan said. He started to climb out of the gully.

Earl caught hold of his arm and stopped him. "Wait a minute," the little scientist said. "Ford and Parker told us to wait here."

"Yeah, well, we been waitin' for a couple of hours now, and there's been all sorts of shootin' in town. I reckon something could've happened to those boys, and it's up to us now to put a stop to whatever hell-raisin' is going on here."

"I don't know," Earl said dubiously. "They told us to wait—"

"Yeah, you said that," Callahan cut in. "You can squat out here if you want to, son, but I'm gonna get right in the middle of that ruckus." The rancher nodded toward the town and then abruptly exclaimed, "What the hell?"

Earl looked and saw a column of smoke rising from something on the edge of town. Shots began to ring out again, more of them than ever now. He sensed that whatever was happening in Home, it was starting to reach its climax.

Callahan scrambled out of the gully and took off toward town, carrying the rifle at a slant across his chest. Earl hesitated for a moment as he pondered his choices. Plunge right into the middle of that violent chaos, he thought, or stay here by himself and maybe risk being alone when the bad guys came looking for him, as they inevitably would?

"Damn it," he muttered. That was no choice at all. How come life didn't offer a "none of the above" option?

But it didn't, so he climbed out of the gully and trotted after Callahan, his short legs moving fast as he tried to catch up to the rancher.

With the rotors beating the air, the helicopter flew toward Home. General Weldon Stone opened the steel case that sat at his feet and looked at the hardened plastic canister nestled within it. The canister had a simple nozzle on it that could be attached to a hose. Stone had such a hose. All he had to do was attach it to the canister, run the other end out of the helicopter, fly over Home, and turn the handle on the canister's valve. The gas would do the rest. It was possible that some of the people in town might survive, but the general and his men could dispose of them a short time later, after the gas had become inert.

It should have bothered him, the idea of killing fellow Americans. He had been a career military man, after all. He had devoted his life to serving his country. But over the years he had come to realize that those on the political left were right . . . sometimes the few had to suffer for the good of the many. Sometimes the many had to suffer for the good of even more. He had seen how the poor and those of color had flocked to the military because civilian life held nothing for them but injustice. He had seen how the rich and powerful—most of them Jews—always got richer and more powerful, and the unfairness of it ate at him. The politicians never seemed to do anything about it, even the ones who had once shown promise, like the previous president.

Then a special politician, a different politician, had come along, and General Stone had recognized at last a kindred spirit, although the man had no service experience and generally held the military in disdain, like most of his ilk. But he had a dream of transforming the country, of spreading the wealth and making the United States a kinder, gentler nation.

And when General Stone looked in the President's eyes, he knew the son of a bitch was willing to kill anybody he had to in order to make that dream of tolerance and equity come true. The President, to Stone's way of thinking, was the perfect blend of ideals and utter ruthlessness.

Kill for good. Murder for equality. Wipe out a whole town if you had to in order to be sure nobody found out the truth.

It was all collateral damage, and General Stone was enough of a pragmatist to know that such things were inevitable if true change was to come about.

"General!"

Stone looked up from the canister and all the dreams it held. "What is it, Lieutenant?" he asked his aide.

"There's a big cloud of smoke up ahead. It looks like it's coming from the direction of the town."

Stone stood up, bracing himself against the side of the helicopter, and looked past the pilot and co-pilot. He saw the column of smoke rising in the distance.

"What do you think it is, sir?" the lieutenant asked.

"I don't know, son," Stone replied, "and in a few minutes, whatever it is won't matter."

Jack, Rowdy, and J. P. Delgado crouched behind a parked car on Main Street, trading shots with a squad of Rey del Sol killers. Jack was more scared than he had ever been in his life, but a certain calmness had descended on him when the invaders opened fire on him and his companions and forced them to take cover. He knew he might die at any second, but he also knew that he was fighting for a good cause, for the very survival of his hometown. For his mom and his friends and for everybody who lived here, even the assholes. They didn't deserve to have a bunch of drug-running, power-hungry thugs come waltzing in and take over, slaughtering people right and left. It wasn't right.

And if Jack had to die to put a stop to it, well, he supposed he could be at peace with that.

But he was still scared, and he tried to channel that fright into making every shot count.

Up and down Main Street, similar skirmishes were going on as the resistance forces converged on the police station. A few minutes earlier, what looked like most of the invading force had gathered and started toward the smoke coming from the burning warehouse. Out in the open like that, they had made good targets for the citizens of Home who opened fire on them from alleys and rooftops. The resistance was still heavily outnumbered, though, and the invaders seemed to be intent on wiping them out. The wave of Rey del Sol killers was slowly sweeping up the street, killing the defenders as they came to them. Jack had seen half a dozen townspeople die already, riddled with bullets.

The same fate awaited him, probably within minutes. The invaders were closing in.

Rowdy let out an excited whoop. "Got another one!" he said.

"Keep your head down, kid," Delgado warned. The cop fired another round. They all had the rifles on single fire now, since their ammunition was starting to run low.

One of the invaders tried to dash from one parked car to another. Jack was waiting for him and drilled him through the body. The man tumbled to the ground and flopped around like a fish out of water as he died.

That ought to bother me, Jack thought, but it doesn't. They came in here ready to murder anybody who stood up to them. They were getting a lot hotter welcome than they had expected. Maybe later, the human lives he had taken would haunt him.

But he wasn't going to have to worry about that, he told himself, because there was no way he was going to live through this.

Rowdy suddenly frowned and asked, "Hey, am I goin' nuts, or do I hear a helicopter?"

As the fighting spread down Main Street, Ford, Parker, and Bud crouched behind the Dumpster they had used as an observation post earlier. Some of the invaders were still clustered around the two trucks parked in front of the police station, but most of them had hurried off down the street to check on that smoke and stayed to fight the resistance forces.

"We're not gonna get a better chance than this," Ford said. "I say we go."

Parker nodded. "So do I. Ready, Bud?"

"Yeah, let's do this," the cameraman said, his voice shaking a little despite his unhesitating answer.

The three men burst out from cover and headed toward the trucks at a dead run. They wanted to cover as much ground as possible before the invaders saw them coming.

That lasted only a couple of seconds, but it was enough for them to close the gap to about fifty yards. Then several of the enemy whirled around and started to raise their guns.

Ford and Parker were in front. They opened fire, cutting down the invaders before the men could pull their triggers. The shots drew more attention, though.

"Split up!" Parker yelled. "Bud, go with Fargo!"

The two agents veered apart. Their rifles were still chattering death. From the corner of his eye, Ford saw Parker suddenly stumble. Parker didn't go down, though. He stayed on his feet and kept firing, mowing down several more of the invaders before he finally lost his balance and tumbled to the ground.

Ford bit back an oath. He couldn't worry about his friend now. He and Bud had almost reached their destination. One of the invaders appeared at the rear door of the truck where the jamming equipment was located. Ford's rifle blasted at the same time as flame spewed from the muzzle of the invader's weapon. Bullets chewed at Ford's left leg like the teeth of a rabid animal. It collapsed under him.

The guy in the truck was doubled over, though, blood spurting between his fingers as he pressed his hands to his midsection. He toppled out of the vehicle and thudded to the street.

"Go!" Ford shouted to Bud from the ground. "Get in there and destroy that equipment!"

Bud was pale and terrified looking, but he jumped over the corpse and started climbing into the truck. Ford rolled over on his belly and lifted his rifle, hoping to be able to cover Parker, who lay unmoving on the asphalt now. Ford loosed several shots at a group of thugs who started toward the fallen agent.

Footsteps slapped on the pavement behind him. Ford glanced around, convinced he was about to be shot to pieces.

Instead, he saw Earl Trussell and Rye Callahan firing their rifles as they flanked him. Earl dropped to a knee beside him and shouted over the racket of gunfire, "Are you all right, you big gorilla?"

"Better now," Ford yelled back. There was no time for explanations, so he added, "We gotta keep those bastards outta this truck!"

"They'll have to come through us," Callahan grated. He sprayed lead up the street at the invaders.

Earl suddenly looked up. "What th— Is that a *helicopter* I hear?"

Ford heard the distinctive eggbeater sound and knew Earl was right. A chopper was coming toward Home.

Had help somehow gotten here already?

CHAPTER 48

"Damn it, no!"

The woman's angry shout made Jimmy and Eloise turned swiftly from the library window. They were shocked to see the blond reporter struggling with Clayton Cochrum. The lawyer had a pair of scissors he must have gotten from the librarian's desk.

Worse that that, one of General Garaldo's arms was free, and he was struggling to get the other ropes off himself.

"You son of a bitch!" Wilma yelled at Cochrum. "I didn't think you'd really do it!"

She was grappling with him and had hold of his arms, but he suddenly pulled loose from her and struck her with a vicious backhanded blow that sent her sprawling back over one of the library tables.

That brought her within reach of Garaldo, who abandoned his efforts to free himself and lunged toward her instead, reaching out as much as he could while still tied in the chair. He grabbed her arm and jerked her into his lap. Wilma was too stunned by the blow Cochrum had landed to fight back until it was too late. Garaldo looped his arm around her neck and held her in front of him like a human shield.

Eloise had started to lift her rifle, but she stopped when she saw she couldn't get a clear shot at the general. "Drop your guns!" Garaldo shouted. "Drop your guns and free me, or I snap her neck!"

"The hell I will!" Eloise yelled back at him. "Let that girl go!"

Garaldo smirked. "You will not shoot her, any more than you shot me when you had your chance."

"I wouldn't be so sure about that," Eloise warned. "All she and her kind ever do is tell lies about the American people."

"All right, go ahead," Garaldo taunted. "Those weapons will shoot right through her into me. Kill us both."

Cochrum began circling, getting to the side where Eloise couldn't cover both him and Garaldo.

"Watch him, Jimmy," Eloise said.

"I don't want to . . . shoot anybody," Jimmy said.

"Neither do I, honey, but we may have to."

"Look, just let the general go," Cochrum urged. "Nobody else has to die here."

"You weasel," Eloise practically spat. "What'd you do, sell out to him?"

Garaldo laughed. "The counselor has been working for Rey del Sol all along. Who do you think paid him to represent Emilio Navarre?"

"Hey, those fees were paid by an anonymous donor interested in justice," Cochrum protested.

Another harsh laugh came from Garaldo. "That was cartel money, and you know it. Now, take the gun away from that halfwit and let's get out of here."

"You shouldn't call people names," Jimmy scolded.

Cochrum held out a hand. "Gimme the gun, kid. You know you don't want to hurt anybody. I'll bet your parents always taught you to stay away from guns."

"Well . . . they said I might hurt myself or somebody else."

"Jimmy!" Eloise said. "Don't listen to him."

"Take it easy, Jimmy," Cochrum said. "Nobody's gonna get hurt—"

He was close enough to lunge forward, grab the barrel of Jimmy's rifle, and shove it toward the ceiling. Eloise spun toward them, but she couldn't fire because Jimmy was between her and Cochrum.

The lawyer didn't have to worry about that. He tore the rifle out of Jimmy's hands, flipped it around, and pulled the trigger.

The bullets punched into Jimmy's thick-bodied figure and spun him out of the way. Eloise screamed and fired, but she was too late. Slugs pounded her off her feet. She dropped the rifle as she went down.

One of her bullets had found its mark, though. Cochrum staggered a little as he lowered the rifle he had taken away from Jimmy. Blood stained his white shirt under the expensive suit coat.

"Cochrum!" Garaldo said. "Cut me loose!"

Cochrum dropped the rifle and picked up the scissors again. He stumbled over to the general. Wilma watched him with wide, terrified eyes.

"Five million bucks, right, General?" Cochrum

asked as he used the scissors to saw through the last of the bonds holding Garaldo in the chair.

"Of course. That was our arrangement." Garaldo got to his feet, holding the blonde with his left arm now as he held out his right hand. "Give me the scissors."

Cochrum handed them over and asked, "What do you need them for?"

"This," Garaldo said, and plunged the sharp tips into Cochrum's neck. With a savage twist and jerk, he ripped the lawyer's throat out. Wilma screamed as blood flew everywhere, spurting from severed arteries.

Gagging, Cochrum clapped his hands to his ravaged throat, but of course he couldn't do any good. He fell to his knees, then pitched forward onto his face. A crimson puddle began to spread around his head.

Wilma managed to gasp, "Wh-what are you going to do with me?"

Garaldo grinned at her. "Why, you're coming with me, *señorita.* Imagine what a scoop you're going to have! You're about to witness the balance of power in the world shifting. . . ."

Bud stuck his head out the back of the truck. "I got it!" he yelled to Ford. "The jamming signal's down! And there's a radio in here, so I started it broadcasting a mayday loop!"

"Good work, kid," Ford said. His leg had hurt like blazes at first, but he couldn't even feel it now.

And he was getting cold, which wasn't a good sign. He figured he was bleeding out.

But somewhere, somebody would pick up that emergency signal, and the cavalry would come galloping in, just like in the old movies. Ford glanced up. Smoke from the burning warehouse clogged the sky above Home now, and he couldn't see the approaching helicopter. He could hear it, though, and he figured everybody else in town could, too. The shooting had stopped. A feeling of tense expectancy hung in the air along with the smoke.

Ford grasped Earl's arm. "You make sure the truth gets out, you hear?" he said. "Don't let the . . . sons of bitches get away with this."

Earl nodded. "Yeah, sure, but you can tell the story, too. You and Parker both. People are gonna be a lot more likely to believe a couple of upright government agents than a lowlife scientist like me."

"Forget it," Ford said. "This is . . . your job now . . . kid."

Yeah, it was cold, cold and dark, and Ford felt consciousness slipping away.

The last thing he heard before the icy blackness claimed him was an explosion.

With the terrified blonde's arm tightly gripped in one hand and a rifle in the other, General Jose Luis Garaldo strode down the street toward the police station. Some of his men noticed him and came running up to him. They didn't salute, as they should have, but they were low-level thugs and there was only so much that could be done with such inferior raw material.

"Report!" Garaldo snapped at them.

"We are under attack, General," one of the men said.

"I can see that, you fool! Where is all that smoke coming from?"

The men shook their heads. One of them explained, "When we went to see, someone opened fire on us. And now a helicopter comes!"

Garaldo jerked his head in a nod. He had heard the chopper approaching, too, as he dragged the reporter downtown from the high school. Now it was almost on top of them.

One of the men carried a grenade launcher. Garaldo shoved the blonde into the arms of another man and took the grenade launcher. He loaded a grenade into it and brought the weapon to his shoulder, angling it toward the sky.

If whoever was in that helicopter thought they were going to help the Americans, they were in for a big surprise. Garaldo's forces had already shot down one chopper today.

With any luck, the general himself would make it two.

All he needed was for those clouds of smoke to clear. . . .

"General, we can't really see what's going on down there!" the pilot called over his shoulder to Stone.

"Get lower," Stone ordered. It didn't really matter what sort of fight was taking place in Home. Soon all the combatants would be dead. But with the deadly power of the gas on his side, he could afford to indulge his curiosity, he supposed. The apparatus was already hooked up. All he had to do was twist the valve, and that wouldn't take but a second.

The helicopter swooped down through the smoke, and the propwash from the rotors helped to disperse it. The chopper emerged abruptly from the smoke above one end of what had to be Main Street. It was littered with shot-up cars and sprawled bodies. This was war, Stone thought, but it was about to be over.

"General!" the pilot suddenly screamed. "Incoming!"

Stone's eyes widened as he looked past the man and saw something streaking toward the chopper. The pilot reacted instinctively, trying to swerve the helicopter out of the way.

Stone's hand flashed to the valve on the gas canister.

Before he could turn it, something slammed into the chopper's tail section and exploded. The impact jolted Stone off his feet. As he slammed to the deck, the aircraft began to spin wildly. Somebody was cursing at the top of his lungs. Stone groped toward the canister but before he could reach it, the damaged chopper crash-landed on the pavement in the middle of Main Street.

The pilot had done a masterful job of retaining some control and getting the bird down in one piece. It would never fly again, though. Flames broke out and spread toward the fuel tank.

The lieutenant, bleeding from a gash on his forehead suffered in the crash, grabbed Stone's arm and tried to haul him to his feet. "Sir, we've gotta get out of here! Now!"

Stone struggled to reach the canister. He got his hands on it and ripped the tubing free. The valve was still closed, and the canister was intact. The deadly contents were still in there.

With his aide's help, Stone staggered to his feet. The dozen or so FPS officers who were also in the helicopter looked to him for orders. They were shaken up and had some cuts and scrapes but seemed to be largely all right.

"Get out there and fight!" Stone barked as he waved a hand at the hatch while he cradled the canister against his chest with the other hand.

"Fight who, sir?" one of the men asked.

"Whoever's out there, damn it! Everybody in this town is an enemy! Go, go, go!"

The men piled out of the chopper and started shooting as soon as their boots hit the pavement. In a matter of seconds, chaos once again reigned in Home as the three-way battle raged along Main Street.

Pain shot through Stone every time he took a breath. He had broken some ribs when he fell, he thought, and he had a hunch at least one of them had pierced a lung. He would soon be drowning in his own blood.

But that didn't matter, because he wouldn't live that long. He would die quickly and painlessly, with one twist of that valve. He would be the first to die, in fact, but the gas would spread and kill everyone else who breathed it. He could only hope that the winds would disperse it throughout the town and wipe out everyone, so the President's hands would remain clean, and the media and the gullible voters would continue to worship at his feet and America would continue to be transformed into a country where the Jews didn't run everything.

That was a dream worth dying for, wasn't it, Stone asked himself as he climbed out of the wrecked chopper and stumbled into the middle of the street.

"This is Bud Conway reporting from Home, Texas," Bud said into the portable radio he had patched into the big set inside the truck. "If anyone is hearing me, please record this. I don't know how long I'll be able to broadcast."

He had taped dozens of reporters doing remotes during his career. It had never seemed that hard to him. Now he had a chance to try it for himself. Nobody had told him to. It had just occurred to him that somebody ought to try to document the momentous events that were going on here today.

"War has broken out here in this small Texas town, war between paramilitary killers from the Rey del Sol drug cartel and the embattled citizens of Home. There's something else happening, too. A helicopter has just crash-landed in the street, and armed men are pouring from it and joining in the fight, cutting down whoever happens to get in front of their guns. That appears to be mostly the cartel gunmen. People are dying all around me. It's like a scene out of a nightmare. Blood and smoke and bullets are everywhere. Please, if you're listening, record this."

A little blond-haired guy with a mustache suddenly loomed out of the smoke and grabbed Bud's arm. "Are you a reporter?" he demanded.

"Yeah, I guess," Bud answered. "Who're you?"

"Earl Trussell. I'm a scientist from Casa del Diablo. Gimme that radio."

Before Bud could stop him, Earl had ripped the radio out of his hands and brought it to his mouth.

"Listen to me, world! Put this out on the Internet as quick as you can, as often as you can. Upload it everywhere! The President has a secret bio-weapons lab in the mountains west of Home, Texas. I know it's true, because I worked there. They've been making nerve gas to use on his political enemies. He's going to wipe out all the opposition and make himself president for life! I know it sounds crazy, but it's true! Somebody has to stop—"

A shot rang out. The radio slipped from Earl's fingers as he crumpled, but Bud caught it before it hit the ground.

A tall, red-faced man in a black combat outfit strode toward Bud and Earl, smoke curling from the barrel of the pistol in his hand. In his other hand he carried some sort of blue plastic canister.

Bud slipped the radio in his pocket but left it on. He thrust his hands in the air and said, "Don't shoot!"

With an angry snarl on his face, the man said, "I heard what he was saying. Who was he talking to?"

"To . . . to me," Bud stammered. "Just to me. He was talking crazy, I don't know what was wrong with him."

"Do you know who I am, son?"

"N-no, sir."

"General Weldon Stone," the man snapped. "A true patriot! That's why you have to die, and I have to die, and everybody in this town has to die, so that America can be transformed."

Bud swallowed hard. "Then . . . then it's true? What he was saying?"

"Of course, it's true!" The shooting was dying away now. The battle seemed to be coming to an end. That made it easier to hear General Stone as his voice rang out clearly. "You don't think a visionary like our President would let a little thing like the death of a few citizens stand in the way of bringing our country the change it needs, do you? Of course, he'll do whatever's necessary to put his policies forward. That's why he ordered those scientists at Casa del Diablo to develop that nerve gas. It's for the good of the country! That's what all those damned Jew-loving right-wingers never seem to understand! It's for the good of the country!"

"So . . . we all have to die?" Bud asked.

Stone held up the canister. "As soon as I open this valve, the nerve gas inside it will spread all over Home. No one will be left to tell the truth of what happened here, and the President will be safe to continue his work."

"His work of murdering everybody who disagrees with him, you mean?"

Stone smiled and holstered his gun. "It's not murder if it's in a good cause."

He reached for the valve on the canister.

Bud was ready to jump him and try to stop that valve from being turned, even though he knew he'd probably get a faceful of the gas and die instantly. But before he could make a move, a shot blasted somewhere behind him. Stone's head jerked back as a red-rimmed black hole appeared in the center of his forehead. His knees unhinged and the canister slipped from his fingers as he fell.

Bud didn't know if being dropped would make the gas start to escape, but he didn't want to take that chance. He made a desperate dive forward, stretching out his arms as far as he could.

The canister dropped into them, and he stopped its fall a handful of inches before it struck the pavement.

Realizing that he held death in his hands, Bud cradled the canister carefully against him and rolled over. He saw Chief Alex Bonner standing at the corner, her service revolver grasped in her right hand while her left gripped the other wrist to steady it. Bud knew she was the one who had made the shot that killed Stone.

She lowered the gun and started toward him. "Is that—" she called.

"Yeah," Bud said. "It is."

A harsh voice demanded, "Give it to me!"

Now what the hell?

Bud hoped the radio was still transmitting. He looked over his shoulder and saw a dark-faced man in military fatigues stalking toward him, covering him with a rifle he held one-handed while dragging Wilma along with the other. Bud was happy to see that she was still alive, even though she was a pain in the ass sometimes.

"Give me the canister!" the man said again.

Alex called, "Drop it, Garaldo!"

So this was General Garaldo, the leader of the cartel forces, Bud thought. It figured. No sooner was one dangerous maniac put down than another one popped up to take his place.

"Back off, bitch!" Garaldo snarled at Alex. "I'll

shoot that fool and the canister, and the gas will be released."

"Then you'll die, too," Alex warned.

"Better death than defeat!"

"Wilma!" Bud yelled. "Catch it!"

He threw the canister high in the air.

Just as Bud had figured would happen, Garaldo let go of Wilma and turned his head to follow the flight of the canister. She turned and sprinted to get under it.

Alex shouted, "Bud, get down!"

He sprawled on the pavement, getting as far out of the line of fire as he could. Garaldo pulled the trigger, making his rifle chatter insanely, but shots came from all around him and slammed into him. The impacts jarred him back and forth in a bizarre dance for what seemed longer than the two or three seconds it really was.

Then the rifle slipped from his fingers and he followed it to the pavement, landing in a bloody heap that didn't move again.

Bud watched as Wilma caught the canister. He pulled the radio from his pocket and saw that the switch was still locked in the transmit position.

"This has been Bud Conway reporting," he said hollowly. "I hope you folks got all that."

Then he fainted dead away.

"Mom! Mom!"

Her son's voice was the sweetest thing Alex had ever heard. She saw him rushing toward her and ran to meet him. Rowdy and Delgado limped after him, bloody from minor wounds but still alive.

Alex caught Jack in her arms and hugged him like she never intended to let him go. She whispered his name over and over and asked if he was all right. She felt his tear-streaked face against hers as he nodded.

"What about you?" he asked.

"I'm fine, I'm fine," she said, and at that moment, she was. She was surrounded by death, destruction, and tragedy, but she had never been finer.

Her son was alive.

EPILOGUE

Emergency responders from the county seat arrived less than fifteen minutes later, followed shortly by the State Police, the Texas Rangers, and the National Guard. They were able to contain the fires that had broken out, as well as arresting the members of Rey del Sol who had survived the battle. There were only a handful of them.

All the members of the Federal Protective Service had been killed in the fierce fighting. For a short time, bureaucrats in Washington tried to deny that the helicopter and the black-uniformed men came from the FPS, but the presence of General Weldon Stone's body, plus the broadcast that had gone out over the radio, made it impossible to sell that story.

Within an hour, the audio of that broadcast was the most downloaded file on the Internet, with billions of hits on thousands of websites. The genie was so far out of the bottle that it could never be put back. At first the White House claimed that General Stone had gone rogue, acting on his own to establish the nerve gas project at Casa del Diablo. The man was obviously deranged, the White House press secretary said over and over again. It didn't matter that everyone had heard Stone saying the President had ordered those criminal actions. For a day, the media seemed to be on the verge of buying the story and trying to sell it to the rest of the country.

Then the President's Chief of Staff had murdered a woman named Julia Hernandez and followed that up by taking his own life, leaving a long, detailed letter telling everything he knew about Casa del Diablo, which was plenty.

That left everything in the hands of the politicians in Congress, and the country held its breath, waiting to see if once, just once, those men and women would finally do the right thing.

In Home, people were too busy to pay all that much attention to what was going on in Washington.

There were multiple funerals, every day for a week.

Clint and Eloise Barrigan, Jimmy Clifton, Jerry Houston, Lester Simms, Betsy Carlyle, and Antonio Ruiz were all buried with full honors and hundreds of fellow law enforcement personnel from all over the country in attendance. Dave Sutherland, the city attorney, had been killed in the fighting, too. Alex hadn't even known he was part of it until it was all over. Twenty-seven other citizens of Home, twenty-one men and six women, had met their deaths in the battle, too, and they were laid to rest in solemn ceremonies.

Brad Parker's body was taken back to his home in California for burial. Alex didn't know where

Clayton Cochrum was buried and didn't care. They could have cinched up his body in a garbage bag and left it at the curb, as far as she was concerned.

Lawrence "Fargo" Ford, although badly shot up, survived the battle and was in the hospital, as was Earl Trussell, who had been questioned by every law enforcement agency under the sun about his involvement with Casa del Diablo, which had been closed down and sealed by the FBI, pending a full investigation.

Rye Callahan, the leathery old rancher, had come through the ruckus without a scratch and gone to see what was left of his home.

There were so many government lawyers and personal injury attorneys in Home that the sidewalks were always crowded. It was a lawsuit boomtown. Alex wished they would just all go away. She craved normalcy.

But as one of the heroes of the Battle of Home, she knew she might not ever get that again.

"Don't wear him out," Dr. Boone advised her as he left her in Ford's room at the Home Community Hospital. Ford could have been transferred out to a big-city hospital, but he had insisted on staying right where he was.

"I'll try not to," Alex said with a smile.

Ford grinned up at her from the hospital bed when they were alone. His leg was twice its normal size under the covers from all the bandages. He slapped it anyway and tried not to wince.

"Doc says I ought to be able to walk again. Probably not without a limp, though."

"You'll still be able to get around," Alex said. "That's what matters."

"Yeah." He looked at her uniform. "You've probably been pretty busy keeping the peace. I assume that's why you haven't come to see me until now."

"The county sheriff has sent a bunch of deputies in to help out until I can recruit some more officers," she said. "Anyway, I was here several times. You just didn't know it because you were laying around taking it easy."

"In a coma, you mean."

"Well . . . yeah, if you want to get technical about it."

Ford's eyes narrowed. "Have you, uh, heard anything through the grapevine about whether there'll be any charges against me?"

"You're overestimating my connections, Fargo. I'm just a small-town police chief. Nobody at the CIA talks to me." She paused. "I don't see how they could take any action against you, though. Everything you did was justified."

"Some people won't see it that way. And some of them are pretty powerful."

"If you're worried about the President, I think he's got plenty on his mind right now without plotting vengeance against you."

"I wouldn't be so sure about that." Ford sighed. "Anyway, I think it's a foregone conclusion that I won't be doing any more field work. Not with a bum leg and a cloud over my head. It might be time for me to retire and go into some other line of work."

"I have openings for police officers," Alex said. "My son and his friend Rowdy have decided to go to college and major in criminal justice so they can become cops, but it'll be a while before they're ready to step in." She shrugged. "The pay's not very good, but it's a nice place to live."

"You know," Ford drawled, "that's not a bad idea."

Alex looked at him in surprise. She had been halfway joking, but she saw something in Ford's eyes that told her he wasn't taking the offer as a joke. Not at all.

And suddenly, deep inside, she was glad.

She rested her hand on his and squeezed, then looked out the window at what she could see of Home. Satellite news trucks were still everywhere, competing for space with the lawyers. Bud and Wilma were stars now and could write their own tickets at any network. Alex still didn't like the blonde, but Bud had turned out to be an okay guy.

No, Home wasn't back to normal yet, she thought as she smiled at Ford, but maybe someday it would be.

She was willing to wait.

"The stand-off at the White House continues today as the former President, although impeached and removed from office, refuses to leave. In her first act as president, following the resignation of the former vice-president, the former Speaker of the House has ordered the Secret Service not to use force to make the former President vacate the premises. 'We will allow this unfortunate situation to run its course,' she was quoted as saying. 'I'm sure that in time the poor man will come to his senses and realize that he's no longer the Commander-in-Chief.'

"In other news, the new President vowed to see that Congress acts swiftly to pass the National Education and Re-education Act. 'In times so obviously perilous as these,' she said, 'it's imperative that we do everything in our power to see to it that each and every student in our schools knows exactly what to think. . . .'"